THE ECHO MAKER

Richard Powers is the author of nine novels, including *Galatea 2.2* and *The Gold Bug Variations*, both of which were nominated for the US National Book Critics Circle Award; *Operation Wandering Soul*, which was nominated for the US National Book Award for Fiction; *Plowing the Dark*; *Gain*; and, most recently, *The Time of Our Singing*, winner of the WH Smith Literary Award. *The Echo Maker* won the US National Book Award in 2006. Richard Powers lives in Illinois.

D0529195

ALSO BY RICHARD POWERS

RICHARD POWERS

The Echo Maker

VINTAGE BOOKS
London

Published by Vintage 2007

2 4 6 8 10 9 7 5 3 1

Copyright © Richard Powers 2006

Richard Powers has asserted his right under the Copyright, Designs
and Patents Act 1988 to be identified as the author of this work

This book is sold subject to the condition that it shall not,
by way of trade or otherwise, be lent, resold, hired out,
or otherwise circulated without the publisher's prior
consent in any form of binding or cover other than that
in which it is published and without a similar condition,
including this condition, being imposed on the
subsequent purchaser

This novel is a work of fiction. Names and characters are the product
of the author's imagination and any resemblance to actual persons,
living or dead, is entirely coincidental.

A portion of this work was originally published, in slightly different
form, in *Black Clock* no.3

First published in the United States by Farrar, Straus & Giroux,
New York in 2006

First published in Great Britain in 2006 by William Heinemann

Random House, 20 Vauxhall Bridge Road,
London SW1V 2SA

www.vintage-books.co.uk

Addresses for companies within The Random House Group Limited
can be found at: www.randomhouse.co.uk/offices.htm

The Random House Group Limited Reg. No. 954009

A CIP catalogue record for this book
is available from the British Library

ISBN 9780099506027

The Random House Group Limited makes every effort to ensure that
the papers used in its books are made from trees that have been
legally sourced from well-managed and credibly certified forests. Our
paper procurement policy can be found at:
www.randomhouse.co.uk/paper.htm

Mixed Sources
Product group from well-managed
forests and other controlled sources
www.fsc.org   Cert no. TT-COC-2139
© 1996 Forest Stewardship Council
FSC

Typeset by SX Composing DTP, Rayleigh, Essex
Printed in the UK by CPI Bookmarque, Croydon, CR0 4TD

To find the soul it is necessary to lose it.
—A. R. Luria

PART ONE

I AM NO ONE

We are all potential fossils still carrying within our
bodies the crudities of former existences, the marks
of a world in which living creatures flow with little
more consistency than clouds from age to age.

—Loren Eiseley, *The Immense Journey*, "The Slit"

Cranes keep landing as night falls. Ribbons of them roll down, slack against the sky. They float in from all compass points, in kettles of a dozen, dropping with the dusk. Scores of *Grus canadensis* settle on the thawing river. They gather on the island flats, grazing, beating their wings, trumpeting: the advance wave of a mass evacuation. More birds land by the minute, the air red with calls.

A neck stretches long; legs drape behind. Wings curl forward, the length of a man. Spread like fingers, primaries tip the bird into the wind's plane. The blood-red head bows and the wings sweep together, a cloaked priest giving benediction. Tail cups and belly buckles, surprised by the upsurge of ground. Legs kick out, their backward knees flapping like broken landing gear. Another bird plummets and stumbles forward, fighting for a spot in the packed staging ground along those few miles of water still clear and wide enough to pass as safe.

Twilight comes early, as it will for a few more weeks. The sky, ice blue through the encroaching willows and cotton-woods, flares up, a brief rose, before collapsing to indigo. Late February on the Platte, and the night's chill haze hangs over this river, frosting the stubble from last fall that still fills the bordering fields. The nervous birds, tall as children, crowd together wing by wing on this stretch of river, one that they've learned to find by memory.

They converge on the river at winter's end as they have for eons, carpeting the wetlands. In this light, something saurian still clings to them: the oldest flying things on earth, one stutter-step away from pterodactyls. As darkness falls for real, it's a beginner's world again, the same evening as that day sixty million years ago when this migration began.

Half a million birds—four-fifths of all the sandhill cranes on earth—home in on this river. They trace the Central Flyway, an hourglass laid over the continent. They push up from New Mexico, Texas, and Mexico, hundreds of miles each day, with thousands more ahead before they reach their remembered nests. For a few weeks, this stretch of river shelters the miles-long flock. Then, by the start of spring, they'll rise and head away, feeling their way up to Saskatchewan, Alaska, or beyond.

This year's flight has always been. Something in the birds retraces a route laid down centuries before their parents showed it to them. And each crane recalls the route still to come.

Tonight's cranes mill again on the braided water. For another hour, their massed calls carry on the emptying air. The birds flap and fidget, edgy with migration. Some tear up frosty twigs and toss them in the air. Their jitters spill over into combat. At last the sandhills settle down into wary, stilt-legged sleep, most standing in the water, a few farther up in the stubbled fields.

A squeal of brakes, the crunch of metal on asphalt, one broken scream and then another rouse the flock. The truck arcs through the air, corkscrewing into the field. A plume shoots through the birds. They lurch off the ground, wings beating. The panicked carpet lifts, circles, and falls again. Calls that seem to come from creatures twice their size carry miles before fading.

By morning, that sound never happened. Again there is only here, now, the river's braid, a feast of waste grain that will carry these flocks north, beyond the Arctic Circle. As first light breaks, the fossils return to life, testing their legs, tasting the frozen air, leaping free, bills skyward and throats open. And then, as if the night took nothing, forgetting everything but this moment, the dawn sandhills start to dance. Dance as they have since before this river started.

Her brother needed her. The thought protected Karin through the alien night. She drove in a trance, keeping to the long dogleg, south down Nebraska 77 from Siouxland, then west on 30, tracking the Platte. The back roads were impossible, in her condition. Still shattered from the telephone's stab at two a.m.: *Karin Schluter? This is Good Samaritan Hospital in Kearney. Your brother has had an accident.*

The aide wouldn't say anything over the phone. Just that Mark had flipped over on the shoulder of North Line Road and had lain pinned in his cab, almost frozen by the time the paramedics found and freed him. For a long time after hanging up, she couldn't feel her fingers until she found them pressed into her cheeks. Her face was numb, as if *she* had been the one lying out there, in the freezing February night.

Her hands, stiff and blue, clawed the wheel as she slipped through the reservations. First the Winnebago, then the rolling Omaha. The scrub trees along the patchy road bowed under tufts of snow. Winnebago Junction, the Pow Wow grounds, the tribal court and volunteer fire department, the station where she bought her tax-free gas, the hand-painted wooden shingle reading "Native Arts Gift Shop," the high school — *Home of the*

5

Indians—where she'd volunteer-tutored until despair drove her off: the scene turned away from her, hostile. On the long, empty stretch east of Rosalie, a lone male her brother's age in a too-light coat and hat—*Go Big Red*—tracked through the roadside drift. He turned and snarled as she passed, repelling the intrusion.

The suture of the centerline drew her downward into the snowy black. It made no sense: Mark, a near-professional driver, rolling off an arrow-straight country road that was as familiar to him as breathing. Driving off the road, in central Nebraska—like falling off a wooden horse. She toyed with the date: 02/20/02. Did it mean anything? Her palms butted the wheel, and the car shook. *Your brother has had an accident.* In fact, he'd long ago taken every wrong turn you could take in life, and from the wrong lane. Telephone calls coming in at awful hours, as far back as she could remember. But never one like this.

She used the radio to keep herself awake. She tuned in to a crackpot talk-radio show about the best way to protect your pets from water-borne terrorist poisonings. All the deranged, static voices in the dark seeped into her, whispering what she was: alone on a deserted road, half a mile from her own disaster.

What a loving child Mark had been, staffing his earthworm hospital, selling his toys to stave off the farm foreclosure, throwing his eight-year-old body between their parents that hideous night nineteen years ago when Cappy took a loop of power cord to Joan. That was how she pictured her brother, as she fell headlong into the dark. The root of all his accidents: too caring by half.

Outside Grand Island, two hundred miles down from Sioux, as the day broke and the sky went peach, she glimpsed

6

the Platte. First light glinted off its muddy brown, calming her. Something caught her eye, bobbing pearl waves flecked with red. Even she thought highway hypnosis, at first. A carpet of four-foot birds spread as far as the distant tree line. She'd seen them every spring for more than thirty years, and still the dancing mass made her jerk the wheel, almost following her brother.

He'd waited until the birds returned to spin out. He'd been a mess already, back in October, when she drove this same route for their mother's wake. Camping out with his beef-packing friends in the ninth circle of Nintendo hell, starting in on the six-packs for liquid brunch, fully loaded by the time he headed in to work on the swing shift. *Traditions to protect, Rabbit; family honor.* She hadn't had the will then, to talk sense to him. He wouldn't have heard her, if she had. But he'd made it through the winter, even pulled himself together a little. Only for this.

Kearney rose up: the scattered outskirts, the newly extruded superstore strip, the fast-food grease trough along Second, the old main drag. The whole town suddenly struck her as a glorified I-80 exit ramp. Familiarity filled her with a weird, inappropriate calm. Home.

She found Good Samaritan the way the birds found the Platte. She spoke to the trauma doctor, working hard to follow him. He kept saying *moderate severity*, *stable*, and *lucky*. He looked young enough to have been out partying with Mark earlier that night. She wanted to ask to see his med school diploma. Instead she asked what "moderate severity" meant, and nodded politely at the opaque answer. She asked about "lucky," and the trauma doctor explained: "Lucky to be alive."

Firemen had cut him out of his cab with an acetylene torch. He might have lain there all night, coffined against the windshield, freezing and bleeding to death, just off the shoulder of the country road, except for the anonymous call from a gas station on the edge of town.

They let her into the unit to see him. A nurse tried to prepare her, but Karin heard nothing. She stood in front of a nest of cables and monitors. On the bed lay a lump of white wrapping. A face cradled inside the tangle of tubes, swollen and rainbowed, coated in abrasions. His bloody lips and cheeks were flecked with embedded gravel. The matted hair gave way to a patch of bare skull sprouting wires. The forehead had been pressed to a hot grill. In a flimsy robin's-egg gown, her brother struggled to inhale.

She heard herself call him, from a distance. "Mark?" The eyes opened at the sound, like the hard plastic eyes of her girlhood dolls. Nothing moved, not even his eyelids. Nothing, until his mouth pumped, without sound. She leaned down into the equipment. Air hissed through his lips, above the hum of the monitors. Wind through a field of ready wheat.

His face knew her. But nothing came out of his mouth except a trickle of saliva. His eyes pleaded, terrified. He needed something from her, life or death. "It's okay; I'm here," she said. But assurance only made him worse. She was exciting him, exactly what the nurses had forbidden. She looked away, anywhere but at his animal eyes. The room burned into her memory: the drawn curtain, the two racks of threatening electronic equipment, the lime sherbet-colored wall, the rolling table alongside his bed.

She tried again. "Markie, it's Karin. You're going to be all right." Saying it made a kind of truth. A groan escaped his sealed mouth. His hand, stuck with an IV tube, reached up and grabbed her wrist. His aim stunned her. The grip was feeble but deadly, drawing her down into the mesh of tubes.

His fingers feathered at her, frantic, as if, in this split second, she might still keep his truck from wiping out.

The nurse made her leave. Karin Schluter sat in the trauma waiting room, a glass terrarium at the end of a long corridor smelling of antiseptics, dread, and ancient health magazines. Rows of head-bowed farmers and their wives, in dark sweatshirts and overalls, sat in the squared-off, padded apricot chairs alongside her. She figured them: *Father heart attack*; *husband hunting accident*; *child overdose*. Off in the corner, a muted television beamed images of a mountain wasteland scattered with guerrillas. Afghanistan, winter, 2002. After a while, she noticed a thread of blood wicking down her right index finger, where she'd bitten through her cuticle. She found herself rising and drifting to the restroom, where she vomited.

Later, she ate, something warm and sticky from the hospital cafeteria. At one point, she stood in one of those half-finished stairwells of poured concrete meant to be seen only when the building was on fire, calling back to Sioux City, the massive computer and home electronics company where she worked in consumer relations. She stood smoothing her rumpled bouclé skirt as if her supervisor could see her over the line. She told her boss, as vaguely as she could, about the accident. A remarkably level account: thirty years of practice hiding Schluter truths. She asked for two days off. He offered her three. She started to protest, but switched at once to grateful acceptance.

Back in the waiting room, she witnessed eight middle-aged men in flannel standing in a ring, their slow eyes scanning the floor. A murmur issued from them, wind teasing the lonely screens of a farmhouse. The sound rose and fell in waves. It took her a moment to realize: a prayer circle, for another victim who'd come in just after Mark. A makeshift Pentecostal service, covering anything that scalpels, drugs, and lasers couldn't. The gift of tongues descended on the circle of men, like small talk at a family reunion. Home was the place you never escape, even in nightmare.

Stable. Lucky. The words got Karin through to midday. But when the trauma doctor next talked to her, the words had become *cerebral edema*. Something had spiked the pressure inside her brother's skull. Nurses tried cooling his body. The doctor mentioned a ventilator and ventricular drain. Luck and stability were gone.

When they let her see Mark again, she no longer knew him. The person they took her to the second time lay comatose, his face collapsed into some stranger's. His eyes wouldn't open when she called his name. His arms hung still, even when she squeezed them.

Hospital personnel came to talk to her. They spoke to her as if she were brain-damaged. She pumped them for information. Mark's blood alcohol content had been just under the Nebraska limit—three or four beers in the hours before rolling his truck. Nothing else noticeable in his system. His truck was destroyed.

Two policemen took her aside in the corridor and asked her questions. She answered what she knew, which was nothing. An hour later, she wondered if she'd imagined the conversation. Late that afternoon, a man of fifty in a blue work shirt sat down next to her where she waited. She managed to turn and blink. Not possible, not even in this town: hit on, in the trauma-unit waiting room.

"You should get a lawyer," the man said.

She blinked again and shook her head. Sleep deprivation.

"You're with the fellow who rolled his truck? Read about him in the *Telegraph*. You should definitely get a lawyer."

10

Her head would not stop shaking. "Are you one?"

The man jerked back. "Good God, no. Just ne
advice."

She hunted down the newspaper and read the flimsy accident account until it crumbled. She sat in the glass terrarium as long as she could, then circled the ward, then sat again. Every hour, she begged to see him. Each time, they denied her. She dozed for five minutes at a shot, propped in the sculpted apricot chair. Mark rose up in her dreams, like buffalo grass after a prairie fire. A child who, out of pity, always picked the worst players for his team. An adult who called only when weepy drunk. Her eyes stung and her mouth thickened with scum. She checked the mirror in the floor's bathroom: blotchy and teetering, her fall of red hair a tangled bead-curtain. But still presentable, given everything.

"There has been some reversal," the doctor explained. He spoke in B waves and millimeters of mercury, lobes and ventricles and hematomas. Karin finally understood. Mark would need surgery.

They slit his throat and put a bolt into his skull. The nurses stopped answering Karin's questions. Hours later, in her best consumer-relations voice, she asked again to see him. They said he was too weakened by the procedures. The nurses offered to get something for her, and Karin only slowly realized they meant medication.

"Oh, no thanks," she said. "I'm good."

"Go home for a while," the trauma doctor advised. "Doctor's orders. You need some rest."

"Other people are sleeping on the floor of the waiting room. I can get a sleeping bag and be right back."

"There's nothing you can do right now," the doctor claimed. But that couldn't be; not in the world she came from.

11

She promised to go rest if they let her see Mark, just for a moment. They did. His eyes were still closed, and he responded to nothing.

Then she saw the note. It lay on the bed stand, waiting. No one could tell her when it had appeared. Some messenger had slipped into the room unseen, even while Karin was shut out. The writing was spidery, ethereal: immigrant scrawl from a century ago.

I am No One
but Tonight on North Line Road
GOD led me to you
so You could Live
and bring back someone else.

A flock of birds, each one burning. Stars swoop down to bullets. Hot red specks take flesh, nest there, a body part, part body.

Lasts forever: no change to measure.

Flock of fiery cinders. When gray pain of them thins, then always water. Flattest width so slow it fails as liquid. Nothing in the end but flow. Nextless stream, lowest thing above knowing. A thing itself the cold and so can't feel it.

Body flat water, falling an inch a mile. Torso long as the world. Frozen run all the way from open to close. Great oxbows, age bends, lazy delayed S, switch current to still as long as possible the one long drop it already finishes.

Not even river, not even *wet brown slow west*, no now or then except in now and then rising. Face forcing up into soundless scream. White column, lit in a river of light. Then pure terror, pealing into air, flipping and falling, anything but hit target.

One sound gets not a word but still says: *come*. Come with. Try death.

At last only water. Flat water spreading to its level. Water that is nothing but into nothing falls.

She checked into one of those crane-tourist places off the interstate. It seemed to have just fallen off the back of a truck. They gouged her for a room. But she was close to the hospital—all that mattered. She stayed one night, then had to find something else. As next of kin, she qualified for the shelter house a block from the hospital, a hostel subsidized with the pocket change of the world's largest global fast-food cartel. The Clown House, she and Mark had called it, back when their father was dying of fatal insomnia four years before. It had taken the man forty days to die, and at the last, when he finally agreed to go to the hospital, their mother sometimes stayed overnight at the Clown House to be near him. Karin could not face that memory, not now. Instead, she drove to Mark's place, half an hour away.

She navigated out to Farview, where Mark had bought a catalog house just months after their father's death with his portion of the meager inheritance. She got lost and had to ask for directions to River Run Estates from the Walter Brennan impersonator at the Four Corners Texaco. Psychological. She'd never wanted Mark living there. But after Cappy died, Mark listened to no one.

At last she found the modular Homestar, the pride of Mark's adulthood. He'd bought it just before starting as a Maintenance and Repair Technician II at the meat packing plant in Lexington. The day Mark wrote the down-payment check, he ran around town celebrating as if he'd just gotten engaged.

A fresh loop of dog shit welcomed her inside the front door. Blackie cowered in the living room corner, whimpering in guilty confusion. Karin let the poor creature out and fed her. In the postage-stamp yard, the border collie reverted to herding things—squirrels, snow motes, fence posts—anything to convince the humans that she was still worthy of love.

The heat was down. Only her brother's habit of never completely shutting off a tap had kept the pipes from bursting. She scooped the cone of shit into the frosty yard. The dog crept up to her, willing to make friends, but wanting first to know Mark's whereabouts. Karin lowered herself to the stoop and pressed her face into the frozen railing.

Shivering, she went back inside. She could ready the house for him, at least: cleaning that hadn't been done in weeks. In what her brother called the family room, she straightened the stacks of truck-customization and cheese-cake magazines. She gathered scattered discs and stacked them behind the paneled bar that Mark, with limited success, had installed himself. A poster of a girl in a black leather bikini slung over a vintage truck's hood sagged off the bedroom wall. Disgusted, she tore it down. Only when she looked at the scraps in her hands did she see what she'd done. She found a hammer in the utility closet and tried to tack the poster back up, but it was too torn. She threw it in the bin, cursing herself.

The bathroom was a science-fair project in full bloom. Mark had no cleaning supplies except pipe cleaners and Black Leather Soap. She searched the kitchen for vinegar or ammonia, but found nothing more solvent than Old Style. Under the sink, she turned up a rag-filled bucket with a can of

14

scouring powder that thumped when she lifted it. She twisted the lid and it popped open. Inside was a packet of pills.

She sat down on the kitchen floor and cried. She considered heading back to Sioux City, cutting her losses and resuming her life. She picked at the pills, her fingers flipping them. Dollhouse accessories or sports equipment: white plates, red barbells, tiny purple saucers with unreadable monograms. Who was he hiding them from, down there, besides himself? She thought she recognized the local favorite: Ecstasy. She'd taken some once, two years ago in Boulder. Had spent the evening mind-merging with friends and hugging perfect strangers. Numb, she held a pill and rubbed it against her sagging tongue. She tore it away and fed the whole stash down the disposal. She let the yipping Blackie back inside. The dog nosed around her calves, needing her. "It's all right," she promised the creature. "Everything's going to be back again, soon."

She moved on to the bedroom, a museum of cows' teeth, colored minerals, and hundreds of exotic bottle caps mounted on homemade stands. She inspected the closet. Alongside the mostly dark denim and corduroy, three grease-stained jumpsuits with the IBP logo hung on a hook above his caked work boots, the ones he wore every day, heading to the slaughter. The thought sliced through her: things she should have handled the day before. She phoned the plant. Iowa Beef Processors: *World's largest supplier of premium beef, pork, and allied products.* She got an automated menu. Then another. Then chirpy music, then a chirpy person, then a croaky person who kept calling her *ma'am.* Ma'am. Somewhere along the line, she'd become her own mother. A personnel counselor walked her through the steps to start Mark's disability. For the hour it took to transact the forms, she felt the release of being useful. The pleasure of it burned.

She called her own employers, up in Sioux. They were a big outfit, the third-largest computer vendor in the country. Years ago, in the early days of the PC clone boom, they'd broken out of the pack of identical mail-order vendors on the simple gimmick of running herds of Holsteins in their ads. Mark had laughed at her when she'd dragged back to Nebraska from Colorado and got a job with them. *You're going to work complaints for the Cow Computer Company?* She couldn't explain. After years of what she'd thought of as career advancement—graduating from phone receptionist in Chicago to ad-copy saleswoman for trendy trade magazines in Los Angeles, progressing to right-hand woman and finally company face for two dot-com entrepreneurs in Boulder who were going to make millions with an online world where people could develop rich alter egos, but who ended up suing each other—she'd slammed back down to earth. Past thirty, she had no more time or pride to risk on ambition. Nothing wrong with honest gruntwork for a secure company that lacked all pretension. If her fate lay in consumer relations, she would relate to consumers as expertly as humanly possible. In fact, she'd discovered a hidden aptitude for complaint-handling. Two e-mails and fifteen minutes on the phone, and she could convince a customer ready to firebomb the outfit that she and her multi-thousand-employee firm wanted nothing more than the man's lifelong friendship and respect.

She couldn't explain to her brother or anyone: status and satisfaction meant nothing. Competence was all. At long last, her life had stopped misleading her. She had a job she performed well, a new one-bedroom condo near the river in South Sioux, even a nice little shared nervousness with a friendly mammal in tech support that threatened to turn into a relationship any month now. Then this. One phone call, and reality found her out again.

No matter. Nothing in Sioux needed her. The one that really needed her lay in the hospital, on a dark island, with no other family to look out for him.

She reached her office manager, smoothing her hair as he came on the line. He looked up her vacation days and said she could stay out until a week from the coming Monday. As self-effacingly as she could, she explained that she wasn't sure that would be enough. It probably had to be enough, her manager said. She thanked him, apologized again, hung up, and returned to more furious cleaning.

With only dish soap and paper towels, she brought Mark's place back to livable. She studied herself in the bathroom mirror as she cleaned the spatter-spots: a thirty-one-year-old professional soother, three and a half pounds overweight with red hair eighteen inches too long for her age, desperate for something to fix. She could rise to this. Mark would be back soon, gleefully respattering the mirror. She would return to Cow Computer country, where people respected the work she did and only strangers asked her for help. She smoothed her dry cheeks back toward her ears and slowed her breathing. She finished the sink and tub, then went out to the car and checked her backpack: two pullovers, a pair of twill slacks, and three changes of underwear. She drove out to the Kearney outlet strip and bought a sweater, two pairs of jeans, and some moisturizer. Even that much tempted fate.

I am No One, but Tonight on North Line Road . . . She asked around the trauma unit about the note. By all accounts, it had simply appeared on the bedside stand shortly after Mark's admission. A Hispanic clerical nurse with an elaborate crucifix necklace studded with turquoise boulders insisted that no one but Karin and hospital personnel had been allowed to see him for the first thirty-six hours. She produced the paperwork to prove it. The nurse tried to confiscate the slip of paper, but Karin refused to surrender it. She needed it for Mark, when he came to.

They moved him from trauma to a room where she could sit with him. He lay stretched on the bed, a felled mannequin. Two days later, he opened his eyes for half a minute, only to squeeze them shut. But they opened again, at dusk that evening. Over the next day, she counted six more eye openings. Each time, he looked out on some living horror film.

His face began moving like a rubber costume mask. His unplugged gaze sought her out. She sat at bedside, slipping on scree at the lip of a deep quarry. "What is it, Mark? Tell me. I'm here."

She begged the nurses for something to do, anything, however small, that might help. They gave her special nylon socks and basketball high-tops to put on Mark and remove again, every few hours. She did this every forty minutes, massaging his feet as well. It kept his blood circulating and prevented clots. She sat at bedside, squeezing and kneading. Once, she caught herself sub-vocalizing her old 4-H pledge:

> my Head to clearer thinking,
> my Heart to greater loyalty,
> my Hands to larger service,
> and my Health to better living . . .

as if she were back in high school and Mark were her project for the county fair.

Larger service: she'd looked for it her whole life, armed with nothing more than a bachelor's in sociology from UNK. Teacher's aide on the Winnebago reservation, volunteer at homeless feeding stations in downtown L.A., pro bono clerical worker for a law firm in Chicago. For the sake of a prospective boyfriend in Boulder, she'd even briefly served as street demonstrator in antiglobalization marches, chanting out the protests with a zeal that could not mask her profound sense of silliness. She would have stayed home forever, given herself to keeping her family intact, had it not been for her family. Now the last other member of it lay next to her, inert, unable to object to her services.

The doctor put a metal tap in her brother's brain, draining it. Monstrous, but it worked. The pressure in his skull dropped. The cysts and sacs shrank. His brain now had all the room it needed. She told him as much. "All you need to do now is heal."

Hours went by in a heartbeat. But the days stretched out without end. She sat by the bed, cooling his body with special chilling blankets, taking off his shoes and putting them on again. All the while, she spoke to him. He never showed any hint of hearing, but she kept talking. The eardrums still had to move, the nerves behind them ripple. "Brought you some roses from the IGA. Aren't they pretty? They smell good, too. The nurse is changing the empties on the drip again, Markie. Don't worry; I'm still here. You've got to get up and see the cranes this year, before they go. They're out of this world. I've never seen so many of them. Coming into town in packs. Bunch of them landed on the roof of the McDonald's. They're up to something. Jeez, Mark. Your feet are ripe. They smell like a bad Roquefort."

Smell my feet. Her ritual punishment for any transgression, starting the year he passed her in strength. She smelled his stagnant body again, for the first time since they were children. Roquefort and curdled puke. Like the feral kitten they found

19

hiding under the porch when she was nine. Sweet-sour, like the forest of mold on the slice of moist bread Mark left in a covered dish on top of the furnace vent in fifth grade, for a science fair, and forgot about. "We'll draw you a good bubble bath when you get home."

She told him about the stream of visitors to his comatose neighbor's bed: women in smock dresses; men in white shirts and black trousers, like 1960s Mormons on their missions. He took in all her stories, stonelike, his smallest face muscles stilled.

In week two, an older man came into the shared room wearing a puffy coat that made him look like a shiny blue Michelin man. He stood at the bed of Mark's unconscious roommate, shouting. "Gilbert. Boy? You hear me? Wake up, now. We don't have time for such foolishness. That's enough, hear. We got to get on back home." A nurse came to check on the commotion and led the protesting man away. After that, Karin stopped speaking to Mark. He didn't seem to notice.

Dr. Hayes said that the fifteenth day was the point of no return. Nine-tenths of closed-head trauma victims who came back came back by then. "The eyes are good news," he told her. "His reptilian brain is showing nice activity."

"He has a reptile brain?"

Dr. Hayes smiled, like a doctor in an old public health film. "We all do. A record of the long way here."

Clearly he wasn't from around these parts. Most locals hadn't come the long way. Both Schluter parents believed evolution was Communist propaganda. Mark himself had his doubts. *If all the millions of species are constantly evolving, how come we're the only ones who got smart?*

The doctor elaborated. "The brain is a mind-boggling redesign. But it can't escape its past. It can only add to what's already there."

She pictured those mangled Kearney mansions, glorious old wooden Victorians enlarged with brick in the 1930s and again in the 1970s with pressboard and aluminum. "What's his reptile brain . . . doing? What kind of nice activity?"

Dr. Hayes reeled off names: medulla, pons, midbrain, cerebellum. She copied the words into a tiny spiral notebook where she recorded everything, to look up later. The neurologist made the brain sound more rickety than the old toy trucks Mark used to assemble from discarded cabinet parts and sawn-off detergent bottles.

"What about his higher . . . ? What's above reptile—some kind of bird?"

"The next higher structure is the mammalian."

Her lips moved as he talked, assisting. She couldn't help it. "And my brother's?"

Dr. Hayes grew guarded. "That's harder to say. We don't see any explicit damage. There is activity. Regulation. The hippocampus and amygdala seem intact, but we did see some spiking in the amygdala, where some of the negative emotions, like fear, start."

"You're saying my brother is *afraid*?" She waved off the doctor's reassurances, thrilled. Mark was feeling. Fear or anything: it didn't matter. "What about his . . . human brain? The part above the mammal?"

"He's piecing himself back together. Activity in his prefrontal cortex is struggling to synchronize into consciousness."

She asked Dr. Hayes for every pamphlet the hospital had on head injury. She underlined all the hopeful suggestions in green fine-line marker. *The brain is our last frontier. The more we learn about it, the more we see how much more there is to know.* The next time she met Dr. Hayes, she was ready.

"Doctor, have you considered any of the new head-injury treatments?" She scrambled in her shoulder bag for her little spiral notebook. "Neuroprotective agents? Cerestat? PEG-SOD?"

"Wow. I'm impressed. You've done your homework."

She tried to look as competent as she wanted him to be.

Dr. Hayes steepled his fingers and touched them to his lips. "Things happen fast in this field. PEG-SOD has been discontinued, after poor results in a second Phase III trial. And I don't think you want cerestat."

"Doctor." Her client-relations voice. "My brother is struggling to open his eyes. You say he may be terrified. We'll take anything you can give him."

"All research on cerestat—Aptiganel—has been halted. A fifth of all patients taking it have died."

"But you have other drugs, don't you?" She looked down at her notebook, tremoring. At any moment, her hands would turn to doves and fly away.

"Most are still in the early testing. You'd have to be in a clinical trial."

"Aren't we, already? I mean . . ." She waved toward her brother's room. In the back of her mind, she heard the radio jingle: *Good Samaritan Hospital . . . the largest medical facility between Lincoln and Denver.*

"You'd have to change hospitals. Go where they're running the studies."

She looked at the man. With proper grooming, he could be the advice doctor on breakfast television. If he saw her at all, it was only as a complication. He probably found her pathetic, in every measurable way. Something in her reptilian brain hated him.

22

Rises up in flooded fields. There is a wave, a rocking in the reeds. Pain again, then nothing.

When sense returns, he is drowning. Father teaching him to swim. Current in his limbs. Four years old, and his father floating him. Flying, then flailing, then falling. His father grabbing his leg, pulling him under. Holding him beneath the surface, stiff hand pressing down his head until all bubbles stop. *River will bite, boy. Be ready.*

But there is no *bite*, no *ready*. There is only *drown*.

There comes a pyramid of light, burning diamonds, twisting fields of stars. His body threads triangles of neon, a tunnel rising. The water over him, his lungs on fire, and then he explodes upward, toward air.

Where his mouth was, just smooth skin. Solid swallows up that hole. House remodeled; windows papered over. Door no more a door. Muscles pull lips but no space to open. Wires only, where words were. Face bent wrong and folded up into its own eyes. Slipped in a metal bed, the hell he must be in. His smallest move a pain worse than dying. Maybe death is done already. Done all ways, in one tip of his life and lifting. Who'd want to live after such a fall?

A room of machines, the space he can't reach. Something splits out from him. People move in and smooth away too fast. Faces push up to his mouthless face, pushing words into him. He chews them and puffs sound back. Someone says be patient, but to not him. *Be patient, be a patient* is what he must be.

This may be days. No saying. Time flaps about, wings broken. Voices pass, some circle back, but one's as close to always there as there is. A face almost his face, so close it wants something of him, if only at least words. That face a she and like water weeping. Nothing she is will say what happened.

One need tries to tear out of him. Need to *say*, more than the need to be. If a mouth, then all would be out. Then this she would know what happened, know his death wasn't what it seems.

Pressure fills, like fluid crushed. His head: endless pressure, buried already. Sap streams out of his inner ear. Blood out his gorged eyes. Killing pressure, even after all that seeps out of him. A million more schooling thoughts than his brain can hold.

A face hovers near, forming words on fire. Says *Mark, stay*, and he would die to make her stop keeping him alive. He pushes back against the thing collapsing him. Muscles pull but skin won't move. Something slack. He works forever to winch the tendons in his neck. At last his head tilts. Later, lifetimes, lifts the edge of his upper lip.

Three words would save him. But all muscles can't free one sound.

Thoughts throb in a vein. Red pulses his eyes again, then that one white shaft shooting up from the black he blasted through. Something in the road he'll never reach now. Screaming up close as his life rolled. Someone here in this room, who will die with him.

The first word comes. It surfaces through a bruise wider than his throat. The skin grown over his mouth tears clear and a word forces through the bloody opening. *I.* The word hisses, taking so long she'll never hear. *I didn't mean.*

But words change to flying things as they hit the air.

Two weeks in, Mark sat up and moaned. Karin was at his bedside, five feet from his face. He buckled at the waist, and she screamed. His eyes twisted around and found her. Her scream turned into a laugh, then a sob, while his eyes twitched over her. She called his name, and the face underneath the tubes and scars flinched. Soon a raft of caregivers filled the room.

Much had happened underground, in the days he lay frozen. Now he poked out, like winter wheat through snow. He turned his head, craning his neck. His hands thrust out clumsily. His fingers picked at the invasive hardware. He hated most his gastric feeding tube. As his arms got better at clawing it, the nurses imposed soft restraints.

Now and then, something spooked him, and he thrashed to escape it. Nights were the worst. Once when Karin was leaving for the day, a wave of chemicals bucked through him and he surged upright, scrambling almost to his knees on his hospital bed. She had to wrestle him down to keep him from tearing out his hoses.

She watched him return, hour by hour, as in some grim Scandinavian film. Sometimes he gazed at her, weighing if she was edible or a threat. Once, a surge of animal sexuality, forgotten in the next moment. At times she was a crust he tried to brush from his eyes. He shot her that liquid, amused look he'd given her one night when they were teens, each of them crawling home from their respective assignations, drunk. *You, too? I didn't know you had it in you.*

He started vocalizing—groans muffled by the tracheotomy tube, a secret, vowel-free language. Every rasp lacerated Karin. She badgered the doctors to do something. They measured scar tissue and cranial fluid, listening to everything but his frantic gurgling. They swapped his trach tube for a fenestrated one, pierced with tiny holes, a window in Mark's throat wide enough for sounds to pass through. And every one of her brother's cries begged for something Karin couldn't identify.

He was back to how she'd first seen him, when she was four, staring down from the second-story landing on a lump of meat wrapped in a blue baby blanket her parents had just dragged home. Her earliest memory: standing at the top of the stairs, wondering why her parents bothered cooing over something far stupider than the outdoor cats. But she soon learned to love this baby, the greatest toy a girl could ask for. She hauled him around like a doll for a year until he finally took a few dazed steps without her. She jabbered at him, wheedled and bribed, kept crayons and bits of food just out of reach until he called for them by their real names. She'd raised her brother, while her mother was busy laying up treasures in heaven. Karin had gotten Mark to walk and talk once already. Surely, with help from Good Samaritan, she could do it twice. Something in her almost prized this second chance to raise him right this time.

Alone by his bed between nurses' visits, she started talking to him again. Her words might focus his brain. None of the neurology books she pored over denied that possibility. No one knew enough about the brain to say what her brother might or might not hear. She felt as she had through childhood, putting him to bed while their parents were out wailing on home-steader hymns around the neighbor's Hammond chord organ, before their parents' first bankruptcy and the end of socializing. Karin, from the earliest age, playing babysitter, earning her two dollars by keeping her little brother alive for another night. Markie, skyrocketing from an overdose of Milk

Duds and cherry colas, demanding they count to infinity or run telepathic experiments on each other or relate long epics from Animalia, the country humans couldn't get to, populated by heroes, rogues, tricksters, and victims, all based on the creatures of their family farm.

Always animals. The good ones and the evil, the ones to protect and the ones to destroy. "You remember the bull snake in the barn?" she asked him. His eyes flickered, watching the idea of the creature. "You must have been nine. Took a stick and killed it all by yourself. Protecting everyone. Went to Cappy and bragged, and he beat the shit out of you. *You just cost us eight hundred dollars' worth of grain. Don't you know what those creatures eat? What have you got for brains, boy?* Last snake you ever killed."

He studied her, the edges of his mouth working. He seemed to be listening.

"Remember Horace?" The injured crane they'd adopted when Mark was ten and Karin fourteen. Winged by a power line, the bird had ditched on their property during the spring migration. It went into a dance of total panic as they approached. They spent an afternoon closing in, letting the bird adjust to them, until it resigned itself to capture.

"Remember, when we washed him, how he took the towel from you with his beak and started drying himself? Instinct, like how they coat themselves with mud to darken their feathers. But God. We thought that bird was smarter than any human being alive. Remember how we tried to teach it to shake?"

All at once, Mark started keening. One arm tomahawked and the other swung wide. His torso slashed upward and his head thrust out. Tubes tore off and the monitor alarm squealed. Karin called the attendants while Mark flapped about on the sheets, his body lurching toward her. She was in tears by the time the orderly showed. "I don't know what I did. What's wrong with him?"

"Would you look at that," the orderly said. "He's trying to hug you!"

She ran up to Sioux, to put out fires. She'd missed her return-to-work date, and she'd reached the limit of what she could ask for by phone. She went in to talk to her supervisor. He listened to the details, shaking his head with concern. He had a cousin, hit in the skull with a seven iron once. Damaged a lobe that sounded like *varietal*. Never the same afterward. Her supervisor hoped that wouldn't happen to Karin's brother.

She thanked him, and asked if she could stay out just a little while longer.

How much longer?

She couldn't say.

Wasn't her brother in the hospital? Didn't he have professional care?

She could take an unpaid leave, she bargained. Just for a month.

Her supervisor explained that the Family Medical Leave Act did not extend to siblings. A brother, in the eyes of the medical-leave law, was not family.

Maybe she might give notice, and they could hire her back when her brother was better.

It wasn't impossible, the supervisor said. But he could guarantee nothing.

This hurt. "I'm good," she said. "I'm as good as anyone else on the lines."

"You're better than good," the supervisor conceded, and even now she swelled with pride. "But I don't need good. I just need *here*."

28

She cleaned out her cubicle in a daze. A few embarrassed officemates expressed concern and wished her well. Over before she'd really started. A year ago, she'd thought she might rise in the firm, make a career, start a life up here with people who knew only her friendly readiness and nothing of her messy past. She should have known that Kearney—the Schluter touch—would come back to claim her. She considered walking down to tech support, to break the news to her flirtation, Chris. Instead, she called him on her cell phone from the parking lot. When he heard her voice, he gave her the silent treatment, both barrels. Two weeks without a call or e-mail. She kept apologizing until he talked. When he got over his sulk, Chris was all concern. He asked what had happened. Bottomless familial shame blocked her from telling all. She'd made herself witty for him, light, easygoing, even sophisticated, by local standards. In fact, she was just a shit-kicker raised by zealots, with a shiftless brother who'd managed to reduce himself to infancy. *Family emergency*, she just repeated.

"When are you coming back?"

She told him the emergency had just cost her her job. Chris cursed the firm nobly. He even threatened to go have it out with her supervisor. She thanked him, but said he had to think about himself. His own job. She didn't know this man, and he didn't know her. Yet when he didn't argue with her, she felt betrayed.

"Where are you?" he asked. She panicked and said *home*. "I can come down," he volunteered. "This weekend, or some time. Help out. Anything you need."

She held the phone away from her spasming face. She told him he was too good, that he shouldn't have to worry like that about her. This made him sullen again. "That's okay, then," he said. "Nice knowing you. Take care. Have a good life."

29

She hung up, cursing. But life in Sioux had never really belonged to her. It was, at most, a binge of simplicity that she now had to detox from. She drove to her condo to check on the place and pack a more realistic wardrobe. The trash hadn't been taken out in weeks and the place reeked. Mice had chewed through her matching plastic sealable bowls, and lentils covered the counters and beautiful new floor. The philodendrons, schefflera, and peace lily were all past saving.

She cleaned up, shut off the water main, and paid the delinquent bills. No new monthly paycheck would cover them. Locking the door behind her as she left, she wondered how much more she might have to give up, for Mark. On the ride back south, she tapped all the anger-management tricks they'd given her in job training. They played across her windshield like PowerPoint slides. Number One: It's not about you. Number Two: Your plan is not the world's. Number Three: The mind can make a heaven of hell, a hell of heaven.

She owed her own competence to raising her brother. He was her psychology experiment: Given another parent, with everything else the same, could her own flesh and blood grow up worthwhile? But in exchange for her selfless care, he gave her back, at best, an endless supply of his chief attribute: total aimlessness. *Animals like me,* the eleven-year-old claimed. And they did, without fail. Everything on the farm trusted him. Even ladybugs would crawl fearlessly across his face, finding a place in his eyebrows to nest. *What do you want to be when you grow up?* she once made the mistake of asking. His face burst with excitement: *I could be a real good chicken calmer.*

But when it came to humans, no one quite knew what to make of the boy. He'd made some mistakes as a kid: burning down the corn crib while shooting off tinfoil-wrapped matches. Getting caught playing with himself behind the rotting chicken coop. Killing a five-hundred-pound newly weaned calf by lacing its feed with a bowl of mixed medicines, convinced it was in pain. Worse, he spoke with a lisp until the age of six, which pretty much convinced both parents he was possessed. For weeks, their mother made him sleep under a wall exorcised with a cross anointed with oil, which shed droplets on his head as he slept.

At seven, he took to spending long hours in the afternoons in a meadow half a mile from their house. When their mother asked him what he did there for hours at a time, he replied, "Just play." When she asked with who, he said, at first, "No one," and later, "With a friend." She refused to let him leave the house until he told her the friend's name. He answered with a shy smile: "His name is Mr. Thurman." He went on to tell the panicked woman all the great times that he and Mr. Thurman had together. Joan Schluter called in the entire Kearney police force. After a stakeout of the meadow and a thorough cross-examination of the boy, the police told the frantic parents that Mr. Thurman not only had no criminal record, he had no record whatsoever, outside of their son's head.

Karin was Mark's only hope of surviving adolescence. When he turned thirteen, she tried to show him how to save himself. *It's easy*, she claimed. She'd discovered in high school, to her shock, that she could make even the elites like her by letting them dress her and instruct her musical tastes. *People like people who make them feel secure.* He didn't know what the word meant. *You need a brand*, she told him. *Something recognizable.* She pushed him into chess club, cross-country, Future Farmers, even the thespians. Nothing stuck until he stumbled upon the group that would take him

31

in because he passed the simple audition of failing to fit in anywhere else—the group of losers that freed him from her.

After he found his tribe, she could do little more for him. She concentrated on saving herself, finishing her sociology degree, the first ever in a family that looked on college as a form of witchcraft. She pressured Mark to follow her at UNK. He made it through one year, never having the heart to upset his many advisors by actually declaring a major. She moved to Chicago, answering phones for a Big Five accounting firm on the eighty-sixth floor of the Standard Oil Building. Her mother used to call long-distance, just to listen to her phone-receptionist voice. "How'd you learn how to sound like that? That's not right! That can't be good for your vocal cords." From Chicago she went to Los Angeles, the greatest city on earth. She tried to tell Mark: *You could be lots of things out here. You could find work anywhere. They're begging for easygoing people out here. Your parents aren't your fault,* she told him. *You could come out here and nobody would ever have to know about them.* Even when her own launch began to fall back to earth, she still believed: people liked people who made them feel more secure.

When Mark was himself again, she would restart them both. She'd get him on his feet, listen to him, help him find what he needed to be. And this time she'd take him away with her, someplace reasonable.

She'd saved the note, and read it daily. A kind of magic charm: *Tonight on North Line Road GOD led me to you.* Surely that note writer—the saint who had discovered the wreck and come to the hospital on the night of the accident—would return to make real contact, now that Mark was awake. Karin waited patiently, for a long-delayed explanation. But no one came by to identify himself or explain anything.

A spring bouquet arrived from the IBP plant. Two dozen of Mark's coworkers signed the *Get Well Soon* card, some adding jokey, off-color encouragements Karin couldn't decode. The whole county knew what had happened to Mark: a police siren couldn't go off in the Big Bend region without everyone between Grand Island and North Platte telling you exactly who had screwed up, and how.

A few days after the trach tube change, Mark's best friends at last visited. Karin heard them when they were still down the hall.

"Damn, it's a cold universe out there."

"Tell me about it. My 'nads have migrated up into my eye-sockets."

They rolled into the room, Tommy Rupp in black flak jacket and Duane Cain in Thinsulate-stuffed camouflage. The Three Muskrateers, reunited for the first time since the accident. They showered Karin with upbeat greetings. She fought the urge to ask where they'd been. Rupp strode up to Mark where he lay whimpering in bed and offered him a palm. Mark, from some deep reflex, flipped him a high five.

"Jesus, Gus. They really did a number on you." Rupp waved at the monitors. "Can you believe this? All this gear, just for you."

Duane hung back, squeezing his neck. "He's making headway, don't you think?" He turned to Karin, standing behind him at bedside. Tattoos crept out from under the collar of his long underwear, a cartoon of red muscles stung onto his hairless chest, as detailed and realistic as an anatomy text. He looked flayed alive. He whispered to Karin, slow and booming, for all those just emerging from a coma. "This is fucking incon-ceivable. Happened to exactly the person who didn't deserve it."

Rupp took her elbow. "Our man's in pretty rough shape."

Her arm went hot from the wrist up. The curse of the red-headed: she flushed faster than a pheasant from the brush. She withdrew her arm and smoothed her cheeks. "You should have seen him last week." She couldn't control her tone.

A look passed from Cain to Rupp: *The woman is hurting, man. Don't let the Madame Mao thing get you.* Cain's face was clear, earnest, working with her. "We've been calling in. We understand he just recently woke up."

Rupp had Mark's clipboard chart and was shaking his head. "Are they doing anything at all useful for him?" The world needed new management, a fact so obvious that only a select few knew it.

"They had to reduce pressure on his brain. He wasn't responding to anything."

"But he's coming back now," Rupp declared. He turned back to Mark and fisted his shoulder. "Isn't that right, Gus? Full return. Old times again."

Mark lay still, staring.

Karin blurted, "You're seeing him at the best he's been since . . ."

"We've been keeping track," Duane insisted. He scratched his tattoo muscles. "We've been following."

A river of phonemes flowed from the bed. Mark's arms snaked out. His mouth went *Ah . . . ah, kee-kee-kee.*

"You're upsetting him," Karin said. "He shouldn't get worked up." She wanted to kick them out, but Mark's activity excited her.

"Are you kidding?" Rupp pulled an empty chair up to the bedside. "A visit is the best thing for him. Any non-insane doctor will tell you that."

"Man needs his friends," Duane echoed. "Raise his serotonin levels. You're familiar with serotonin?"

Karin stopped her hands from flying upward. She nodded, despite herself. She grabbed her elbows for balance and walked out of the room. On her way out the door, she heard the chairs shuffle and Tommy Rupp say, "Slow down there, bro. Chill. What do you want to say? One tap for yes, two for no . . ."

If anyone knew what had happened that night, those two did. But she refused to ask them in front of Mark. She left the hospital, drifting toward Woodland Park. Late afternoon, under a purple-brown sky. March had launched one of its false springs, the kind that got the whole town to lower its guard before slamming it with another arctic blast. Steam trails rose up from the dirty piles of snow. She cut through downtown Kearney, a business district hosed for as far into the future as anyone could see. Falling commodities prices, rising unemployment, aging population, youth flight, family farms selling out to agribusiness for dirt and change: geography had decided Mark's fate long before his birth. Only the doomed stayed on to collect.

She walked past solid A-frames crumbling away to tar-paper shacks. She wove from Avenue E to Avenue I, between Thirty-first and Twenty-fifth, inside a life-sized photo album of her past. The house of the boy she first loved; the house of the boy she first failed to make love with. The house of her girlfriend of twenty years, who disowned her one day, six weeks after getting married: apparently something the new husband said. This was the town she'd tried three times to escape, each time recalled by perverse family disaster. Kearney had a headstone all picked out for her, and her job was only to walk randomly around these graveyard streets until she stumbled upon it.

Before Joan Schluter died, she'd given her daughter a stiff cardboard photograph of Great-Grandfather Swanson standing in front of his crumbling house, that chapel to desolation, twenty-five miles northwest of what would become Kearney. The man in the picture held half of his library—either *Pilgrim's Progress* or the Bible: the photo was too blurry to tell. On the mud wall of the soddie behind him, dangling from a stag's antler, hung a gilded birdcage, purchased out east at great expense and dragged a thousand miles overland in an oxcart, taking up precious cargo space that might have stored tools or medicines. The birdcage was more urgent. The body could survive any isolation. Then there was the mind.

Now residents had a cage still more gilded: cheap broadband. The Internet had hit Nebraska like liquor hitting a Stone Age tribe—the godsend every sandhills homesteader descendant had been waiting for, the only way to survive such vacancy. Karin herself abused the Web daily, up in the Sioux metropole: travel sites, auction sites selling discounted but very serviceable clothes, fancy gift foods for winning over her workmates, and, once or twice, the occasional dating service. The Net: a last-ditch cure for prairie blindness. But her dabbling was nothing compared to Mark's addiction. He and his friends manned two dozen online avatars between them, talking Pig Latin to chat-room housewives, posting long comments on conspiracy theory blogs, uploading questionable images to crazedpics.com. Half their after-plant hours consisted of building up experience points for fantasy characters in various alternate worlds. It panicked her, the number of hours he was willing to spend somewhere purely imaginary. Now he was locked in deeper space, a place where instant messages couldn't reach. And everything she'd feared the Web might do to him now seemed like heaven.

She wandered around town long enough to outlast his friends' click-impaired attention spans. The streetlights came on, on those streets that had lights. Now the blocks scrolled and repeated, the streets a simulation more predictable than one of Mark's online games. She doubled back on Central toward the hospital, keen to get her brother back to herself again.

But Rupp and Cain were still there, kicked back in their hospital chairs. Mark was sitting up in bed. The three of them were playing catch with a wadded-up ball of paper. Mark's throws were wild. Some went backward, hitting the wall behind him. He threw the way a sailor-suited chimp might ride a tricycle. But he was throwing. The resurrection froze her, Mark's biggest leap since his truck left the road. Cain and Rupp lobbed him underhand bloopers, which he stabbed at, half a second late. The makeshift ball bounced off his chest, his face, his flailing hands. And every humiliating hit produced a sound that could only be the thickest laughter. She wanted to scream. She wanted to clap with joy.

In the hallway, as they left, she thanked her brother's friends. What did it matter? The surviving part of her was beyond pride.

Rupp waved her off. "He's still in there. Don't worry. We'll dig him out."

She started to ask whether they'd been together, the night of the accident. But she didn't want to jeopardize this brief alliance. She showed them the note. "Do you know anything about this?"

They both shrugged. "No idea."

"It's important," she said. But they denied all knowledge.

Duane Cain, retreating crablike down the corridor, called back to her. "You wouldn't know what happened to the Ram, by any chance?"

She stared at him, baffled. Old Testament sacrifices. Barnyard rituals.

"I mean: Was his truck totally totaled? We could, you know . . . We could look it over for you, if you want."

The police questioned her again. She'd spoken to them the day after the accident but had no memory of the meeting. Later, when she was in better shape, they came back for details. Two officers kept her for forty minutes in a hospital conference room. They asked if she knew anything about her brother's activities on the evening of the accident. Had he been with anyone? Had he spoken to her about any recent personal problems, any change at work, anything he might have been struggling with? Was he distressed or depressed?

The questions skidded inside her. Her brother trying to off himself—the idea was so crazy she couldn't answer it. She'd lived fifteen feet away from Mark for more than half of her life. She knew his junior high school social studies grades, the brand of his underwear, his favorite color jujube, the middle name and perfume of every girl he'd ever craved. She could complete any sentence he spoke before it left his mouth. Even in jest, he'd never once mentioned wanting to die.

They asked if he'd been angry or aggressive in recent weeks. Not unusually so, she told them. They said he'd been at the Silver Bullet, a seedy bar on Route 183. She told them he went there often, after work. He was a controlled driver. He never drove unless he felt sober. The truck was his baby.

They wanted to know if he ever did anything more than drink. She told them no, and it felt just like the truth. She would have sworn to it in a court of law.

Did her brother recently make or receive any threats? Did he ever mention involvement in violent or dangerous activities?

It was winter. The roads were slick. Something like this happened every other week. Were they saying this wasn't a simple accident?

They had calculated Mark's velocity from his skid marks. As his truck left the road, he was braking from a top speed of eighty miles an hour.

The figure shook her. But she gave away nothing. She tried again: he was out in the middle of the night, driving too fast for conditions, and he lost the edge of the road.

He wasn't alone, the police told her. There were three sets of tire tracks on the stretch of North Line where he lost control. As they reconstructed it, an eastbound light truck had veered over the center line into Mark's lane, cutting him off before straightening out and leaving the scene. Mark, heading west, had veered in front of this skid, first hard to the right, then across the road, ending up flipped over in the left-hand ditch. A third vehicle, a midsized sedan also heading west, drove off the shoulder on the right-hand side of the road, its tailing distance apparently giving it barely enough time to shoulder safely.

The description unfolded in front of her, some weirdly cut, handheld-camera reality show. Somebody had lost control, right in front of Mark. He couldn't slam on his brakes, because of the person behind him.

The investigating officers pointed out the odds against three vehicles converging by chance on an empty stretch of country road, after midnight on a weekday, at least one of them traveling at eighty miles an hour. They explained that Mark fell into a high-risk group: Nebraska small-town male under the age of thirty. They asked if her brother ever raced. Racing on deserted highways at night—one of the area's occasional pastimes.

If they were racing, she asked, wouldn't they all have been heading the same direction?

There were more dangerous games, the police hinted. Could she tell them anything about his friends?

She said something vague about coworkers from IBP. A group of them, she claimed; a circle. She made Mark sound almost popular. Bizarre: she wanted even the police to think well of him. Even these men who wanted her to believe that someone had run her brother off the road. They didn't care what happened to Mark. Mark was just a set of skids. Throughout the interview, she fingered the note hiding in her cloth shoulder bag. The note from Mark's finder, the one who'd brought him back. *I am No One* . . . Could they charge her with suppressing evidence? But if she showed them, they would confiscate it, and she would lose her only talisman.

She asked who reported the accident. They said the accident was called in from a pay phone at the Mobil station just off the Kearney interstate exit, by a male of indeterminate age who refused to give a name.

The driver of one of the other two vehicles?

The cops couldn't say, or wouldn't. They thanked her as they let her go. They said she'd been very helpful. They said they were sorry for her brother, and wished him a speedy recovery.

So they can arrest him, she thought, smiling brightly and waving goodbye.

A rising comes that isn't always death. A flight that doesn't always end in breaking. He lies still through every imaginable light, the beams passing through him like he is water. He solidifies, but not all at once. He collects like salt when the sea evaporates. Flaking apart, even as he sets.

Now and then, a current floats him. Flings through his broken body. Mostly he falls back into accident. But sometimes a river lifts him, over the low gray hills, elsewhere.

His pieces still send and receive, but no longer to one another. Words trickle through his head. Less words than sounds. *Goat head. Goat head.* Just a clock ticking, no less than his heart. Sound spatters, like spilled oil. Goat head. Ram truck. Ram tough. Ram horn. Ghost ahead. Ram a ghost. Goat dead. Slam horn. Done. Breaking. Falling. Plunging under again, no bottom. Words click through his head, an endless freight. Sometimes he runs alongside, peering in. Sometimes these words peer out, finding him.

He is awake, or someplace near it. His body drifts on and off. Possible that he himself is here straight through. Only he doesn't know it, when what his mind hooks to comes and goes.

Ideas hit him, or he hits them. A game always, scores pouring in, as standings change. Surrounded by people—seas of them—the crowd a huge, changing thought. He never knew himself. Every single human a separate line in a play so large and slow no one can hear it.

Time is just a yardstick for pain. And he's got all the time in the world. Sometimes he jerks up, remembering, desperate to go, fix, undo. Mostly he lies still, signals of the disconnected world buzzing through him, a swarm of gnats he would catch and kill. They scatter when he reaches for them.

Something wonderful: he could count to anything, even all these swarms, just by adding one. Covering debts, bets. Hovering up by the highest number. In a lookout tower on a hill. People could do anything. They don't know they're gods, that they live through even death. People might make a

41

hospital where they could keep every possible life alive. And then someday, life might return the favor.

A good kid once, the one he was in.

Little by little, there is no need. No falling, no rising. Just is.

People don't have ideas. Ideas have everything.

Once he looks down and sees himself, his hand, throwing. So he has a hand, and the hand can catch. His body, formed through the flung ball. Knows repeats. Even without him, or anyone thinking so.

Something else he is supposed to remember. Something else to save someone. Desperate message. But maybe no more than *this*.

The health professionals descended on him. Increasingly, Karin got in the way, worthless as the therapists took over. But she stayed nearby, to help, where possible, bring her twenty-seven-year-old brother back from infancy. She opened up the possibility a crack, allowing herself to feel a hint of something that might in time become relief.

She wrote down the therapists' routines, the relentless exercises. On page after perfect, empty page, she ordered Mark's days. She noted the hour when he rose and put his feet on the floor. She described his first failed efforts to stand, grappled to the side of the bed. Looked at from up close, his eyebrows' smallest spasm was a miracle. Her notebook was her punishment and her reward. Every word was like rebirth. Only Mark's naked struggle kept her going. He would need these days replayed for him, months from now. And she would be ready.

The days of rehab drill numbed with crushing repetition. An orangutan would have started walking and talking, just to escape the torture. When Mark at last stood upright, Karin walked him in circles, first around the room, then around the nurses' station, then around the floor. The tubes came off, untethering him. Together, in short, shuffling steps, they made a tiny solar system, orbits within orbits. Ungodly relief, a feeling she thought would never come again: just walking alongside him.

The windowed tube came out of his throat, leaving the passage open for words. Still, Mark didn't talk. Karin copied his speech therapist, endlessly repeating: *Ah. Oh. Oo. Muh muh muh. Tuh tuh tuh.* Mark stared at her moving mouth, but wouldn't imitate. He just lay in bed murmuring, an animal trapped under a bushel, afraid that the speaking creatures might silence it for good.

He alternated between docility and rage. Watching the therapists, she learned how to play each mood. She tried him out on television. Weeks before, he would have wallowed in it. But something about the quick cuts, flashing lights, and riotous soundtracks made him whimper until she shut it off.

One evening, she asked if he'd like her to read to him. He groaned a sound that wasn't *no*. She started on an old issue of *People*; he didn't seem to mind. The next morning, she picked through The Second Story, the used book store on Twenty-fifth, until she found what she was after. The Boxcar Children. *Surprise Island, Mystery Ranch,* and *Caboose Mystery*: three of the original nineteen, volumes that floated through resale the way those orphaned children floated through their adult-damaged world. She stood in the store's moldy stacks, flipping through the used inside covers until she found one with a shaky, imperious "M. S." The curse of small-town life on a shallow river: your most prized possessions always turned up again, eternally resold.

She sat and read to him for hours. She read out loud until the visitors on the other side of the sliding curtain began to curse her under their breath. Reading calmed him, especially at night, when he slipped downward, back into the accident. As she read, his face struggled with the mystery of forgotten places. Sometimes, halfway through a sentence, she'd hit a word—*button, pillow, Violet*—that caused Mark to struggle up, trying to speak. She stopped calling the nurses. They only sedated him.

Years had passed since she'd read aloud. She mangled sentences and mispronounced words. Mark listened, his eyes like half-dollars, as if words were a new life form. Surely their mother must have read to them, in childhood. But Karin could form no image of Joan Schluter reading anything but advance accounts of End Time, even then, already breaking out all over.

Joan had gotten her first real glimpse of End Time at last, eighteen months earlier. Karin had kept a bedside vigil then, too, the opposite of this one. Their mother was struck by an eleventh-hour burst of words, all the words avoided in years of child rearing. *Babe? Swear to me that if I start repeating myself, you'll put me out of my misery. Hemlock in my prune juice.*

This, spoken while clutching Karin's wrist, forcing her gaze.

If you ever see the signs. Going on and on? About nothing? Even if it seems like no big deal. Promise me, Kar. Bag over my head. I do not care to stick around for that particular last act.

But, Ma, that's against the Word of God.

Not in my Bible. Show me where.

Ending your own life?

That's just the thing, Kar. I wouldn't be!

I see. You want me *to go to hell* for *you. Thou shalt not kill.*

This isn't killing. This is Christian charity. We did it for animals all the time, back on the farm. Promise me, Kar. Promise me.

Ma, watch out. You're repeating yourself. Don't put me into a difficult situation here.

You see what I'm saying. No fun.

Fun was not something Joan Schluter had ever had to worry about. Yet in extremity, she'd said tender things: ghastly, loving apologies for her failure as a parent. Near the end, she asked: *Karin, will you pray with me?* and Karin, who'd sworn never to talk to God again, even if He started the conversation, bowed her head and mouthed along.

There will be some insurance money, Joan told her. *Not a lot, but some. For both of you. Can you do something good with it?*

What do you mean, Ma? What good do you want me to do?

But her mother no longer knew what good was. Only that it needed doing.

From the thick of *The Woodshed Mystery*, Karin said, "You know what, Mark? After an upbringing like ours? We're lucky there's anything left of us at all."

"Left us," her brother agreed. "Anything."

She surged to her feet, clapping a cry back into her mouth. She stared at him. He just sank in the sheets, hiding until the danger passed. "Jesus, Mark. You talked. You can say things."

"Jesus Jesus. Mark. Jesus," he said. And then fell silent.

"Echolalia," Dr. Hayes called it. "Perseveration. He's imitating what he hears."

Karin would not be dimmed. "If he can say a word, it must mean *something*, right?"

"Ah! You're pushing up against questions neurology can't answer yet."

Mark's speech traced the same tight loops his walking did. One afternoon it was "chick, chick, chick, chick," for most of an hour. It sounded like a symphony to her. Rousing him for a walk, Karin said, "Come on, Mark, let's tie your shoes." This launched a barrage of "tie shoes, tissues, die your noose." He kept it up until she, too, felt brain-damaged. But exhilarated: in the hypnotic repetition, she thought she heard "too tight shoes." A few loops later, he produced, "Shoofly, don't tie me."

The words had to mean something. Even if they weren't quite thoughts, he flung them with the force of meaning. She was walking him down a crowded hospital corridor when Mark popped out with "Got a lot on our plates right now."

She threw her arms around him and squeezed him in joy. He knew. He could *say*. All the reward she needed.

He pulled free and turned away. "You're turning that dirt into clay."

She followed his gaze. There in the hall's hum, she finally heard it. With an animal precision hers had lost, his ears picked up stray pieces of the surrounding conversations and wove them together. Parrots exhibited more native intelligence. She pulled his chest up against her face and began to cry.

"We'll get through this," he said, his arms dead at his sides. She pushed him back and examined his face. His eyes said less than nothing.

But she fed and walked and read to him tirelessly, never doubting that he would come back. She had more energy for rehabilitation than she'd had for any job she'd ever worked.

Brother and sister were alone together the next morning when a voice like a cartoon mouse broke over them. "Hey! How's today treating the two of you?"

Karin jumped up with a shout and threw her arms around the intruder. "Bonnie Travis. Where have you been? What took you so long?"

"My bad!" the mouse girl said. "I wasn't sure whether . . ."

Her eyes pinched and she worked her lower lip. She touched Karin's shoulders in a burst of fear. *Brain damage.* Worse than contagious. It turned the innocent cagey and unnerved the surest believer.

Mark sat on the end of the bed in jeans and a green work shirt, his palms curled on his knees and his head erect. He might have been pretending to be the Lincoln Memorial. Bonnie Travis hugged him. He made no sign of feeling the embrace. She sprang up from the botched gesture. "Oh, Marker! I wasn't sure how you were going to look. But you look real good to me."

His head was shaved, with two great riverbeds scarring the patchy watershed. His face, still scabbed over, looked like a ten-inch peach pit. "Real good," Mark said. "Wasn't sure, but could good should be good."

Bonnie laughed and her Camay face flushed cherry Kool-Aid. "Wow! Would you listen to you! I heard from Duane you couldn't talk, but I am reading you loud and clear."

"You talked to those two?" Karin asked. "What are they telling people?"

"Looking good," Mark said. "Pretty pretty pretty." The reptile brain, creeping out to sun itself.

Bonnie Travis giggled. "Well, I did clean up a little before I came."

Words came flowing out of the mouse girl, meaningless, trivial, stupid, lifesaving words. The Travis high-speed pelting, which for years had maddened Karin, now felt like a steady April downpour, raising the water table, recharging the soil. Babbling, Bonnie Travis picked at her plum wool skirt and lumpy hand-knit sweater, its patches of olive yarn converging on the color of the Platte in August. On her neck chain, a Kokopelli danced and played the flute.

The year before, after their mother's funeral, Karin had asked Mark, *Are you two an item? She your woman now?* Wanting some protection for him, however little.

Mark had just grunted. *Even if she was, she wouldn't realize.*

Bonnie told a motionless Mark all about her new job, the latest change from her steady waitressing. "I'm telling you, I've just landed every woman's dream occupation. You'll never guess what it is in a million years. I didn't even know it existed. Docent for the new Great Platte River Road Archway Monument. Did you two know that our new arch is the only monument in the whole world that straddles an interstate? I can't understand why it's still not doing very well."

Mark listened, mouth open. Karin closed her eyes and basked in beautiful human inanity.

"I get to dress up as a pioneer woman. I've a floor-length cotton dress? And a truly sweet bonnet with a little beak. The whole nine yards. And I have to answer any visitor's questions as if I were the real deal. You know, like it's still one hundred and fifty years ago. You'd be amazed at what people ask."

Karin had forgotten just how intoxicatingly pointless existence could be. Mark hung on the edge of the bed, a sandstone pharaoh, staring at Bonnie's intricate, moving mouth. Afraid to stop talking, she chattered on about the tepees lining the I-80 exit ramp, the simulated buffalo stampede, the life-size Pony Express station, and the epic story

48

of the building of the Lincoln Highway. "And you get all that for only $8.25. Can you believe some people think that's expensive?"

"It's a steal," Karin said.

"You'd be amazed, all the places people come from. Czech Republic. Bombay. Naples, Florida. Most of the folks stop to see the birds. They're getting incredibly famous, those birds. Ten times as many crane peepers as we used to get just six years ago, according to my boss. Those birds are putting our town on the map."

Mark started laughing. At least it sounded like laughter, slowed to a crawl. Even Bonnie flinched. She stuttered and laughed, herself. She could think of nothing more to say. Her lips curdled, her cheeks flushed, and her eyes filled with tears.

It came time for Karin to change Mark's shoes and socks, the old circulation ritual from bed-bound weeks that she kept up because she had nothing else to do. Mark sat docile as she removed his Converse All-Stars. Bonnie pulled herself together and helped with the other foot. Holding Mark's bare feet, she asked, "Want me to do your toes?"

He seemed to mull over the idea.

"You want to paint his . . . ? He'd have a fit."

"Just for fun. It's something we've played with, in the past. He loves it. Calls them his hind claws. I know what you're thinking, but it's really not that kinky. Marker?"

He didn't move his head or blink. "He loves it," he said, his voice thick and sad. Bonnie clapped her hands and looked at Karin. Karin shrugged. The girl dove into her fringed bag, digging out a supply of nail polish stashed away for just this possibility. Bonnie made Mark lie back and surrender his feet to the process. "Iced Cherry? How about Bruise? No. Frostbite? Frostbite it is."

Karin sat and watched the ritual. She'd come back six years too late to help Mark. Whatever she did for him now, however far she rehabilitated him, he would return to this. "I'll be right back," she promised, and left the room. Coatless, she cut a surveyor's line to the Shell station she'd been daydreaming about for a week. She pasted a sum on the counter and asked for a pack of Marlboros. The cashier laughed at her: two dollars short. Six years since she'd thought of buying a cigarette, and the price had doubled while she was stupidly staying clean. She made up the difference and dragged the prize outside. She put one to her lips, already buzzing from the taste of the filter. With a shaking hand, she lit it and drew in. A cloud of indescribable relief expanded in her lungs and inked into her limbs. Eyes closed, she smoked half the cigarette, then carefully stubbed it out and slipped the unsmoked half back into the pack. When she returned to the hospital, she sat on a cold bench in the horseshoe drive, just outside the sliding glass doors, and smoked the other half. She would brake her descent as much as possible, a long, slow ride back to exactly where she'd been before her six brutally won years. But she'd savor every baby step back down into enslavement.

In Mark's room, the pedicure was wrapping up. Mark sat on the bed, studying his toes the way a sloth might study a film of a tree branch. Bonnie fluttered about him, twittering. "Perfect timing," she told Karin. "Could you take our picture?" Bonnie rooted through her magic bag and produced a disposable camera. She lined up alongside Mark's hind claws, the lime of her eyes wildly complimenting the purple she'd applied to him.

As Karin swung the plastic viewfinder up to her eye, her brother smiled. Who knew what he knew? Karin couldn't even vouch for Bonnie.

Blissful Bonnie retrieved her camera. "I'll make copies for you both." She rubbed Mark's shoulder. "We're going to have a lot of fun when you're one hundred percent together again."

He grinned and studied her. Then one hand shot out for her sweater-covered breasts while the other grabbed his crotch. Syllables dripped from his mouth: *Fork, fuck a fox, sock suck cunt me . . .*

She squealed, jumped back, and swatted away his hand. She clutched her chest and caught her breath, shaking. The shaking turned to high-strung giggles. "Well, maybe not *that* much fun." But she kissed his healing skull as she left. "Love you, Marker!" He tried to stand up and follow her. Karin held him back, petting and calming him until he shrugged her off and swung away onto the bed, arching upward, his eyes full of pain. Karin followed Bonnie out into the hallway. Around the door frame, out of sight, Bonnie stood crying.

"Oh, Karin! I am so sorry. I tried my hardest to be up. I had no idea. They told me to be ready for anything. But not this."

"It's okay," Karin lied. "This is just how he is right now."

Bonnie insisted on a long embrace, which Karin returned, for her brother's sake.

Pulling away at last, Karin asked, "Do you know what happened that . . . ? Did the boys tell you anything . . . ?"

Bonnie waited, eager to answer anything. But Karin just turned away and let her go. Back in the room, she found Mark on the bed, leaning back on his arms, head tilted up, inspecting the ceiling, as if he'd paused while exercising and forgot to resume living.

"Mark? I'm back. Just the two of us again. Are you all right?"

"One hundred percent," he said. "Back together." He shook his head sagely and turned toward her. "Maybe not *that* much fun."

First he's nowhere, then he's not. The change steals over, one life stepping through another. Just as he crosses back, he sees the nowhere he's been. Not even a place until feeling flows in. And then, he loses all the nothing he was.

Here is a bed he lives in. But a bed bigger than the town. He lies along its giant length, a whale in the street. Beached creature blocks long. Off-beam ocean thing come back to life-crushing weight, dying of gravity.

Nothing large enough to carry him here or lift him away. Flattened belly running the whole road length. Flukes snagged on fences, stabbed by sharp tree peaks. Lying alongside white wooden boxes with pitched roofs, smoke curling from crayon chimneys, a child's scribbled *home*.

This whale is pain, and searing cold. Bursts of fact his skin tells him. Planted in this flat prairie, dumped by a wave that went out too fast. Great jaws bigger than a garage flap on the ground, sounding. Every cry from the cavern throat shakes walls and breaks windows. Far away, blocks down—the stranded beast's tail flaps. Hemmed in by houses, pinned by this instant low tide.

Miles of air above press down so hard the whale can't breathe. Can't lift his own lungs. Dying in dried ocean, smothered underneath the thing it now must inhale. Largest living thing, almost God, stretched out flat, muscles beaten. Only his heart, as big as the courthouse, keeps pounding.

He wants death, if he wants anything. But death rolls away with the retreating water. His breathing is an earthquake. The whale gasps and rolls, crushing lives underneath it, as it is crushed by air. Storms rage in its head. Spears and cables drape down his sides. His skin peels off in sheets of blubber.

Weeks, months, and the groans of the rotting mountain of animal subside. The scattered town drifts back. Tiny, land-born lives poke at the monster with pins and needles, hack at him, reclaiming their crushed homes. Birds pick at his decaying flesh. Squirrels tear off chunks, bury them for the coming winter. Coyotes polish his bones to shining ivory. Cars drive under his huge, vaulting ribs. Stoplights hang from the knobs of his spine.

Soon, his bones sprout branches and leaves. Residents crawl through him, seeing no more than *street, stone, trees.*

His parts come back to him, so slowly he can't know. He lies in the shrinking bed, taking stock. Ribs: yes. Belly: check. Arms: two. Legs: too. Fingers: many. Toes: maybe. He does this always, with changing results. Makes a list of himself, like old rebuilt machines. Remove. Clean. Replace. List again.

The place that threw him away now wants him back too bad. People push sounds on him, endless free samples. Words, by the way people say them. *How how how now now now?* Something he might hear in the fields at night, if he stopped to listen. *Mark mark mark,* they make him. Cackles, copying with every new user. No use. Silence can't cover him. They read him off of papers, speak him out. They merge him, move him on, make him up from scratch. Words without tongue. He, tongue without words.

Mark Schluter. Shoes, shirt, service. Huge loops of him. Steps he takes. Round around and back again. Repeat as needed. Something settles out, a him big enough for him to climb back in. In noise and rush, he keeps deep down. Sometimes a field of corn, the popping stalks talking to him. He never knew that all things talk. Had to slow to hear. Other times, a mud flat, flow in an inch of water. His body a small craft. The hairs on his limbs are oars, beating the current. His body, countless microscopic creatures banded together in need.

At last notions climb out his throat. Belching, birthing words. Baby wolf spiders, scattering off the back of their mother sound. Every curved line in the world is saying. Branches tapping the glass. Tracks in the snow. "Lucky" is there, circling alongside. "Pretty," panting, happy to see him. "Good," a purple flower stabbing up through the lawn.

One last broken moment and he might still feel: *something in the road that ruined me*. But then mending brings him back, to the smear of thoughts and words.

Some days his rage was so bad that even lying still infuriated him. Then the therapists asked her to leave. Help out by vanishing. She camped out in Farview, in her brother's modular home. She fed his dog, paid his bills, ate off of his plates, watched his television, slept in his bed. She smoked only out on the deck, in the frosty March wind, on a damp director's chair inscribed BORN SCHLUTER, so his living room wouldn't stink of cigarettes when he finally came home. She tried to keep to one cigarette an hour. She forced herself to slow, taste the smoke, close her eyes, and just listen. At dawn and dusk, as her ears sensitized, she could hear the sandhills' bugle call underneath the neighbor's militant exercise videos and the long-haul eighteen-wheelers pounding up and down the interstate. She would hit the filter in seven minutes, and be checking her watch again fifteen minutes later.

She might have called half a dozen old friends, but didn't. When she went into town to shop, she hid from old classmates. But she couldn't avoid them all. Acquaintances stepped out of some movie version of her past, playing themselves, only nicer than they'd ever been in real life. Their sympathy hungered for details. What was Mark like? Would he ever be back to normal? She told them he was almost there.

She had one phone number, still in her fingers. On those days when Mark defeated her, she would come home with half a gallon of her old college-favorite Gallo, get quietly smashed while watching the Classic Movies Channel, then dial a few digits, just for the surge of the forbidden. Four numbers in, and she remembered that she wasn't dead yet. Anything might still happen. She'd quit him like cigarettes, though purging him from her system had taken longer. Karsh: slick, dexterous, unrepentant Robert Karsh, Kearney HS Class of '89, Most Likely to Make a Difference, the eternal angle-worker whom she'd once had to order out of a car 150 miles from anywhere, the only soul other than her brother who could always see right through her. She heard his voice, part evangelist, part porn-ographer, already bringing her back to herself, only three more digits away from her probing fingers.

A decade of chemical craving—anger and longing, guilt and resentment, nostalgia and fatigue—flooded through her as she dialed the reflex number. But she always stopped short of follow-through. She didn't really want *him*: just some proof that her brother wouldn't drag her down with him into the buried kingdom of brain damage.

The intoxicating ritual self-abasement mixed with the Gallo and the ever-denser cigarettes to make her glow, a color all hers again. She would put on one of Mark's bootlegged CDs—his one-hit thrasher bands, masters of the blissfully relentless. Then she'd spread back onto his bed and fall endlessly down into the mattress, skydiving through pure air. She'd touch herself as Robert had—*still alive*—while Mark's dog looked on from the doorway, baffled. The simple tests of her body graduated by degrees into pleasure, so long as she could keep her hands from thinking.

A point of moral pride: she dialed the whole number only once. In late March, the days lengthening, she took her brother for one of his first spins outside the hospital. They walked around the grounds, Mark deep in a focus she couldn't penetrate. The air around them filled with spring's first insect drones. The winter aconite was already fading, and the crocuses and daffodils pushed through the last clumps of snow. A white-fronted goose flew overhead. Mark's head snapped back. He couldn't see the bird, but when he looked down, his face burned with memory. He broke into a smile wider than any she'd seen on him since their father died. His mouth hung open, readying the word *goose*. She urged him on with her hands and eyes.

"G-G-G-go goo god damn. Damn it to hell. God shit piss bitch. Suck a flaming cunt up your ass."

He smiled proudly. She gasped and pulled away, and his face fell. She fought off the rush of tears, took his arm again in fake calm, and turned him back toward the building. "It's a goose, Mark. You remember them. You're kind of a silly goose yourself, you know that."

"Shit piss fuck," he chanted, studying his shuffling feet.

This was injury, not her brother. Just sounds: meaningless, buried things brought up by trauma. He didn't mean to assault her. She told herself this all the way back to Farview. But she no longer believed anything she told herself. All the hopes that had carried her for weeks dissolved in that stream of mocking profanity. She found her way to the Homestar in the pitch dark. Inside, she went straight to the phone and dialed Robert Karsh. Her steady, years-long rise to self-sufficiency was ready to submit again.

56

The little girl answered. Better her than her older brother. The girl's drawled "Hello" had two too many syllables. Seven years old. What kind of parents let their seven-year-old girl answer the phone after dark?

Karin fished up the girl's name. "Ashley?"

The tiny voice returned a broad, trusting, Cartoon Network "Yeesss!" Austin and Ashley: names that could scar a child for life. Karin hung up, and instinctively dialed another number, one she'd considered calling for weeks.

When he picked up, she said, simply, "Daniel." After an ambushed pause, Daniel Riegel said, "It's you." Such relief surged through Karin that she couldn't imagine why she hadn't called him earlier. He might have helped, as early as the night of the accident. Someone who knew Mark. The real Mark, the kind one. Someone she could talk to about both past and future.

"Where are you?" he asked.

She started to giggle. Horrified, she got hold of herself. "Here. I mean, Farview."

In his naturalist's voice, the hush he used in the field to point out things that were easily scared away, Daniel said, "For your brother."

It felt like telepathy. Then she remembered: small town. She sunk into his soft questions. The release of answering was beyond description. She reversed herself with every sentence: Mark was getting better by leaps and bounds; he was worse than helpless. He could think and identify things and even talk; he was still trapped in the wreck, walking like a trained bear and chattering like a perverted parrot. Daniel asked how she was coping. She was doing fine, considering. The days were long, but she could handle them. *With help*, her voice begged, despite herself.

She considered asking Daniel to meet her somewhere, but couldn't risk scaring him. So she just talked, her voice curling like surf. She tried to sound for him like the capable woman she had almost become. She had no right even to contact the man. But her brother had nearly died. Disaster trumped the past and gave her temporary asylum.

Until the age of thirteen, her brother and Daniel had been joined at the hip, twin nature boys turning up ornate box turtles, stumbling on bobwhite nests, camped outside burrows that they dreamed of inhabiting. Then, in high school, something happened. Sometime during sophomore year, from one class period to the next, they fell out. Long, protracted war, with a static front. Danny stayed with the animals and Mark abandoned them for people. "Growing up," Mark explained, as if love of nature were an adolescent fixation. He never had anything to do with Daniel again. Years later, when Karin started dabbling with Daniel herself, neither boy ever mentioned the other to her.

She and Daniel spun out, almost as soon as they'd started. She ran off to Chicago, then on to Los Angeles, before crawling home, humbled. Daniel, untiring idealist, welcomed her back without questions. Only when he overheard her mimicking him in whispers on the phone to Karsh did Daniel kick her out. She fled to her brother for support. But when Mark, loyal to her, started bad-mouthing Daniel, hinting at dark secrets in the past, Karin turned on him so harshly they didn't speak for weeks.

Now Daniel's voice reassured her: she was better than her past. He'd always said as much, and now life had dealt her a challenge that would prove him right. Daniel's tone threatened to convince her. Human stupidity meant nothing, least of all what humans thought it meant. You could brush it away like a wisp of insect silk grazing your face. Unintended cruelties didn't matter. All that mattered now was her brother. Daniel asked about Mark's care, good questions she should have asked the therapists long before. She listened to him as if to a forgotten favorite song, one that distilled a whole chapter of life into three minutes. "I'd be happy to come to the hospital," he said.

"Well, he's not making much of anyone, just yet." Something in her didn't want him seeing Mark as he was now. What she wanted from Daniel was stories, stories of Mark, before. Things she wasn't sure she was remembering right, after too many days at bedside.

She did remember to ask Daniel about his own life. The distraction helped, even if she couldn't focus on the details. "How are things at the Sanctuary?"

He had quit the Sanctuary in despair at their compromises. He now worked for the Buffalo County Crane Refuge, a smaller, more limber and confrontational group. Work at the Sanctuary had been steady and well-intentioned, but far too accommodating. The Refuge was harder-line. "If you want to save something that's been around for millions of years, you can't be moderate."

How contemptible she'd been, ever to take this man lightly. His gentle firmness was worth ten of her and Karsh put together. She couldn't believe that he would still talk to her. The accident permitted that, too. Made everyone briefly better than they were. Put the present above the past. She'd been circling in a snowstorm, frostbitten and near collapse, and she'd stumbled on a lean-to with a fire. She wanted this conversation to go on, slowly meandering nowhere. For the first time since the hospital's call, she felt she could do whatever disaster required. If she could just call this man from time to time.

59

Daniel asked about her life before the wreck. He asked in a soft aside, as if lying motionless in a field, looking through binoculars. "I've been managing," she told him. "Learning a lot about myself. It turns out I have some skill, working with upset people." She described all the responsibilities she'd had, in the job she'd just lost. "They say they might be able to hire me back, when this is all over."

"Have you been seeing anyone?"

She started to giggle again. Something was truly wrong with her. Something skidding out of control. "Only my brother. Nine or ten hours a day." Even telling him that much terrified her. But how infinitely better it was to be terrified than dead. "Daniel? It would be really good if we could sit for a minute. If you have the time to see me. I don't want to burden you. This is . . . a handful, is all. I know I'm the last person with any right to ask you . . . But I don't quite know how to do this by myself."

Long after they hung up, she heard him saying, "Of course. I would like that. Too."

She could learn, she told herself, falling asleep. Learn how not to be her knee-jerk, self-protecting self. The time for constantly rebuffing imagined slights was over. The accident changed everything, gave her a chance to undo all her old hit-and-runs. The last few weeks had emptied her—just having to look at Mark laid bare. How easy now, to float above herself, gaze down on all the killing needs that controlled her, and see them for the phantoms they were. Nothing had the power to hurt her except for what power she gave it. Every barrier she'd ever chafed against was no more than a Chinese finger lock that opened instantly when she stopped pulling. She could simply watch, learn about the new Mark, listen to Daniel without having to understand him. Other people were about themselves, not about her. Everyone alive was at least as scared as she was. Remember that, and a person might come to love anyone.

Echo caca. Cocky locky. Caca lala. Living things, always talking. How you know they're living. Always with the *look*, with the *listen*, with the *see what I mean*. What can things mean, that they aren't already? Live things make such sounds, just to say what silence says better. Dead things are what they are already, and can shut up in peace.

Humans the worst. All over him with their words. Worse than cicadas on a warm night. Or all frog, more or legs. Listen to the spurts. Listen to those birds. But birds might be louder. His mother told him. The less the thing, the louder the ring. Take the wind: all that noise, just going nowhere from nothing for no reason, and there's no thing on earth less than the wind.

Someone says he's missing the birds. How can that be? The birds are always coming. How can he miss them, when they aren't even missing? Animals must be more like rocks. Saying only what they are. A longer now, a shorter then, living in the place he's just come from.

He knew what that place is, but now it's just saying.

They make him say a lot, humans. They take him out spinning, and it's murder. Hell in a hall, bumper to bumper, worse than freeways, people flying all ways too fast to miss. And still they want talk, even while moving. Like talk isn't crazy enough. But once they work him, they let him lie. Sleeping old dogs, up to new tricks. This he loves: when they give him his body back, and no need. Loves just lying still in the world buzz, all channels at once pouring through his skin.

61

He has to work some, with time come back. Up and attic, there and bath again. Have him living in a boxcar now. Old train with others orphaned like him. He's lived in worse. Not easy to say just where he is. So he says nothing. Some things say him. What's on his mind hops off. Thoughts come out, not thoughts he knew he had. No one always knows what he means. This can't bother him. He doesn't really, either.

A girl comes by he'd like to do. Maybe already did. That would make it good, though. Could go. Do each other, always. Encore. One car, for the two of them, doing it. Those birds mate for good, after all. The birds he's missing. Who are humans, to do better? Pair forever. Teach their kids to reach the top of the earth and find their way back, the way-back way he found.

Those birds are smart. His father always told him. A dad who knew those birds so well he used to kill them.

Something killing him to remember, just now, but it goes.

Small talk, but all talk. Say it, say if, say *at*. Say it's an easy it. Echo. Lala.

Finished, over and done, just then. Now he's not. That's why they make him talk. Prove he's with the living things, not stones.

Not sure why he's here, or how. He's taken an acid dent. Something else dented worse, but wordy people won't say. All those things to talk about, millions of moving things, and that's never one anyone mentions. Most times when they're talking, nothing happens. Nothing but what's already right here. What happened to him is a thing even living things won't say.

She kept reading to Mark: all she could do. Mark's face stayed placid through the stories' struggles. He just rode those sentences, their boxcar rhythm. But the most predictable read-aloud went right up Karin's spine. The scene where the twelve-year-old boy is felled by a blow to the skull as he sneaks into a derelict house and is bound and gagged in the root cellar made her shut the book, unable to read on. Closed head trauma had ruined her. Even children's fiction now went real.

The Muskrateers came by for repeat offenses. "Didn't we promise?" Tommy Rupp asked. "Didn't we say we'd help bring the man back?" He and Cain produced foam footballs outfitted with tail fins, handheld electronic games, even radio-controlled cars. Mark responded, first with flattened baffle-ment, then with machine-like glee. He made more hand-eye headway in half an hour with his friends than he did in days with the physical therapist.

Duane was all consultation. "What're you doing with your rotator cuff there, Mark? Watch the rotator cuff. It's what you call a flashpoint."

Rupp kept them on task. "Will you hold up with the medicine man bit and let Gus here throw the ball? Am I right, Gus?"

"Right, Gus," Mark said, watching the commotion as if in instant replay.

Bonnie showed up every few days. Mark reveled in her visits. She always brought *joy stuff*: rubber animals wrapped in metallic paper, washable tattoos, fortunes sealed in orna-mental envelopes. *You will soon embark on an unforeseen adventure* . . . She was better than a book. She could go on forever with funny stories of living in a covered wagon along the interstate that never quite reached its homestead tract. She showed up once in her faux pioneer outfit. Mark looked at her in wonder, half birthday boy, half child molester. Bonnie brought him a disc player and ear buds, something Karin had failed to think of. She produced a box of discs—chick music, sighs about the blindness of guys—nothing Mark would ever have been caught dead listening to. But under the head-phones, Mark closed his eyes, smiled, and tapped his thigh with his fingers.

Bonnie liked to listen along to the stories that Karin read aloud. "He's following every word," she insisted.

"You think?" Karin asked, grasping at any hope.

"You can see it in his eyes."

Her optimism was an opiate. Karin already depended on her, worse than cigarettes.

"Can I try something?" Bonnie asked, touching her shoulder. Her hands probed Karin incessantly, turning every word into a confidence. She cozied up to Mark, one palm coaxing, the other restraining. "Ready, Marker? Show us what you're made of. Here we go. One, two, buckle my . . . ?"

He gazed at her, slack-jawed, smitten.

"Come on, buddy. Focus!" She sang again: "One, two, buckle my . . ."

"Shoe." The syllable came out, a pitched moan. Karin gasped at the first proof that somewhere deep down, Mark still made meaning. Her brother, who only a few weeks before, had repaired complex slaughterhouse machinery, could now complete the first line of a nursery rhyme. She pressed her jaw, mouthing, *Yes!*

Bonnie carried on, giggling like water in a brook. "Three, four. Knock at the . . ."

". . . door!"

"Five, six, pick up . . ."

". . . shit."

Karin broke into mortified laughter. Bonnie reassured the crestfallen Mark. "Hey! Two out of three. You're doing fantastic."

They tried him on "Hickory Dickory Dock." Mark, his face strained with ecstatic concentration, scored perfectly on *dock*, *clock*, *down*, and *dock*. Bonnie began, "It's Raining, It's Pouring," but getting far enough in to remember the words that came next, broke off in mumbled apologies.

Karin took over. She tried him on a verse Bonnie had never heard. But for the two Schluter siblings, the four lines condensed all the icy chill of childhood. "I see the moon," Karin prompted, sounding just like their mother, back when Joan Schluter's rhymes weren't yet devil exorcisms. "And the moon . . ."

Mark's eyes widened, a rush of comprehension. His lips closed around a hopeful grimace. "Sees me!"

"God bless the moon," Karin assured him, that old singsong. "And . . . ?"

But her brother held still, pressed against his chair, staring at some creature unknown to science that suddenly appeared in silhouette on the horizon at dusk.

Karin sat beside Mark one afternoon, refreshing him on the rules for checkers, when a shadow moved across the board. She twisted to see a familiar figure in a navy pea coat hovering over her shoulder. Daniel's hand reached for her but didn't touch. He called to Mark, a gentle hello, as if the two of them hadn't shunned each other for the last decade. As if Mark weren't sitting robot-like in a hospital chair.

Mark's head snapped back. He scrambled up onto the chair, faster than he'd moved since the accident, pointing and wailing, "God, oh God! Help me. See see see?"

Daniel stepped forward to calm Mark. Mark climbed up over the chair back, screaming, "Miss it, miss it." Karin backed Daniel out of the room as a floor nurse rushed in. "I'll call you," she said. Their first face-to-face in three years. She squeezed his hand, criminal. Then she rushed back to calm her brother.

Mark was still seeing things. Karin worked to comfort him. But she couldn't figure out what he'd seen, in the long shadow falling out of nowhere. He lay in bed, still shaking. "See?" She hushed and lied to him, saying she saw.

She went to Daniel, after the hospital calamity. He felt just as she remembered him: steady, mammalian, familiar. He looked unchanged since high school: the long, sandy hair, the wisp of goatee, the narrow, vertical face: a gentle seed-eater. His continuity comforted her, now that all else had changed. They talked for fifteen minutes, four feet from each other across his kitchen table, nervous and sick with reassurance. She rushed away before breaking anything, but not before they agreed to meet again.

Their difference in age had vanished. Daniel had always been a child: Markie's grade, Markie's friend. Now he was older than she was, and Mark was an infant between them. She started calling Daniel at all hours for help with the endless overwhelming decisions: claims forms, disability, the papers for Mark's move to rehab. She trusted Daniel as she should have trusted him, years ago. He could always find the best available answer. More: he knew her brother, and could guess what Mark would want.

Daniel didn't open to her all at once. He couldn't have, this time around. He was no longer who he'd been, if only because of what she had done to him. That he spent time with her at all left her amazed, ashamed, and grateful. She didn't know what their new contact meant or what, if anything, might be in it for him. For her, seeing him meant the difference between bobbing and going under. After another day in the chaos of Mark's new kingdom, she found herself inventing reasons to contact Daniel. She could voice anything with him, from the wildest hope for Mark's latest tiny triumph to her fear that he was sliding back. Daniel would meet her every word with inward reserve, and keep her to some middle, steady path.

They could have no real future, after the humiliations of their past. But they could make a better past than the one they'd mangled. Mark's struggles engaged them. Their vicarious work, undoing old pettiness: measuring how far Mark had come, and how far he had to go.

Daniel brought Karin books from libraries as far away as Lincoln, accounts of brain damage, carefully selected to lift her hope. He copied articles, the latest neurological research, which he helped her decode. He called to check in, prompting her on what to ask the therapists. It felt like life again, letting him carry her for a while. Once, her gratitude so overwhelmed her that she couldn't resist a rushed, deniable hug.

She began to see Daniel with new eyes. Some part of her had always dismissed him, a neo-hippie inclined to righteousness, a little too organically pure, hovering above the herd. Now she felt her long unfairness. He simply wanted people to be as selfless as they should be, humbled by the million supporting links that kept them alive, as generous with others as nature was with them. Why did he waste his time with her, after what she'd done to him? Because she asked him to. What could he possibly get from their new connection? Simply the chance to do things right, at last. Reduce, reuse, recycle, retrieve, redeem.

They took walks. She dragged him to Fondel's Auction, the old Wednesday-night county-wide ritual. It felt like the guiltiest of heavens, being anywhere but the hospital. Daniel never bid on anything, but he approved of all secondhand resale: *Keeps things out of the landfill*. For her part, she indulged her old childhood obsession with the ghosts of previous owners still hiding out in discarded things. She walked up and down the long folding tables, fingering every dented pan and frayed rug, inventing stories for how they'd gotten here. They bought a lamp together, its stem made out of a statue of the Buddha. How such a thing had ever come to Buffalo County or why it was abandoned there only the wildest invention could explain.

On their seventh outing, shopping in the vegetable section of the Sun Mart for an impromptu dinner, he called her *K.S.* for the first time in years. She'd always loved the nickname. It made her feel like someone else, a key team member in an efficient organization. *You'll make a difference somewhere*, he told her, back before either of them had a clue how little difference the world allowed. *A real contribution, K.S. I know it*. Now, lifetimes later, choosing mushrooms, he slipped back into the name, as if no time had passed. "If anyone can bring him back, it's you, K.S." She might still make a difference, if only to her brother.

She invented destinations for them, errands they needed to run. One warming weekend, she suggested a walk down by the river. Almost by accident, they found themselves at the old Kilgore bridge. Neither of them hinted that the place meant anything. Ice still crusted the water's edge. The last cranes were departing on the long run north to their summer breeding grounds. But she could still hear them, invisible overhead.

Daniel scooped up small pebbles and angled them into the river. "Our Platte. I do love this river. A mile wide and an inch deep."

She nodded, grinning. "Too thick to drink and too thin to plow." Grade school lessons, as familiar as the times tables. Under the skin, just from growing up here. "Some river, if you stand it on its side."

"No place like it, huh?" His mouth hooked sideways, a look almost mocking, in anyone but Daniel.

She shoved him gently. "You know, growing up? I was convinced that Kearney was totally hot shit." He winced. She'd forgotten; he hated when she swore. "The center of the continent. Mormon Trail, Oregon Trail, Transcontinental Railroad, Interstate 80?"

He nodded. "And a trillion birds passing through on the Central Flyway."

"Exactly. Everything crossing, right through town. I figured it was just a matter of time before we became the next St. Louis."

Daniel smiled, bowed his head, and stuck his hands in his navy pea coat. "Crossroads of the nation."

Being together—just being—was easier than she dared believe. She hated the girlish waves of anticipation, almost obscene, given what had brought them back. She was trading on disaster, using her damaged brother to make things right with her own past. But she couldn't help herself. Something was about to happen, a good thing she hadn't engineered, somehow the result of Mark's catastrophe. She and Daniel were edging toward new territory, quiet, stable, and maybe even guiltless, a place she'd never thought possible. A place that could only help Mark.

They walked halfway out across the bridge. The pinned pony trusses swayed beneath their feet. The Platte's north channel slipped beneath them. Daniel pointed out dens and burrows, encroaching vegetation, slight changes in the riverbed that she couldn't make out. "Lots of action today. Blue-winged teal, there. Pintail. The grebes are early this year, for some reason. Look there! Is that a phoebe? Who are you? Come back. I can't see who you are!"

The old bridge shook and she slipped her arm under the sleeve of his coat. He stopped and appraised her: a shocking accidental. She looked down and saw her hand swinging his like some schoolchild's. Valentine's and Memorial Day rolled into one. He grazed the back of his fingers over the new copper penny of her hair. A naturalist's experiment.

"Do you remember when I used to quiz you on the species?"

She held still under his hand. "Hated it. I was so pitiful."

His hand lifted to point to a cottonwood, barely budding. Something sat in the branch, small, flecked with yellow, and as jittery as she felt. No name she knew. Names would only have obliterated the thing. The nameless bird opened its throat, and out came the wildest music. It sang senselessly, sure that she could follow. All around, answers sprang up—the cottonwood and the Platte, the March breeze and rabbits in the undergrowth, something downstream slapping the water in alarm, secrets and rumors, news and negotiation, all of inter-locked life talking at once. The clicks and cries came from everywhere and ended nowhere, making no judgment and promising nothing, just multiplying one another, filling the air like the river its bed. Nothing at all was her, and for the first time since Mark's accident, she felt free of herself, a release bordering on bliss. The bird sang on, inserting its own collapsed song inside all conversation. The timelessness of animals: the kinds of sounds her brother made, crawling out of his coma. This was where her brother now lived. This was the song she would have to learn, if she wanted to know Mark again.

Something trumpeted overhead, a last, late remnant of the mass now on their way to the Arctic. Daniel looked up, searching. Karin saw nothing except gray cirrus.

"Those birds are doomed," Daniel said.

She grabbed his arm. "That was a whooper?"

"Whooper? Oh no. Sandhills. You'd know a whooper."

"I didn't think . . . But the whoopers are the ones . . ."

"The whoopers are already gone. Couple hundred left. They're just ghosts. Have you ever seen one? They're like . . . hallucinations. Dissolving as you look at them. No: the whoopers are over. But the sandhills are just now staring down the barrel."

"The sandhills? You're kidding. There must be thousands . . ."

"Half a million, give or take."

"Whatever. You know me and numbers. I've never seen so many sandhills as I've seen this year."

"That's a symptom. The river's being used up. Fifteen dams, irrigation for three states. Every drop used eight times before it reaches us. The flow is a quarter of what it was before development. The river slows; the trees and vegetation fill in. The trees spook the cranes. They need the flats—someplace to roost where nothing can sneak up on you." He spun in a slow half-circle, eyes scouring. "This is their only safe stopover. No other spot in the center of the continent they can use. They're brittle—a low annual recruitment rate. Any large habitat break will be the end. Remember, the whoopers used to be as plentiful as the sandhills. A few more years, and we can say goodbye to something that's been around since the Eocene."

He was still that straggler her brother had adopted, the scrawny long-distance walker who saw things the rest of them couldn't. He was the person Markie might once have become. Little Mark. *Animals like me.*

71

"If they're so threatened, why are there so many . . . ?"

"They used to roost along the whole Big Bend: a hundred and twenty miles or more. They're down to sixty, and shrinking. The same number of birds crammed into half the space. Disease, stress, anxiety. It's worse than Manhattan."

Anxiety-stricken birds: she stifled a laugh. Something in Daniel mourned more than the cranes. He needed humans to rise to their station: conscious and godlike, nature's one shot at knowing and preserving itself. Instead, the one aware animal in creation had torched the place.

"We're crowding them into one of the greatest spectacles going. That's why crane tourism has exploded. Big business now, and every spring we use even more water. So the show will be even more spectacular next year." Daniel spoke almost sympathetically, straining to understand. But his own ability to grasp the race was shrinking faster than the habitat.

He shuddered. She touched his chest, and by impulse, he folded her into a mournful kiss confused by its cause. His hand slipped across the spark of her hair into her suede jacket's open collar. She took him against her, wrong in more ways than she could count. Excitement was shameful, under the circumstances. But that thought just excited her worse. The embrace lifted her up above the last few weeks. Her body gave in to cold spring elation. Whatever happened, she wouldn't be alone.

Stealing back to town on that surveyor's plumb line of a road, through rolling fields fuzzed with their first green, she asked him. "He's never going to be the same, is he?"

Daniel watched the road. She'd always loved that about him. He never spoke until he meant to. He tilted his head and at last said, "Nobody's ever who they were. We just have to watch and listen. See where he's going. Meet him there."

She put her hand up under his coat. She rubbed his flank

without thinking, imagined them running off the road, flipping over, until he gently held her wrist and stole a puzzled look at her.

They sat in his apartment, by candlelight, as if they were still young and sharing a first Christmas. She huddled in front of his space heater. Daniel smelled like a woolen blanket just out of storage. He cradled her from behind and unbuttoned her shirt. She curled into the threat of doing this again.

The down on her lower back stiffened under his stroking fingers. He traced the curve of her abdomen, looking on with the same hungry surprise as he had the first time, eight years ago. "See?" she repeated from memory. "My appendectomy scar. Had it since I was eleven. Not very attractive, is it?"

He laughed again. "Wrong the first time. Still wrong, years later!" He nuzzled her armpit with the tip of his nose. "Some women never learn."

She rolled him over and rose, one of his feathered, gray priestesses, neck extended. Another endangered species, in need of conserving. She straightened herself above him, displaying.

When they were still again, she gave him the surrender he hadn't asked for. "Daniel? What was it? That bird in the tree?"

He lay on his back, a scarecrow vegan. His slack muscles held his own years of suppressed questions that he would never dare ask. In the dark, he scanned their shared life list, the species they had seen that day. "It's . . . called a lot of things. You and me, K.S.? We can call it anything we want."

Karin was looping Mark around the floor in their daily steeplechase when he had his first abstract thought. Mark still walked as if tethered. He stopped to listen at a patient's room. Someone was sobbing, and an older voice said, "It's all right. Never mind all this."

73

Mark listened, smiling. He raised his hand and announced, "Sadness." There in the corridor, the feat of intellect startled Karin into tears.

She was there again, for his first complete sentence. The occupational therapist was helping Mark cope with buttons, and Mark just spit out the words like an oracle: "There are magnetism waves in my skull." He covered his face in both fists, seeing what he was, now that he could name it. In a dam-burst, sentences began pouring out of him.

By the next evening, he was conversing—slow, fuzzy, but understandable. "Why is this room so weird? This isn't the food I eat. This place is just like a hospital." Eight times an hour, he asked what had happened to him. Each time, he sat shocked by the news of the accident.

That night, as she said goodbye, Mark jumped up and pressed the windows, trying to open the sealed safety glass. "Am I asleep? Am I gone? Wake me up—this is someone else's dream."

She went to the window and embraced him. She led him away from banging on the glass. "Markie, you're awake. You've had a very big day. Rabbit is here. I'll be back tomorrow morning."

He followed her back to his plastic bedside chair, his prison. But when she sat him down, he looked up, dazed. He shoved at the apron of her coat. "What are you doing here, anyway? Who sent you?"

Her skin went metal. "Stop it, Mark," she said, harsher than intended. Sweet again, she teased, "You think your sister wouldn't look after you?"

"My sister? You think you're my sister?" His eyes drilled her. "If you think you're my sister, there's something wrong with your head."

She grew eerily clinical. She reasoned with him, laying out the evidence, like reading aloud another children's story. The calmer she was, the more it upset him. "Wake me up," he wailed. "This isn't me. I'm stuck in someone else's thoughts."

She kept Daniel up all night, shuddering with the memory of it. "You can't imagine what he looked like when he said it. 'You think you're my sister?' So certain. Not even a second thought. You can't know what that felt like."

All night long, Daniel listened. She'd forgotten how patient he was. "He's made a big step. He's still putting everything together. The rest will come quickly."

By morning, she was ready again to believe him.

Days later, Mark was still denying her. He assembled everything else: who he was, where he worked, what had happened to him. But he insisted that Karin was an actress who looked very much like his sister. After many tests, Dr. Hayes gave it a name. "Your brother is manifesting a condition called Capgras syndrome. It's one of a family of misidentification delusions. It can occur in certain psychiatric conditions."

"My brother is not mentally ill."

Dr. Hayes winced. "No. But he's facing some massive challenges. Capgras is also reported in closed-head trauma, although that's incredibly rare. Damage in precise, probably multiple spots . . . there are only a couple of cases in the literature. Your brother is the first accident-induced Capgras patient I've ever seen."

"How can the same symptom have two completely different causes?"

"That's not clear. It may not be a single syndrome."

Multiple ways of mistaking your blood relations. "Why is he doing it?"

"In some hard-to-measure way, you don't match up with his image of you. He knows he has a sister. He remembers everything about her. He knows you look like her and act like her and dress like her. He just doesn't think you *are* her."

"He knows his friends. He recognizes *you*. How can he know strangers, and not—"

"The Capgras sufferer almost always misidentifies his loved ones. A mother or father. A spouse. The part of his brain that recognizes faces is intact. So is his memory. But the part that processes emotional association has somehow disconnected from them."

"I don't *seem* like his sister to him? What does he see when he looks at me?"

"He sees what he always sees. He just doesn't . . . feel you sufficiently to believe you."

A lesion that damaged only the sense of loved ones. "He's blind to me emotionally? And so he decides . . . ?" Dr. Hayes gave a chilling nod. "But his brain, his . . . *thinking* isn't damaged, is it? Is this the worst thing we'll have to face? Because if it is, I'm sure I can . . ."

The doctor lifted a palm. "The only thing certain in head injury is uncertainty."

"What's the treatment?"

"For now, we need to watch, see how he develops. There may be other issues. Secondary deficits. Memory, cognition, perception. Capgras sometimes shows spontaneous improvement. The best thing now is time and tests."

He used the phrase again, two weeks later.

She didn't believe Mark had any syndrome. His mind was just sorting out the chaos of injury. Every day left him more like his old self. A little patience, and the cloud would lift. He'd already come back from the dead; he would come back from this smaller loss. She was who she was; he'd *have* to see that, as he got clearer. She took the setback the way the therapists told her to, one baby step in front of the other. She worked on Mark, not pushing anything. She walked him down to the cafeteria. She answered his strange questions. She brought him copies of his two favorite truck-modding magazines. She encouraged and reinforced his memories, vaguely alluding to family history. But she had to pretend not to know too much about him. She tried once or twice; any claim of intimacy led immediately to trouble.

One day he asked, "Can you at least find out how my dog is doing?" She promised to. "And for God's sake, would you please get my sister here, already? She probably hasn't even heard." She had learned enough by then to say nothing.

She held herself together in front of Mark. But at night, alone with Daniel, she nursed her worst fears. "I quit my job. I'm back in a town I can't escape, in my brother's house, living off savings. I've been sitting for weeks, helpless, reading children's stories. And now he says I'm not me. It's like he's punishing me for something."

Daniel only nodded and warmed her hands. She did like that about him: if there was nothing to say, he said nothing.

"I've been doing so well, for so long. He's so much better than he was. He couldn't even open his eyes. Why should this be so scary? Why can't I just sit still with this, wait it out?"

His fingers soothed the knobs of her spine, drawing all the static charge out of her. "Pace yourself," he said. "He's going to need you for a long time."

"I wish he *did* need me. He looks at me like I'm worse than a stranger. Cuts right through me. If I could just . . . if he would just say what he needs."

77

"Hiding is natural," Daniel said. "A bird will do anything, not to reveal that it's hurt."

Her brother drove his body like the worst student driver. Sometimes he lurched ahead, blasting past all speed limits. Other times, a crack in the linoleum would rattle him. Some days he solved every puzzle the therapists invented. Other days, he couldn't chew without biting his tongue.

He remembered nothing of the accident. But he could make new memories again. For that, Karin was ready to thank any power. He still asked twice a day how he'd gotten here, but now mostly to challenge her smallest change in phrasing. "That's not what you said last time." He asked often about his truck, whether it was as banged up as he was. She gave him the vaguest answers.

His outward progress was breathtaking. Even his friends were shocked by the great leaps of evolution, from one visit to the next. He talked more than he had before the accident. He swung from bouts of rage into a sweetness he'd lost at the age of eight. She told him the doctors wanted to move him out of the hospital. Mark glowed. He thought he was going home. "Can you tell my sister I've got the green light? Tell her Mark Schluter is out of here. Whatever's been holding her up, she'll know where to find me."

She bit her lip and refused even to nod. She'd read in one of Daniel's neurology books never to humor delusions.

"She'll be worried about me. Man, you have to promise me. Wherever she's gone, she needs to know what's happening. She was like always looking after me? That's her big thing. Personal claim to fame. Saved my life once. My father came this close to snapping my neck like a pencil. I'll tell you about it someday. Personal stuff. But trust me: I'd be dead without my sister."

It tore her up, to look on and say nothing. And yet, she felt a sick fascination at the chance to learn what Mark really said about her when talking to someone else. She could survive this, for however long it took him to come back to reason. And his reason was solidifying daily.

"Maybe they're keeping her away from me. Why won't they let me talk to her? Am I somebody's science project? They want to see if I'll mistake you for her?" He saw her distress, but mistook it for indignation. "Hey, okay. You've helped me, too, in your own way. You're here every day. Walking, reading, whatever. I don't know what you want. But I'm the grateful recipe."

"Recipient," she said. He stared at her, baffled. "You said 'recipe.' You mean 'recipient.'"

He scowled. "I was using the singular. You look a lot like her, you know? Maybe not quite as pretty. But damn close."

A wave of vertigo rolled over her. Steadying herself, she reached into her shoulder pouch and pulled out the note. "Look at this, Mark! I'm not the only one who has been looking out for you." Unplanned therapy. She knew he needed to recover more, before plunging back into the accident. But she thought it might shake him loose, bring him back to himself. Prove her authority, somehow.

He fisted the paper and stared at it. He squinted from different distances, then handed it back to her. "Tell me what it says."

"Mark! You can read. You just read two pages for the therapist this morning."

"Holy jump up and sit down. Anybody ever tell you you sound exactly like my mother?"

The woman she'd spent her life trying not to become. "Here. Have another look."

"Hey! It's not my problem, all right? I mean, look at that creeping thing. That's not writing. Some kind of spiderweb. Tree bark or something. You tell me what it says."

The writing *was* spectral. It snaked like their Swedish grandmother's illegible longhand. Karin put the writer at eighty years old, an ancient immigrant afraid of making any contact that would require surrendering information to a database. She read the words off the scrap, although she'd long ago memorized them. *I am No One but Tonight on North Line Road GOD led me to you so You could Live and bring back someone else.*

Mark pressed the scar that flowed up his forehead. He took the note back from her. "What's that supposed to mean? God led somebody? Well, if God's so big on me, how come He took my perfect truck and flipped it in the first place? Whoosh. Like shooting craps with me."

She took his arm. "You remember that?"

He shook off her hand. "So you've been telling me. Like twenty times a day. How could you forget?" He fingered the note. "No, man. That's too many steps. Just to get my attention? Not even God takes that many steps."

What their mother had said the year before, about her wasting death: *You'd think the Lord would be a little more efficient.*

"Whoever wrote this note found you, Mark. They came to see you in Intensive Care. They left you this. They wanted you to know."

A noise tore out of him, the squeal of a dog whose hind legs were just run over by his master's station wagon. "Know *what?* What am I supposed to do with this? Go help somebody else come back from the dead? How do I do that? I don't even know where the dead *are.*"

Cold clawed up Karin's spine. Dark things, games the police had hinted at. "What do you mean, Mark? What are you saying?"

He waved his arms around his head, warding off evil like a swarm of bees. "How am I supposed to know what I mean?"

"What . . . dead people don't you . . . ?"

"I don't even know who *is* dead. I don't know where my sister is. I don't even know where *I* am. This whole so-called hospital could be a movie studio where they take people to fool them into thinking that everything's regular."

She mumbled apologies. The note meant nothing. She reached to take it back. But he grabbed it away from her.

"I need to find who wrote this. This person knows what happened to me." He scrambled in his back pockets, his favorite baggy, low-riding, black jeans that Karin had brought him from home. "Shit! I don't even have a wallet to put this in. No social certificate card. No fucking photo ID! No wonder I'm nowhere."

"I'll bring your wallet tomorrow."

He stared up at her, his face flared. "How are you going to get into my home to get it?" When she said nothing, his shoulders collapsed. "Well, I suppose if they can operate on your brain without you even knowing, they've probably got the keys to your damn house."

They ask Mark Schluter who he thinks he's supposed to be. Sounds like an easy one, but their questions all have little tricks. Always more to them than you might think. God knows why, but they try to trip him up. All he can do is answer and stay cool.

81

They ask him where he lives. He points to all the medical crap, everybody running around in whites. Shouldn't they be telling him? They change the question: Does he know his home address? Mark Schluter, 6737 Sherman, Kearney, Nebraska. Reporting for duty. They go: Is he *sure*? How sure do they want him to be? They ask if his house is in Kearney or Farview. Just another desperate attempt to confuse him. Sure, he lives in Farview *now*. But they never said he needed to answer in the present tense.

They ask him what he does. Trick question. Hang with his friends. Go hear bands, at the Bullet or elsewhere. Check for ground effects on eBay. Do vids. Watch TV. Run the dog. He's got a thief character online whose stats he builds up when nothing else is happening. He does not say the obvious: that they're treating him like an online character himself.

Is that all? All he does? Well, they don't have to know *all*. Not their business, what goes on behind closed doors. But no; they're like: What does he do to make a living? Where does he *work*? Well, why didn't they ask as much in the first place?

He tells them about Utility Maintenance and Repair II. Which machines are a bitch and which are cake to maintain. Only in his third year, and already earning sixteen big ones an hour. They don't ask him how he feels about the animals, which is just as well. He hates it when people ask. Everybody eats the damn animals; somebody has to kill them. And that's not even him: all he does is watch over the gear. He gets to wondering why they want to know so much about the plant. He hasn't been in for a few days, and perhaps there's funny stuff afoot. Certain people might want his job. It's decent money and good work, especially in a recession. Tons of guys would kill for worse.

They ask him who's the vice president under the first bush.

Insane. What next? Senators in the trees? They tell him to count backward from a hundred by threes. Is this a particularly useful skill, might one inquire? They give him tons of quizzes—circling things, crossing them out, and whatnot. Even here, they jerk him around, make the print way too small, or give him ten seconds to do half an hour of work. He tells them he likes his life and doesn't really want to audition for anything else; if they want to fire him from the test program, feel free. They just laugh and give him more tests.

Something weird about all this grilling. Doctors saying they're his friends. Tests proving he can't do certain things, when obviously he can. They should be testing the woman who's impersonating his sister.

His buds come by, but even they are strange. Duane-o seems regular enough. You can't duplicate him. Get him started on any topic—terrorism, whatever: *Are you familiar with the concept of jihad? Here's the thing the State Department doesn't understand about the Islamicists. They can't help belonging to a foreign country.*

Islamicists? I thought they were called Muslims. Am I wrong in calling them Muslims?

Well, "wrong." Wrong is a relative term. Nobody's going to call you "wrong," per se . . .

A stream of unbelievably meaningless crap, like only the Cain Man can deliver. Rupp looks and sounds okay, too, but there's something off with his timing. Tommy Rupp is never off. The man who got Mark hired at the plant, who taught him how to shoot, who turned Mark on to undreamed-of alternate experiences: One-shot Rupp, of everyone, should be able to explain what's going on.

He asks Rupp if he knows anything about the chick who's pretending to be Karin. The guy gives him a look like Mark's turned werewolf. Something has infiltrated the man's food supply. He's so uptight all the time, like it's always somebody's funeral. Real Ruppie never gave a shit. He knew how to have a time. Real Ruppie could stand in the cooler all day long, toting cow quarters around and not even feel it. Nothing ever froze that guy. This guy is frozen constantly.

The whole setup is deeply disturbing, and all Mark can do is roll with it. They're hiding something from him, something bad. His truck, destroyed. His sister, missing. Everyone claims innocence. No one will tell him about the accident or the hours just before and after it. He can only sit tight, play dumb, and see what he can learn.

Duane-o and Rupp make him play five-card. Therapy, they say. So okay: he's not doing anything else. But they use trick cards where the clubs and spades look the same. The deck is funny, too, with way too many sixes, sevens, and eights. They play for IBP packing stickers; Mark's stack vanishes like the buffalo. They keep telling him he's already drawn cards, when he hasn't. A dumbass game for pissants. He tells them as much. They're like: *Schluter, this is your favorite game of all time.* He doesn't bother correcting them.

They spend a lot of time listening to mix CDs that Duane downloads and burns. A lot has happened to music while Mark was away. The songs jack with him. Jesus! Would you listen to this? Weirdest stuff I've ever heard. What is this, country metal?

This upsets Rupp. Stop squirming and use your ears, Gus. Country metal! You still on morphine, or something?

Country metal exists, Cain insists. It's a totally recognized genre. You're not onto that? Duane's the real Cain, no matter what.

But the looks those two shoot each other make Mark want to hide. When they're near, he can't hear himself think. Too much happening at once for him to see what's wrong. But when they're gone, he has no leads to follow. You can't explain what you can't see.

Problem is, the Karin look-alike seems so real. He's sitting by himself, respecting the laws, listening to something restful, when she comes by to harass him. She won't quit with the sister act. She hears the music. Hawaiian vocal trios?

I don't know. They're like Polynesian polkas, or something. She's all: Where'd you get this?

No say. An orderly gave it to me, for being a nice guy.

Mark? Are you *serious*?

What? You think I stole it from some Alzheimer's spaceman? What do you care? Are you tracking my activities now?

She goes: You really enjoy listening to this?

Well, come on. What's not to love?

It's just that . . . No, I'm sure you do. I bet it's good. Her eyes, all red and puffy, like someone's salted them.

You don't know me. I listen to this stuff all the time. I like to listen to, you know, stupid music. When nobody's around. Under the helmet—the, the earmuffs.

Like he's just told her he's into cross dressing, or something. All cranked up. I'm sure, she says. Me, too.

He doesn't quite get it. It really tortures her. He doesn't get anything. He needs to talk less, watch more. He could write things down, but the pages might be used as evidence.

Even Bonnie, beautiful simple Bonnie, has changed on him. She's like a ghost, something out of an old TV show, little pioneer cap and dress down to the floor. She's got some new life or something, living on roots, in a grass-covered trench, like a giant prairie dog, out by the Interstate Arch. She has to pretend her mother dies in a snowstorm and her father dies from drought, like something out of the freaking Bible, even though her parents are both alive and living in a gated community outside Tucson. Nobody's quite what they say they are, and he's just supposed to laugh and play along.

But she's still sexy as a pay channel, even in the ankle-length dress. So he doesn't argue with her. In fact, the whole getup is kind of hot, especially the antique cap. It cheers him to sit next to her and gawk while she designs little cards and such. Get Well thingies for total strangers in the rooms next to his. Postcards of newborns in bassinets to send to lawmakers in Washington. He sits up close, helping, painting inside the lines with one hand while keeping his other on her. If nobody else is there, she'll let him put his fingers just about anywhere.

But the cards won't cooperate. He stabs one, and the tip of his pen dents the tabletop. What the hell is wrong with these things? he asks. This looks like shit.

She jumps. She's *scared* of him. But she puts her arm around him. You're doing great, Marker. It's amazing how good. You were pretty beaten up there, for a while.

Was I? But I'm getting back now, right? To where I was?

Already are. Just look at you!

He studies her, but can't tell if she's lying. He wipes his fucked-up eyes. He pulls out his own Get Well card, for comparison: *I am No One . . .* Well, join the club. You're not alone.

Weeks passed that Karin couldn't account for. While the therapists were examining her brother, testing his memory and grasp of ordinary detail, she was losing days. Some part of her was out of sync. Small wonder, with Mark twice a day calling her an impostor. Not days she much cared to remember.

They moved Mark to the rehab facility. It crushed him. "So this is what 'discharge' means. This place is worse than where I was. It's just a minimum-security hospital. What happens if I jump bail?"

In fact, Dedham Glen was a fair step up from Good Samaritan. All pastels and river stone, the place might have been a low-end retirement community. He never mentioned recognizing the place where they'd consigned their mother in her final illness. Mark had his own room, the halls were cheerier, the food better, and the staff more capable than at the colder, more sterile hospital.

Best of all was Barbara Gillespie, the nurse's aide for his wing. Though new to the facility and surely pushing forty, Barbara worked with the zeal of the self-employed. From the start, she and Mark seemed to have known each other forever. Barbara could always tell, better than Karin, what Mark was asking for, even when Mark himself didn't know. Barbara made the rehab clinic feel like a family holiday timeshare. She was so assuring that both Schluter siblings tried to please her by acting healthier than they really were. Around Barbara, Karin found herself believing in total cures. Mark fell in love with her within days, and Karin soon followed. She lived for her exchanges with the attendant, inventing little problems to consult her about. In Karin's dreams, she and Barbara Gillespie were as close as sisters, consoling each other over Mark's damage as if they'd both known him since infancy. In waking life, Barbara was almost as consoling, preparing Karin for the hurdles still ahead.

Karin studied Barbara at every chance, trying to imitate her self-possession and easy grace. She described her to Daniel one night in his dark monk's cell. She tried not to sound too fawning. "She's always completely *with you* when she talks to you. More present than any person I've ever met. Never out in front of or behind herself. Not working on the next patient, or the last one. Wherever she happens to be, that's where she is. I'm always either undoing the last three stupid things I've done or fending off the next three. But Barbara, she's just . . . *centered*. Right there. You have to see her in action. She's the perfect nurse for Mark. Completely comfortable with him. Listens to all his theories, even when I want to press his face into a pillow. She's more at home in her body than anyone I've ever seen. I'll bet you there's no one in the world she'd rather be."

Daniel put a hand on her forearm, cautioning her in the dark. She lay back on his futon on the floor of a room so bare his three potted plants seemed like remainders in nature's clearance sale. His basement apartment's few furnishings were all retreads. His bookshelves—full of USGS publications, Conservation Service pamphlets, and field guides—were made from stacked orange crates. His work desk was an old oak door recovered from a demolition and laid out on sawhorses. Even his refrigerator was a refurbished dorm-room mini-cube, picked up at Goodwill for ten dollars. He kept his apartment a dim sixty degrees. Of course he was right: the only defensible way of life. But she already had plans to make the place livable.

"The woman has her own internal thermometer," she said. "Her own atomic clock. The last person on earth who's not prorating her time. She's just so *even*. So tranquil. A bubble of steady attentiveness."

"Sounds like she'd make a good birder."

"Mark never rattles her, even when he's completely out there. None of the residents unnerve her, and some are as spooky as you get. She has no expectations about who people are supposed to be. She just sees you, sees whoever is in front of her."

"What does she do for him?"

"Officially? She's the general attendant. Keeps the schedule, does light therapy, takes care of his routine needs, checks in five times a day, monitors his craziness, cleans up after him. She's the most underemployed person I know, including me. I can't understand why she's not running the place."

"If she were running the place, she wouldn't be caring for your brother."

"True." Fake sagacious monosyllable: copying Daniel. Her old chameleon complex. Be the one you're with.

"Career advancement can be toxic," Daniel said. "A person should do what they love, whatever the status."

"Well, that's Barbara, all right. She picks his dirty underwear off the floor like she's doing ballet." Daniel's hand traced cautious circles on her arm. It dawned on her: he was jealous of this woman, of Karin's description. Patience was his secret vanity, something he wanted to do better than anyone else. "She sits and listens to Mark while he launches these bizarre notions, like everything he's saying is totally plausible. Like she completely respects him. Then she just explores things with him, without condescension, until he sees where he's gone wrong."

"Hmm. Was she ever in the Scouts?"

"But she seems somehow sad to me. Totally stoic, but sad. No wedding ring, or any tan lines from one. Who knows? It's just so odd. She's exactly who I've tried to be my whole life. Daniel? Do you believe there are purposes out there?"

He pretended confusion. The man lived like an anchorite and meditated four times a day. He'd sacrificed his life to protecting a river tens of thousands of years old. He worshipped nature. He'd put Karin herself on a pedestal since childhood. By any measure, he was faith incarnate. And still, the word *purpose* made him nervous.

She waffled. "It doesn't have to be . . . Call it anything. Ever since the accident, I've thought: Maybe we're all on invisible paths? Paths we're supposed to follow, without knowing. Ones that really lead somewhere?"

He tensed on the bed. The rapids of his breath cascaded across her breasts. "I don't know, K.S. Do you mean your brother's accident was meant to lead you to this woman?"

"Not me. Him. You know what his life was like, before. Look at his friends, for God's sake. Barbara Gillespie is the first nonloser he's been taken with since . . ." She rolled to face him, draping her arm over his flank. "Since you, all right?"

He winced at the forlorn compliment. The bond of childhood, broken with puberty. The Danny Riegel whom Mark once loved was not this man lying across a foot-wide gap from her. "You think this might be his . . . path? This woman has arrived to save him from himself?"

She drew back her arm. "Don't make it sound so crude." At least he didn't mock her, as the other man would have. But she heard herself, how desperate she was. She'd end up like her mother, using the *Living Scriptures* volume like a Magic 8 Ball.

"Does this woman need to be fate?" Daniel asked. "Couldn't she just be something lucky in his life, for a change?"

"But he would never have met her without the accident."

Daniel stood and walked to the window, stark naked, oblivious. Like a wild child. The chill of his apartment didn't touch him. He tried on the idea. She loved that in him, his eternal willingness to try her on. "No one is on a separate path. Everything connects. His life, yours, hers, his friends' . . . mine. Other . . ."

Watching him stare out the window on all those tangled paths, she thought of the policemen's three sets of linked tracks. Three that they saw and measured. How many drivers sped by that night, leaving no trace? She sat up in bed, covering her bareness with the blanket. "You're the most mystical person I know. You're always proclaiming some living essence we can't even . . ." Robert Karsh had mocked him mercilessly. *The Ent Man. The Druid. Green Giant Junior.* Karin had joined in—any cruelty, to be affirmed.

Daniel spoke to something out the window. "One million species heading toward extinction. We can't be too choosy about our private paths."

The words reproached her. She felt the slap. "My brother was almost killed. I don't know what's going to happen to him. Whether he'll be able to work again, whether his brain, his personality . . . Don't begrudge me for needing a little faith to survive this."

In silhouette against the window, he grabbed the crown of his head. "Begrudge? My God, no!" He came back to the bed. "Never." He stroked her hair, contrite. "Of course there are forces bigger than us."

She felt it in his stroking hand: forces so big that our paths mean nothing to them.

"I love you," he said. Ten years after the fact, yet somehow premature. "You seem to me everything that's best about humans. You've never felt more decent to me than you do right now." Frail, he meant. Needy. Mistaken.

She let his judgment ride. She burrowed into his meager chest, trying to smother her own words even as they came out. "Tell me that something right could still come out of this."

"It can," he said. Any cruelty, to affirm. "If this woman can help Mark, then she's our path."

Daniel meditated: his version of a plan. She had to leave the apartment whenever he drew his legs up into the lotus. She wasn't afraid of bothering him; he was oblivious, once tuned to his breathing. It just upset her to see him so tranquil and removed. She felt abandoned, as if all her problems with Mark were just impediments to Daniel's transcendence. He never tranced out for more than twenty minutes at a time, at least by her watch. But to Karin, that always threatened to become forever.

"What do you want from it?" she asked, trying to sound neutral.

"Nothing! I want it to help me want nothing."

She fisted her skirt hem. "What does it do for you?"

"It makes me more . . . an object to myself. Disidentified." He rubbed his cheek and glanced upward, eleven o'clock. "Makes my insides more transparent. Reduces resistance. Frees up my beliefs, so that every new idea, every new change isn't so much . . . like the death of me."

"You want it to make you more fluid?"

His head bobbed, like she'd just met him halfway. She found the idea almost hideous. Mark had become fluid. She could not be any more fluid than Mark's accident now forced her to be. What she wanted—what she needed from Daniel— was dry land.

The last crane disappeared, and Kearney returned to itself. The crane peepers—twice as many as had visited just five years before—vanished with the migrants. The whole town relaxed at not having to play itself for another ten months. Famous each spring, for something that at best resented you: it screwed up a place's self-image.

Other birds came in the cranes' wake. Wave after wave, birds by the millions passed through the tiny waist of a continent-sized hourglass. Birds Karin Schluter had seen since childhood but had never noticed: Daniel knew them all by name. He carried around alphabetized life lists of all 446 Nebraska species—*Anas*, *Anthus*, and *Anser*, *Buteo*, *Branta*, and *Bucephala*, *Calidris*, *Catharus*, *Carduelis*—covered in penciled checks and smudged, unreadable field notes.

Karin went birding with him, a way of staying sane. On afternoons when Mark raged against her and she needed to escape, she and her birder went northwest into the sandhills, northeast into the loess, or east and west along the twisting braids of river. She whipsawed between elation and guilt over abandoning her brother, even for an afternoon. She felt as she had at ten, returning home from a summer's evening of hide-and-seek to realize, only when her mother shrieked at her, that she'd left her little brother curled up in a concrete culvert, waiting to be found.

Only outside, in the warming air, did Karin sense how close she'd come to collapse. Another week of caring for Mark and she'd have begun believing his theories about her. She and Daniel picnicked near the sandpit wetlands just southwest of town. She'd just bitten down on a slice of cucumber when her whole body began trembling so hard she couldn't swallow. She bent down and covered her quaking face. "Oh my God. What would I have done, back here, with what's happened to him, without you?"

He lifted her shoulders. "I've done nothing. I wish there was something I *could* do." He offered her his handkerchief, the last man in North America to blow his nose into cloth. She used it, making horrible noises and not caring.

"I can't get away from here. I've tried, so many times.

Chicago. L.A. Even Boulder. Every time I make a start, try to pass myself off as normal, this place drags me back. My whole life, I've dreamed of self-sufficiency, far away. Look how far I've gotten! South Sioux."

"Everyone comes home, sometime."

She coughed a phlegmy laugh. "Never really left! Stuck in a stupid loop." She swept her hand in the air. "Worse than the damn birds."

He flinched, but forgave her.

After lunch, they made fresh sightings: redstarts, pipits, a solitary golden-crowned kinglet, even a vagrant male Lewis's woodpecker passing through. Grassland gave few hiding places. Daniel taught her how to see without being seen. "The trick is to make yourself small. Shrink your sphere of sound inside your sphere of sight. Widen your periphery; watch only motion." He made her sit still for fifteen minutes, then forty, then an hour, just watching, until her backbone threatened to split open and eject some other creature from her cracked shell. But stillness was salutary, like most pain. Her concentration was shot. She needed slowing, focusing. She needed to sit silent with someone from choice, not from injury. Her brother still refused to recognize her; his persistence had grown truly spooky. She could not imagine the bizarre, unstable symptom lasting as long as it had. Motionless for an hour, on a rise of returning bluestem, inside a bubble of wild silence, she felt her helplessness. As she shrank and the sea of grass expanded, she saw the scale of life—millions of tangled tests, more answers than there were questions, and a nature so swarmingly wasteful that no single experiment mattered. The prairie would try out every story. One hundred thousand pairs of breeding swifts pumped eggs into everything from rotting telephone poles to smoking chimneys. A plague of starlings wheeled overhead, descended, Daniel said, from a handful of birds released into Central Park a century ago by a drug maker who wanted America to have all the birds mentioned in Shakespeare. Nature could sell at a loss; it made up in volume. Guess relentlessly, and it didn't matter if almost every guess was wrong.

Daniel was just as profligate. The man who denied himself even hot showers lavished her with attentions all afternoon. He interpreted markings and tracks for her. He found her a wasp's nest, an owl pellet, and a tiny bleached warbler skull beyond the skill of any jeweler. "Do you know that Whitman line?" he asked her. " 'After you have exhausted what there is in business, politics, conviviality, and so on—have found that none of these finally satisfy, or permanently wear—what remains? Nature remains.' "

He meant to give comfort. But it sounded to her relentless, indiscriminate, indifferent: much like what her brother had become.

When they got home from the day's exploration, Daniel handed her a shirt box that had sat in the back of his twenty-year-old Duster for the last month. She'd guessed it was for her, waiting for him to find the nerve to give it. She opened the flimsy carton, already preparing some show of gratitude for whatever natural-history exhibit he'd found her. The box flapped open, and she was the specimen inside. Every trinket she'd ever given him. They sat in the lot behind his apartment as she sifted through the embalmed past. Notes in her elvish scrawl, written in colors of pen she never could have owned, punch lines of running jokes that now meant nothing to her, even half-finished attempts at poems. Pairs of ticket stubs to films she couldn't have seen with him. Sketches from back when she could draw. A postcard from her mishap in Boulder:

"I knew I should have sold the stock options last month." A plastic action figure of Mary Jane, Spiderman's object of desire. Karsh had given it to her, claiming she was the spitting image. Karin had passed it on to Daniel—stupid tease—instead of melting the thing down to dioxins as she should have.

By all evidence, she'd never given him anything of value. But he'd kept it all. He even had her mother's obituary from *The Hub*, clipped long after he should have consigned the whole box to an incinerator. His zeal was as spooky as Mark's distance. She looked at this time capsule of scraps, horrified. She wasn't worth preservation.

Daniel watched her, stiller than when birding. "I just thought, if you were feeling a little rootless, K.S., that you might like . . ." He held out his hand, ten years snug in his palm. "I hope this doesn't seem obsessive."

She clutched the box, unnerved by his pointless conservation, but unable to scold him. His entire worldly possessions fit into two suitcases, and he'd kept this. She could start to give him real things, gifts she picked out just for him, things it wouldn't be pathetic to preserve. He could use a light spring coat, for starters.

"Can I just . . . Could I hang on to this for a little? I need to . . ." She pressed the box, then her forehead. "It's all still yours. I'm just . . ."

He seemed pleased, but she was too shaken to be sure. "Keep them," he said. "Keep them as long as you like. Show Mark, if you feel like it."

Never, she thought. *Never.* Not the sister she wanted him to recognize.

Despite Mark's refusal to acknowledge her, he rebuked her when she skipped an afternoon. "Where were you? Had to meet your handlers or something? My sister would never have cut out like that, without saying. My sister is very loyal. You should have learned that when you trained to replace her."

The words filled her with hope, even as they demoralized her.

"Tell me something. What the hell am I still doing in rehab?"

"You were really hurting, Mark. They just want to make sure you're one hundred percent before they send you back home."

"I *am* a hundred percent. One hundred and ten. Fifteen. Don't you think *I'm* the best judge of that? Why would they believe their tests before they believe me?"

"They're just being careful."

"My sister wouldn't have left me in here to rot."

She was beginning to wonder. Even though any small change in routine still rattled him, Mark grew steadily more like himself. He spoke clearer, confusing fewer words. He scored higher on the cognition tests. He could answer more questions about his past, from before the accident. As he grew more reasonable, she couldn't help trying to prove herself. She dropped casual details, things only a Schluter could know. She would wear him down with common sense, inescapable logic. One gray April afternoon, taking him for a spin around Dedham Glen's artificial duck pond in the drizzle, she mentioned their father's stint as a rainmaker, flying his converted crop duster.

Mark shook his head. "Now, where in the world did you learn that? Bonnie tell you? Rupp? They think it's weird, too, how much like Karin you are." His face grew overcast. She saw him think: *She should be here by now. They won't tell her where I am.* But he was too suspicious to speak the thought out loud.

What did it mean to be related, if he refused relations? You couldn't call yourself someone's wife unless they agreed; years with Karsh had taught her that. You weren't someone's friend just by decree, or she'd be surrounded by support. Sister was no different, except technically. If he never again recognized her as his flesh and blood, what difference would all her objections make?

Their father had a brother once. Luther Schluter. They learned about him overnight, when Karin was just thirteen and Mark almost nine. Cappy Schluter suddenly insisted upon taking them to a mountainside in Idaho, even though it meant missing a week of school. *We're going to visit your uncle.* As if they should have suspected such a person's existence all along.

Cappy Schluter dragged his children across Wyoming in a burgundy and mint Rambler station wagon while Joan rode shotgun. Neither child could read in a moving car without vomiting, and Cappy forbade the radio because of all the subliminal messages that manipulated the unconscious listener. So they had only their father's stories of the young Schluter brothers to see them across 890 miles of the earth's most ruthless scenery. He got them from Ogallala to Broadwater on tales of his family's Sandhills days, first as Kincaid Act homesteaders, and then, when the government pulled the land out from underneath them, as ranchers. From Broadwater to the Wyoming border, he entertained them with accounts of his older brother's hunting skills: four dozen rabbits nailed to the barn's southern wall, seeing the family through the winter of '38.

To get his children through Wyoming, Cappy Schluter resorted to grim detail about every opponent Luther Schluter had bested on his way to third place in the Nebraska state wrestling championship. "Your uncle is a powerful man," he repeated, three times over a two-mile stretch. "A powerful man who could take anything. Saw three men die before he was old enough to vote. The first was a grade school friend who drowned in grain while the two boys were playing in a silo. The second was an old ranch hand who popped an aneurysm while arm-wrestling and expired in the crook of Luther's arm. The third was his own father, when the two of them went out to rescue fourteen head of cattle stranded in a snowstorm."

"Uncle Luther's father?" Mark asked, from the backseat. Karin shushed him, but Cappy just sat ramrod straight, his Korean War-vet posture, hearing nothing.

"Three men before voting age, and one woman, not long after."

The kids sat in the backseat, traumatized. For most of the trip, Mark withdrew into a cocoon against his door handle and muttered to his secret friend, Mr. Thurman. The hundreds of miles of confidential murmuring between boy and phantasm infuriated Karin; she couldn't visualize her own best flesh-and-blood girlfriend, ten hours away, let alone an imaginary companion. By Casper, she was riding Mark. Their mother took to whacking them from the front seat, first with the rolled up Rand McNally and then with her hardback copy of *Come Judgement*. Cappy just gripped the wheel and drove, that grotesque Adam's apple jutting from his throat making him look like a stalking heron.

At last they arrived at their uncle's, a man who, until three weeks ago, hadn't even figured in a family photograph. Whatever power the man had possessed was long gone. This uncle could not have withstood the breeze from a flapping barn door. Luther Schluter, a furnace repairman holed up on a solitary cliff near Idaho Falls, began almost immediately to spout even more bountiful theories than their father. Washington and Moscow had concocted the Cold War together to keep their populations in line. The world was awash in oil that multinationals kept a spigot on for their own profits. The AMA knew that television caused brain cancer, but kept quiet about it for the kickbacks. How was the drive? Car give any trouble?

Of their years of estrangement, Cappy and Luther said nothing. They sat at opposite ends of a ratty sofa in front of the river stone hearth in Luther's hand-built cabin, one of them calling out a name from their Nebraska childhood and the other identifying. Luther told his niece and nephew fantastic tales about young Cappy: how he'd gotten the gash through the bridge of his nose by dropping a granite boulder that he was lifting over his head on a dare. How he was married to a girl before Joan. How he did time over a misunderstanding involving a two-ton Chevy grain truck and thirty-eight bales of hay. With every fable, their father grew stranger. Strangest of all was how Cappy Schluter sat still and abided the remembrances, in awe of this sallow, shaky old man. The children had never seen their father so cowed by anyone. Their mother, too, put up with comments from the recovered relative that she wouldn't have suffered from Satan.

They left after two days. Luther gave each child five dollars in silver and a copy of *The Outdoor Survival Field Manual* to share. Karin made him promise to come out to Nebraska, pretending not to understand that the man would be dead within four months. As they left, Karin's new uncle grasped Cappy with two talons. "She did what she did. I never meant her memory no disrespect."

Cappy barely nodded. "I made things worse," he said. The two men shook stiff hands, and took leave. Karin remembered nothing of the trip home.

Uncles from nowhere and siblings disappearing. On Dedham Glen's fake duck pond, she felt Mark's distress. She was causing it, by not being who she was. *His amygdala*, she remembered. *His amygdala can't talk with his cortex.* "Do you remember Uncle Luther?" she asked. Tugging at him, maybe unfairly.

Mark hunched against the wind in the baseball jacket and blue knit stocking cap he'd taken to wearing to hide the scars under his returning hair. He walked as if performing acrobatics. "Don't know about you, but I got no uncles."

"Come on, Mark. You remember that trip. A third of the United States, to visit a guy they hadn't even bothered to tell us about." She grabbed his arm too hard. "You remember. Sitting in the backseat for hundreds of miles, not even allowed to pee, you and your friend Mr. Thurman, chatting away like the two of you . . ."

He pulled his arm free and froze. He narrowed his eyes and pressed his cap. "Man, do *not* mess with the insides of my head."

She apologized. Mark, shaken, asked to go back in. She steered him toward the building. Mark zipped and unzipped his coat, thoughts racing. He seemed for a moment about to break free, to know her. At the door of the lobby, he murmured, "I wonder whatever happened to that guy."

"He died. Right after we got back home. That was the point of the trip."

Mark stumbled, his face twisted. "What the fuck?"

"Serious. They'd had some fight about their mother's death. Cappy had cut the man off, for saying . . . But the minute he heard Luther was dying . . ."

Mark snorted and waved her off. "Not that guy. He was never anything to me. I mean Mr. Thurman."

She stood gaping, appalled.

Mark just laughed, low and clicking. "I mean, imaginary

friends: do they go bug another whacko kid when you're done with them? And hey!" His face screwed up, mystified. "Whoever told you about that trip? They got it all wrong."

Jack is that person's father, but that person isn't Jack's son. Who is that person? The question's obviously meaningless, to anybody who thinks twice. The questioner should be in rehab, not him. How in living hell should he know who *that person* is? Could be anyone. But they keep asking him such crap, even when he politely points out that it might all be just a wee bit screwy. Today the questioner is a woman fresh from the university in Lincoln, about Mark's age. Not a dog, but with an awful growl, spewing out craziness like:

A girl goes into a store to apply for a job. She fills in the application form. The manager looks at her data and says: "Yesterday we got an application from someone with your same last name, same parents, and exact same birthday, down to the year." "Yes," the girl explains. "That was my sister." "So you must be twins," the manager concludes. "No," the girl says. "We're not."

And Mark is supposed to figure out what the hell they are. So . . . what? One of them is adopted or something?

But no, the university chick tells him, with a mouth like two little bait worms doing it. Useful little mouth, probably, in a pinch. But a pain in the ass at the moment, with its trick questions. She tells him: two girls with the same last name, the same parents, the same date of birth. Yes, they're sisters. But no, not twins.

Do they look alike, or anything?

Super Questioner says it's not important.

102

It *is* important, Mark tells her. You're telling me that if two girls who have to be twins say they aren't twins and you can't tell whether they're lying or not by looking at them and seeing if they look identical, that's not *important*?

Let's go on to the next question, Super Questioner says.

I've a better idea, Mark says. We go into that supply closet and get to know each other.

I don't think so, the worms say. But they twitch a bit.

Why not? Might be nice. I'm a good guy.

I know that. But we're supposed to be learning about you.

Uh, what *better* way to learn about me?

Let's try the next question.

So you're saying, if I get the next question right . . . ?

Well, not exactly.

Let me ask *you* a sister question: Where's mine? Can you talk to the authorities, please?

But she won't. She won't even tell him the twins answer. She says if he comes up with anything, let her know. It bugs the crap out of him. The question is so supremely fucked up it keeps him awake at night. He thinks about it, in his little room in the Cripple Home. He just lies there, in the bed they've made for him, thinking about the twins who claim they aren't twins. Thinking about Karin, where she might be, the truth about what has happened to her, the facts that no one will mention. The docs say he's got a syndrome. The docs must be in on the con.

Maybe it's some kind of sex riddle. You know, like: Want to meet my *sister*? He tries it on Duane and Ruppie. Duane-o says: It may have something to do with Parthian Genesis. Are you familiar with Parthian Genesis? Also known as the phenomenon of virgin birth.

Rupp busts Cain's chops. You been eating mad cow? It has

no answer, Rupp declares. And he's one smart bastard. If Rupp can't figure it out, it's unfigurable.

Maybe you've confused the question, Duane-o suggests. There's a phenomena called garbling. It's like the game of telephone . . .

Chill, Potato Head, Ruppie blasts him. Too much mercury ingestion. You're in a tuna-fish fog. The game of telephone! *Christ.*

I've got Collapse on my cell, Mark says. Used to be great. But somebody screwed with my settings.

Look, Rupp says. It's simple logic. What's the definition of twin? Two people, born of the same parents, at the same time.

Just what I said, Mark says. How come they don't examine you, too?

Rupp gets upset. What're you complaining about? You're living *la vida loca*, man. Maid service, hot meals. Cable. Skilled women giving you workouts.

Could be worse, Duane agrees. You could be one of those Afghani terrorists down in Gitmo. None of them going anywhere, anytime soon. How about that American they captured? Was that guy high, drunk, crazy, brainwashed, or what?

Mark shakes his head. The whole world's on crack. The therapists, working overtime to get Mark to think there's something wrong with him. The fake Karin, trying to distract him. Rupp and Duane, as clueless as he is. The only one he trusts is his friend Barbara. But she works for the enemy, just a lowly guard here at Sing Sing Lite.

Rupp is deep in thought. Maybe they're two test-tube babies, he says. Those sisters. Two different embryos, implanted . . .

Remember the Schellenberger twins? Duane-o asks, all stoked. Anybody ever have sex with them?

Rupp scowls. Clearly someone had sex with them, Einstein. Didn't one of them go away to foal, senior year?

I knew it had something to do with sex, Mark says. You can't have twins without sex, right?

I meant anybody of the three of us, Duane-o whines.

Rupp shakes his head. I wish that Barbara Gillespie had a twin. Can you imagine? What you call your twofer!

Duane-o howls like a coyote. That chick's *old*, man.

So? Means you don't have to teach her anything. The woman's killer, I tell you. You gotta know she's got some deep waves going, under those still waters.

She does have a great walk. If they gave an Oscar for walking, she'd have a shelf full of little bald homonculi. You two are familiar with the concept of the homunculus?

Then Mark is raging. He's shouting, and can't stop himself. Get the hell out of here. I don't want you here.

He frightens them. His friends—if they are his friends—are *scared* of him. They're all: What? What did we do? What's got into you?

Leave me alone. I've got things to figure out.

He's on his feet, pushing them out of the room while they try to reason with him. But he's sick of reason. All three of them are shouting at one another when Barbara appears from nowhere. What's wrong? she asks. And he starts spraying. He's sick of it all. Sick of being kept in this holding tank. Sick of the deceptions, everybody pretending things are exactly normal. Sick of trick questions with no answer, and people pretending there is one.

What questions? Barbara asks. And just the sound of her, coming from that moon-round face, calms him a little.

Two sisters, Mark says. Born at the same time, to the same parents. But they say they're not twins.

Barbara sits him down, and she's soothing his shoulders. Maybe they're two-thirds of triplets, she says.

Rupp smacks himself on the forehead. Brilliant. The woman is brilliant.

Duane waves his hands in the air for a timeout. You know, I was thinking about triplets. Right at the beginning. But I didn't say it.

Of course you were, latent boy. We were all thinking about triplets. It's obvious. Face it. You're a idiot. I'm a idiot. The whole human race is a idiot.

Mark Schluter tenses under the woman's arm, fighting rage. So why am I the only one locked up?

Two days later, Barbara Gillespie comes to take him for a walk.

Don't I need to check with my parole board? he asks.

Very funny, she says. This place isn't that bad and you know it. Come on. Let's go outside.

Outside is not exactly to be trusted. Much wilder than before his bang-up. They say it's April, but one confused April, doing a pretty good January imitation. The wind cuts through his jacket and his skull freezes, even underneath his cap. His head is always cold now. His hair takes forever to grow back; something to do with the feed here.

Barbara practically pushes him out of the foyer. Watch your step there, sweetie. But once they're out, all she wants to do is hang around the bench by the parking lot.

Fine, he says. The Great Out of Doors. I give it five stars. Can we go back inside?

But Barbara keeps him out, teasing. She takes his arm as if they're an old couple. Which would be okay with him. In a pinch.

Five more minutes, friend. You never know what might come along and surprise you, if you wait long enough.

Tell me about it. Like this terrible accident I apparently had.

Barbara points her finger, all excited. Well, would you look who's here!

A car rolls up to the curb, as if by chance. Unmistakably feeb Corolla, with the big dimple on the passenger door. His sister's car. His *sister*, at last. Like rising from the dead. He jumps up and starts shouting.

Then he sees through the windshield, and crashes again. He can't take it anymore. It isn't Karin, but the not-so-secret agent who has replaced her. There's a dog in the passenger seat, pressed to the glass, clawing at the top of the window to make it go down. Another border collie, like Mark's. Smartest breed there is. The dog sees Mark through the window, and it's frantic to get at him. It bursts through the door the instant Barbara opens it. Before Mark can move, the pretty creature is all over him, herding. Up on its hind legs, muzzle skyward, letting out these pathetic yips and howls. That's the thing about dogs. There isn't a human being in the world worthy of any dog's welcome.

The actress Karin comes out of the driver's door. She's crying and laughing all at once. Look at that, she says. You'd think she thought she'd never see you again!

The dog is leaping dead vertical into the air. Mark puts out his arms to fend off the attack. Barbara braces him. Would you look who's here! Barbara says. Look who has been dying to see you. She leans down and nuzzles at the dog. Yes, yes, yes you are—back together! The dog yips at Barbara, that border collie-crazed affection, then assaults Mark again.

Quit with the licking. Get out of my face, will you? Can somebody please leash this thing?

Pretend sister hangs on the driver's door, her face one of those birthday streamers gone soggy. You'd think he punched the woman in the gut or something. She starts to rag him again. Mark! Look at her! What other animal on earth could love you like that?

The dog starts this confused little squealing. Barbara moves toward the fake Karin, calling her sweetie, saying: It's okay. It doesn't matter. You did a good thing. We can try again later.

What later? Mark groans. Try what? What the hell is this about? This dog is mad. Rabies or something. Somebody put this beast down, before it bites me.

Mark! Look at her! It's Blackie.

The agent's dog starts yapping in bafflement. It's got that much right. Blackie? You gotta be *shitting* me. Down!

Maybe he makes a motion, like he's gonna strike the dog, because Barbara steps in between Mark and the howling thing. She gathers up the dog and waves at the imitation Karin like it's time to get back in the car.

Mark goes a little wild. You think I'm nuts! You think I'm blind. It's going to take a lot more than this to fool me.

Barbara bundles the howling animal back into the car and Karin starts the ridiculous four-cylinder engine. The miserable cur spins in circles on the passenger seat, whining and staring at Kopy Karin. Mark curses everything that moves. Don't bug me anymore. Don't *ever* let that thing back in my sight.

Later, when he's alone again, he feels a little bad about it all. It's still eating at him the next day, after he sleeps on it. When Barbara comes to check on him, he tells her. I shouldn't have yelled at that dog. It wasn't the dog's fault. Certain human beings were just using it.

Karin dragged Daniel out to North Line Road. She'd shunned the scene for two months, as if it might harm her. But she needed to understand what had happened that night. When she at last summoned the courage to see the site, she brought protection.

Daniel pulled off the road where Mark must have spun out. The intervening weeks had erased most of the evidence the police had mentioned. The two of them picked through the shallow shoulder ditch on the south side of the road, looking for all the world as if they were tracking an animal. *Bring your sphere of sound inside your sphere of sight.* They crawled over the new spring sedge and grasses, the pokeweed, thistle, and vetch. Nature's job was to grow over, turn the past into now.

Daniel found a patch of ground dusted with glass, invisible to anyone but a naturalist. Karin's eyes adjusted. She saw where the truck must have lain for hours, upside down. They climbed to the road, crossed over to the north side, and drifted back east, toward where Mark had lost control. The road was empty, the middle of the afternoon in the thaw of the year. The surface was layered in smears. She couldn't tell the age of a given track, or what had made it. She walked two hundred yards in each direction, with Daniel in her wake. The forensics investigators must have combed this stretch, re-creating that night from a few ambiguous measurements.

Daniel saw it first—a faint pair of westbound burn marks, all but erased by the weather, that swerved into the eastbound lane. Karin's eyes picked it out; the violent skid feinted to the right before veering, as close to a left turn as a light truck at high speed could make. She worked her way along the lip of the skid, head down, searching for something. Against the long, low, bathwater-gray horizon, with her fall of carrot hair hanging in the windless air, she might have been some Bohemian immigrant farm girl gleaning the fields for grain. She spun around like a struck animal, flinching as the accident unfolded in front of her. When Daniel reached her, she was still shuddering. She pointed down at a second set of tire skids at her feet.

The second skid broke one hundred feet in front of the first. Another vehicle coming from the west had careened into the oncoming lane, where it fishtailed before swinging back into its own. From the start of the second car's jag, Karin looked east and downward into the ditch where her brother had landed, the hole down which her own solidity disappeared.

She read the snaking lines: the car coming from town, perhaps blinded by Mark's headlights, must have lost control and swerved into Mark's lane, just in front of him. Startled, Mark dipped right, then swung back hard to the left, the only slim chance of survival. The swing was too sharp, and his truck left the road.

She stood with her toe on the tire mark, shaking. A car approached; she and Daniel drifted to the southern shoulder. A townie woman of about forty in a Ford Explorer with a ten-year-old girl strapped in the backseat pulled over to ask if everything was okay. Karin tried to smile and waved her on.

The police had mentioned a third set of tracks. She took Daniel and crossed to the north side of the road. Side by side, they tracked back eastward, like foraging juncos. Daniel's tracking eye again discovered the invisible signs, a patch of crushed, sandy ground, two faint hints of wheel scrape that had not yet vanished in the spring thaw. Karin pinned Daniel's arm. "We should have brought a camera. By summer, every one of these tracks will be gone."

"The police must have photographs on file."

"I don't trust their pictures." She sounded like her brother. He tried gentle reassurance, which she shook off. She scanned the tracks. "These people must have come up behind Mark. The whole thing happened in front of them. They had to roll off the road here. They must have sat awhile, level with him, then pulled back onto the road and headed on to Kearney. Left him lying in the ditch. Didn't even step out of their car."

"Maybe they saw how bad it was. Better to get to a phone fast."

She scowled. "From the Mobil station on Second, halfway through town?" She scanned the road, from the modest rise toward the east to the shallow declivity in the direction of Kearney. "What are the odds? It's five o'clock on a beautiful spring weekday, and look at the traffic this road gets. A car every four minutes? What are the odds, after midnight, at the end of February . . . ?" She studied Daniel. But Daniel wasn't calculating. Asked for numbers, Daniel returned only consolation. "I'll tell you the odds," she said. "Somebody swerving by accident in front of you on a deserted country road? Zero. But there's something that would make those odds a lot higher."

He stared at her, as if another Schluter had just gone delusional.

"Party games," she told him. "The police were right."

The wind picked up, the early evening turning. Daniel hunched, swinging his head through a half-circle. He had gone to school with all three boys; he knew their proclivities. It wasn't hard to see: a punishing February night, machines with too much horsepower, young men in their twenties in a country sick with thrills, sports, war, and their many combinations. "What kind of party games?" He looked down at the oily pavement as if he were meditating. In profile, his face framed by shoulder-length sandy hair, he looked even more like an elfin archer escaped from a marathon dice-dungeon crawl. How had he grown up in rural Nebraska without her brother's friends beating the life out of him?

She grasped his skinny upper arm and drew him back down the road toward their car. "Daniel." She shook her head. "You wouldn't know how to play if they strapped you in a NASCAR racer and put a cinder block on the accelerator."

Mark still limped and contusions still lined his face, but otherwise he seemed almost healed. Two months after the accident, strangers who talked to him might have found him a little slow and inclined toward strange theories, but nothing outside the local norm. Karin alone knew how unready he was to fend for himself, let alone tend to complex packing plant equipment. His days were laced with flashes of paranoia, outbursts of pleasure and rage, and increasingly elaborate explanations.

She worked tirelessly for his protection, even as he tortured her. "My sister would have got me out of this place by now." My sister always got me out of all my jams. I'm in the biggest jam of my life. You've failed to get me out. Therefore, you can't be my sister. The syllogism made a kind of demented sense.

She'd heard the complaint countless times before. But reaching some limit, she melted down. "Stop it, Mark. I've had enough. You're doing this to me for no reason. I know you're suffering, but this whole denial thing is not helping any. I'm your damn sister, and I'll prove it to you in a court of law if I have to. So just stop jerking me around and get over it. Now."

The instant the words were out of her mouth, she knew she'd set her cause back by weeks. And the look he flashed her then was like some wild thing, cornered. He looked almost ready to hurt her. She'd read the articles: the rate of violent behavior in Capgras patients was well above average. A young Capgras sufferer from the British Midlands, to prove that his father was a robot, had cut the man open to expose the wires. There were worse things than being called an impostor.

"Never mind," she said. "Forget I said that."

His face went from wild to bewildered. "Exactly," he said, a little tentative. "Now you're talking my language."

He was not ready to face the world. She fought to delay Mark's discharge, and to keep both the HMO and the IBP insurance people at bay. She worked on Dr. Hayes, almost flirting with him, to keep him signing off on the necessary paperwork.

But even with excellent medical coverage, Mark could not stay in rehabilitation much longer. Karin, unemployed now, was tapping her savings. She began to dip into her mother's life-insurance legacy. *Do some good with this.* "I'm not sure this is the kind of thing she intended the money for," she told Daniel. "Not exactly an emergency. Not exactly world-changing."

"Of course this is good," Daniel assured her. "And please don't worry about money." Almost too polite to say the word. Lilies of the field, etc. The ease of Daniel's assurance almost angered her. But she started letting Daniel pay all the daily expenses—groceries and gas—and each time he did, she felt stranger. Mark, she insisted, would be more or less back to himself any week now. But time and institutional patience were running out. And her own sense of competence was fading.

Daniel did what he could to stave off her money panic. One afternoon, apropos of nothing, he said, "You could come work for the Refuge."

"Doing what?" she asked, half hoping this might be an answer.

He looked away, embarrassed. "Office help? We need a congenial, competent set of hands. Maybe do some fund raising."

She tried to grin, grateful. Of course: fund raising. The core of every job description in the nation, from school-children on up to the president.

"We need people who can make others feel good about themselves. Experience in customer relations would be perfect!"

"Yes," she said, thoughtfully. Meaning he was too good and she relied on him for too much already. Added to her mother's money, a little part-time income could stabilize her. But she could not shake the belief that Mark would soon recover fully and she could go reclaim her own job—the *she* that she had made, out of nothing.

No war chest she might build could stave off the bills she'd face, if the insurance people signed off. When claims anxieties and physician consultations defeated her, Karin sought out Barbara Gillespie. She hit up the aide for pep talks so often that she worried that Barbara would start fleeing her on sight. But the woman had bottomless patience. She listened to Karin's fears and groaned in sympathy at tales of the medical bureaucracy. "Off the record? It's a business, as market-driven as a used-car dealership."

"Only not as up-front. At least you can trust a used-car salesman."

"I'm with you on that," Barbara said. "Just don't tell my boss, or I'll be selling some fine pre-owned vehicles myself."

114

"Never, Barbara. They need you."

The woman waved off the compliment. "Everyone's replaceable." The smallest turn of her wrist had something classic to it—the urban proficiency that Karin had aspired to for fifteen years. "I'm only doing my job."

"But it's not just a job for you. I watch you. He tests you."

"Nonsense. You're the one being tested here."

These graceful rebuffs only fed Karin's admiration. She probed Barbara for anything from her professional experience that gave hope of further improvement. Barbara wouldn't talk about other patients. She focused on Mark, as if he were the sum of her experience. The extreme tact frustrated Karin. She needed a female confidante, someone to commiserate with. Someone who would remind her that she was who she was. Someone who could reassure her that persistence wasn't stupid.

But Barbara's professional care turned all topics back to Mark. "I wish I knew more about things he really cares about. Beef packing. Truck customization. Not my strongest subjects, I'm afraid. But the things he'll talk about—it's a surprise a day. Yesterday, he wanted my considered opinion on the war."

Karin felt a twinge of jealousy. "Which war?"

Barbara grimaced. "The latest one, in fact. He's fascinated with Afghanistan. How many recent trauma sufferers pay any attention to the outside world?"

"Mark? *Afghanistan?*"

"He's a remarkably alert young man."

The phrase, its curt insistence, accused Karin. "I wish you could have seen him . . . before."

Barbara gave her patent head-tilt, both ready and reserved. "Why do you say that?"

"Mark was a real number. He could be incredibly sensitive. He had his wild moments—mostly getting back at our father and mother. And he ran with the wrong crowd. But he was really a sweet guy. Instinctively kind."

"But he's a sweet guy now. The sweetest! When he's not confused."

"This isn't him. Mark wasn't cruel or stupid. Mark wasn't so angry all the time."

"He's just scared. You must be, too. I'd be a mess, if I were you."

Karin wanted to melt into the woman, hand over everything, let Barbara take care of her, the way she had tried to take care of Mark. "You would've liked him. He cared for everybody."

"I do like him," Barbara said. "As he is." And her words filled Karin with shame.

By May, Karin was beside herself. "They're not doing anything for him," she told Daniel.

"You say they work with him all day long."

"Busy work. Mindless stuff. Daniel? Do you think I should move him?"

He spread his fingers. *Where?* "You said that Barbara woman was wonderful with him."

"Barbara, sure. If Barbara were his primary physician, we'd be cured. Okay, so the therapists get him to tie his shoes. That doesn't help much, does it?"

"It helps a little."

"You sound just like Dr. Hayes. How did that man ever get certified? He won't do anything. 'Wait and watch.' We need to do something real. Surgery. Drugs."

"Drugs? You mean mask the symptoms?"

"You think I'm just a symptom? His fake sister?"

"That's not what I'm saying," Daniel said. And for a minute, he turned foreign.

She held out her palms, apologizing and defending all at once. "Look. Please don't . . . please just stay with me on this. I just feel so helpless. I've done nothing at all for him." And to his look of utter incredulity, she said, "His real sister would have."

Trying to make himself useful, Daniel brought her two more paperbacks. The books were written by a Gerald Weber, an apparently well-known cognitive neurologist from New York. Daniel had come across the name in the news, regarding a much-anticipated new book about to appear. He apologized for not finding him sooner. Karin studied the author's photo, a gentle, gray-haired man in his fifties who looked like a playwright. The contemplative eyes gazed just alongside the lens. They seemed to find her out, already half-suspecting her story.

She devoured the books in three straight nights. For chapter after bewildering chapter, she could not stop reading. Dr. Weber's books compiled a travelogue of every state that consciousness could enter, and from his first words, she felt the shock of discovering a new continent where none had been. His accounts revealed the brain's mind-boggling plasticity and neurology's endless ignorance. He wrote in a modest voice and ordinary style that placed more faith in individuals' stories than in prevailing medical wisdom. "Now more than ever," he declared, in *Wider Than the Sky*, "especially in the age of digital diagnosis, our combined well-being depends less on telling than on listening." No one had yet listened to her. This man suggested that she might be worth hearing.

Dr. Weber wrote:

Mental space is larger than anyone can think. A single brain's 100 billion cells make thousands of connections each. The strength and nature of these connections changes every time use triggers them. Any given brain can put itself into more unique states than there are elementary particles in the universe . . . If you were to ask a random group of neuroscientists how much we know about how the brain forms the self, the best would have to answer, "Almost nothing."

In a succession of personal case histories, Weber showed the endless surprise folded inside the most complex structure in the universe. The books filled Karin with an awe she'd forgotten she could still feel. She read of split brains fighting over their oblivious owners; of a man who could speak sentences but not repeat them; of a woman who could smell purple and hear orange. Many of the stories made her thankful that Mark had avoided all the fates worse than Capgras. But even when Dr. Weber wrote about people stripped of words, stuck in time, or frozen in premammalian states, he seemed to treat them all like his nearest kin.

For the first time since Mark sat up and spoke, she felt guarded optimism. She was not alone; half of humanity was partly brain-damaged. She read every word of both books, her synapses changing as she devoured the pages. The writer sounded like some masterful, future intelligence. She couldn't be sure of the path that Mark's accident laid out for her. But somehow, she knew it crossed this man's.

By his own accounts, Dr. Weber had never visited any land quite like the one her brother now inhabited. Karin sat down to write him, consciously mimicking his style. It felt like the longest of long shots, to somehow win the attention of this larger-than-life researcher. But she might make the very wildness of Mark's Capgras irresistible to such a man.

She wrote with little hope that Gerald Weber would

respond. But already, she imagined what would happen if he did. He would see in Mark a story like the ones his books described. "The people inside these changed lives differ from us only in degree. Each of us has inhabited these baffling islands, if only briefly." The odds against his even reading her note were great. But his books described far stranger things as if they were commonplace.

"These books are incredible," she told her lover. "The author is amazing. How did you find him?"

She was in Daniel's debt again. On top of everything else, he had given her this thread of possibility. And she, once again, had given him nothing. But Daniel, as ever, seemed to need nothing but the chance to give. Of all the alien, damaged brain states this writing doctor described, none was as strange as care.

PART TWO

BUT TONIGHT ON NORTH LINE ROAD

I know a painting so evanescent that it is seldom viewed at all.

—Aldo Leopold, *A Sand County Almanac*

Faster than they gathered, the only witnesses disappear. They crowd together on the river for a few weeks, fattening; then they're gone. On an invisible signal, the carpet unravels into skeins. Birds by the thousands thread away, taking their memory of the Platte with them. Half a million cranes disperse across the continent. They press north, a state or more a day. The heartiest will cover thousands more miles, on top of the thousand that brought them to this river.

Cranes that crowded into dense bird cities now scatter. They fly in families, lifelong mates with their one or two offspring, any that have survived the previous year. They head for the tundra, peat bogs and muskegs, a remembered origin. They follow landmarks—water, mountains, woods—places recovered from previous years, by a crane map, inside a crane's head. Hours before the onset of bad weather, they will stop for the day, predicting storms on no evidence. By May, they find the nesting spots they left the previous year.

Spring spreads across the Arctic to their archaic cries. A pair that roosted at the roadside on the night of the accident, near to the overturned truck, home in on a remote stretch of coastal Alaska on the Kotzebue Sound. A seasonal switch flips in their brains as they near their nest. They turn fiercely territorial. They attack even their baffled yearling, the one they have nursed all this way back, driving it off with beak jabs and beating wings.

The blue-gray pair turn brown, from the iron rusting in these bogs. They coat themselves with mud and leaves, seasonal camouflage. Their nest is a moated heap of plants and feathers, three feet wide. They call to each other, with coiled, booming trombone windpipes. They dance, bowing deeply, kicking the brisk salt air, bowing again, leaping, spinning, cowling their wings, their throats arched backward in some impulse between stress and joy: ritual spring at the northern edge of being.

Suppose birds store, fixed as a photograph, the outlines of what they have seen. This pair is in their fifteenth year. They will have five more. By June, two new eggs, spotted gray ovals, will follow all the pairs already laid on this spot, a spot all those earlier years had stored in memory.

The pair take turns, as they always have, caring for the clutch. The northern days lengthen until, by the time the eggs hatch, light is continuous. Two colts emerge, already walking and ravenous. The parents trade off hunting for the voracious young, feeding them constantly—seeds and insects, small rodents, the trapped spare energy of the Arctic.

In July, the younger colt starves to death, killed by his older brother's appetite. It has happened before, in most years: a life begun with fratricide. Alone, the surviving bird shoots up. In two months, he is fledged. As the long northern days collapse, his short test flights expand. Frost forms on the family's nest these nights; ice crusting the bogs. By autumn, the young bird is ready to replace last year's ousted child on the long trip back to winter grounds.

But first the birds molt, reverting to native gray. Something happens to their late-summer brains, and this isolated family of three recovers a larger motion. They shed the solitary need. They feed with others, roosting together at night. They hear nearby families passing overhead, threading the great funnel of the Tanana Valley. One day they lift up and join a self-forming V. They lose themselves in the moving strand. Strands converge in kettles, kettles merge in sheets. Soon, fifty thousand birds a day mass down the startled valley, their prehistoric blasts brilliant and deafening, a sky-wide braided river of cranes, tributaries that run for days.

There must be symbols in the birds' heads, something that says *again*. They trace one single, continuous, repeating loop of plains, mountains, tundra, mountains, plains, desert, plains. On no clear signal, these flocks ascend a slow spiral, great twisting columns of lifting thermals that, with one glance at its parents, the new bird learns to ride.

Once, long ago, as the cranes massed for their autumn departure, they passed above an Aleut girl standing alone in a meadow. The birds flew down on her, beat their wings together, and lifted the girl upward in a great turning cloud, hiding her, trumpeting to drown out her calls. The girl rose on that twisting shaft of air and disappeared into the southward flock. So cranes still circle and call when they leave each autumn, reliving that capture of the humans' daughter.

Long afterward, Weber could still pinpoint the moment when Capgras entered his life. Inked into his planner: Friday, May 31, 2002, 1:00 p.m., Cavanaugh, Union Square Cafe. The first copies of *The Country of Surprise* had just come off the press, and Weber's editor wanted him in the city to celebrate. His third book: publication was hardly a novelty anymore. The two-hour train ride in from Stony Brook, by this point in Gerald Weber's career, was more duty than thrill. But Bob Cavanaugh was eager to meet. *Pumped*, the young editor had said. *Publishers Weekly* had called the book "a wild tour of the human brain by a sage writing at the height of his powers." *Wild tour* would play harshly in neurological circles, circles that hadn't forgiven the success of Weber's previous books. And something about *the height of his powers* depressed him. Nowhere but down, from there.

Weber dragged himself into Manhattan, walking from Penn Station down to Union Square briskly enough to get some aerobic benefit. The shadows were all wrong: still disorienting, more than eight months on. A patch of sky where there should be none. Weber hadn't been in since early spring, when witnessing the unnerving light show—two massive banks of spotlights pointing into the air, like something out of his book's chapter on phantom limbs. The images flared up in him again, the ones that had slowly extinguished over three-quarters of a year. That one, unthinkable morning was real; everything since had been a narcoleptic lie. He walked south through the unbearably normal streets, thinking he might get by just fine without ever seeing this city again.

Bob Cavanaugh greeted him at the restaurant with a bear hug, which Weber abided. His editor was trying not to snicker. "I told you not to dress up."

Weber spread his arms. "This isn't dressed up."

"You can't help yourself, can you? We really should do a coffee-table book full of sepia photos of you. The natty neuroscientist. The Beau Brummell of brain research."

"I'm not that bad. Am I really that bad?"

"Not 'bad,' sir. Just delightfully . . . archaic."

Lunch was Cavanaugh at his most charming. He ran down the latest buzz books and described how well *Surprise* was faring with the European agents. "Your biggest, by far, Gerald. I'm sure of that."

"No need to set any records, Bob."

They talked more high-speed industry gossip. Over an entirely gratuitous cappuccino, Cavanaugh at last said, "Okay, enough pleasantries. Let's see your hole card, man."

Thirty-three years had passed since Weber's last hand of blackjack. Junior year of college, Columbus, teaching Sylvie the game. She'd wanted to play for sex favors. Nice game; no losers. But insufficient strategic depth to hold their interest for long.

"I'm not holding anything too surprising, Bob. I want to write about memory."

Cavanaugh perked up. "Alzheimer's? That kind of thing? Aging population. Declining abilities. Very hot topic."

"No, not about forgetting. I want to write about remembering."

"Interesting. Fantastic, in fact. *Fifty-two Weeks to a Better*—no, wait. Who's got that kind of time? How about *Ten Days to—*"

"A lay overview of current research. What goes on in the hippocampus."

"Ah! I see. Are the little dollar signs over my irises fading?"

"You're a good sport, Robert."

"I'm a shitty sport. But a terrific editor." As he picked up the check, Cavanaugh asked, "Can you at least include a chapter on pharmaceutical enhancement?"

Back in Penn Station, as Weber stood under the departure board, waiting for the train out to Stony Brook, a man in a battered blue ski vest and grease-smeared corduroys waved at him in happy recognition.

He might have been a former interview subject; Weber no longer recognized them all. More likely, this was one of many readers who didn't realize that publicity photos and television

127

were one-way media. They saw Weber's receding snow line, the blue glint behind his wire-rims, the soft, avuncular half-dome and flowing gray beard—a cross between Charles Darwin and Santa Claus—and greeted him as if he were their harmless grandfather.

The ruined man drew up, smoothing his greasy vest, bobbing and chattering. Weber was too intrigued by the facial tics to move away. The words came in a babbling stream. "Hi, hey there. Great to run into you again. You remember our little venture out west—just the three of us? That illuminating expedition? Listen, can you do me something? No, no cash today, thanks. I'm flush. Just tell Angela, everything that happened out there is copasetic. It's all okay, whoever she wants to be. Everyone's okay, just who they are. You know that. Am I right? Tell me: Am I right?"

"You are most certainly right," Weber said. Some form of Korsakoff's. Confabulation: inventing stories to patch over the missing bits. Malnutrition from extended alcohol abuse; the fabric of reality rewoven by a vitamin-B deficiency. Weber spent the two-hour train ride back to Stony Brook scribbling notes about humans probably being the only creatures who can have memories of things that never happened.

Only: he had no idea where the notes were headed. He was suffering from something, perhaps the sadness of professional consummation. For a long time, longer than he had deserved, he'd known exactly what he wanted to write next. Now, everything seemed to be already written.

Back home, Sylvie hadn't yet returned from Wayfinders. He sat down to the e-mail in that mix of buzz and dread that came from opening the inbox after too long. The last person north of the Yucatán to go online, he was now suffocating to death under instant communication. He flinched at the message count. He'd spend the rest of the evening just digging out. And yet, some ten-year-old in him still thrilled at diving into the day's mail sack, as if it might yet hold a prize from a contest he'd forgotten having entered.

Several e-mails promised to resize any of Weber's body parts to the scale of his choosing. Others offered offshore drugs to address every imaginable deficit. Mood changers and confidence boosters. Valium, Xanax, Zyban, Cialis. Lowest cost anywhere in the world. Also, his share of vast fortunes offered by exiled government officials of turbulent nations, apparently old friends. Interleaved among these were two conference invitations and another reading-tour request. A correspondent Weber had stopped replying to months before sent another objection to the treatment of religious feelings and the temporal lobe in *The Three-Pound Infinity*. And of course, the usual help-me petitions, which he referred to the Stony Brook Health Sciences Center.

That's where he almost consigned the note from Nebraska, after the opening line. *Dear Dr. Gerald Weber, my brother has recently survived a horrible automobile accident.* Weber was finished with horrible accidents. He'd explored enough broken histories for a lifetime. With what time he had left, he wanted to return to an account of the brain in full flower.

But the next line kept him from hitting the Forward button. *Since starting to talk again, my brother has refused to recognize me. He knows he has a sister. He knows all about her. He says she looks just like me. But I'm not her.*

Accident-induced Capgras. Unbelievably rare, and immensely resonant. A species he'd never seen. But he was finished with that kind of ethnography.

He read the whole brief note twice through. He printed it out, reading it again on the page. He set it aside and worked on his new outline. Making little headway, he scanned the day's headlines. Agitated, he rose and went to the kitchen, where he spooned several hundred illicit milk-fat calories straight from the pint container of organic ice cream. He returned to his study and fought time in a preoccupied cloud until Sylvie came home.

True Capgras resulting from closed-head trauma: the odds against it were unimaginable. A case so definitive challenged any psychological account of the condition and undermined basic assumptions about cognition and recognition. To selectively reject one's next of kin, in the face of all evidence . . . He read the letter again, swept up by his old addiction. Another chance to see, up close, through the rarest imaginable lens, just how treacherous the logic of consciousness was.

Sylvie got back late. She fell through the front door, her mock sigh of relief unable to disguise the kick she'd gotten from her long day's work. "Yo, Man—I'm home!" she chanted from the foyer. "No place like it. Where'd I put that husband?"

He was in the kitchen, pacing, the printed letter clutched behind his back. They kissed, subtler than in their blackjack days, a third of a century ago. More historical.

"The pair bond," Sylvie decreed. She buried her nose in his sternum. "Name a more ingenious invention."

"Clock radio?" Weber suggested.

She pushed him away and slapped his chest. "Bad husband."

"How's the new clubhouse holding up?" he asked.

"Still a dream. We should have moved offices years ago."

They compared days. She was still racing from hers. Wayfinders was thriving, finding ways for a variety of clients even Sylvie hadn't anticipated when she started the social services referral outfit, three years before. After years of drifting through unsatisfactory employment, she had at last come home to a vocation she'd never suspected. Careful to violate no professional confidences, she sketched out the gist of her most interesting cases while they prepared a squash risotto together. By the time they sat down to eat, Weber could recall exactly none of her stories.

They ate side by side, on barstools at the raised kitchen counter where they'd taken their meals together in nearly unbroken pleasure for the last ten years, since their lone daughter had left for college. He told her about lunch in the city with Cavanaugh. He described the Korsakoff's sufferer in Penn Station. He waited until they were washing dishes to mention the e-mail. Stupid, really. They'd been together so long that any attempt to fake a casual tone only blurted the thing out, louder than intended.

She suspected at once. "I thought you were moving on to the memory book. That you wanted to graduate from . . ." She seemed dismayed, or perhaps he was projecting.

He held up his dish-towel hand, before she could repeat all his recent arguments. "Syl, you're right. I really shouldn't spend any more . . ."

She squinted at him and tested a grin. "Not fair, Man. This isn't about my being right."

"No. No, that's true. You're absolutely . . . I mean . . ." She laughed and shook her head. He draped the towel around his neck, a prizefighter between rounds. "It's about what *I've* been wrestling with for the last several months. What *I* should be doing next."

"Well, for heaven's sake. It's not like you're backsliding on a crack cocaine habit or anything."

She would know; she'd worked in a Brooklyn rehab center for almost a decade before bailing out to save herself and start

131

Wayfinders. She shot him a look of skeptical trust, and he felt as he had, through all their years of changing climates: the undeserving beneficiary of her social-worker understanding.

"So what's the crisis? It's not like anyone's holding you to public promises. If this is something that interests you, where's the guilt?" She leaned toward him and picked a stray fleck of risotto out of his beard. "It's just you and me, Man." She grinned. "The general public don't have to know that you don't know your own mind!"

He groaned and pulled the folded-up e-mail out of the pocket of his still-creased trousers. He flicked the offending document with the nails of his right hand. He offered her the printout, as if the sheet exonerated him. "Accidental Capgras. Can you imagine?"

She just smiled. "So when will you see him? When's he coming out?"

"Well, that's the thing. He's a bit banged up. And a bit hard up, too, I gather."

"They want *you* to go *there*? I'm not saying . . . I'm just a little surprised."

"Well, I do have to spend down the travel account. And for studying something like this, seeing him in situ is actually best. But maybe you're right."

She growled, exasperated. "Husband! We've been over this!"

"Seriously. I don't know. Half a continent, for a volunteer consultation? I'd be without a lab. And traveling has become such a hassle. You practically have to strip before boarding the plane."

"Hey! Doesn't Tour Director take care of those things?"

He winced and nodded. *Tour Director*: all that was left of their combined religious upbringings. "Of course. I just think

132

my field-examining days might be over. I need to reconstitute myself, Syl. I just want to stay home, write a harmless little science-journalism book. Keep the lab running, maybe sail a little. The whole domestic tranquility thing."

"What you call your fifty-five-year-old's exit strategy?"

"Spend some quality time with the wife . . ."

"The wife's been neglecting *you* recently, I'm afraid. So stay home, already!" Her eyes taunted his. "Aha! I thought as much."

He wagged his head, bemused by himself. She reached up and polished his bald spot, her ancient good-luck ritual. "You know?" he said. "I really thought I'd acquired a certain degree of self-mastery, at this point in my life."

" 'Much of the work of the brain consists of hiding its work from us,' " she quoted.

"Nice. Has a ring to it. Where's it from?"

"It'll come back to you."

"People." He rubbed his temples.

"Quite the species," Sylvia agreed. "Can't live with them, can't vivisect 'em. So what is it about this particular people that has you hooked again?" Her job, to talk him into what he'd already decided.

"A man who recognizes his sister, but does not credit the recognition. Apparently otherwise reasonable and cognitively unimpaired."

She whistled low, even after a lifetime of hearing his tales. "Sounds like something for Sigmund."

"It does have that ring. But at the same time, the clear result of injury. That's what makes it so fantastic. It's the kind of neither-both case that could help arbitrate between two very different paradigms of mind."

"This is something you would like to see before you die?"

133

"Ah! Can we put that a little less terminally? The patient's sister is aware of my work. She's not sure that his doctors have fully grasped the case."

"They do have neurologists in Nebraska, don't they?"

"If they've come across Capgras at all outside their medical texts, it'll have been as a feature of schizophrenia or Alzheimer's." He took the dish towel from around his neck and dried their two wineglasses. "The sister is asking for my help." Sylvie studied him: *Those are the ones you swore to stay away from.* "Anyway, misidentification syndromes might reveal a lot about memory."

"How do you mean?" He'd always loved that phrase of hers.

"In Capgras, the person believes their loved ones have been swapped with lifelike robots, doubles, or aliens. They properly identify everyone else. The loved one's face elicits memory, but no feeling. Lack of emotional ratification overrides the rational assembly of memory. Or put it this way: reason invents elaborately unreasonable explanations to explain a deficit in emotion. Logic depends upon feeling."

She chuckled. "This just in: male scientists confirm the bleeding obvious. So, sweetie. Take a trip. See the world. Nothing's stopping you."

"You wouldn't mind if I went out? Just for a couple of days?"

"You know how much I'm scrambling myself right now. It would give me a chance to clear my own backlog. In fact, I think I'd better skip our video date for tonight. There's a child HIV assessment I need to work up for tomorrow."

"You wouldn't think less of me if I . . . backslide?"

She looked up from the empty sink, startled. "Oh, my poor little Man. Backslide? This is your calling. It's what you *do*."

They kissed again. Amazing that the gesture still communicated so much, after three decades. He held back a lock of her mocha hair and grazed her forehead. Her hair was thinner than it had been in college, when they'd met. How searchingly beautiful she'd been. But lovelier to him now, at peace with herself at last. Lovelier, because graying.

She looked up at him, curious. Open.

"Thanks," he said. "Now, if I can just survive the damn airport security . . ."

"You leave that to Tour Director. That's what *he* does best."

He called them all by fictional names. When the details of a life threatened anyone's privacy, he substituted others. Sometimes he created a single case history from a composite of several people he'd studied. That much was standard professional practice, for everyone's protection.

He described a woman once, well-known in the literature. In *The Three-Pound Infinity*, he called her "Sarah M." Bilateral extrastriate damage to the middle temporal area left her suffering from akinetopsia, a rare, near-complete motion blindness. Sarah's world had fallen under a perpetual strobe light. She couldn't see things move. Life appeared to her as a series of still photographs, connected only by ghostly motion trails.

She washed and dressed and ate in time lapse. A turn of her head launched a series of clunking carousel slides. She couldn't pour coffee; the liquid hung from the pot spout in icicles, and from one stopped moment to the next the table would fill with frozen coffee lakes. Her pet cat terrified her, blinking out and rematerializing elsewhere. The television stabbed at her eyes. A bird in flight made bullet holes in the windowpane of sky.

Of course, Sarah M. couldn't drive, couldn't walk in crowds, couldn't even cross the street. She stood on the curb of her quiet town, paralyzed, the film stuck. A truck at a distance might mow her down, the second she placed her foot in the gutter. Still images piled up one after the other—incoherent, bisecting cubist tracers. Cars and people and objects reappeared at random.

Even her own moving body was no more than a series of sequential stiff poses, a game of Statuemaker. And yet, strangest of all: Sarah M. alone of all the world saw a kind of truth about sight, hidden from normal eyes. If vision depends upon the discrete flash of neurons, then there is no continuous motion, however fast the switches, except in some trick of mental smoothing.

Her brain was like anyone's, except in losing this last trick. Her name was not Sarah. It might have been anything. She was there, in Weber's strobing mind, when he stepped into the jetway at LaGuardia, and gone when he found himself, that same afternoon, dead center in the evacuated prairie, with no transition but a jump cut.

He stayed at a motel just off the interstate. The MotoRest—he chose it for its sign: WELCOME CRANE PEEPERS. The utter estrangement of it: *I've a feeling we're not in New York anymore.* He and Sylvie had left the Midwest in 1970 and never looked back. Now the rolling openness of his birthright seemed as alien to him as *Sojourner's* pictures beamed back from Mars.

Outside the Lincoln airport rental, he'd panicked for a moment, finding himself with neither passport nor local currency.

Once inside the MotoRest lobby, he might have been anywhere. Pittsburgh, Santa Fe, Addis Ababa: the comforting, neutral pastels of global commuting. He'd stood on the same tawny carpet in front of the same teal check-in counter countless times before. A dozen brilliant, shiny apples sat in a basket on the reception desk, all the same shape and size. Real or decoration, he couldn't tell until he sank a fingernail into one.

While the check-in clerk processed his credit card, Weber thumbed the stacks of tourist brochures. All of them were flush with red-crested birds. Masses of birds: like nothing he'd ever seen. "Where can I go see these?" he asked the clerk.

She looked embarrassed, as if his card had been rejected. "They've been gone for two months. They're all up north now, sir. But you want to see them, just sit tight. They'll be back." She handed him his Visa, along with a key card. He went up to a room that pretended it had never been inhabited by anyone, one that promised to disappear, traceless, the instant Weber checked out.

Every surface in the room spouted cardboard messages. The staff welcomed him personally. They offered him a full range of goods and services. One piece of cardstock in the bathroom said that if he'd like to save the earth, he should leave his towel over the shower bar, and if not, he should throw it on the floor. The messages had been put out fresh that morning and would be replaced at his departure. Thousands like them, from Seattle to St. Petersburg. He might have been in any hotel room anywhere, except for the crane pictures above the bed.

He'd spoken with Karin Schluter before leaving New York. She'd been remarkably poised and informed. But when she phoned from downstairs, half an hour after he checked in, she was a different person. She sounded timid, nervous about coming up to the room. Clearly it was time for him to update the publicity shot. Perfect thing to tease Sylvie about, when he called her that night.

He came down to the lobby and met the victim's only near relation. She was in her early thirties, dressed in tan cotton slacks and rose cotton blouse, what Sylvie called universal passport clothes. Weber's dark suit—his standard travel fare—startled her and left her apologizing with her eyes before she could say hello. Dead-straight copper hair—her sole striking feature—hung down beneath the bottom of her shoulder blades. That spectacular fall upstaged her face, which, with some generosity, might be called fresh. Her decidedly corn-fed body was heading prematurely toward solemn. Healthy midwestern woman who might have run hurdles in college. As he looked at her, she primped unconsciously. But when she stood and walked toward him, her hand extended, she flashed him a brave, side-mouthed smile, altogether worth aiding.

They shook hands, Karin Schluter thanking him too profusely, as if he'd already cured her brother. Just the sight of him seemed to lift her. When he deflected her gratitude, she said, "I brought some documents." She sat on a couch next to the lobby's fake fireplace and spread a dossier on the coffee table: three months of handwritten notes combined with copies of everything the hospital and rehab center had given her. Hands weaving, she launched into her brother's story.

Weber sat next to her. After a bit, he touched her wrist. "We should probably check in with Dr. Hayes, before anything else. Did he get my letter?"

"I spoke with him this morning. He knows you're here. He says feel free to go see Mark, this afternoon. I have his notes somewhere."

The paperwork spread in front of Weber, a guidebook to a new planet. He forced himself to ignore the file and listen to Karin Schluter's version. Through three successive books, he'd championed the idea: facts are only a small part of any case history. What counted was the telling.

Karin said, "Mark accepts that there was an accident. But he doesn't remember any of it. His mind's a blank. Nothing, for twelve hours before he rolled the truck."

Weber raked his salt-and-pepper beard. "Yes. That can happen." Twenty years, and he'd almost mastered it: how to tell people that others had been there before them, without denying their private disaster. "It sounds like what's called retrograde amnesia. Ribot's law: older memories are more resilient than newer ones. *The new perishes before the old.*"

Her lips mirrored his as he spoke, struggling to stay alongside. She spread a palm on the stack of forms. "Amnesia? But his memory's fine. He knows who everyone is. He remembers everything about . . . his sister. He just refuses to . . ." She pulled her lips against her teeth and bowed her head. The fall of red hair spilled across the papers. He could not imagine where such a refusal must leave her.

"You say he's talking again without struggling. Does he sound different?"

She studied the air. "Slower. Mark was always a fast talker."

"Does he search for words? Have you noticed any difference in his vocabulary?"

Her lopsided smile returned. "Aphasia, you mean?"

She botched the pronunciation. Weber just nodded.

"Vocabulary was never his big thing."

He made a stab. "You're close to your brother?" Capgras prerequisite. "You always have been?"

Her neck jerked back, defensively. "We're the only family either of us has left. I've tried to look out for him, over the years. I'm a little older than him, but . . . I always tried to be around, until I absolutely had to go, for my own sanity. Mark's not quite cut out for the world. He's always depended on me, a bit. He and I have gone through some pretty strange family times together." Flustered, she turned back to the file. She extracted two sheets. Her head turned, scanning the lines, lips moving again. "Here. This is what keeps nagging at me. When they first brought him into the emergency room after the accident, he was awake. He wasn't even . . . Here: Glasgow Coma Scale. He wasn't even in the danger area. They let me see him that night, just for a minute. He recognized me then. He was trying to talk to me. I know it. But you see, there's this spike later in the morning. His intracranial pressure shoots way up."

She might have been studying to become a surgical nurse. He thumbed his beard from underneath. Over the years, the gesture had managed to calm almost everyone. "Yes, that can happen. The skull is a fixed volume. If delayed swelling causes the brain to expand, it can be worse than the original impact."

"Sure, I read about that. But shouldn't his doctors have been monitoring? If I understand right, in the first few hours, they should have . . ."

Weber looked around the MotoRest lobby. Foolish, talking to her here. She'd been so measured over the phone. In person, she presented all the complications of need that Weber meant to retire from. But true Capgras from an accident: a phenomenon that could crown or crash any theory of consciousness. Something worth seeing.

"Karin? We spoke about this. I'm not a lawyer. I'm a scientist. I value your invitation to come talk to your brother. But I'm not here to second-guess anyone."

She caught her breath. Her face flamed. She pulled at her shirt collar. She gathered her spray of hair and tied it up like a hank of rope. "Yes, of course. I'm sorry. I thought you . . . I should probably just take you to see Mark."

Dedham Glen Nursing and Rehabilitation Center looked to Weber like an elite suburban high school. Peach, single-story, modular— something you'd never notice, unless a loved one were trapped inside.

"They won't be keeping him here much longer," Karin said. "The therapy has been great, but the coverage is topping out and he's crazy to go home. His muscle strength is pretty much back. He's dressing and bathing himself, getting along with people, mostly making sense. Compared to a few weeks ago, he's as good as normal. Except when it comes to ideas about me."

She piloted the car toward the visitors' spaces near the front walk. "We put our mother here, when she got ill. She passed, five and a half weeks later. I thought I'd rather die myself than put Mark here. But it was the only choice."

"Do you think he holds that against you?" Old habit: probing for psychological mechanism.

She reddened again. Her skin was instant litmus. She pointed to a picture window at the building's corner. A medium-height, thin twenty-seven-year-old in a black sweatshirt and baby-blue knit cap stood stranded in mid-wave, his hand pressed to the glass. "You can ask him yourself, in a minute."

Mark Schluter met his visitors halfway down the hall of his wing. He walked as if on crutches, pressing a hand to his right thigh. His face still bloomed with half-healed scars. Across his throat ran the telltale necklace of a tracheotomy. His black jeans sagged and his long-sleeve sweatshirt—too heavy for June—crept down his arms to his fingers. The shirt sported a card-playing, beer-drinking dog saying, *What The Hell Do I Know?* Tufts of returning hair stuck out from under the lip of his cap. He swung down the hall, playing at being a pendulum. He pulled up in front of Karin. "Is this the guy who's going to get me out of this hellhole?"

The woman's hands fled into the air. Her knot of hair came undone. "Mark. I told you Dr. Weber was coming today. Couldn't you have put on a decent shirt?"

"Favorite shirt."

"It isn't appropriate, when talking to a doctor."

He raised a stiff arm and pointed at her. "You're not the boss of me. I don't even know where you came from. The damn Arab terrorists could have parachuted you in here, special forces, as far as I know." The storm blew over as fast as it appeared. Righteous indignation collapsed in sighs. He spread his palms, grinning at Weber. "You with the FBI or something?" A finger reached out and flipped Weber's maroon dress tie. "I talked to you guys already."

Karin was mortified. "It's just a suit, Mark. You act like you've never seen a suit before."

"I'm sorry. He looks like 'The Fuzz.' " His fingers hung quote hooks in the air.

"He's a neuropsychologist. And a famous writer."

"Cognitive neurologist," Weber corrected.

Mark Schluter rocked on his heels. Dank laughter poured out of him. "What's that? Some kind of shrink?" Weber shook his head. "A *shrink!* So, like, who are you supposed to be?"

Weber tilted his head. "Tell me what you mean."

"I mean: I already know who this lady thinks she is. How about you?"

Karin exhaled. "We discussed him yesterday, Mark. He just wants to talk to you. Let's go back to your room and sit."

Mark wheeled on her. "I warned you once. You're not my damn mother, either." He turned back to Weber. "I'm sorry. It's just painful to me. She has these ideas. It's hard to describe." But when Karin headed down the hall, he hobbled along beside her, like a puppy on a leash.

The room was a modest version of Weber's at the MotoRest, although hugely more expensive. Bed, dresser, desk, television set, coffee table, two chairs. A pair of cartoon Get Well cards in loud colors stood on the dresser. Next to them lay an ancient stuffed Curious George, missing one button eye. A boom box sat on the desk, surrounded by a pile of CD jewel boxes. A truck magazine sporting way too much chrome on its cover lay next to it, still shrink-wrapped. Weber flipped on his pocket digital tape recorder. He could ask permission later. "Nice room," he prompted.

Mark frowned and looked around. "Well, I haven't done much with it. But I'm not gonna be here long. Sooner torch this place than move in."

"What kind of place is this?" Weber asked.

Mark sized him up out of the corner of his eye. "Isn't it obvious?" Karin sat on the foot of the bed, her hair a cape around her shoulders. Her brother eased himself into a chair, flapping his tennis shoes on the floor and enjoying the clatter. He waved for Weber to sit in the chair opposite him. Weber lowered himself to the cushions. Mark giggled. "You supposed to be old, or something?"

143

"Ach. Not my favorite topic. So what exactly do they call this place?"

"Well, Doc." Mark inclined his head. He gazed out from under his bunched eyebrows and whispered, "Some folks in these parts call it Dead Man's Glands."

Weber blinked, and Mark barked with pleasure. Karin sat despairing on the bed, picking at her slacks.

"How long have you been here?"

Mark shot an anxious glance at the bed. Karin averted her eyes, looking back at Weber. Mark cleared his throat. "Well, I'll tell you. Pretty much forever?"

"Do you know why you're here?"

"Do you mean why I'm here and not home? Or why I'm here and not dead? Same answer, on both counts." Mark pulled his sweatshirt taut and leaned forward. "Read the script-shirt, man." The card-playing, beer-drinking dog asking, *What The Hell Do I Know?*

"You don't have to perform for him, Mark."

"Hey! What do you care? You're the one who wants me here."

Weber asked, "So what do they do for you here?"

The boy-man turned contemplative. He stroked his bare chin. They might have been talking politics or religion. "Well, you know what this is. It's—well, you know: a nursery home. Where they take you when you're banged up and no good to anybody?"

"You got banged up?"

The face yanked back, snorting. "Put it this way? The doctors claim I'm not exactly what I was before."

"Do you think they're right?"

Mark shrugged. A spasm shot through him. One hand

tugged the baby-blue cap over his brows. The other thrust out. "Ask her. She keeps telling them what I *was*."

Karin pressed one wrist to her temple and stood. "Excuse me," she apologized, and stumbled from the room.

Weber persisted. "You had an accident?"

Mark considered this: one of many possibilities. He slumped deeper into his chair, toeing the floor in front of him. "Well, I rolled my truck, you know. Totaled it. At least that's what they tell me. They haven't actually produced the evidence or anything. They're not real big on evidence here."

"I'm sorry to hear that."

"Are you?" He sat up and leaned forward again. "Fantastic '84 cherry-red Dodge Ram. Rebuilt engine block. Modified drive shaft. Totally pimped. You'd love it."

He sounded like a typical American man in his twenties, from any of the big, empty states. Weber hooked his thumb toward the empty hallway. "Tell me about her."

Mark's hands picked at the knit cap. "Well, Doc. You know? It gets pretty complicated, pretty fast."

"I can see that."

"She thinks that if she does a perfect imitation, I'll take her for my sister."

"She isn't?"

Mark tsked and waved his index finger in the air, a stubby, pink window wiper. "Not even close! Okay, so she looks a lot like Karin. But there are some obvious differences. My sister is like . . . a Labor Day picnic. This one's a business lunch. You know: eye on the clock. My sister makes you feel safe. Easy. This one's totally high maintenance. Plus, Karin is heavier. Actually a bit of a tub. This woman is almost sexy."

"Does she sound at all—?"

"And they messed up the face a little. Know what I'm

saying? Her expressions, or such. My sister laughs at my jokes. This one's scared all the time. Weepy. Talk about hair trigger? Real easy to freak out." He shook his head. Something long and silent passed through him. "Similar. Very similar. But worlds apart."

Weber toyed with his ancient wire-rims. He stroked the crown of his balding head. Mark unconsciously fingered his cap. "Is she the only one?" Weber asked. Mark just stared at him. "I mean, is anyone else not what they seem?"

"Jesus, you're the doctor, right? You ought to know that nobody's 'What They Seem.'" He hunched, peeking out through the scare quotes he formed next to his ears. "But I know what you're saying. I've got this buddy, Rupp. That bastard and me do everything together. Something weird has happened to him, too. The fake Karin has him brainwashed or something. And they swapped my damn dog. Can you believe that? Beautiful border collie, black and white, with a little gold around the shoulders. Now what kind of sick person would want to . . . ?" He stopped playing hockey with his toes. His hands fell to his lap. He leaned forward. "It's like some horror flick, sometimes. I can't figure out what's going on." His eyes filled with animal alarm, ready to ask even this stranger for help.

"Does . . . this woman know things that only your sister should know?"

"Well, you know. She could've learned that shit any-where." Mark twisted on his cushions, fists near his face, like a fetus warding off the world's first blows. "Just when I most need my real sister, I'm supposed to accept this imitation."

"Why do you suppose this is happening?"

Mark straightened and gazed at Weber. "Now, that's a damn good question. Best question I've heard in a long time." He stared off into the middle distance. "It's got to have

146

something to do with . . . what you were talking about. Rolling the rig." For a minute, he was gone, wrestling with something too big for him. Then Mark came back. "Here's what I'm thinking. Something happened to me, after . . . whatever happened." He held his palm out, not even glancing at Weber. "My sister—my real sister—and Rupp, maybe, took the Ram somewhere where I wouldn't be able to see it. Where it wouldn't upset me. Then they got this other woman who looked like Karin, so I wouldn't notice she was gone." He looked up at Weber, hopeful.

Weber tilted one shoulder. "And how long has she been gone?"

Mark threw two hands above his head, then brought them back down across his chest. "For as long as this other one's been here." His face clouded in pain. "She's not at her old place. I've tried her number. And it sounds like that job of hers canned her."

"What do you suppose your sister might be doing?"

"Well, I don't know. Getting the truck fixed up, like I said? Maybe she's holding off contact until it's ready. To surprise me?"

"For months?"

Mark curled his lip, sarcastically. "Have you ever repaired a truck? Takes some time, you know. To get it like new."

"Your sister knows how to work on trucks?"

Mark snorted. "Does the pope shit on Catholics? She could probably strip that cheap Jap four-cylinder of hers down to washers and put it back together into something halfway decent, if she wanted to."

"What kind of car does the other woman drive?"

"Ah!" Mark glanced sidelong at Weber, refusing to surrender. "You've noticed. Yes, she's been pretty complete at copying the details. That's what's so scary."

"Do you remember anything about the accident?"

Mark's head spun through half a circle, cornered. "Shrink, let's just relax and regroup for a minute, shall we?"

"Sure. I'm with you." Weber leaned back and tucked his hands behind his head.

Mark regarded him, his mouth open. Slowly, the jaw firmed into a chuckle. "Serious? You for real?" A series of low, clunking thuds came out of him, the laughter of someone stuck in puberty. He kicked out his legs and folded his own hands behind his head, like a toddler imitating his father. "This is more like it! The good life." He smiled and flashed Weber a thumbs-up. "You hear that Antarctica is breaking up?"

"I heard something like that," Weber said. "Did you read that in the paper?"

"Naw. The tube. Newspapers are too full of conspiracy theories these days." After a moment, he grew troubled again. "Listen. You're a shrink. Let me ask you something. How easy would it be for a really good actress to . . ."

Karin returned, distressed to find the two of them stretched out as if on some vacation cruise. Mark jackknifed up. "Speak of the devil. Eavesdropping. I might've known." He looked at Weber. "You want to get something to drink? Nice cold brew or something?"

"They let you have beer here?"

"Ha! Gotcha. Well, there's a Coke machine out there, anyway."

"Would you like to try some puzzles, first?"

"Beats a pig in a poke with a sharp stick."

Mark seemed eager to play. The puzzles were timed. Weber had Mark cancel out lines scattered on a sheet of paper. He showed Mark a cartoon and asked him to circle as many objects whose names started with the letter O as he could find. "Can I just circle the whole thing and call it 'obnoxious'?" Weber asked him to trace routes on a street map, following simple directions. He asked him to name all the two-legged animals he could think of. Mark rubbed his head, infuriated. "Pretty tricky of you. When you put it that way, you're forcing me to think of only four-legged ones."

Weber had Mark strike out all the numerals from a sheet of paper filled with letters. When Weber called time, Mark threw his pencil across the room in disgust, almost hitting Karin, who cowered by one wall. "You call these games? These are more screwed up than the stuff the therapists make me do."

"How do you mean?" Weber asked.

"What do you mean, '*How* do you mean?' Who the hell says, '*How* do you mean?' Here. Look at this. See how you made everything so small? Deliberately trying to mess me up. And look at this 'three.' It looks exactly like a capital B. B for *bastard*. Then you try to distract me, by telling me I only have two minutes left." His lip twisted and his eyes shut against their dampening.

Weber touched his shoulder. "Want to try another? Here's one with shapes . . ."

"You do them, Shrink. You're an educated man. I'm sure you can figure it out by yourself." He swung his head, opened his mouth, and groaned.

Summoned by the sound, a woman appeared in the doorway. She wore a russet pleated skirt and a cream silk blouse. Weber felt he'd met her in some other capacity—the airport, the car rental, or the hotel front desk. A youthful forty, medium build, five foot nine, round cheekbones, cautious, inquiring eyes, a blue-black shoulder-length cowl of hair: the kind of face that imitated a minor celebrity. The woman seemed briefly to recognize Weber, as well. Not unheard of: his face got around. People who knew nothing about brain research sometimes remembered him from talk shows or magazines. But as quickly as she noticed, she looked away. She cocked an eyebrow at Karin, who beamed. "Oh, Barbara! Just in time, as always."

"Any difficulties, here?" Her voice was wry, a little self-mocking. *Difficulties Are Us.* At the sound of his attendant, Mark's twisting anger dissolved. He sat up, beaming. The aide beamed back. "Problems, friend?"

"I got no problems! That's the guy with all the problems."

The caretaker wheeled on Weber. She studied him, her face a nurse's mask, the barest curl to her lips. "New admit?"

"The man is nothing *but* problems," Mark shouted. "Check out his so-called puzzles, if you want to make yourself nuts."

The woman stepped toward him and held out her hand. Stupidly, Weber handed over his battery of tests as if she were the chairman of a human subjects review board. She studied the documents. She riffled the pages, then looked him in the eye. "How much are the answers worth to you?" She glanced at Mark, her audience, now a ball of glee. Weber felt grateful for her defusing. Karin made the introductions. Barbara Gillespie returned Weber's tests, a little sheepish.

"Ask her anything, Doc. She's the only reliable thing around here. Best thing I've currently got on my side."

Barbara crossed toward Mark, clucking in objection at the compliment. Weber watched the graceful woman bond with her charge. The pair reminded him of something—bonobos grooming each other, chattering in easy and instinctual reassurance. He felt a twinge of envy. Her rapport was natural and unstudied, more than Weber had felt with any of his patients for a long time, if ever. She embodied that open fellow feeling his books preached.

The two whispered to each other, one anxious and the other soothing. "Do you think I can ask him?" Mark asked.

Barbara patted Mark's folder, suddenly all registered professional. "Absolutely. He's a distinguished man. If you can talk to anyone, it's him. I'll come back later, for your workup."

"Can I get that in writing?" Mark called after her.

Ms. Gillespie waved goodbye to Karin. Karin grazed the attendant's forearm. Barbara curled her fingers at Weber as she left. *Distinguished.* So she *had* placed him. He turned to Karin, who shook her head in admiration. "My brother's keeper."

"I wish," Mark snapped. "I wish she'd keep me. From you. Would you mind if I talked with the doctor here for a moment, in private? Person to person?"

Karin folded her hands together in front of her and left the room again. Weber stood, one hand holding the briefcase, the other pumping his milky beard. Question time had turned. Mark swung to face him.

"Look. You're not working for her or anything? You're not, like, involved with her or anything? Physically? Then would you mind getting in touch with my real sister? I can give you all the info I have for her. I'm starting to really worry. She may have no idea what's happened to me. They may be feeding her a bunch of lies. If you could just make contact, it would help a lot."

"Tell me a little bit more about her. Her character." How did a Capgras patient see character? Could logic, stripped of feeling, see past the performance of personality? Could anyone?

Mark waved him off, squeezing his head. "How about

151

tomorrow? My brain is bleeding. Come back tomorrow, if you feel like it. Just lose the suit and briefcase, all right? We're all good people here."

"You've got it," Weber said.

"My kind of shrink." Mark thrust out his hand, and Weber shook it.

Weber found Karin in the reception area, seated on a hard green vinyl sofa, the kind that could be sponged off in an emergency. Her eyes looked allergic to air. Two papery women with walkers slid past her, a foot race in suspended animation. One greeted Weber as if he were her son. Karin was explaining before he could sit down. "I'm sorry. It kills me to see him like that. The more he says he doesn't know me, the less I know how to be toward him."

"What does he think is different about you?"

She pulled herself together. "It's strange. He glorifies me now. I mean *her*. In fact, he and I—I mean *this* me—struggle pretty much the same way we always did. We had kind of a rough time, growing up. I've tried to keep him from doing all the stupid things I've done, over the years. He needs me to be the voice of reason; he's never had anyone else for that. Used to resent it like crazy, the straighter I kept him. But now he just resents *me*, and thinks *she* was some kind of saint."

She stopped and smiled in apology, her mouth pumping like a trout's. Weber offered his arm—clumsy, archaic, something he never did. He blamed Nebraska, the level, dry, buzz-filled June. The flat accents, the broad, stolid, agrarian faces—so chalky and secret— disoriented him, after decades in the loud, brown turmoil of New York. The faces out here shared a furtive knowledge—of land, weather, impending crisis—that sealed them off from interlopers. Half a day in this place, and already he felt how reticent a person might get, surrounded by so much grain.

She took his arm and stood. He led her out the main doors, down the sidewalk to the parking lot. He felt unsettled, the hamstrung sense that had plagued him throughout his neurology residency. He'd curtailed medical practice years ago, in favor of research and writing, in part, perhaps, to protect himself. In the last eighteen months, he'd grown worse. Just watching someone wire a macaque would soon prove crippling.

Karin Schluter hung on his arm, heading toward the parking lot.

"You have a nice way with him," she conceded. "I think he liked you." She stared straight ahead as she spoke. She'd wanted more. Not even finished with the screening, and already Weber had let her down.

"Your brother is a lively personality. I like him very much."

She stopped on the sidewalk. Her face turned raw. "What do you mean, 'lively'? He's not going to stay this way, is he? You can help him, right? Like the things you try, in your books . . ."

The real work was never with the injured. "Karin? Think back to the night of Mark's accident. Do you remember imagining what might happen to him?"

She stood clasping herself, her face aflame. He kept a distance now. The June wind whipped her hair into a dozen tow lines. She pinched her eyes. "This isn't what he's like. He was quick. Sharp. A little crude. But he cared for everyone . . ."

Her hands were folded across her breasts, her face a ruddy mess, her eyes welling. He cupped her elbow and urged her down the walk toward the car. A casual observer might have seen a lovers' quarrel. Weber turned and saw Mark, standing at his window. *You're not, like, involved with her?* He swung back

153

to the sister. "No," Weber said. "This is not who he was. And he'll be someone else a year from now." As soon as he said it, he regretted even that harmless truism. Too easily turned into a promise.

The color in her face deepened. "I'm sure whatever you can do for him will help."

More sure than he was. He could still make it back to Lincoln in time for an evening flight. Weber pressed his thumbnail into his palm and mastered himself. "To do anything for him, we have to learn who he has become. And to do that, we have to win his trust."

"Trust *me*? He hates the sight of me. He thinks I've abducted his real sister. He thinks I'm a government robot spy."

They reached her car. She stood still, keys in hand, waiting for him to work a miracle. "Tell me something," he said. "Have you lost weight recently?"

Her mouth made a shocked O. "What—?"

He tried to smile. "Forgive me. Mark said that his real sister was considerably heavier."

"Not *considerably*." She straightened her belt. "I've lost a few pounds. Since our mother passed. I've been . . . working on myself. Starting over."

"Do you know much about cars?"

She stared at him as if brain damage were endemic. Then guilty understanding stole into her eyes. "Unbelievable. I tried to get him to teach me, one summer, a few years ago. I was trying to impress . . . someone. Mark wouldn't let me do anything but hand him wrenches. It was just a few days. But ever since, he's been convinced that I have this secret love for camshafts, or what have you."

She pressed the key fob and the car unlocked. He walked

around to the passenger side and slid in. "And the way he was with the nurse, with Ms. . . . ?" He knew the name, but let her say it.

"Barbara. She does have a way with him, doesn't she?"

"Would you say the way he talks to her is different from how he would have, before?"

She stared out the window at the open fields. The lime blush of the June prairie. She shook her head. "Hard to say. He didn't know her before."

He called Sylvie that night, from the MotoRest. He actually felt nervous dialing. "Hey, it's me."

"Man! I was hoping it might be you."

"As opposed to the telemarketers?"

"Don't shout, sweetie. I can hear you."

"You know, I truly hate talking into this ridiculous thing. It's like holding a saltine up to your face."

"They're supposed to be small, my love. That's what makes them mobile. I take it this case isn't going so great?"

"On the contrary, Woman. It's staggering."

"That's good. Staggering is good, right? I'm glad for you. So tell me about it. I could use a good story right now."

"Rough day?"

"That probation kid from Poquott who we were getting employment letters for mistook the UPS man for a SWAT team."

Her voice still caught, even after years of such disasters. He searched for something useful, or just kind. "Anyone hurt?"

"Everyone will live. Including me. So tell me about your Capgras. Impaired recognition?"

"It feels like the opposite, in fact. Too attentive to small difference."

Aside from the absurd makeup compact passing itself off as

a phone, they might have been back in college, trading appraisals late into the night, long after curfew had sealed each of them in their separate dorms. He'd first fallen in love with Sylvie over the phone. Every time he traveled, the fact came back to him. They fell into a cadence, talking as they had almost every evening of their lives for a third of a century.

He described the bewildered man, his terrified sister, the antiseptic nursing facility, the oddly familiar attendant, the desolate town of twenty-five thousand, the dry June, the vacant, floating terrain in the dead center of nowhere. He wasn't violating professional ethics; his wife was his colleague in these matters, in every way except the payroll. He described how bottomless it felt, watching recognition atomize into ever more exacting, distinct pieces. *That woman laughed; this one's scared. This one's facial expressions are wrong.* Doubles, aliens: splitting individuality into a hundred parts, preserving distinctions too subtle for normality to see.

"I'm telling you, Woman. No matter how often I see it, it chills me."

"I thought you'd never seen this before."

"Not Capgras. I mean the naked brain. Scrambling to fit everything together. Unable to recognize that it's suffering from any disorder."

"That's only reasonable. Can't afford to admit what's happened. Sounds like a lot of my clients. Like me, in fact, sometimes."

He hadn't realized how much he needed to talk. The afternoon's interview had excited him in a way that no one but Sylvie would understand. She asked for more details about Mark Schluter. He read her some notes. She asked, "Does he look her in the eyes when he talks to her?"

"I didn't really notice."

156

"Hm. That's the kind of thing we here on Venus look for first."

They wandered onto current events: the wildfires out west, the guilty verdict against the crooked giant accounting firm, and at last the indigo bunting she saw that morning at the feeder.

"Remember to renew your passport," he said. "September'll be here any minute."

"*Viva Italia. La dolce vita!* Hey. By the way. When is your return flight? I jotted it down and stuck it on the refrigerator. I just seem to have misplaced the refrigerator."

"Hang on. Let me get my briefcase."

When he came back and picked up the phone, she was laughing. "Did you just put down your cell so that you could walk across the room?"

"What about it?"

"My sage. My sage at the height of his powers."

"I can barely force myself to use one of these shoehorns. I absolutely refuse to walk around with one clamped to my face. It's schizophrenia."

She couldn't stop chuckling. "Not even in private?"

"Private? What's that?"

He gave her his flight information. They traded a few more stalling phrases, reluctant to say goodbye. He was still talking to her in his head for several sentences, after they hung up. He showered, hanging the towel over the bar—*Help save the earth.* He retrieved his digital voice recorder from his briefcase, then slipped between the stiff, cool sheets, where he replayed the day's taped conversation. He listened again to the twenty-seven-year-old boy, lost to himself, busy exposing impostors the world could not make out.

Years ago, in Stony Brook, Weber had worked with a patient suffering from hemispatial neglect: the notorious "Neil," from Weber's first book, *Wider Than the Sky*. A stroke at fifty-five — the age Weber had now reached unscathed — left the office machine repairman with a lesion in his right hemisphere that overnight blotted out half his world. Everything to the left of Neil's sight midline folded into nothing. When he shaved, Neil left the left side of his face untouched. When he sat down to breakfast, he failed to eat the left side of his omelette. He never acknowledged people who approached him from the left-hand side. Weber asked Neil to draw a baseball diamond. Neil's third base trickled just off the edge of the pitcher's mound. Even in Neil's memory, recounting the day's events, the left half of the world crumpled and collapsed. Closing his eyes and imagining himself in front of his house, Neil could see the garage on the right but not the sunroom on the left. When giving directions, he gave them all exclusively as a series of right turns.

This deficit went beyond vision. Neil couldn't see that he wasn't seeing. Half the map where he stored space itself was gone. Weber tried a simple experiment, a scene he dramatized in *Wider Than the Sky*. He held a mirror perpendicular to Neil's right shoulder and made Neil look at an angle into the mirror. The area to the left of Neil's body now appeared to Neil's right. Weber held a silver good luck charm above Neil's left shoulder and told Neil to reach for the charm. He might as well have asked the man to sail to a bearing that had fallen off the compass. Neil hesitated, then stabbed out. His hand crashed into the mirror. He fumbled against the glass, even groping behind it. Weber asked what he was doing. Neil insisted that the charm was "inside the mirror." He knew what mirrors were; the stroke had left that intact. He knew it was crazy to think that the charm could be in the glass. But in his new world, space extended only to the right. Inside the mirror was the more likely of two unreachable places.

Cases such as Neil—thousands of them a year—suggested two truths about every normal brain, both of them shattering. First: what we took for a priori, absolute apprehension of real space in fact depended upon a fragile chain of perceptual processing. "Left" was as much in here as out there. Second: even a brain that thought it was measuring, orienting, and inhabiting plain-old given space might already, without the slightest notion, have lost as much as half a world.

No brain, of course, could completely credit this. Weber had liked Neil. The man absorbed a crushing blow without bitterness or self-pity. He made his adjustments and pressed on—if not forward, then northeasterly. But after the last set of examinations, Weber never saw Neil again. He had no idea what became of the man. Some other neglect wiped him out, reduced him to story. The man Weber had met and interviewed at length passed into the man he described in the pages of his book. He'd left "Neil" behind in the prose looking glass, lost somewhere, off in an imperceivable direction, an unreachable place deep inside the narrative mirror . . .

Weber woke early, from rough sleep. He showered to wick off the sluggishness, remembering, with a pang of conscience as the hot stream revived him, that he'd taken one just hours before. He made himself a packet of coffee in the complimentary coffeemaker, housed, for some reason, next to the bathroom sink. Then he sat at the writing desk, flipping through a rustic, hand-illustrated guidebook provided there.

> The name "Nebraska" comes from an Oto word meaning flat water. The French, too, called the river that ran through it "Platte."

Precisely how he'd pictured the place: a wide, flat hollow at the heart of the map, so level it would make Euclid blush. The real, rolling landscape surprised him. He sipped the grim coffee and examined the guidebook's cartoon map. Towns dotted the blank space like so many circled wagons. He found Kearney—at 25,000, the fifth-biggest settlement in the state—in the southernmost oxbow of the Platte, cowering from too much openness.

> To the north and west, the Gangplank, a great swatch of eroded sediment, juts out across what was once, 100 million years ago, the floor of a vast ocean . . .
> Major Stephen Long's 1820 expedition of Army Engineers called the area the Great American Desert. In his report to Washington, Major Long declared the crust of land "wholly unfit for cultivation and of course uninhabitable by a people depending upon agriculture." The expedition's botanist and geologist concurred, noting the "hopeless and irreclaimable sterility" of a country that should "forever remain the unmolested haunt of the native hunter, the bison and the jackal."
> Herds of bison once scoured this basin. Brown rivers of meat flowed across the prairie, holding up wagon trains for days . . .

Herds all done away with, the book said. The jackal and the native hunter, too: cleared off. Prairie dog cities, their underground streets stretching for miles, drowned in poison. River otters, all but eliminated. Pronghorn, gray wolves: all shot. Page 23 showed a color plate of two mounted, moth-eaten carcasses in the State Museum in Lincoln. Only two larger species now survived in the region in any quantities:

For six weeks out of every year, cranes along the Platte outnumber humans several times over. They migrate over a quarter of the earth's circumference, briefly stopping here for whatever scraps of waste grain they can scavenge.

He finished the coffee and rinsed the cup. He donned his coat and tie, then, remembering his promise to Mark Schluter, removed them. In his shirtsleeves, he felt naked. Down at the front desk, he snatched a cosmetically perfect if tasteless apple and called it breakfast. He followed his directions to Good Samaritan Hospital and made his way up to Neurology. Dr. Hayes's nurse showed Weber into the office at once, trying not to stare at the famous personality.

The neurologist looked young enough to be Weber's son. Gawky ectomorph with angry skin who steered his body like a legacy device. "I just want to tell you what an honor this is. I can't believe I'm talking to you! I used to read your books like comics, back in med school." Weber thanked him as graciously as he could. Dr. Hayes spoke deliberately, as if delivering a belated lifetime achievement award to a silent-film actor. "Incredible case, isn't it? Like seeing Bigfoot stroll out of the Rockies and into your neighborhood supermarket. I actually thought of your stories when we worked him up."

Fresh copies of Weber's last two books sat on Hayes's desk. The young neurologist picked them up.

"Before I forget, would you mind . . . ?" He handed them to Weber, along with a heavy Waterman pen. "Could you make them out: 'To Chris Hayes, my Watson in the strange case of The Man Who Doubled His Sister.'"

Weber searched the neurologist's face for irony but found only earnestness. "I . . . Could I just . . . ?"

"Or whatever you feel like writing," Dr. Hayes said, crestfallen.

Weber wrote: *For Chris Hayes, with thanks. Nebraska, June 2002.* Man was not only *the commemorating animal*; he was the animal who insisted on commemorating in advance. Weber handed the books back to Hayes, who read the inscription with a tight-lipped smile. "So you met him yesterday. Eerie, isn't it? I'm still disconcerted, talking to him, and it's been months. Of course, our group will be writing him up for the journals."

Bow shot. Weber held up his hands. "I don't want to do anything to . . ."

"No, of course not. You're writing for a popular audience." Broadside. "There's no overlap." Hayes rolled out the complete history, including the pages no one had shown Karin Schluter. He showed Weber the paramedics' notes, three lines of green ballpoint on a form dated Feb. 20, 2002: *'84 Dodge Ram, rolled off south shoulder of North Line Road, between 3200 and 3400W. Driver pinned upside down in vehicle.* Unbelted, unreachable, and unresponsive. The one accessible door was crumpled beyond opening. The paramedics couldn't enter or move the truck, for fear of crushing the victim. They could only wait for support and watch the police take photographs. Weber studied one of the pictures. "Wrong way

162

up," Hayes said. Weber flipped the image. A long-haired Mark Schluter hunched on top of himself, a glaze of blood seeping up his face through his open collar. His head bowed against the roof of the cab, in inverted prayer.

When the firemen arrived, they had to burn their way through a roof post with an acetylene torch. Weber pictured the scene: police lights strobing across frozen fields, flares circling the truck where it lay flipped in the roadside ditch. Uniformed people, their breath steaming, moving about in dreamlike, methodical activity. When the firemen at last torched through the roof post, the wreck shifted and the truck settled. The body crumpled on itself. The firemen scrambled under the wreck and drew the body clear. Mark Schluter briefly regained consciousness in the ambulance. The paramedics raced him to Kearney, the only hospital within six counties with any shot at keeping him alive.

Hayes proceeded to the medical charts. White male, twenty-seven, five ten, 160 pounds. He had lost considerable blood, most of it from a gash between his right third and fourth ribs, where he'd impaled himself on the spike of a metal model Prussian helmet fastened to his truck's gear shift. His front scalp and face were heavily abraded. His right arm was dislocated and his right femur fractured. The rest of his body was badly scratched and bruised, but he was otherwise astonishingly intact.

"We use the word *miracle* a lot out here in the Plains States, Dr. Weber. But you don't often hear the term thrown around a Level II trauma center."

Weber studied the images that Hayes clipped to the light box. "This one qualifies," he agreed.

"The closest thing to a Lazarus walk-away I've ever seen, even in my residency days in Chicago. Eighty miles an hour, on an icy country road in the dark. The man should have been dead, many times over."

"BAC?"

"Funny you should ask. We see a lot of that, in the Kearney Emergency Room. But he came in at .07. Under the legal limit, even in the Cornhusker State. A few beers in the three hours before rolling his vehicle."

Weber nodded. "Was he on anything else?"

"Not that we found. The ER attending logged him in at a Glasgow solid ten. E3-V3-M4. Eyes opening to speech. Withdrawing from pain. Some verbal response, although mostly inappropriate."

Eight was the magic number. After six hours, half of all patients with Glasgow Coma Scale numbers of eight or lower gave up and died. Ten was considered moderate injury. "Something happened to him after admission?"

Weber was just playing professional detective. But Hayes grew defensive. "They stabilized him. All the protocols, even before determining whether he was insured. We have one of the highest rates of medical indigence in the country, out here."

Weber had seen higher. Half the country couldn't afford insurance. But he murmured approval.

"It took the paper-pushers an hour before they could locate his next of kin."

Weber studied the paperwork. The victim's pockets contained only thirteen dollars, a knock-off Swiss Army knife, a receipt for a tank of gas at a place in Minden dated that afternoon, and a single cyan-colored condom in a transparent package. Probably his good-luck charm.

"Apparently, his license flipped up under the dash when the truck rolled. The police found it while searching the vehicle for drugs. They located the sister up in Sioux City, and she gave phone consent for anything we needed. The trauma service got him going on mannitol, Dilantin . . . You can read everything. Pretty standard fare. Intracranial pressure steady at around 16 mm Hg. We got a little improvement right away. Motor response climbed. Some increase in verbal. Marked him up to a Glasgow twelve. Five hours after the admit, I would've told you that we were heading out of the woods."

He took the file back from Weber and searched it, as if he still had a chance to head off what happened next. He shook his head. "Here's the note from the next morning. ICP up to twenty, then spiking even higher. He had a small seizure. Some delayed bleeding, as well. We went to a ventilator as soon as we could. We decided to drill. Tracheotomy clearly indicated. His sister was here by then. She approved everything." Dr. Hayes scoured the papers, looking for some shred that refused to come forward. "If you're asking me, I'd say we caught everything as it arose."

"It seems like it," Weber said. Only, intracranial pressure had to be caught *before* it arose. Dr. Hayes blinked at him, perhaps resenting the national celebrity brought in to aid the poor locals. Weber stroked his beard. "I can't imagine doing anything differently." He glanced around Dr. Hayes's office. All the right journals on the shelves, up to date and orderly. Framed diploma from Rush Medical and Nebraska Board Certification. On the desk, a picture of Hayes and a slim, honey-haired model, shoulder to shoulder on a ski lift. A world inconceivable to Mark Schluter, before or after his accident.

"Would you say that Mark shows any tendency toward confabulation?"

Hayes followed Weber's glance, to the picture, the beautiful woman on the lift. "Not that I've noted."

165

"I tried him on a battery of the standard tests yesterday."

"Did you? I gave him everything, already. Here. Any scores you might need."

"Yes, of course. I didn't mean to suggest . . . But some time has passed . . ."

Dr. Hayes measured him. "He's still under observation." He offered Weber the folder again. "The data are all here, if you care for a look."

"I'd love to see the scans," Weber said.

Hayes produced a series of images and clipped them to his light box: Mark Schluter's brain in cross section. The young neurologist saw only structure. Weber still saw the rarest of butterflies, fluttering mind, its paired wings pinned to the film in obscene detail. Hayes traced over the surreal art. Each shade of gray spoke of function or failure. This subsystem still chattered; this one had fallen silent. "You see what we're dealing with, here." Weber just listened to the younger man step through the disaster. "Something that looks like possible discrete injury near the anterior right fusiform gyrus, as well as the anterior middle and inferior temporal gyri."

Weber leaned toward the light box and cleared his throat. He didn't quite see it.

"If that's what we're looking at," Hayes said, "it would fit the prevailing understanding. Both the amygdala and the inferotemporal cortex intact, but a possible interruption of connection between them."

Weber nodded. The current dominant hypothesis. Three parts needed to complete a recognition, and the oldest trumped all. "He gets an intact facial match, and that generates the appropriate associated memories. He knows his sister looks exactly like . . . his sister."

"But no emotional ratification. Getting all the associations for a face without that gut feeling of familiarity. Pushed to a choice, cortex has to defer to amygdala."

Weber smiled, despite himself. "So it's not what you think you feel that wins out, it's what you feel you think." He fiddled with his wire frames, feeling out loud. "Call me archaic, but I still see some problems. For one, Mark doesn't double every person that he cared for before the accident. He should still be able to draw upon auditory cues, behavioral patterns: all sorts of identification tools other than facial. Can flattened emotional response really defeat cognitive recognition? I've seen bilateral damage to the amygdala—patients with destroyed emotional responses. They don't report that their loved ones have been replaced by impostors." He sounded too effusive, even to himself.

Hayes was ready. "Well, you've heard of the emerging 'two-deficit' theory? Perhaps insult to the right frontal cortex is impeding his consistency-testing . . ."

Weber felt himself turning reactionary. The odds against multiple lesions, all exactly in the right place, had to be enormous. But the odds against recognition itself were even greater. "You know he thinks his dog is a double? That seems like more than just a rupture between the amygdala and the inferotemporal cortex. I don't doubt the contribution of lesions. Right hemisphere damage is no doubt implicated in the process. I just think we need to look for a more comprehensive explanation."

Hayes's tiniest facial muscles betrayed incredulity. "Something more than neurons, you mean?"

"Not at all. But there's a higher-order component to all this, too. Whatever lesions he has suffered, he's also producing psychodynamic responses to trauma. Capgras may not be caused so much by the lesion per se as by large-scale psychological

167

reactions to the disorientation. His sister represents the most complex combination of psychological vectors in his life. He stops recognizing his sister because some part of him has stopped recognizing himself. I have always found it worthwhile to consider a delusion as both the attempt to make sense—as well as the result—of a deeply upsetting development."

After a beat, Hayes nodded. "I'm . . . sure it's all worth thinking about, if that interests you, Dr. Weber."

Fifteen years ago, Weber would have launched a counterstrike. Now he found it comical: two docs marking their territory, ready to rear up and batter at each other like bighorn sheep. *Ram tough.* Wellbeing coursed through Weber, the simple poise of self-reflection. He felt like mussing Dr. Hayes's hair. "When I was your age, the prevailing psychoanalytic bias had Capgras resulting from taboo feelings toward a loved one. 'I can't be feeling lust for my sister, ergo she's not my sister.' The thermodynamic model of cognition. Very popular in its day."

Hayes rubbed his neck, embarrassed into silence.

"On the face of it, this case would single-handedly refute that possibility. Clearly Mark Schluter's Capgras isn't primarily psychiatric. But his brain is struggling with complex interactions. We owe him more than a simple, one-way, functionalist, causal model." He surprised himself. Not by his belief, but by his willingness to speak it aloud to a physician this young.

The neurologist tapped the film on his light box. "All I know is what happened to his brain early on the morning of February 20."

"Yes," Weber said, bowing. All that medicine ever wanted to know. "It's amazing that he has any integrated sense of self left at all, isn't it?"

168

Dr. Hayes accepted the truce. "We're lucky this particular circuit is so hard to disrupt. A handful of documented cases. If it were as common as, say, Parkinson's, we'd all be strangers to each other. Listen, I'd like to help in any way possible. If we can do any further tests or imaging here at the hospital . . ."

"I have a few low-tech examinations I'd like to try before that. The first thing I want to do is get some galvanic skin response."

The neurologist's eyebrows shot up. "Something to try, I guess."

Dr. Hayes walked Weber back to the parking lot. They'd been sealed in the consulting room long enough that the return to stark, prairie June caught Weber out. The still air expanded in his lungs, smelling like some archaic summer holiday. It hinted of something he'd last tasted in Ohio at age ten. He turned to see Dr. Hayes hunching next to him, his hand extended.

"Pleasure meeting you, Dr. Weber."

"Please. Gerald."

"Gerald. I look forward to seeing the new book. A nice break from work. And I want you to know I'm your biggest fan."

He did not say *still*, but Weber heard it. Weber stood, one foot in the street. "I was hoping we could touch base again, before I head back east?"

Hayes brightened, ready to fawn or fight all over again. "Ah! Of course, if you have the time and interest."

Time and interest . . . For years, he'd strictly rationed both. A name chair at a Research One University, a long list of respected articles about perceptual processing and cognitive assembly, and a pair of popular neuropsychology books that sold to wide audiences in a dozen languages: he'd never had much time or interest to spare. He'd already outlived his father by three years and had greatly outproduced him. And yet, Weber chanced to be working at the precise moment when the race was making its first real headway into the basic riddle of conscious existence: How does the brain erect a mind, and how does the mind erect everything else? Do we have free will? What is the self, and where are the neurological correlates of consciousness? Questions that had been embarrassingly speculative since the beginnings of awareness were now on the verge of empirical answer. Weber's growing, dazed suspicion that he might live to see such wild philosophical phantoms solved, that he might even contribute to solving them, had pretty much driven out any other semblance of what, in popular parlance, had come to be called *a real life*. Some days it seemed that every problem facing the species was awaiting the insight that neuroscience might bring. Politics, technology, sociology, art: all originated in the brain. Master the neural assemblage, and we might at long last master *us*.

Weber had long ago commenced that extended retreat from the world that ambitious men begin to make around their fortieth year. All he wanted was to work. His old hobbies— guitar, paint box, tennis racket, verse notebooks—sat tucked away in corners of the too-big house, waiting for the day he might resurrect them. Only the sailboat gave him any sustained enjoyment now, and that, only as a platform for more cognitive reflection. He struggled to sit through feature films. He dreaded the periodic dinner-party invitation, although, truth be told, he generally enjoyed himself once the evening was under way, and hosts could always count on him to produce a bizarre conversational firework or two. Tales from the crypt, Sylvie called them: stories that proved to the assembled dinner guests that nothing they thought, saw, or felt was necessarily true.

He had lost no capacity for mundane delights. A walk around the mill pond still pleased him in any season, although he now used such strolls more to jog stalled thoughts than to see the ducks or trees. He still indulged in what Sylvie called foraging—constant low-level snacking, a weakness for sweets that he'd nursed since childhood. His wife first fell in love with him when he declared to her, at twenty-one, that heavy glucose metabolism was essential for sustained mental effort. When, at twice that age, his body began to change so profoundly that he no longer recognized it, he briefly struggled to curb the familiar pleasure before accepting the alien new shape as his own.

He still enjoyed his wife's bedrock companionship. He and Sylvie still touched incessantly. *Monkey grooming*, they called it. Constant hand rubs while they read together, shoulder massages as they washed the dishes. "You know what you are?" she accused, pinching him. "Nothing but a dirty old neck-rub-philiac." He answered only with happy groans.

At growing intervals that neither of them cared to calculate, they still played with each other. However fitful, the persistence of desire surprised them both. The previous year, on their thirtieth anniversary, he estimated the number of climaxes that he and little Sylvie Bolan had shared since their first foray in the top bunk in her dorm room in Columbus. One every third day, on average, for a third of a century. Four thousand detonations, joining them at the hip. Nights of animal ecstasy always amused them, coming back to themselves, to the embarrassment of speech. Curled up against his flank, giggling a little, Sylvie might say, "Thank you for the beautiful human sexuality, Man," before padding off to the bathroom to clean herself. A person could only howl in abandonment so many times. Time didn't age you; memory did.

Yes, the slowing body, the gradually depleting pleasure neurotransmitters had cooled them. But something else as well: what you loved well, you grew to resemble. He and the wife of his years now resembled each other so much that there could be no strangeness of desire between them. None except that impenetrable strangeness he'd given himself over to. The country of perpetual surprise. The naked brain. The basic riddle, on the verge of being solved.

He stood in throbbing music, waiting for Karin Schluter. Above his head, someone growled in techno-pain, begging for euthanasia. A lunch dive, a long line of kids in retro, acid-washed jeans, Weber stark among them, having forgone the coat and tie in favor of khakis and a knit vest. Karin suppressed her giggles as she walked up. "Aren't you warm in that?"

"My thermostat runs a little low."

"So I've noticed," she teased. "Is that from all the science?"

She'd chosen a place on the local college campus called Pioneer Pizza. Her nerves from yesterday had settled. She played less with her hair. She smiled at the surrounding flock of students as the hostess seated them.

"I went to school here. Back when it was still Kearney State College."

"When was that?"

She blushed. "Ten years. Twelve."

"No way." The words sounded ludicrous on his lips. They'd have sent Sylvie into convulsions. Karin just beamed.

"Those were wild days. A little too close to home for me, but still. My friends and I were the only people between Berkeley and the Mississippi to protest the Gulf War. This gang of Young Republicans manhandled my then-boyfriend, just for wearing a "No Blood For Oil" button. Tied him up with a yellow ribbon!" Her glee hid as fast as it had surfaced. She cast a guilty look around the restaurant.

"How about your brother?"

"You mean school? They pretty much had to give Mark an honorary high school diploma. Don't get me wrong. He's no idiot." She worked her mouth, hearing her present tense. "He was always shrewd. He could read a teacher and figure out the barest minimum needed to pass her tests. Not that it took a genius to outsmart the Kearney High faculty. But Mark just wanted to fix up trucks and dink around with video games. He could twitch over a new game cartridge for twenty-four hours without even getting up to pee. I told him he should get a job as a play-tester."

"How did he make a living, after graduation?"

"Well, 'a living' . . . He flipped burgers until Dad threw him out of the house. Then he worked at the Napa parts store and lived like an Indian for a long time. His buddy Tom Rupp got him a job at the IBP plant in Lexington."

"IBP?"

She wrinkled her nose, surprised at his ignorance. "Infernal Beef Packers."

"Infernal . . . ?"

Her face flushed. She pressed three fingers to her lips and blew on them. "I mean, Iowa. Although, you know: Iowa, Infernal. You have to squint to tell the difference."

"He worked for a slaughterhouse?"

"He's not a cow killer, or anything. That's Rupp. Markie repairs their equipment." She looked down again. "I guess I mean 'repaired.'" She lifted her head and studied him. Her eyes were the color of oxidized pennies. "He's not going back there anytime soon, is he?"

Weber shook his head. "I've learned not to make

173

predictions, over the years. What we need, as in most things, is patience and cautious optimism."

"Yes," she said. "I'm trying."

"Tell me what you do." Her lips traced his words, and she looked at him blankly. "Your work."

"Oh!" She pressed her bangs with her right hand. "I'm a consumer relations agent for . . ." She stopped, surprised at herself. "Actually, I'm between job opportunities."

"Your employers let you go? Because of this?"

Beneath the table, her knee pumped like a sewing machine. "I didn't have any choice. I had to be down here. My brother comes first. It's just the two of us, you know." Weber nodded. She bubbled over with explanations. "I have a little war chest. My mother left us some life insurance money. It's the right thing. I can start again, once he's . . ." Her tone was optimistic, fishing.

The waitress came to take their orders. With a guilty glance around the room, Karin ordered the Supreme. Weber chose at random. When the waitress left, Karin eyed him. "I can't believe it. You do it, too."

"I'm sorry? What do I do?"

She shook her head. "I just thought that someone with your accomplishments . . ."

Weber grinned, puzzled. "I really have no idea . . ."

She flicked the air with her left hand. "Never mind. It's nothing important. Something I notice in men, sometimes."

Weber waited for Karin to explain. When she didn't, he asked, "Did you bring the pictures?"

She nodded. She reached into her shoulder bag, a brightly patterned knit sack made by some indigenous people, and withdrew an envelope. "I picked ones that would mean the most to him."

Weber took the photos and thumbed through them.

"That's our father," Karin said. "What can I say? Blind in one eye from an argument with the livestock. Ready to recite 'The Face on the Barroom Floor' anytime after the night's third shot, at least when we were young; he didn't go in much for poetry, in his later days. He started out as a farmer, but spent most of his life trying to break into the commercial class with a parade of get-rich-quick schemes. On a Christmas-card basis with every bailiff in bankruptcy court. He lost a lot of money selling privacy boxes. You hooked them up to your TV so the cable company couldn't track what you watched. He came up with this idea for peddling identity-theft insurance. He only sold things that he couldn't buy enough of himself. That was his downfall. The man thought the nine-digit zip code was a Democratic Party plot to control the movements of ordinary citizens. Even the local militia guys thought he was a little out there."

"And he died . . . ?"

"Four years ago. He couldn't sleep. He just couldn't sleep, and then he died."

"I'm sorry," Weber said, pointlessly. "How would you describe their relationship?"

She screwed up her mouth. "Nonstop slow-mo death match? Give or take a couple of happy camping trips. They liked to fish together, back when. Or working together on engines. Stuff where they didn't have to talk. That next one's our mom, Joan. She didn't look quite that good by the end. Which was a year or so ago, I think I said."

"You say she was a religious woman?"

"A big, big speaker in tongues. Even her ordinary English was pretty colorful. She often had the house exorcised. She was convinced that it hid the souls of children in torment. I was like, 'Hello! Earth to Mom! I'll name those tormented child souls for a dime!'" Karin took the picture of the pretty, chestnut-haired farm wife from Weber and studied it, sucking in her cheeks. "But she kept us alive through all the years of Dad's self-employment schemes. Clerk-Typist III, here at the college."

"How did Mark get along with her?"

"He worshiped the woman. Worshiped them both, really. He just sometimes did it while shouting and waving a blunt weapon around."

"He was violent?"

She exhaled. "I don't know. What's 'violent' anymore? He was a teenage guy. Then, a guy in his twenties."

"Did he share your mother's . . . ? Was he religious?"

She laughed until she had to hold her hands in the air. "Not unless you count Devil worship. No. That's unfair. The black-magic phase was me. Here, look. Karin Schluter, high school senior. Your advanced Goth vampire look. Pretty scary, huh? Two years before that, I was a cheerleader. I know what you're thinking. If my brother hadn't had an accident to explain this Capgras, you'd be looking for a schizophrenia gene. That's the Schluter family. Let's see what else I've got."

She talked him through the rest of the loose scrapbook. She had family photos going back to a great-grandfather, Bartlett Schluter, standing in front of the ancestral sod house as a young boy, his hair like corn silk. She had pictures of the beef-packing plant in Lexington, a five-hundred-thousand-square-foot, windowless box with a hundred forty-foot containers lined up alongside it, waiting to be hauled away by semis. She had portraits of Mark's best friends, two scraggly men in their mid-twenties enjoying themselves with smoke, drink, and pool cues, one in a camouflage tee and the other in a shirt reading "Got Meth?" She had a photo of a gangly, black-haired, pale-blue woman in a hand-knit olive V-neck, radiating a fragile smile. "Bonnie Travis. The group's moll."

"This is in the hospital?"

"Mid-March. Those are Mark's toes, with the little pedicure treatment. She thought it would be cute to paint them fuchsia." Her words thickened with the injustice of affection. "Here: you wanted pictures that would excite him."

A familiar face flashed in front of Weber. His own skin would have registered a change in conductivity.

"You've met Barbara. As you noticed, he's completely gaga over her."

The woman smiled sadly into the camera, forgiving the machine and its operator. "Yes," Weber said. "Do you know why?"

"Well, I've been thinking. He responds to something in her. Her trust. Respect." A note filled her voice: an envy that could go either way. *I'd give him what this woman does, if he'd let me.* Karin stroked the photo. "I can't tell you what I owe this woman. Can you believe she works down at the bottom of the food chain? One baby step up from a volunteer. That's for-profit health care for you. Put three greedy humans together, and they can't tell their assets from their armpits."

Weber smiled noncommittally.

"Here's Mark's pride and joy." She fingered a picture of a narrow, vinyl-sided modular home, something Weber's generation would have called a prefab. "This is the Homestar. That's actually the name of the catalog building company. But that's what he calls his, like it's the only one in the world. My bad-ass, rebel brother, never prouder than the day he finally scraped together the six-thousand-dollar down payment, his toehold on the bottom rung of the middle class." She bit her thumb tip. "What you call fleeing a precarious upbringing."

"That's where you're living, while you're in town?"

He might have served her a warrant. "Where else can I go? I'm out of a job. I don't know how long this is going to go on."

"Makes perfect sense," he declared.

"It's not like I'm rooting through his things." She shut her eyes and blanched. He picked up a photo of five hirsute men with guitars and a trap set. She looked again. "That's Cattle Call. A sorry house band at a bar called the Silver Bullet, outside town. Mark loves them. They were playing the night of his accident. That's where Mark was, right before. Here's his truck; I found a whole shoe box full of truck shots, in a closet at the Homestar. This could upset him."

"Yes. Maybe we should skip that one for now."

The pizzas came. His choice dismayed him: pineapple and ham. He couldn't imagine having ordered it. Karin dug into her Supreme with gusto. "I shouldn't be having pizza. I know I could eat better. Still, I don't do much meat, except when I eat out. I'm surprised they can sell any cow parts at all, in this part of the country. You should hear what goes on at that plant. Ask Mark. It'll put you off your feed for good. You know, they have to clip the horns to keep the crazed beasts from goring each other."

It didn't much hinder her appetite. Weber poked at his Hawaiian as if he were doing ethnography. At last the food gave out, along with their words.

"You ready?" she asked doubtfully, pretending she was.

At Dedham Glen, he asked for an hour alone with Mark. Her presence might jeopardize a clean skin response test.

"You're the boss." She smoothed her eyebrows and backed away, bobbing.

Mark was alone in his room, studying a bodybuilding

178

magazine. He looked up and beamed. "Shrink! You're back. Give me that one with crossing out the numbers and letters again. I'm ready for it now. I wasn't ready for it yesterday."

They shook hands. Mark was in a different shirt, this one listing a dozen Nebraska laws still on the books. *Mothers may not perm their daughters' hair without a state license. If a child burps in church, his parents may be arrested.* He wore the knit cap from the day before, even in the close, summer room. "You by yourself today, or . . . ?"

Weber just raised his eyebrows.

"Here. Have a seat. Take a load off. You're supposed to be an old guy, remember?" He cawed like a raven.

Weber took his chair from yesterday, across from Mark, making the same groans to the same laughter. "Would you mind if I use a tape recorder while we talk?"

"That's a tape recorder? You're shitting me! Lemme see that thing. Looks more like a cigarette lighter. You sure you aren't some Special-Ops . . . ?" Mark tucked the machine up to his cheek. " 'Hello? Hello? If you can hear me, I'm being held hostage here against my will.' Hey! Don't look like that. Just busting your balls, is all." He handed back the tiny machine. "So, how come you need a tape recorder? You got problems or something?" He spun his fingers around each ear.

"Something like that," Weber admitted.

He'd used a tape recorder the day before. There'd been no way to ask permission, out of the gate. Yet he needed to be able to reproduce that first contact verbatim. He'd banked on getting retroactive permission. And now he had it, or close enough.

"Wow. Cool. Live on tape. You want me to sing?"

"You're on. Hit it."

Mark launched into a dead monotone, tone-deaf tune.

179

Gonna open you up, gonna peel you out . . . He broke off. "So come on. Give me one of your so-called puzzles. Beats lying around and dying."

"I've got some new ones. Picture mysteries." He pulled the Benton Facial Recognition Test out of his briefcase.

"Mysteries? My whole damn life is a mystery."

Mark recognized images of the same face from different angles, in different poses, under different lighting. But he couldn't always tell when a glance was aimed at him. He did reasonably well identifying celebrities, although he called Lyndon Johnson "some high-ranking corporate goon" and Malcolm X "that guy Dr. Chandler on the hospital show." He enjoyed the whole process. "This guy? He's supposed to be a comedian, if yelling like there's Ben-Gay on your scrotum is funny. So okay. This chick calls herself a singer, but that's just because they took her dancing pole away." He also did well separating actual faces from facelike shapes in drawings and photographs. Overall, his recognition scores were high normal. But he struggled with the emotions of conventional facial expressions. His responses tended to skew toward fear and anger. Given the circumstances, however, Mark's numbers showed nothing that Weber could call pathological.

"Can we try one more thing?" Weber asked, as if it were the most natural request in the world.

"Whatever. Knock yourself out."

He dove into his briefcase and pulled out a small galvanic skin response amplifier and meter. "How would you feel about me wiring you up?" He showed Mark the finger-clip electrodes. "It basically measures your skin conductivity. If you get excited, or feel tense . . ."

"You mean like a lie detector?"

"Yes, a little like that."

Mark cackled. "No shit! Now we're talking. Bring it on! I always wanted to try to bust one of those things." He held out his hands. "Wire me up, Mr. Spock."

Weber did, explaining every step. "Most people show a rise in skin conductivity when they see a picture of someone close to them. Friends, family . . ."

"Everybody sweats when they see Mom?"

"Exactly! I wish I'd put it that way in my last book."

Of course the methodology was all wrong. There should have been a separate device operator and reader. His calibration trials were primitive at best. No randomizing, no double blind. No controls. Nothing in Karin's pictures gave him any baseline. But he was not sending this data to a refereed journal. He was just getting a rough sense of this shattered man, of Mark's attempts to tell himself back into a continuous story.

Mark raised his unwired hand. "I promise to tell the truth . . . etcetera, etcetera. So help me, Gosh."

They looked at pictures together. Weber flipped through Karin's photos, watched the bobbing needle, and scribbled down numbers.

"Hey! The Homestar! That's my house. It's a beautiful thing. They built that sucker to my personal specifications."

The needle danced again. "There's Duane-o. Look at that pudgy bastard. Knows a lot, even if he's not the race's brightest bulb. And that's the Rupture. Check the cue technique. You'd want this guy on your side, in any—you know—situation. If you're looking for your overall good times, these are the two to call."

The picture of his sister—Karin as Goth vampire—produced little conductance. He closed his eyes and pushed the picture away. Weber fished. "Anyone you know?"

181

Mark looked down at the four-by-six glossy picture. "It's . . . you know. The daughter from the Addams Family."

The needle flickered at the picture of his great-grandfather. "The patriarch. This guy? He was sitting in that sod house when he was a kid, and a cow came crashing through the roof. Good times, back then."

The IBP packing plant produced an anxious twitch. "That's where I work. Christ, it's been weeks. I hope to God they're holding my spot. You think?"

Conscientiousness outliving its usefulness: Weber had seen it hundreds of times. Twenty years before, his eight-year-old daughter, Jessica, almost killed by a burst appendix, came back to awareness frantic that her oral report on the honey-dance of bees would be late.

"I can't lose that job, man. It's the best thing to happen to me since my father died. They need me to keep those hoppers going. I've got to get in touch with the boss, ASAP."

"I'll see what I can find out," Weber told him.

The needle spiked again with the picture of Mark's attendant. "Barbie Doll! So, all right, I know this Gillespie woman is like practically your age. But she's still great. Sometimes I think she's the only real person to survive the Android Invasion."

He responded to the picture of Bonnie Travis as well. In fact, watching the meter as Mark studied her picture, Weber made out something Karin Schluter hadn't mentioned.

Mark nodded at the photo of Cattle Call. The needle failed to suggest that Mark associated the local band with the anxiety of his last intact night. "These guys are okay. They're not ready to play Omaha, or anything. But they've got a groove and a little bit of the High Lonesome, two things that aren't easy to combine, I'm telling you. I'll take you to hear them, if you'd like."

"Might be interesting," Weber said.

For Mark's parents, another flat line. Mark stuck his unwired hand up underneath his knit cap, stretching it from the inside. "I know what you want me to say. This one looks like Harrison Ford, pretending to be my father. This one—somebody's idea of my mother on a good day. But not even in the minor-league ballpark, really. Hang on a minute." He gathered the stack of pictures and crumpled them. "Where'd you get these?"

Stupidly, Weber wasn't ready for the question. He ran through the possible lies. He rested his face on his fist, looked Mark in the eye, and said nothing.

Mark grew frantic with theories. "You get these from her? Don't you see what's going on? I thought you were supposed to be some famous East Coast freak of intellect. She steals these good pictures from my friends. Then she hires actors who look a little like my family. Snaps a few shots. Boom! Suddenly, I've got a whole new history. And because nobody else knows any better, I'm stuck with it." He slapped the picture of his parents with the back of his hand. He threw the stack of pictures on the table between them and tore the electrode leads off his fingers.

Weber picked up the photo of Mark Schluter's father. "Can you say what exactly doesn't seem . . . ?"

Mark plucked the photo from his hands. He tore it down the middle, neatly bisecting his father's head. He offered the pieces to Weber. "A gift for Miss Deep Space . . ." A gasp came from the hall. Mark scrambled to his feet. "Hey! You want to spy on me, come spy . . ." He swung toward the door, ready for a chase. Karin tumbled into the room.

She brushed past him and snatched the torn photo pieces. "What do you think you're doing, tearing your own father?" She threatened him with the scraps. "How many of these do you think we have?"

It stopped him in place. Her sheer rage baffled him. Docile, he stood by as she fit the scraps together and inspected the damage.

"It can be taped," she declared at last. She glared at her brother, shaking her head. "Why are you *doing* this?" She sat down on the bed, shaking. Mark sat down again, too, chastened by something too big to dope out. Weber just watched. His job description: watch and report. For twenty years, he'd built a reputation on exposing the inadequacy of all neural theory in the face of the great humbler, observation.

"What are you feeling right now?" he asked.

"Anger!" Karin shouted, before realizing the question wasn't for her.

Mark's voice, when it came, was even more mechanical than his eerie baseline. "What do you care?" He tilted his head toward heaven. "You don't understand this. You come from New York, where everybody's God, or something. Out here, people . . . My sister? She's weird, but she's my only ally on earth. Me and her, basically, against everybody. This woman?" He pointed and snorted. "You saw her try to attack me." He sat down at the testing table and started to cry. "Where is she? I just *miss* her. I'd just like to see her again for five seconds. I'm afraid something may have happened to her."

Karin Schluter echoed the moan. She raised her palms and took two steps toward the door, then stopped and sat down. The tape recorder was running. A part of Weber was already writing up this uncanny moment. Mark sat fiddling with the GSR meter. His eyes cast terrified looks around the room. He held the electrical leads in one hand. Then, as if convulsed by current, his fist clenched and he sat up. "Listen. I just had an idea. Can we try something? Can you just . . . ?"

Mark offered Weber the leads. Weber thought to refuse, as affectionately as possible. But in two decades of field research, no one had ever refused his testing. He smiled and attached the contacts to his fingertips. "Fire when ready."

Mark Schluter slid his pelvis forward. His limbs flailed like the blades of a tin windmill. From his jeans pocket he extracted a crumpled note. At the sight of it, his sister groaned again. Mark fixed his eyes on the meter. He unfolded the paper and handed it to Weber. In a frantic, leaky hand, almost unreadable, someone had scribbled:

I am No One
but Tonight on North Line Road
GOD led me to you
so You could Live
and bring back someone else.

"Look!" Mark cried out. "It moved. The needle jerked. It went right up to here. What does that mean? Tell me what that means."

"You have to calibrate it," Weber said.

"Have you seen this note before?" Mark kept his eye fixed on the meter. "Do you know who wrote this?"

Weber shook his head. "No." Pure alien curiosity.

"It moved again! Man. Please don't jerk me. We're talking about my *life*, here."

"I'm sorry. I wish I could tell you. But I don't know anything about it." Even to himself, he sounded fake.

Disgusted, Mark waved for him to remove the finger clips. He pointed toward the bed. "Hook her up."

Karin was on her feet, both hands slicing the air. "Mark, I've told you all I know about the thing a hundred times."

He wouldn't quit until she sat and attached the leads to her fingers. Then, the barrage of questions. *Who wrote this? Who found it? What does it mean? What am I supposed to do with it?* She answered every accusation with increasing impatience.

"Nothing's happening," Mark cried. "Does that mean she's telling the truth?"

It meant her skin was not changing conductance. "It doesn't mean anything," Weber said. "You have to calibrate it."

Before Weber left that afternoon, he put it to Mark. "There's a condition called Capgras. Very rarely, when the brain is hurt, people lose their ability to recognize—"

A primal howl cut him off. "Fuck. Don't *start* with that, man. That's what the Haz-doctor keeps saying. But he's in on the whole thing. That woman is sucking his cock or something." Mark, bare, stared at Weber, eyes begging. "I thought I could trust you, Shrinky."

Weber fingered his beard. "You can," he said, and fell silent.

"Besides," the thin voice pleaded. "Isn't it more scientific, just to go with the more likely explanation?"

Sylvie's words that night from the MotoRest were honey out of stone. "Ah! I know that voice. Wait—don't tell me. It's the man who used to hang around here."

He couldn't remember everything he wanted to tell her. It didn't matter. She was primed with her own stories.

"Your very clever daughter Jessica has just won an NSF grant for young researchers. Apparently, planet-hunting is still fundable, this year." She quoted a handsome figure. "California will have to tenure her, just for the loot she's bringing in."

186

Jess, his Jess. *My daughter, my ducats.*

Sylvie launched into the day's long adventure, her attempts to trap a family of raccoons that was holding regular book-club gatherings in the Weber attic. She planned to catch them alive and drive them around in circles for a long time in broad daylight, to bewilder them, before dropping them off behind a strip mall in Centereach.

At last she asked, "So what did you learn from your misidentifier today?"

He lay back on the rented bed, closed his eyes, and held the shoehorn of a phone against his cheek. "He's got one thin scrap of sheet tin propped up between himself and dissolving. Just looking at him makes everything I think I know about consciousness melt into air."

The conversation shifted; he had some trouble following where it wanted to go. He asked about the weather on Chickadee Way, how the place looked.

"Conscience Bay was just gorgeous, Man. Like glass. Like frozen time."

"I can imagine," he said. The needle would have jumped.

He worked late, going over his notes. A moist June chill that mocked his whole image of the Great Plains saturated his room. He could find no way to shut off the air conditioner or open a window. He lay in bed, in the amber glow of the clock, appraising himself. Midnight came and went, and his eyes wouldn't close. He *had* seen the note before. Karin Schluter had Xeroxed it and stuffed the copy into the thick portfolio she'd shown him on his first day. Now, as he lay miles from sleep, he tried to decide whether he'd lied about not knowing it, or had just forgotten.

He'd seen true face blindness, and this wasn't it. All his books described some flavor of agnosia—blindness to objects, blindness to places, blindness to age or expression or gaze. He'd written about people who couldn't distinguish foods, cars, or coins, although some part of their brains still knew how to interact with the baffling objects. He'd told the story of Martha T., a devoted ornithologist, who overnight lost the ability to tell a wren from a red-bellied sapsucker, yet could still describe, in detail, how the birds differed. Several times in the books he described prosopagnosia. For truly vertiginous diseases, the brain was endlessly accommodating.

The Country of Surprise portrayed Joseph S. In his early twenties, he was shot in the head by a mugger's small-caliber handgun, damaging a small region in his right inferotemporal region—the fusiform gyrus. He lost his ability to recognize acquaintances, friends, family, loved ones, or celebrities. He could walk past anyone and not know him, however often or recently they'd met. He even had trouble picking out his own mirror image.

"I know they are faces," Joseph S. told Weber. "I can see the differences in each feature. But they aren't distinctive. They mean nothing to me. Think of the leaves of an enormous maple. Put any two next to each other and you can see how different they are. But look up into the tree and try to name the leaves."

Nothing to do with memory: Joseph could list in some detail accurate descriptions of features that friends of his *ought* to have. He just couldn't recognize those features, when assembled into a face.

Despite his crippling damage, Joseph S. earned a doctorate in mathematics and pursued a successful university career. He scored off the charts on standard IQ tests, especially spatial reasoning, navigation, memory, and mental rotation. He described to Weber his elaborate compensatory systems: cues of voice, clothing, body type, and minute ratios of eye width to nose length to lip thickness. "I've gotten fast enough to fool a lot of people."

Faces only: nothing else gave him trouble. In fact, he was better than most at picking out slight differences in nearly identical objects: pebbles, socks, sheep. But surviving in society depended upon performing staggering facial calculations constantly, as if they were child's play. Joseph S. lived like a spy behind enemy lines, doing by laborious math and algorithm what everyone else did like breathing. Every moment out in public demanded vigilance. He said that the problem contributed to the breakup of his first marriage. His wife couldn't bear his having to study her in order to pick her out of a crowd. "It very nearly cost me my current marriage, too." He described seeing his second wife on campus one afternoon and embracing her. Only it wasn't his wife. It was no one he knew.

"What we think of as a single, simple process," Weber wrote,

> is in fact a long assembly line. Vision requires careful coordination between thirty-two or more separate brain modules. Recognizing a face takes at least a dozen . . . We are hard-wired for finding faces. Two Oreo cookies and a carrot can make an infant howl or laugh. Only: the many, delicate hard-wires between modules can break at several different spots . . .

With varying damage to different areas, a person might lose his ability to distinguish sex, age, the emotional expression of a face, or the direction of someone's attention. Weber described a patient who was completely unable to decide how attractive a given face seemed. In his own lab, he gathered data suggesting that some sufferers from face blindness were actually matching faces without their conscious minds knowing.

Few weeks went by when he didn't receive letters from anxious readers struggling with some attenuated form of failing to recognize old acquaintances. Some were consoled by Weber's bombshell: a simple neurological quirk that revealed how everyone suffered from a form of prosopagnosia. Even normal recognition fails when the observed face is upside down.

Mark Schluter was not face-blind. Just the reverse: he saw differences that were not there. He most resembled those people Weber had met for whom every change in expression could split into a new and separate person. That nightmare flashed across Weber's closed lids just before he fell asleep, looking up into the million leaves of a tree towering above him, each leaf a life he had met once, a moment in a life, even a particular emotional aspect of that isolated moment, every look a separate object to identify, unique and multiplying into the billions, beyond anyone's ability to simplify into names . . .

The third morning, he went alone to Dedham Glen. He needed more psychometry, to test for broader delusional tendencies. He found the place easily. Despite the tangled river valley, the town was a sheet of graph paper. Two days in this perfect grid and—barring any spatial-orienting lesions—one could find anything.

Three gigantic children were camped on the floor around Mark's television. Mark, in his knit cap, sat between a badger

190

in a prison outfit and a keg-chested man in hunting cap and sweats. Weber recognized them from Karin's photographs.

On screen, a road through a rolling brown landscape reeled out from the horizon. The taillights of low-slung cars clawed across the veering asphalt. The three seated males jerked in unison with the taillights, jolting the way diabetic Jessica sometimes did, in the middle stages of insulin shock. The footage looked like home movies, handheld vérité motor sports overdubbed with a throbbing techno soundtrack. Then Weber saw the wires. Each of the trio was tethered by an umbilical to a game box. The race—part film, part cartoon— half derived from this trio's brains.

The wires recalled Weber to graduate student days, the sunset of behaviorism: old laboratory experiments with pigeons and monkeys, creatures taught to want nothing except to press buttons and slide levers all day long, merging with the machine until they dropped from exhaustion. The three men had become the sinuous music, the serpentine road, the engine roar. But they showed no sign of dropping anytime soon. Changes on the screen produced changes in physiology, which fed back into the screen world.

The ribboning road bore hard to the right, floating, then falling. The cars lifted free, nosing into the air. Then the crunch of steel when chassis slammed back to earth and the three bodies absorbed the impact. The engines whined, choking on the pavement. The noise crashed like surf as the drivers ground for higher gears. Specks far down the chute of scenery swelled into other speeding vehicles, which the foreground cars scrambled to pass. No saying where the race unfolded. Somewhere empty. Some square state with more cows than people, midway between prairie and desert. A few tract homes, filling stations, strip malls—the tile set for heartland America. For a few seconds, it rained. Then the rain turned to sleet, sleet to snow. Daytime faded to dark. In another moment night lifted, as the race ground a few dozen more miles down the imaginary road.

Whatever damage Mark Schluter suffered, his thumbs and their wiring were still intact. Recent studies by a colleague of Weber's suggested that enormous areas of the motor cortex of game-cartridge children were devoted to thumbs, and that many in the emerging species *Homo ludens* now favored their thumbs over their index fingers. The game controller had at last consummated one of the three great leaps of primate evolution.

The trio on the floor elbowed one another, their bodies extensions of the cars they piloted. They hit an open stretch where the road stopped whipping and became straightaway through sandy hills toward a looming finish line. The racers accelerated, jostling for position. They banked into a last hard right. One of the cars slid wide through the curve and fishtailed. The driver overcompensated, swinging back onto the road, into his companions' vehicles. All three cars locked up and soared into a spectacular corkscrew. They came down, plowing into a file of slower cars cruising into the finish. One car ricocheted out of the pack and struck the filled grandstand. The screen turned a bright smear. People fled in all directions, termites from a torched hive. The car exploded into an oily flare. An arcing cry cracked open and fell back to earth as laughter. Out of the flames emerged a crash-suited figure, charred from helmet to boots, dancing crazily.

"Holy shit," the badger felon said. "That's what I call a big finish there, Gus."

"Un-fucking-be-lieve-able," the keg-chest confirmed. "Greatest fireball ever."

But the third driver, the one Weber came to see, just droned. "Wait. Give me that puppy back. One more time."

The engines dead, the badger glanced up and saw Weber in the doorway. He nudged Mark. "Company, Gus."

Mark spun around, his eyes both lit and scared. Seeing Weber, he snorted. "That's not company. That's the Incredible Shrinking Man. Hey. This guy's famous. Tons more famous than most people realize."

"Pull up a spot," the hunting cap offered. "We were just winding up, anyway."

Weber reached into his pocket and turned on his voice recorder. "Go ahead," he said. "Take another lap. I'll just sit and collect my thoughts."

"Hey! I'm forgetting myself. Where the hell are my manners?" Mark scrambled to his feet, shoving off of his cursing friends. "Shrinkster, meet Duane-o Cain. And this one here . . ." He pointed to the badger. "Hey, Gus. Who the hell you supposed to be, again?" The badger shot him the finger. Mark laughed, an emptying gas cylinder. "Whatever you say. This one's Tommy Rupp. One of the world's great drivers."

Duane Cain snorted. "Driver? Putter, maybe."

Weber watched the trio maneuver to a new starting line. He was thirty-four years old when he first saw one of these boxes. He'd gone to pick up seven-year-old Jessica from her girlfriend's house. He found the girls parked in front of the tube and scolded them. "What kind of children are you, watching television on such a gorgeous day?"

The question reduced the girls to derisive howls. It wasn't *television*, they sneered. It was, in fact, lobotomized table tennis stood on end. He watched in fascination. Not the game: *them*. The game was chunky, flat, and repetitive. But the two girls: *they* were off somewhere in deep symbolic space.

"How is this better than real Ping-Pong?" he asked tiny Jess. He genuinely wanted to know her answer. The same question haunted his work. What was it about the species that would save the symbol and discard the thing it stood for?

His seven-year-old sighed. "Dad," she told him, with that first hint of contempt for adulthood and all its trouble with the obvious. "It's just *cleaner*."

His daughter never really looked back. Eight years later, she built her own computer from parts. By eighteen, she was using it to analyze the traces of light from a backyard telescope. Now almost thirty, living in Southern California, that most abstract of states, she was winning grants from the NSF for finding new planets, at least one of which would surely turn out to be cleaner than Earth.

The trio of boys conferred without words. They ran laps of intricate ballet beyond the reach of any choreographer. Weber studied Mark for signs of deficit. No saying how coordinated he had once been. But even now, Mark could run rings around Weber in any vehicle, real or phantom. He drove like a maniac. The occasional stunning fireball drew no more than a viscous laugh.

Weber was noting down Mark's eye movements when a shout tore through the room. It seemed just another of the game's shattering sound effects. He turned to see Karin in the doorway, her face aflame. Her hands were up, clutching the back of her skull. Her elbows flared. "*Animals*. What do you think you're doing?"

The males scrambled to their feet. Tom Rupp recovered first. "We thought we'd come keep our friend company. He needed a little diversion."

Her left hand grabbed her neck while her right cut the air. "Are you insane?"

194

Duane Cain twisted under the injustice. "You want to get back on the Prozac for a minute? We're just here to supply companionship."

Karin waved her nails at the video game, the road still snaking mindlessly across the screen. "Companionship? That's what you call putting him through this again?" She shot Weber a look of betrayal.

"The man's not objecting," Rupp said. "Are you, buddy?"

Mark stood grasping his controller, one cheek screwed up. "We were just doing what we always do." He held up the game pad. "What's with the freaking?"

"Exactly." Cain looked at Weber, then back at Karin. "See what we're saying? It's not like this is real, or anything. We're not putting anybody through anything."

"Don't you two have jobs? Or have you become completely unemployable?"

Rupp stepped toward her, and she backed toward the door. "I took home thirty-one hundred dollars this month. How about you?" Karin crossed her arms under her breasts and looked down. Weber felt some old, unfinished business between them.

"Working?" Duane said. "It's Sunday, for Christ's sake."

A giggle leaked out of Mark. "Even God didn't bust his balls all the time, Sarge."

"Go away," she said. "Go kill some cows."

Rupp smiled a little lemonade smile and flicked the back of his fingernails up his cheek. "Give it up, Ms. Gandhi. You take a hit out on a cow every time you bite into a burger. You know what I think? Our man here is right. Arab terrorists kidnaped Karin Schluter and replaced her with a foreign agent."

Duane Cain glanced nervously at Weber. But Mark just laughed like a thudding cowbell. Karin sliced through the men toward her brother. Reaching him, she lifted the controller from his hands and placed it on the console. She popped the disc from the machine and the screen went blue. She crossed to Weber and handed him the platter of offending code. She touched his elbow. "Ask these two what they know about Mark's accident."

A cry issued from her brother. "Uh, hello? Are you on crack?"

"They used to play games like this, only out on real country roads."

Mark leaned close to Weber. He whispered, "This is what I mean about her."

Tom Rupp sneered. "This is defamation. Do you have the slightest evidence . . . ?"

"Evidence! Don't talk to me like I'm some dimwit policeman. Who do you think I am? I'm his sister. You hear me? His own flesh and blood. You want evidence? I've been out there. Three sets of tracks?"

Mark dropped into the chair next to Weber. "Out where? What tracks?" He curled up, clutching his elbows.

Duane Cain formed a T with his hands. "Deep breathing time. Would it kill anyone if we all just chilled for a second?"

"Maybe you've managed to fool the police. But I hold you personally responsible. If things never get better . . ."

"Hey!" Mark said. "It doesn't get any better than this."

Tom Rupp shook his head. "There's something seriously wrong with you, Karin. You might want to consult with the professional while he's here."

"And then to make him play racing games, drag him through all that again, like nothing ever happened? Have you lost your minds?"

Mark sprang from his chair. "Who the hell do you think you are? You've got no power here!" He made for her, arms thrust outward. She turned, instinctively, into the arms of Rupp, who opened to protect her. Mark stopped short, hung his hands on his neck, and whimpered. *Not what I meant. Not what you think.*

Weber watched the free-for-all, already telling Sylvie. She would show him no sympathy. *You're the one who wanted to get out of the lab. Who wanted to see this thing up close, before you died.*

Karin pushed herself from Rupp's arms. "I'm sorry, but you two have to leave."

"Already gone." Rupp gave her a dress salute, snappy National Guard issue, which Mark, by reflex, mimicked.

Duane Cain wobbled his extended thumb and pinky at Mark. "Keep it real, bro. We'll be back."

When they were gone and calm returned, Weber turned to Karin. "Mark and I should probably work alone for a bit." Mark pointed two fingers at her and chuckled. Karin's face fell. She hadn't thought Weber capable of such betrayal. She spun and fled the room. Weber followed her into the hall, calling her until she stopped. "I'm sorry. I needed to watch Mark with his friends."

She exhaled and rubbed her cheeks. "With his friends? That part of him hasn't changed."

Something occurred to Weber, from reviewing the literature the night before. "How does your brother seem when you talk to him on the phone?"

"I . . . haven't called him. I'm just here, every day. I hate phones."

"Ah! We can bond over that."

"I haven't called him since the accident. No point. He'd

just hang up on me. At least that's one thing he can't do face-to-face."

"Would you like to try an experiment?"

She was ready to try anything.

Mark Schluter sat toying with a video-game controller, turning it over in his palms as if it were some sealed bivalve he couldn't open. Something had gone out of the game. He looked up at Weber, imploring. "You making some secret plans with her?"

"Not exactly."

"You think she's right?"

"About what?"

"About those guys," Mark snapped.

"I couldn't say. What do you think?"

Mark flinched. He sucked in a mouthful of air and held it for fifteen seconds, fingering his tracheotomy scar. "You're supposed to be Dr. Brainiac. You gotta explain all this crap to me."

Weber fell back on professional training. "It might help us both figure out what happened if we worked through a few tests." Not exactly a lie, per se. He'd seen stranger things happen. As hopes went, it was qualified enough.

Mark stroked his scarred face and sighed. "Fine. Whatever you got. Knock yourself out."

They worked for a long time. Mark hunched over the tests, gripping a pen as doggedly as he'd gripped the controller. His focus was all over the road, but he managed to complete most of the tasks. He showed little cognitive impairment. His emotional maturity tested below average, but not much lower, Weber guessed, than the other parties to the morning's confrontation. All of America would have tested below average on that, nowadays. Mark showed some features of depression.

Weber would have been stunned if he didn't. Borderline depression was a signal indicator of appropriate response, in the summer of 2002.

Other tests ferreted out paranoia. Until the mid 1970s, many clinicians maintained that Capgras was the by-product of a paranoiac condition. Another quarter-century had reversed cause and effect. Ellis and Young, in the late 1990s, suggested that patients who lose affective response to familiar people would reasonably *become* paranoid. So it always went, with ideas: go back far enough, and moving clouds caused the wind. Wilder reversals were on their way, should Weber live to witness them. The day would come when the last clean cause and effect would disappear into thickets of tangled networks.

But indisputably, Capgras and paranoia correlated. No surprise, then, when Mark's scores showed mild paranoid tendencies. Just what horror the flashes of persecution and clowning held at bay, Weber's tests could not determine.

Mark marveled at Weber's professional patter. "Man! If I could talk like you, I'd be getting laid on a daily basis." He launched into imitative psychobabble, almost convincing enough to earn him a comfortable wage somewhere on the West Coast.

Weber said, "I'm going to read you a story, and I want you to repeat it." He took out the standard text and read at the usual speed. " 'Once upon a time, there was a farmer who fell ill. He went to the town doctor, but the doctor failed to cure him. The doctor told him, "Only a happy look will make you happy again." So the farmer walked all through town looking for someone happy, but he could find no one. He went home. But just before he reached his farm, he saw a happy-looking deer racing across the hills, and began to feel a little better.' Now you tell it back to me."

"Whatever turns you on. So there's this guy," Mark growled. "Who got banged up and was in a depression. He went to the hospital, but nobody would help. They told him to go look for someone happier than he was. So he went downtown, but he couldn't find anyone. So he went home. But on his way home, he saw this animal, and he thought, 'That thing is happier than I am.' The end." He shrugged, waiting for his score and dismissing it at the same time.

That afternoon, at a break in the testing, Mark asked, "Did they build you, too?"

The recorder was still running. Weber turned nonchalant. The creature he was hunting relaxed in a patch of sunlight, just in front of him. "What do you mean?"

"Did they build you from parts, as well?" The simple tone of voice, the bodily ease: he might have been greeting a neighbor over the back fence. Sweetly polite, but poised over the bottomless pit.

"You don't think I'm human?"

" 'I couldn't say,' " Mark mimicked. " 'What do *you* think?' " His grazing eyes swung to some movement behind Weber. "Hey! Barbie Doll!"

Weber turned, startled. Barbara Gillespie stood just next to him, in a tailored, ochre skirt suit fit for a job interview. She greeted him covertly in the fraction of a second before addressing Mark. "Mr. S.! You are due for a complete oil change."

Mark banked a glance at Weber, filled with criminal glee. "Don't worry. It's nowhere near as interesting as it sounds."

Barbara looked at Weber. "Should I come back later? Do you two need more time?"

The tacit alliance unnerved Weber. "We were just wrapping up, in fact."

She peeked at him, almost a question. She turned to Mark and pointed toward the bathroom. "You heard the doctor!"

Mark squeezed himself up on his feet. He bobbed through the bathroom door, then popped right out again. "Oh! I think I might need some help."

Barbara shook her head. "Nice try, darling. Leave the towel on this time, okay?"

"She called me darling! You heard her, right, Shrink? You'll testify in court?"

As the door closed again, Barbara turned to Weber. She held his gaze: again the unnerving connection. "Could you make a note that his sex drive seems unaffected?"

Weber touched his earlobe. "Forgive me for asking the lamest question on earth. Have we run across each other before?"

"You mean before a couple of days ago?"

He failed to smile. He'd reached an age when everyone he met fit into one of the thirty-six available physiognomic templates. The number of people he met once and never saw again had reached devastating proportions. He'd crossed a threshold, around fifty, when every new person he met reminded him of someone else. The problem was exacerbated when total strangers greeted him familiarly. He could pass someone in the halls of the university medical center, then see them six months later at the Stop 'N Shop, overwhelmed by a sense of collegial connection. The virgin prairies of Nebraska were a dream, after the minefields of Long Island and Manhattan. Yet he'd had two days to locate this woman, and still came up empty-handed.

Barbara tried not to smile. "I'd remember if we had."

So she did know who he was, maybe had even read him. What was a nursing-home attendant in her early forties doing reading books like his? The thought was inexcusably bigoted, especially for a man who'd once devoted a whole chapter to the category errors and prejudices that haunt the human circuitry. He studied her, compelled by her unlikelihood. "How long have you been with Dedham Glen?"

She glanced skyward and made a comic calculation. "For a while, now."

"Where were you before?" Absurd, trying to hit the moon with a few scattered stones in the dark.

"Oklahoma City."

Colder and colder. "Same line of work?"

"Similar. I was at a large public facility down there."

"What brought you to Nebraska?"

She smiled and dipped her head, like holding an apple under her chin. "I guess I just couldn't take the hustle and bustle of the metropolis." Something far away held her interest. Discovered, she turned shy. The look flustered him, although he'd asked for it. He looked away. Only the appearance of Mark Schluter in the bathroom doorway saved him. He was holding a towel in front of his naked body. The knit cap had disappeared, exposing the patchy, returning hair. Boyish, he beamed at his caregiver. "I'm ready for my pain now, ma'am."

With two arching eyebrows, Barbara excused herself, weirdly intimate, like the two of them had grown up three houses down from each other, gone to grade school together, written each other hundreds of letters, flirted one evening with testing more serious waters, then backed away, honorary blood relations for life.

Weber gathered his papers and retreated to the lobby. He'd gotten what he'd come for, acquired the requisite data, seen up close one of the most bizarre aberrations the self could suffer. He had enough material now, if not for a write-up in the medical literature, at least for a haunting narrative case history. He could do little more, here. It was time to head home, resume the rounds of colloquium, classroom, laboratory, and writing desk, the routine that had provided his middle age with a degree of productive reflection wholly undeserved.

But before he left, he'd just ask Barbara Gillespie about Mark's changes over the last several weeks. He had Dr. Hayes's observations, of course, and Karin's. But only this woman saw Mark constantly, with no investment to sway her. He sat in the lobby on one end of a dark vinyl sofa across from a palsied woman slightly younger than he in an epic struggle with the zipper on her unnecessary jacket. He wanted to help, but knew enough not to. He felt oddly nervous, waiting for Barbara, as if he were eighteen again, at a graduation dance. He checked his watch every two minutes. At the fourth check, he sprang to his feet, startling the jacket woman, who, frightened, tore her zipper back down to the starting line. He'd forgotten having asked Karin Schluter to phone her brother at exactly three o'clock, now just minutes away.

He hovered outside Mark's closed door, shamelessly eavesdropping. He heard the woman talking, with laughing grunts from Mark. The phone rang. The boy cursed and called out, "I'm coming, I'm coming, already. Hold your damn horsemeat."

Over the sound of banged furniture, Barbara's voice soothed. "Take your time. They'll wait."

Weber knocked at the door and let himself in. A startled Barbara Gillespie looked up from where she had been flipping through magazines with her charge. Weber slipped into the room, closing the door behind him. Mark stood with his back turned, struggling with the phone. His arms shook as he

203

shouted, "Hello? Who is this?" Then shocked silence. "Oh my God! Where are you? Where have you *been*?"

Weber glanced at Gillespie. The attendant was staring at him, guessing not only the caller but Weber's role. Her eyes questioned him. His turn to look away, guilty.

Mark's voice cracked and dampened, welcoming a loved one back from the dead. "You're here? You're in *Kearney*? Jesus. Thank God! Get over here, *now*. No! I am not listening to another word. I'm not talking to the phone, after all this. You won't believe the shit I've been through. I can't believe you weren't around for this. I'm not . . . I'm just saying. Get over here. I need to look at you. I need to see. You know where I am? Oh, right, duh. Hurry your ass. Okay. No. Stop. I'm not talking. I'm hanging up now. You hear that?" He leaned down, demonstrating. "Hanging up." He put the receiver on the hook. He lifted it up again, listening. He turned from the phone toward the others, glowing. He took Weber's reappearance without comment. He was flying. "You are not going to *believe* who that was! Karin the S!"

Barbara cast a glance at Weber and rose. "Lots to do," she announced. She mussed Mark Schluter's bare head and brushed past Weber.

Weber brushed past the elated Mark and followed her out into the hallway. "Miss Gillespie," he called, surprising even himself. "Would you have a minute?"

She stopped and shook her head, waiting for him to come toward her, out of Mark's earshot. "It's not fair."

He nodded, too clinically. Her distress surprised him. Surely she dealt with worse, every day. "It's a severe blow. But people are remarkably pliant. The brain will surprise us."

She raised her eyebrow. "I mean the call."

The accusation irritated him. She knew nothing of the literature, of differential diagnostics, of this man's cognitive or

204

emotional prospects. An hourly-wage staffer. He calmed himself. When the words came out, they were as level as the prairie horizon. "It's something we needed to determine."

The word formed in her face: *We?* "I'm sorry. I'm just an aide. The nurses and therapists can tell you a lot more. Excuse me. I'm running way late." She knocked and disappeared into another patient's room, two doors down.

Flustered, Weber returned to Mark's. Mark was spinning on one heel. Seeing Weber, he pumped both hands in the air. "My damn sister! Can you believe it? She'll be here in a minute. Man, she's got a lot of explaining to do."

Weber hadn't really expected the experiment to succeed. Experimental bias, Dr. Hayes would call it. Redundant: merely proposing an experiment betrayed an expectation. Yes, he suspected this thing was more than a simple short circuit. For a disconnection between the amygdala and the infero-temporal cortex to run roughshod over all higher cognition mocked any trust one put in consciousness. Whatever other reasons Weber's reason had, some part of him hoped that a dramatic phone interaction might prove therapeutic. And maybe that was the greater cruelty, the wishful thinking that signed off on unapproved tests on live subjects.

Mark stopped pacing when Karin Schluter appeared, triumphant, in the doorway. Something had changed: she'd done something to her hair—cut and waved it. Powder-blue eyeliner and apricot lips. A pair of stone-washed jeans and a too-snug T-shirt with a paw print across her breasts reading, *Kearney High School, Home of the Bearcats.* Cheerleader Karin, the one before Goth Karin. Weber had given her one awful sliver of hope, and she'd run with it. She swept into the room, arms out, her face radiant with relief, ready to hug them both. But as she closed the gap, Mark recoiled.

"Don't touch me! That was you on the phone? You haven't tortured me enough? You had to pretend she was here? Where is she? *What have you done with her?*"

A cry came from both siblings. Weber turned away as the noise traveled down the hall, caught up with Barbara Gillespie, and confirmed her. The experiment had gotten away from him. But the results were all his.

That evening, with Sylvie, he recounted the day's stories. How Mark and his friends played at racing, as if it meant nothing. How Karin had melted down, seeing them. How Mark had performed so strangely on the tests, and his explanations for every failure. How he'd soared at the sound of his sister, then shrieked at the sight of her. Weber didn't mention the nurse's aide half-accusing him on an ethics charge.

For every story he gave Sylvie, she told him one back. But by the next morning, he felt as if he'd invented all of hers.

Weber had worked with several patients who could not recognize their own body parts. Asomatognosia: it arose surprisingly often, almost always when strokes in the right hemisphere paralyzed a victim's left side. He combined the subjects in print under the name Mary H. One sixty-year-old woman, the first of the Marys, claimed her ruined arm was "pestering" her.

Pestering how?

"Well, I don't know whose it is. And I find that disturbing, Doctor."

Could it be yours?

"Impossible, Doctor. Don't you think I would know my own hand?"

He made her trace the limb with her own right hand, all the way down from her shoulder. Everything connected. *So whose hand is this, then?*

"It couldn't be yours, could it, Doctor?"

But it's connected to you.

"You're a doctor. You know you can't always believe what you see."

Other, subsequent Marys gave their limbs names. One elderly woman called hers "The Iron Lady." A male ambulance driver in his fifties called his "Mr. Limp Chimp." They ascribed personalities to their arms, whole histories. They talked, argued with, even tried to feed them. "Come on, Mr. Limp Chimp. You know you're hungry."

They did everything but own them. One woman said her father left her his arm when he died. "I wish he hadn't. It just falls on me. Falls on my chest, when I'm sleeping. Why did he want me to have this? It's burdening me something awful."

A forty-eight-year-old auto mechanic told Weber that the paralyzed arm next to him in bed was his wife's. "She's in the hospital, now. She's had a stroke. She's lost control of her arm. So . . . here it is. I guess I'm taking care of it for her."

If that's her arm, Weber asked, *where's yours?*

"Well, right here, of course!"

Can you lift your arm?

"I *am* lifting it, Doctor."

Can you clap your hands?

The lone, good right hand flapped in the air.

Are you clapping?

"Yes."

I can't hear anything, can you?

"Well, it's soft all right. But that's because there's not a whole lot to clap about."

207

Personal confabulation, the neurologist Feinberg called it. A story to link the shifting self back to the senseless facts. Reason was not impaired here; logic still worked on any other topic but this. Only the map of the body, the *feel* of it, had been fractured. And logic was not above redistributing its own indisputable parts in order to make a stubborn sense of wholeness true again. Lying in his rented room at 2:00 a.m., Weber could almost feel the fact in the limbs he lay numbering: a single, solid fiction always beat the truth of our scattering.

He woke fitfully, from a dream where his work had gone terribly wrong. He was still hypnopompic. Elevated pulse and damp skin. A cold process throbbed just below his sternum. Something had happened in New York that he needed to fix. His dream had been on the verge of naming it. Something that marred everything he'd made in the last two decades. Some change in climate, the wind turning against him, exposing the obvious, all the evidence that he was the last to notice. And for a moment before full consciousness, he remembered feeling the same low-grade dread on previous nights.

The spectral red glow of the clock said 4:10 a.m. Irregular meals and a strange environment, crashing blood sugar, sleep-doped prefrontal cortex, ancient physiological cycles linked to the earth's spin: the same chemical flux behind any dark night of the soul. Weber closed his eyes again and tried to bring down his pulse, clear his mind of the night's wild imaginings. He worked to locate himself and settle into the stream of his breathing, but he kept returning to a checklist of hazy indictments. It took until 4:30 a.m. to name what he was feeling: shame.

He'd always slept effortlessly, on demand. Sylvie marveled at him. "You must have the conscience of a choirboy." She herself would miss a night's sleep if she showed up so much as five minutes late for a dentist's appointment. His only bad stretch of insomnia had been in his first months of medical school, after they'd moved from Columbus to Cambridge. Years later, he'd had several rough nights after giving up clinical practice. Then, another restless week after Jessica told the two of them her long-held secret, a disclosure that distressed Weber not because he objected in the slightest but because Jess had needed to hide it from them for so long. His own fault: all the times he'd teased his daughter about boys, admiring her leisurely approach to the hunt, he was killing bits of her.

He'd had stretches—the first year in his new Stony Brook lab; the sudden onset of his writing vocation—when he hadn't needed sleep at all. He'd work past midnight, then rise after an hour or two with fresh ideas. And the same Sylvie who marveled that he could sleep within seconds of his head touching the pillow stood in awe of his ability to go night after night on almost nothing. "A camel, that's what you are. A camel of consciousness."

She wouldn't have recognized him now. He lay still and tried to empty himself. *Resting is as good as sleep,* his mother always claimed, half a century ago. Did researchers ever really disprove folk wisdom? But even resting lay beyond him. By five-thirty, the longest eighty minutes he'd lived through in years, he gave up. He dressed in the dark and went downstairs. The lobby was empty except for a young Hispanic woman behind the desk, who whispered good morning and said that coffee wouldn't be ready for half an hour. Weber gave her a sheepish wave. She was reading a college textbook—organic chemistry.

Dawn was starting to fuse. He made out shapes in the indigo light, but not yet colors. The street was lovely, cool, and dormant. He cut across the asphalt parkway toward the stunted commercial strip. A single light truck nosed around the Mobil station across the street. His ears adjusted, tuning in to complete cacophony. The dawn symphony: hoots and jeers, mocking whistles, chips, slides, arpeggios, and scales. At this hour, he stood little chance of being arrested for vagrancy. He stopped at the far end of the MotoRest parking lot, closed his filmy eyes, and listened.

The songs came on, mathematical, melodious, their elaborate patterns slowly mutating. Some were as singable as any human tune. He counted, sensitizing to the calls that played off one another, each a solo against a mass chorus. He lost count after a dozen, unsure where to lump and where to split. Every complex riff was identifiable, although Weber could identify none. Softer, in the middle distance, he heard the shush of cars along Interstate 80 whooshing like sprung balloons.

He opened his eyes: still in Kearney. A diffident commercial strip marked by a forest of metal sequoias bearing harsh, cheery signage. The usual gamut of franchises—motel, gas, convenience store, and fast food—reassured the accidental pilgrim that he was somewhere just like anywhere. Progress would at last render every place terminally familiar. He wandered into the intersection and sniffed his way toward town.

The arid chain stores along the strip gave way, in a handful of blocks, to gingerbread Victorians with wraparound porches. Just past these lay the core of an old downtown. The ghost of a prairie outpost, circa 1890, still looked out from the high, squared-off brick storefront façades. Light was rising. He could now read the posters in the shop windows: Celebrate Freedom Rally; Corvette Show; Faith In Bloom Garden Tour. He passed something called The Runza Hut, sealed up and dark, hiding its purpose from foreign interlopers.

The town shook itself awake. Three or four people moved along the street across from him. He passed a monument to the local dead of the two world wars. The whole tableau left him uneasy. The streets were too wide, the houses and shops too ample, too much wasted lot between them. Kearney had been conceived on too grand a scale, back when they gave land away for free, back before the place's real destiny became clear. Its lanes were laid out in a grid of numbered streets and avenues, as if it had been in danger of sprouting into a full-scale Manhattan against the epic emptiness enclosing it.

Weber sat on a bench in front of the monument, searching through the last two days for what had so unsettled him. He considered Mark Schluter, the man's uninterrupted, unthinking trust in his shattered self. But stopping and thinking about Mark proved a mistake. There on the too-spacious street, vertigo flooded back over Weber. Something crucial was escaping him. He had left himself vulnerable to some charge. The sidewalk widened and rolled under his feet. No rational explanation.

He stood and walked two more blocks, looking for anything open at this hour. A greasy spoon materialized across the way. He pushed open the door, rattling a Jesus fish on the glass. He recoiled, even as a cowbell on the inside handle announced him. At a central table, four weathered men in denim and caps that sported hybrid seed logos turned to look at him. He shied into the room and hovered by the cash register until a woman called from the kitchen, "Seat yourself, hon."

He stumbled to a booth away from the farmers. As he dropped onto the spongy red seat, the night's ordeal flared up again. Exactly the kind of low-grade agitation that responded nicely to the antianxiety medication that his colleagues now dished out in bulk. Knowing how quickly the body stopped making externally supplied substances, Weber tried not to take anything stronger than a multivitamin. Even these he had forgotten to pack, and so had taken nothing for the last three days. But so slight a change could not possibly account for this bout.

His fingers drummed on the booth's gray Formica. From two feet above them, he watched them type. A laugh bubbled up from his clenched belly and broke over him. He took his typing hands and cradled them in each other. Diagnosis stared him in the face. He, the last life scientist to go online, was suffering from e-mail withdrawal.

The waitress appeared at boothside, dressed like something out of a movie: half ward nurse, half meter maid. His age, if she was a day: thirty years too old to wait on tables. He grinned at her, a reprieved idiot. The waitress shook her head. "Don't you need a license to be that happy before you've had your coffee?" She held up two Pyrex coffee pots. He pointed to the one that wasn't orange.

He'd forgotten about midwesterners. He could no longer read them, his people, the residents of the Great Central Flyover. Or rather, his theories about them, honed through his first twenty years of life, had died from lack of longitudinal data. They were, by various estimates, kinder, colder, duller, shrewder, more forthright, more covert, more taciturn, more guarded, and more gregarious than the mode of the country's bean curve. Or else they *were* that mode: the fat, middle part of the graph that fell away to nothing on both coasts. They'd become an alien species to him, although he was one of them, by habit and birth.

He rubbed his bald spot and shook his head. With a little more edge, she asked, "What can I get you, hon?" He looked around the booth, confused. A half-sigh slipped out of her, the first of a long day. "You need a menu? We've got one of everything."

He raised his eyebrows. "Spinach crêpes?"

Her mouth barely tightened. "Fresh out. Anything else, though."

When she left with his order—*two over easy, with twin pigs*—he fished out his absurd cell phone. Like carrying around a little science-fiction phaser in his pocket. He'd slipped it into his trousers when he left his room, already contemplating a double descent into vice. He checked his watch, adding an hour for New York. Still too early. He eavesdropped on the table of weathered men, but what little they said was pressed into so fierce a shorthand that it might as well have been Pawnee. One of the circle, a bulbous face with luxurious ear and nose hair, whose blood-red cap read "IBP," worked away on a toothpick, carving it into a tiny totem pole with his deft incisors. "You can't let yourself get cocky," the man said. "Those Arabs will walk across a desert to take revenge on a mirage."

"Well, the Bible near says as much, already," his tablemate agreed.

No need to alarm Sylvie, really. She could tell him nothing. Had there been anything wrong, she'd have mentioned it the night before. Besides, if she caught him using a cell phone from a public place to quell a nervous feeling, she'd never let him live it down.

The waitress brought his sausage and eggs. "You did say

wheat toast, didn't you, dear?" He nodded. They hadn't mentioned toast, as far as Weber could remember. She poured him fresh coffee and turned toward the farmers' table. She stopped and swung back around to him. "You're the brain man from New York? The one who came out for a look at Mark Schluter."

He flushed. "That's right. How . . . ?"

"Wish I could tell you it was psychic powers." She spiraled the coffee pots near her ears. "My niece is a friend of the boys. She showed me a book of yours. Said you were out. We all think it's a tragedy, what's happened to Mark. But there's some who say that if it hadn't been that particular accident, it would've been another much like it. Bonnie says he's pretty different these days. Not that he wasn't kinda different before."

"He's bruised up, yes. But the brain is a surprising place. You'd be shocked what it can recover from."

"This is what I am forever trying to tell my husband."

Something clicked in him. He felt the thrill of dredging up something too small to merit remembering. "Your niece. Is she thin, light-complected? Long, straight, black hair down below her shoulders? Does she knit her own clothes?"

The waitress threw out one hip and tipped her head. "Now, I know for a fact she hasn't met you yet."

He spiraled his hands by his ears. "Psychic powers."

"Ho-kay," she said. "You got my dollar. I'll go buy your damn book."

She went to the circle of men and topped off their coffees. They flirted with her outrageously, joking about her pair of hot, bottomless pots. The same jokes that filled Long Island diners, jokes Weber had long ago stopped hearing in his native country. She leaned into the group, and they spoke together in soft voices. Surely about him. The alien species.

214

She came back his way, waving coffee pots in triumph. "You were looking at pictures of her at Pioneer Pizza. That fellow there—" She pointed with the decaf. "I won't say 'gentleman'—has a daughter who waited on you."

Weber pressed his hand to his forehead. "I think I'm outnumbered here."

"Small town for you, i'nit? Everybody's somebody's kin. Take that plate for you, hon? Or are you still working on it?"

"No, no. My labors now have ended."

As soon as his waitress left, dread washed back over him. Coffee was a mistake, after such a night. He never drank caffeinated anymore. Sylvie had kept him clean for close to two years. Sausage, too: a gross miscalculation. Four days in Nebraska; four days away from the lab, the office, the writing desk. He checked his watch; still too early to call out east. But he called Bob Cavanaugh's cell so infrequently that he'd earned the right to abuse it now.

His editor's preemptive "Gerald!" knocked Weber back. Caller ID: one of the world's truly evil technologies. The receiver was not supposed to know the sender before the sender knew the receiver. Weber's own cell phone had Caller ID built into the dial screen. But he always averted his eyes. Cavanaugh sounded pleased. "I know why you're calling!"

The words crawled up Weber's spine. "Do you?"

"You haven't seen them yet? I sent them as attachments, yesterday."

"Seen what? I'm on the road. Nebraska. I haven't—"

"God help you. What is it, still smoke signals out there?"

"No, I'm sure they . . . I just haven't . . ."

"Gerald. Why are you whispering?"

"Well, I'm in a public place." He looked around. No one in the restaurant was looking at him. They didn't have to.

"Gerald Weber!" Affectionate but merciless. "You aren't calling at this hour to ask *how things are going*?"

"Well, not entirely, no. I just—"

"Slippery slope, Gerald. Three more books and you'll be asking for sales figures. I, for one, am delighted to witness your descent into humanity. Well, set your mind at rest. We're off on a pretty good foot."

"A pretty good foot? Is the creature in question a biped?"

"Ah, biology humor. The *Kirkus* review is a little mixed, but the *Booklist* is to die for. Hang on. I'm on the train. I copied myself on the laptop. I'll read you the highlights."

Weber listened. This couldn't be it. He couldn't be worried about the book. *The Country of Surprise* was the richest thing he'd ever written. It consisted of a dozen re-created case histories of patients who'd suffered what Weber studiously refused to call brain damage. Each of his twelve subjects had been changed so profoundly by illness or accident that each called into question the solidity of the self. We were not one, continuous, indivisible whole, but instead, hundreds of separate subsystems, with changes in any one sufficient to disperse the provisional confederation into unrecognizable new countries. Who could take issue with that?

Listening to the review, Weber was all islands. Cavanaugh stopped reading. Weber was supposed to respond. "Does that please you?" he asked his editor.

"Me? *I* think it's great. We're using it for the ad."

Weber nodded, to someone half a continent away. "What didn't *Kirkus* like?"

Another silence at the other end. Cavanaugh, finessing. "Something about the case histories being too anecdotal. Too much philosophy and not enough car chases. They may have used the word *portentous*."

"Portentous in what sense?"

"You know, Gerald, I wouldn't worry about it. Nobody can discover you anymore. You've become a big target; more points for taking you down than for praising you. It won't hold us up in the slightest."

"Do you have the piece handy?"

Cavanaugh sighed and retrieved the file. He read it to Weber. "There. Masochist. Now forget it. Fuck the peasants. So what are you doing in Nebraska? Something to do with the new project, I hope?"

Weber flinched. "Oh, you know me, Bob. Everything's the new project."

"Are you examining someone?"

"A young accident victim who thinks his sister is an impostor."

"Strange. That's what my sister thinks of me."

Weber laughed, dutifully. "We all play ourselves."

"This is for the new one? I thought I was buying a book about memory."

"That's what's so interesting. His sister matches everything he remembers about her, but he's ready to discard memory in favor of gut reaction. All the remembered evidence in the world can't hold a candle to low-level *hunch*."

"Wild. What's the prognosis?"

"You'll have to buy the book, Robert. Twenty-five bucks, at your local chain."

"At that price, I'll wait to read the reviews first."

They hung up. Weber snapped back to the restaurant, the smell of bacon grease. The reception of his work was almost irrelevant. Only the act of honest observation mattered. And on that score he was covered. The morning's anxiety had been an aberration. He couldn't imagine what had triggered it.

217

Perhaps that woman Gillespie's unspoken accusation. He drained his coffee, searching the cup bottom. At the far table, the farmers exchanged jokes about agricultural extension agents. Weber listened without following.

"So the first fella says, 'This bug don't chew and spit up its cud like the other one.' 'Naw,' the second fella tells him. 'This one is a non-compost mantis.'"

His waitress reappeared. "Get you anything else, dear?"

"Just the check, thanks. Oh. And could I ask you something?" He felt mildly queasy again. Nothing. "You say that everyone is somebody's kin out here. How about the Schluters?"

She gazed out the window, on a street slowly filling with moving bodies. "The father was kind of a loner. Joan Swanson had some family down in Hastings. But, you know, she was the kind of person who believed that the Kingdom was coming tomorrow afternoon, at 4:15 p.m. And nobody she knew was ready to make the cut. Tends to drive even family away." She shook her head sadly and stacked the dirty dishes. "No, not much safety net for those two kids."

He returned to Good Samaritan for a follow-up with Dr. Hayes. They reviewed Weber's three days of materials. Hayes studied the GSR results, facial recognition scores, and psychological profiles. He asked a dozen questions, of which Weber could answer only a third. Hayes was impressed. "Strangest thing you could hope to see, and still come out intact!" He smacked the sheaf of notes. "Well, Doctor, you've raised my appreciation for the case. I suppose that's good science for you. But what's indicated now? How do we treat the condition and not just the symptom?"

Weber grimaced. "I'm not sure I know the difference,

here. The literature has no systematic treatment studies. No real sample size to work with. Psychiatric origins are rare enough. Trauma-induced cases are almost fiction. If you want my opinion . . ."

The neurologist bared his palms: no sharp implements. "No turf in medicine. You know that."

If Weber knew anything from a lifetime of research, it was exactly the opposite. "I'd recommend intensive, persistent cognitive behavioral therapy. It's a conservative course, but worth pursuing. Let me give you a recent article."

Hayes raised an eyebrow. "I suppose," he said. "I suppose we could even get spontaneous melioration."

Weber countered the attack. "It has happened. CBT has a track record in delusions. If nothing else, it can help address the anger and paranoia."

Everything about Hayes radiated healthy skepticism. But the first rule of medicine was to do *something*. Useful or worthless, however irrelevant or unlikely—act. Hayes stood and offered Weber his hand. "I'll be happy to refer him to Psych. And I look forward to seeing your piece, wherever it appears. Remember to spell my name with an 'e.'"

There remained only to say goodbye. Weber arrived at Dedham Glen after Mark's afternoon physical therapy. Karin was there, a chance to combine both farewells. He saw them from a distance, out on the front grounds, Karin sprawled on the grass fifty yards off, like some quarantined babysitter, while Mark sat on a metal bench underneath a cottonwood next to a woman Weber instantly recognized without having met. Bonnie Travis wore a sleeveless baby-blue blouse and denim skirt. Having removed his knit cap, she was placing a garland of woven dandelions around Mark Schluter's head. She planted a twig in his hands, a garden Zeus's scepter. Mark wallowed in the treatment. They looked up as Weber approached across the lawn, and Bonnie's face broke out in a smile that could only have arisen in a state with fewer than twenty-two people per square mile. "Hey! I know you. You look just like your photograph."

"You, too," Weber answered.

Mark doubled over giggling. Only grabbing Bonnie kept him from falling off the bench.

"What?" Bonnie begged, laughing along. "What'd I say?"

"You're both nuts." Mark strafed them with his scepter.

"Splain, Markie."

"Well, first off, a photo's flat? And it's, like, this big."

Bonnie Travis cackled like a fiend. It struck Weber that they'd been recreating before his arrival, although he smelled nothing. Karin stood and walked over to Weber, her face filled with suspicion. "This is it, isn't it?"

Mark reeled. "What's happening? You exposed her? You're arresting her?"

Weber addressed Karin. "I've spoken with Dr. Hayes. He'll refer you to intensive cognitive behavioral therapy, as we discussed."

"She's going to the slammer?" Mark grabbed Bonnie's forearm. "See? What'd I tell you? You didn't believe me. This woman's got a problem."

"You'll be involved," Weber told her. As promises went, this was the feeblest.

Karin's eyes interrogated Weber. "You're not coming back?"

He gave her the look of friendly respect that had won him the trust of hundreds of altered, anxious people—all the reassurance he had just last night misplaced.

220

"You're leaving?" Bonnie pouted. In truth, she looked nothing like her picture. "But you just got here."

Mark jerked up. "Hang on. No, Shrinky. Don't go. I forbid you!" He pointed his imperial trident at Weber. "You said you'd get me out of this joint. Who's gonna spring me if you don't?"

Weber arched his eyebrows but said nothing.

"Man! I gotta get home. Get back to work. That job is the only good thing I've got going. They'll shit-can me if I hang out here any longer."

Karin palmed her own temples. "Mark, we've been over this. You're on disability. If the doctors feel you need more therapy, IBP's insurance will . . ."

"I don't need therapy; I need work. If those health people would just get off my back. I don't mean you, Shrinky. Your head's in the right place, at least."

Mark had accepted Weber as spontaneously as he rejected his own sister. Nothing Weber had done deserved such trust. "Keep working on yourself, Mark." Weber cringed at the sound of his own words. "You'll be home in no time."

Mark looked away, crushed. Bonnie leaned over and put her arm around him. He made a sound like a slapped dog. "Handing me back over to her! And after I *proved* . . ."

"Excuse me," Weber said. "I need to check some things with the staff before I go." He headed back to the facility and slipped inside. The reception area looked like the starting line of a wheelchair race. Weber approached the desk and asked for Barbara Gillespie. His pulse raced, vaguely criminal. The receptionist paged Barbara. She appeared, unsettled by the sight of him. Her eyes, that green alert: leave now. She tried for lightness. "Uh-oh. A medical authority."

He found himself wanting to jest back. So he didn't. "I've been speaking with Neurology at Good Samaritan."

"Yes?" Instant professional register. Something in her knew what he was after.

"They've agreed to some CBT. I'd like to enlist your help. You have . . . such good rapport with him. Clearly, he dotes on you."

She turned cautious. "CBT?"

"I'm sorry. Cognitive behavioral therapy." Strange that she didn't know. "Would you be interested?"

She smiled, despite herself. "On some days, yes. Definitely."

He barked a single-syllable laugh. "I'm with you on that. I often . . ."

She nodded, reading him without explanation, the lightest touch. It struck him again, her absurd rank. Yet she excelled at what she did. Who was he to promote her beyond that calling? They shared a nervous moment, both of them searching for the final, forgotten detail. But no such detail existed, and he wouldn't invent one.

"Thank you, then," she told him. "Take care." The words sounded hopelessly midwestern. Yet her voice—so coastal.

He rushed it out. "Can I ask you something? Have you, by any chance, read anything of mine?"

She looked around the room for support. "Yikes. Is this an exam?"

"Of course not." He backed away.

"Because if it is, I'll need to study first."

He waved apology, mumbled his thanks, and broke for the outdoors. He imagined her eyes on his back all the way down the walk. He felt as he rarely did, as if he'd botched an interview. The morning's nausea followed him down the walk.

Flanked by the two women, Mark sat enthroned on his bench while a smattering of rehab residents, caretakers, and visitors wandered the grounds of his lowland Olympus. A garland of dandelions, a scepter of cottonwood: how Weber would remember him. In Weber's brief absence, Mark had changed again. The bitterness at betrayal had fled. He held up his rod and waved it at Weber in benediction. "Godspeed, voyager. We send you back out upon your restless search for new planets."

Weber stopped in mid-step. "How on earth . . . ? What a bizarre coincidence."

"There's no such thing as coincidence," Bonnie said, her words a halo.

"There's nothing *but* coincidence," Karin countered.

Mark giggled. "What do you mean? Wait, wait: I mean . . ." He dropped his voice, mocking Weber's authoritative baritone. "I mean: '*How* do you mean?'"

"My daughter's an astronomer. That's her work. She looks for new planets."

"Dude," Mark drawled. "You already told me."

The fact shook him worse than the imagined coincidence. The sleepless night, the hot, sticky air wrecked his concentration and scattered his memory. He needed to be gone. He had two conference keynotes to deliver over the next three weeks, then a trip to Italy with his wife before classes in the fall.

Karin walked him to the parking lot. Her disappointment had deepened into stoic despair. "I guess I was expecting too much. When you told me about the brain being so surprising . . . ?" She waved her fingers in front of her face. "I know. I'm not saying . . . Can you just tell me one thing? Don't soften this."

Weber braced.

"He must truly hate me, right? Some resentment so deep,

223

to produce this. To single me out. Every night I lie in bed trying to imagine what I did to him, that he needs to erase me. I can't remember anything that deserves this. Am I just repressing . . . ?"

He took her arm again, stupidly, as he had just three days back, when they first walked this path. "This isn't about you. There is probably a lesion . . ." Just the opposite of what he'd argued with Dr. Hayes. Obscuring the dynamics of most interest to him. "We talked about this. It's a feature of Capgras. The subject only misidentifies the people closest to him."

She snorted, acrid. "You always double the one you love?"

"Something like that."

"So it *is* psychological."

Aggravating hunch, in the mouth of another. "Look. You haven't been singled out."

"Yes I have. He's accepting Rupp now."

"I don't mean Rupp. There's his dog."

She freed her arm, ready to be hurt. Then she softened in a way Weber hadn't yet seen. "Yes. You're right. And he loves Blackie more than anything that moves."

At the curb, Weber made to shake her hand. With last-minute guilt, she embraced him. He stood still and suffered it. "Tell me if anything changes," he said.

"Even if it doesn't," she promised, and turned away.

He woke early again, in fresh panic. The ceiling of a foreign room materialized just inches from his face. He sucked air, but his lungs wouldn't expand. Not quite 2:30 a.m. By 3:15, he was still wondering how he'd forgotten telling Mark about Jess. He fought the urge to get up and listen to the session tapes. By 4:00, he took his vitals and thought he might be looking at something serious. When he could no longer lie still, he got up, showered, dressed, packed, checked out, and, hours early, drove the rental back east to the Lincoln airport, on the razor-like, featureless interstate.

As the plane passed over Ohio, he rallied. He looked down on a cloud-covered Columbus, imagining invisible landmarks under the patchy blanket. Places from a third of a century ago: the sprawling, centerless campus. The dilapidated student suburb where he and Sylvie had shared a bungalow. Downtown Columbus, the Scioto, the time warp of German Village, Short North, with its great used bookstore where he'd taken Sylvie on their first date. He still had the entire map, clearer with eyes closed.

By the wrinkled hills of Pennsylvania, his Nebraska interlude began to seem no more than a fleeting deficit. When he touched down at LaGuardia, he was himself again. His Passat waited in the long-term lot. The brittle, collaborative madness of the Long Island Expressway never looked more familiar or more beautiful. And at its far end—the familiar anonymity of home.

PART THREE

GOD LED ME TO YOU

I once saw, on a flowerpot in my own living room, the efforts of a field mouse to build a remembered field. I have lived to see this episode repeated in a thousand guises, and since I have spent a large portion of my life in the shade of a nonexistent tree, I think I am entitled to speak for the field mouse.

—Loren Eiseley, *The Night Country*, "The Brown Wasps"

When animals and humans still shared the same language, the Cree recount, Rabbit wanted to go to the moon. Rabbit asked the strongest birds to take him, but Eagle was busy and Hawk couldn't fly so high. Crane said he would help. He told Rabbit to hold on to his legs. Then he went for the moon. The journey was long and Rabbit was heavy. Rabbit's weight stretched out Crane's legs and bloodied Rabbit's paws. But Crane reached the moon, with Rabbit hanging on to him. Rabbit patted Crane in thanks, his hands still bleeding. So Crane got his long legs and blood-red head.

Back then, too, a Cherokee woman was courted by both Hummingbird and Crane. She wanted to marry Hummingbird, because of his great beauty. But Crane proposed a race around the world. The woman agreed, knowing Hummingbird's speed. She didn't remember that Crane could fly at night. And, unlike Hummingbird, Crane never tired. Crane flew in straight lines, where Hummingbird flew in every direction. Crane won the race with ease, but the woman still rejected him.

All the humans revered Crane, the great orator. Where cranes gathered, their speech carried miles. The Aztecs called themselves the Crane People. One of the Anishinaabe clans was named the Cranes—*Ajijak* or *Businassee*—the Echo Makers. The Cranes were leaders, voices that called all people

229

together. Crow and Cheyenne carved cranes' leg bones into hollow flutes, echoing the echo maker.

Latin *grus*, too, echoed that groan. In Africa, the crowned crane ruled words and thought. The Greek Palamedes invented the letters of the alphabet by watching noisy cranes in flight. In Persian, *kurti*, in Arabic, *ghurnuq*: birds that awaken before the rest of creation, to say their dawn prayers. The Chinese *xian-he*, the birds of heaven, carried messages on their backs between the sky worlds.

Cranes dance in southwestern petroglyphs. Old Crane Man taught the Tewa how to dance. Australian aborigines tell of a beautiful and aloof woman, the perfect dancer, turned by a sorcerer into a crane.

Apollo came and went in crane form, when visiting the world. The poet Ibycus, in the sixth century B.C., beaten senseless and left for dead, called out to a passing flock of cranes, who followed the assailant to a theater and hovered over him until he confessed to the astonished crowd.

In Ovid's *Metamorphoses*, Hera and Artemis turn Gerania into a crane, to punish the Pygmy queen for her vanity. The Irish hero Finn fell off a cliff and was caught in the air by his grandmother, when she changed into a crane. If cranes circled overhead above American slaves, someone would die. The First Warrior who fought to create ancient Japan took the form of a crane at death and flew away.

Tecumseh tried to unite the scattered nations under the banner of Crane Power, but the Hopi mark for the crane's foot became the world's peace symbol. The crane's foot—*pie de grue*—became that genealogist's mark of branching descent, *pedigree*.

To make a wish come true, the Japanese must fold a thousand paper cranes. Twelve-year-old Sadako Sasaki, stricken with "atom bomb sickness," made it to 644. Children worldwide send her thousands, every year.

Cranes help carry a soul to paradise. Pictures of cranes line the windows of mourning houses, and crane-shaped jewelry adorns the dead. Cranes are souls that once were humans and might be again, many lives from now. Or humans are souls that once were cranes and will be again, when the flock is rejoined.

Something in the crane is trapped halfway, in the middle between now and when. A fourteenth-century Vietnamese poet sets the birds forever halfway through the air:

Clouds drift as days pass;
Cypress trees are green beside the altar,
The heart, a chilly pond under moonlight.
Night rain drops tears of flowers.
Below the pagoda, grass traces a path.
Among the pine trees, cranes remember
The music and songs of years ago.
In the immensity of sky and sea,
How to relive the dream before the lamp of that night?

When animals and people all spoke the same language, crane calls said exactly what they meant. Now we live in unclear echoes. The turtledove, swallow, and crane keep the time of their coming, says Jeremiah. Only people fail to recall the order of the Lord.

Something was wrong, the moment Karin called upstairs to his hotel room. His voice didn't match the picture on his books. Its folksy tone broadcast compassion, but his words were pure health professional. In the flesh, he looked like one of those poised, balding experts who sit on New England porch swings in autumn answering questions for edutainment TV in maddeningly soft, self-assured voices. The man who came to Nebraska wasn't the author of those rich, embracing books. When she'd tried to present Mark's history, Gerald Weber failed to honor what he claimed lay at the heart of all good medicine. He didn't listen. She might as well have been speaking to her ex-boss, to Robert Karsh, or even to her own father.

Four days later the national expert disappeared. He did nothing but administer a few tests and tape a few conversations, gathering material for his own ends. Helpless to treat the problem itself, he prescribed nothing but a vague program of cognitive behavioral therapy. He blew into town, toyed with everyone's hopes, even played on Mark's friendship. Then he blew out again, suggesting that all parties just learn to live with the syndrome. She had trusted him, and he'd delivered nothing but philosophy.

Yet true to herself, she never once confronted him. Up to the moment that he turned his back on them, she flattered the man's credentials, sure that if she were just polite enough, this gray-haired, bearded, well-spoken specialist would defeat Capgras and retrieve both her brother and her. Daniel had asked several times to meet the doctor. She'd put him off. Daniel never called her on it, but he didn't have to. A week after Weber left, the obvious hit her: she'd preened for this old man. Anything, to win his help.

Three weeks after the neuroscientist abandoned them, Karin was playing Ping-Pong with Mark, in the day room. Mark liked the game enough that he'd play even with her, providing she never won. Barbara rushed in, excited. "Dr. Weber is going to be on *Book TV* tomorrow. Reading from his new work."

"Shrinky on television? *Real* television? Like, nationwide? I told you that the man was famous, but would you believe me? He's going to be a household word."

"*Book TV?*" Karin asked. How did you hear about this?" The aide shrugged. "Pure luck."

"Were you watching for this?" Karin asked. "Or did he tell you . . . ?"

Barbara flushed. "I keep an eye on that cable program. Old, bad habit. I'm down to only a few shows I can watch safely. The ones where nothing explodes and where they don't tell me when to laugh."

Mark tossed his paddle in the air and almost caught it. "The Incredible Shrinking Man, on the idiot box. Can't miss that, now can we?"

The next day, the three of them huddled around the set in Mark's room. Karin chewed her cuticles, even before they introduced the man. Humiliating, watching someone you knew play himself in front of cameras. Barbara was flinching, too. She chattered more in the six minutes of Gerald Weber's introduction than she had in six weeks of caring for Mark. Karin finally had to shush her.

Only Mark enjoyed the proceedings. "The home-team favorite is stepping up to the plate in the clutch situation. The crowd is nervous. They're looking for the long ball." But when Dr. Weber finally strode out to the podium in front of the restrained *Book TV* audience, Mark cried, "What the hell's going on? Is this some idea of a joke?"

Both women tried to calm him. Mark rose to his feet, a pillar of righteousness. "What kind of bull balls is this? That's supposed to be Shrinky? Not even close."

233

Under the television lights, distorted by broadcast and the strain of public appearance, the man was indeed changed. Karin glanced at Barbara, who returned the look, her thick eyebrows crumpled. Weber's hair now swept back dramatically over his thinning crown. The beard had been teased out, florid, almost French. And the dark suit had vanished in favor of a collarless burgundy shirt that appeared to be silk. He seemed taller on camera, and his shoulders flared, almost combative. When he started to read, prose poured out of him in Old Testament cadences. The words themselves were so wise, so attuned to the subtle nuances of human nature that they seemed written by someone already dead. This was the real Gerald Weber, who, for obscure reasons, on his short Nebraska junket, had hidden himself under an empty wheat bushel.

Mark paced in tight, outraged circles. "Who's this guy supposed to be? Billy Graham or someone?" Karin nodded like a bobblehead. Barbara couldn't take her eyes off the speaking image. "Somebody's taking that studio audience for a ride. None of them have seen the real Shrinky, up close and personal. And nobody knows to ask us!"

Karin blocked out her brother and listened. Weber read:

Conciousness works by telling a story, one that is whole, continuous, and stable. When that story breaks, consciousness rewrites it. Each revised draft claims to be the original. And so, when disease or accident interrupts us, we're often the last to know.

The words of the man rolled over Karin Schluter, seducing her all over again. "You're right," she told Mark. "You are exactly right." Nobody had seen the real Weber. Not the New York studio audience; not the three of them.

Mark stopped pacing to assess her. "What the hell do you know? You probably had something to do with this. You're the one who brought him here. Maybe *that's* the real Shrinky, and the Shrinky you passed off on us is a fraud."

Barbara reached up to rub his shoulders. He froze, like a kitten stroked between its eyes. Placid, Mark sat back down and watched. "We're more like coral reefs," Dr. Weber was reading. "Complex but fragile ecosystems . . ." The three of them stared at the performance of the stranger in the silk shirt. Weber told a story of a forty-year-old woman called Maria who suffered from something named Anton's syndrome.

> I sat and chatted with her in her impeccably furnished Hartford home. She was a lively, attractive woman who'd been a successful attorney for many years. She seemed happy and intact in every way, except that she thought she could see. When I suggested to her that she might actually be blind, she laughed at the absurdity and struggled to disprove me. This she attempted to do with remarkable vigor and skill, giving long, vivid descriptions of what was happening just then, outside her window. These scenes had great consistency and detail; she simply did not realize that the images were not coming in through her eyes . . .

The reading lasted no more than fifteen minutes. But all three were squirming in eternity as Weber finished the passage to polite applause. Then the questions began. A respectful student asked about the difference between scientific writing and writing for the public. A retired woman wanted to address the scandal of national health care. Then someone asked if Weber had any qualms about violating his subjects' privacy.

The cameras caught the writer's surprise. Hesitating, he said, "I hope not. There are protocols. I always disguise the names, and often the biographical details, when they're important. Sometimes one case history actually combines two or more stories, to bring out a condition's most salient features."

"You mean they're fiction?" asked another. Weber paused to think, and the camera grew restive. Karin returned to biting her cuticle and Barbara sat upright, a perfect statuette.

Mark spoke first, for all of them. "This totally blows. Can we see what's on Springer?"

The night Weber flew back east from the empty plains, he was all over Sylvie. Late June, but cool and piercing in Setauket, more like a North Shore golden fall than the start of summer. He picked up his car from the long-term lot at LaGuardia and listened to Brahms piano quartets all the way home on the absurdly clogged LIE. All the way out, he pictured his wife, thirty years of her changing face. He remembered that day, a decade or so into their marriage, when he'd asked her, surprised, "Is your hair getting straighter as we get older?"

"What are you talking about? My hair? I used to perm it. You didn't know that? Ah, scientists."

"Well. If it's not on a scan, it can't really be trusted."

She pummeled his soft underbelly, in reply.

But that first night back from Nebraska, he noticed. *Woman.* Maybe it was the dressing up. They had to go out that evening, to a fund-raiser in Huntington. Some halfway-house shelter that Sylvie's Wayfinders were sponsoring. She was dressed already when he pulled in. "Ger! There you are. I was getting nervous. You should have called me, let me know you were on the way."

"Called? I was in the car, Woman."

She laughed her laugh, helpless but to forgive. "You know that little phone you've been carrying around? It works while you're moving. One of its selling points. Never mind. I'm just glad that Tour Director got you home safely."

She wore a blouse of Italian silk, something new, pale bashful lilac, the color of first buds. Around her still-smooth neck hung a thin hank of freshwater pearls, and two tiny seashells clung to her ears. Who was this woman?

"Man. Don't just stand there! Philanthropists of all stripes have paid to see you in a monkey suit."

He undressed her that night, for the first time in years. Then he gazed on her, looking.

"Mmm," she said, ready to frolic too, if a little abashed at them both. She laughed at his touch. "Hmm? Where did this come from all the sudden? They put something in the water out there in Nebraska?"

They played with each other, with nothing left to learn. After, she lay on her back next to him, still breathing hard, holding his hand as if they were courting. She recovered words first. "As the Behaviorist said, 'That was clearly great for you. Was it good for me?' "

He had to snort, rolling onto his problem back and looking out over the rising hillock of his stomach. "I suppose it has been some time. Sorry about that, Woman. I'm not the man I was, back when."

She rolled onto her side and rubbed his shoulder, the one he'd blown out ten years ago, in his mid-forties, and never managed entirely to repair. "I like this part of life," she said. "Slower, fuller. I like that we don't have sex just all the time."

Vintage Sylvie. She meant: *much at all.* "It makes each experience . . . It's newer, somehow, when there's enough time in between to rediscover . . ."

"Inventive. Absolutely inspired. 'Rediscover.' Most people see the glass nine-tenths empty. My wife sees it one-tenth full."

"That's why you married me."

"Ah! But when I married you . . ."

She groaned. "The glass was one-tenth over the lip."

He spun over onto his sore shoulder and regarded her, alarmed. "Really? Did we have sex too often back then?"

Her laughs bobbled out of her, buggies over speed bumps. She pressed her face into the pillow, delighted and red. "I think that might be the first time in human history anyone ever asked that question anxiously."

He saw it in her face, the thought crossing into her before he could speak it out loud. "The relentlessness of marriage." He chuckled. Their old euphemism, picked up from a classic family saga they'd read out loud to each other, back in grad school. Later, after Jess, they amused each other by calling it *sexuality.* Mock clinical. Foreplay: *Are you at all disposed toward sexuality?* And afterward: *Some top-drawer sexuality, that.* Neuropsychology—the home version.

That night, her gaze found him through the folds of sheets, deeply amused by her pet possession, secure in her knowledge of him, constantly refreshed. "Somebody loves me," she sang, a sturdy tonette of an alto, half muffled by the pillow. "I wonder who?"

She fell asleep in minutes. He lay in the dark, listening to her snore, and after a while, the snore turned, for the first time ever in his ears, away from an inanimate rasp, like the creak of the bed, into the shush of an animal, something trapped but preserved in the body, vestigial, released through sleep by the pull of the moon.

With 100,000 copies in print and generally fair prepublication reviews, *The Country of Surprise* rolled out to a reading public hungry for the alien within. The book felt like the culmination of a long second career, one Weber never expected to have. He'd said nothing to anyone except Cavanaugh and Sylvie, but this book would be his last excursion of its kind. His next book, if he was given time to write it, would be for a very different audience.

He hated promotion, having to perform himself in public. He'd gotten away with it so far, thanks to skilled colleagues and motivated grad students covering in the lab. But he could not afford more time away from research, now that brain research had been thrown wide open. Imaging and pharmaceuticals were opening the locked-room mystery of the mind. The decade since the publication of Weber's first book had produced more knowledge about the final frontier than previous five thousand. Goals unimaginable when Weber began *The Country of Surprise* were now tossed around at the most reputable professional conferences. Esteemed researchers dared to talk about completing a mechanical model of memory, finding the structures behind qualia, even producing a full functional description of consciousness. No popular anthology Weber might compile could match such prizes.

The art of the meditative case history belonged to after-hours. Somehow it had muscled in and become his day job. Too soon for that. Ramon y Cabal, the Cronos in Weber's pantheon, said that scientific problems were never exhausted; only scientists were. Weber wasn't exhausted yet. The best was yet to be.

239

Yet he'd interrupted work to travel thousands of miles to the Central Plains to do the Capgras interview. Granted, his current lab project concerned left-hemisphere orchestration of belief systems and the alteration of memories to fit them. But anything he learned from talking to the Nebraska Capgras sufferer was anecdotal at best. A few days back at Stony Brook and he began to see the trip as the last of a long series of surveys that would now give way to more systematic, solid research.

Yet something in him did not like where knowledge was heading. The rapid convergence of neuroscience around certain functionalist assumptions was beginning to alienate Weber. His field was succumbing to one of those ancient urges that it was supposed to shed light on: the herd mentality. As neuroscience basked in its growing instrumental power, Weber's thoughts drifted perversely away from cognitive maps and neuron-level deterministic mechanisms toward emergent, higher-level psychological processes that could, on his bad days, sound almost like *élan vital*. But in the eternal split between mind and brain, psychology and neurology, needs and neurotransmitters, symbols and synaptic change, the only delusion lay in thinking that the two domains would remain separate for much longer.

Back at Dayton Chaminade High, Weber had begun intellectual life as a confirmed Freudian—brain as hydraulic pipe for mind's spectacular waterworks—anything to confound his priest teachers. By graduate school, he'd taken to persecuting Freudians, although he'd tried to avoid the worst Behaviorist excesses. When the cognitive counterrevolution broke, some small operant-conditioned part of him held back, wanting to insist, *Still not the whole story*. As a clinician, he'd had to embrace the pharmacology onslaught. Yet he'd felt a real sadness—the sadness of consummation—hearing a subject who'd struggled for years with anxiety, suicidal guilt, and religious zeal tell him, after the successful tuning of his doxepin dosages, "Doctor, I'm just not sure what I was so upset about, all that time."

He knew the drill: throughout history, the brain had been compared to the highest prevailing level of technology: steam engine, telephone switchboard, computer. Now, as Weber approached his own professional zenith, the brain became the Internet, a distributed network, more than two hundred modules in loose, mutually modifying chatter with other modules. Some of Weber's tangled subsystems bought the model; others wanted more. Now that the modular theory had gained ascendancy over most brain thinking, Weber drifted back to his origins. In what would surely be the final stage of his intellectual development, he now hoped to find, in the latest solid neuroscience, processes that looked like old depth psychology: repression, sublimation, denial, transference. Find them at some level *above* the module.

In short, it now began to occur to Weber that he may have traveled out to Nebraska and studied Mark Schluter in order to prove, to himself at least, that even if Capgras were entirely understandable in modular terms, as a matter of lesions and severed connections between regions in a distributed network, it still manifested in psychodynamic processes—individual response, personal history, repression, sublimation, and wish fulfillment that couldn't be reduced entirely to low-level phenomena. Theory might be on the verge of describing the brain, but theory alone could not yet exhaust *this brain*, hard-pressed by fact and frantic with survival: Mark Schluter and his impostor sister. The book waiting for Weber to write, after this book tour.

They took Mark home: no other place to take him. When the celebrity brain scientist left, offering his one slight recommendation, Dr. Hayes could no longer keep Mark under observation at Dedham Glen. Karin fought the decision tooth and nail. Mark, for his part, was more than ready to go.

Before he could move back into the Homestar, Karin had to move out. She'd lived in the modular home for months, keeping the dog alive, performing routine maintenance. She'd thrown out Mark's contraband and waged war against the invading plant and animal life. Now she had to erase all evidence that she'd ever occupied the campsite.

"Where will you go?" Daniel asked. They lay side by side, face up on his futon on his bare, oak floor. Six in the morning, Wednesday, deep in June. In recent weeks, she'd spent more nights in his monk's cell. She'd taken over his kitchen and sneaked cigarettes in his bathroom, running the water and blowing the smoke out the open window into the complicit air. But she never kept even a spare pair of socks in the empty drawer he prepared for her.

She rolled on her side, so he might spoon her. Talking was easier that way. Her voice was disembodied. "I don't know. I can't afford two leases. I can't even afford one. I . . . I've put my place in South Sioux up for sale. I didn't want to tell you. I didn't want . . . What am I doing here? How much longer can I . . . ? Back to zero, after everything that I've managed . . . But I can't leave him. You know what he's like now. You know what would happen, if I left him alone."

"He wouldn't be alone."

She spun around and stared at him in the growing light. *Whose side are you on?* "If I leave him to his friends, he'll be dead by the end of the year. They'll shoot him in some hunting accident. They'll have him out racing again."

"There are others of us around, to help look after him. I'm here."

She leaned in and pressed him. "Oh, Daniel. I don't get you. Why are you so good? What's in it for you?"

He put his hand on her flank and stroked, as he might stroke a newborn deer. "I'm a not-for-profit."

She ran a finger along his neck. He was like the birds. Once the route was taught him, he stayed on it, returning, so long as there was still a place, always turning home. "The two of you combined are breaking my heart."

They looked at each other, neither of them volunteering. He nodded just a little: totally ambiguous. "Small steps," he said.

She bowed her head, her copper waterfall. "I don't know what that means."

"Simple. You can be here. You can stay here, with me."

He could not have said it better. Neither concession nor command. Just a statement, the best possibility for them both. "Small steps," she said. Just for a little while. Just until Mark . . . "You won't resent me if . . . ?"

A reflex pain passed across his face. What had she ever let him resent? He shook his head, decency outweighing memory. "If you won't hold it against *me*."

"It won't be long," she promised him. "There's not much more I can do. Either he gets better soon or . . ." She stopped, seeing Daniel's face. She'd meant to reassure that she would not invade his territory. Only as she spoke the words did she hear them as a slap.

She leaned into him again, limbs tangling, fragile, the first time in years that they lingered with each other in broad daylight. She felt it in the pallet of his chest, tasted it in his mouth's pinched bliss. In the interests of getting wrong right, he might forgive her everything. Everything but safety and hiding.

She evacuated the Homestar, erasing her tracks. Daniel, the expert tracker who could hold still and disappear into thin air, helped. She restored Mark's chaos to the state she remembered. She scattered the CDs. She bought another girlie poster to replace the one she'd destroyed: a blond in a slightly torn gingham dress holding a large monkey wrench in greasy hands, poised over a blood-red pickup. She had no idea what to do about Blackie. She considered bringing the dog to Daniel's too, at least until they saw how Mark would be, once home. In his present state, Mark might attack the thing, lock it out of the house, feed it bulk laxatives. Daniel would have been fine with another creature sharing his sanctuary. But Karin couldn't do it to the dog.

Dr. Hayes signed off on the discharge, and Dedham Glen released Mark Schluter to the care of the only kin who recognized him, even if he failed to return the favor. Barbara asked if she could help.

"Bless you," Karin said. "I think I have Moving Day handled. It's next week I'm worried about. And the week after that. Barbara, what am I supposed to do? The insurance won't cover extended nursing, and I'm going to have to start working."

"I'll still be here. He'll have his regular appointments with the cognitive therapist. And I can come check in on him, if that would help."

"How? You've given us too much already. I can't even think about repaying . . ."

The aide radiated eerie calm. Her hand on Karin's shoulder carried absolute certainty. "Things work out. Everybody gets repaid, one way or another. Let's see how things go."

Karin asked Bonnie Travis to help her get Mark home. Mark made the rounds at the facility, saying goodbye to his fellow inmates. "See?" he told them. "It's not a death sentence. They let you go, eventually. If they don't, call me and I'll come bust you out."

But when Karin pulled up in her car, he refused to get in. He stood on the curb, surrounded by his bags. He was capless now, his hair a thin pelt. His face clouded, remembering. "You want to roll this little Jap thing off the road somewhere, with me inside. That's the plan? You want to finish what was supposed to happen the first time?"

"Mark, get in the car. If I wanted to hurt you, would I risk my own life doing it?"

"You hear that, everybody? You heard what the woman said?"

"Mark, please. You'll be fine. Just get in the car."

"Let me drive. I'll get in if you let me drive. See? She won't give me the keys. I always drive my sister everywhere. She never drives when we're together."

"Ride with me," Bonnie said.

He considered the suggestion. "That might work," he said. "But this woman has to wait here for ten minutes after we leave. I don't want her trying anything funny."

The air was ripe with manure and pesticide. The fields—matted soybeans, shin-high corn, pastures flecked with cows resigned to their fate—unrolled in all directions. When Karin reached the Homestar, Mark was on the front stoop, his head in Bonnie's lap, crying. Bonnie stroked the fuzz on his skull, doing her best to console him. Seeing Karin approach, Mark sat up and howled. "Just tell me what's going on. First my truck, then my sister. Now they've got my house."

His elbows flung upward, while his whole body cowered. His neck craned in three directions, as if the next attack might come from anywhere. She looked behind her, and through his eyes, saw the winking, familiar neighborhood go strange. She turned back to where he sat clawing his concrete front steps. He was staring at her, searching for someone, the one she had been once but wasn't any longer. The only one who might help him. His need for her tore her up, worse than her own helplessness.

The women consoled him for a long time. They pointed out the streets, the houses, the lone sugar maple he'd planted in the desert of lawn, the gouge in the left-hand garage edge that he'd made eight months before. Karin prayed for one of the neighbors to come out and say hello. But all living things hid themselves in the face of this epidemic.

Karin considered bundling him back into Bonnie's car and returning him to Dedham Glen. But his moaning gradually gave way to dazed chuckles. "They did an incredible job. They got almost everything right. Jesus! How much did this cost? It's like some billion-dollar film of my life. *The Harry Truman Story*."

At last he went inside. He stood next to Bonnie in the front room, head swiveling in amazement, his tongue clucking. "My father used to tell me they did the moon landing on a sound stage in Southern California. I always thought he was nuts."

Karin snorted. "He *was* nuts, Mark. You remember how he thought the navy could quantum-rearrange the molecules in a battleship to make it invisible?"

Mark studied her. "How do you know they can't?" He checked with Bonnie, who shrugged. He looked back at the life-sized image of his home, shaking his head in disbelief.

Karin sat on the fake sofa, large parts of her dying. This fog would never blow over. Soon her brother would be right: their whole life, a copy of itself. While Bonnie unloaded Mark's things from the car, Karin tried to rally. She took Mark on a tour of the house. She showed him the crack in the corner of the medicine-chest mirror. She raked through his clothes closet, all his summer cutoffs and legible T-shirts waiting for him. She opened the drawer full of loose photos, including dozens of the two of them together. She pointed out the magazine rack, with its three new back issues of *Truckin'* *Magazine*.

In all this sprawl, his eyes landed on her replacement poster. His face darkened. "That's not the picture I had up here."

Karin groaned. "Okay. Let me explain."

"That's not mine. I'd never touch a thing that looked like that. That's the crappiest body molding I've ever seen."

Karin blinked before realizing he meant the truck. "Mark, that's my fault. I tore yours. Accidentally. That's a replacement I put up."

He stopped and squinted at her. "Exactly the kind of shit my sister used to do."

For a moment, she could breathe. Her arms went out to him, tentative but desperate. "Oh, Mark! Mark . . . ? I'm sorry if anything I ever said or did . . ."

"But my sister would have known better than to replace a classic 1957 Chevy Cameo Carrier with some 1990 Mazda piece of crap."

She broke down. Her silent, curdled tears perplexed him enough that he touched one hand to her forearm. The gesture thrilled her more than anything since his return to speech. She composed herself, laughed off her sniffles, and dismissed the

247

moment with a wave. "Listen, Mark. I have to confess something. I never knew as much about the whole truck thing as I probably led you to believe."

"Exactly what I'm saying. But thanks for admitting it. Simplifies life a little."

He took over the tour, pointing out every beer coaster that had been moved since the night of his accident. He tsked as they walked, shaking his head and repeating, "No, no, no. This house is no Homestar."

Bonnie brought in his duffel bags. She started following him around. "We'll fix things, Marker. Get everything just the way you want."

Karin sat on the bed, head in hands, listening to Mark repudiate his beloved mail-order home. But the strength of his memory for the smallest particulars gave her forbidden hope. She herself could no longer recognize her own condo, on those quick trips to South Sioux City to ready it for sale.

"Wait," he said. "I know how to tell once and for all whether this house is real or not. You two stay here. Don't look! Don't let me catch either of you spying."

He headed toward the kitchen. Bonnie quizzed Karin with a look. Karin slumped, knowing what Mark was after. She heard him drop to his knees and root around in the cabinet underneath the sink. Some old, inherited shame stopped her from calling out, old family secrets that sealed them off from each other.

He came back triumphant. "I told you this place is a fake. Something of mine is missing. Something they wouldn't duplicate." He looked at Bonnie, significantly. Bonnie, leaning against a bar stool, glanced at Karin. Karin needed only say: *Mark, I flushed your stash down the toilet.* But she couldn't. Couldn't say she knew he was doing shit, maybe even on the night of the accident. It would make no difference, anyway. He'd just come up with another theory, untroubled by anything so slight as the facts.

Mark came and sat next to her on the sofa. He seemed about to put his arm around her. "I know you have to pretend ignorance. That's your job. I accept that. But just tell me whether I'm in danger. We've gotten to know each other well enough over the last couple of months for you to give me that much. You'd tell me if they were going to hurt me again, wouldn't you?"

Karin waved her hands, a chimp struggling with sign language. Bonnie answered for her. "Nobody's gonna hurt you, Mark. Not while we're around."

"I mean, Christ! They wouldn't go through all this expense if they just meant to finish the job that they bungled back on 2/20/02. Am I right? C'mon. Let's have a look outside."

He left the house and walked up Carson Street. The women followed. All twelve houses on his block were variations on the Homestar. The recently air-dropped subdivision contained the first new structures to be added to the backwater town of Farview since the farm crisis. Drapes fluttered up and down the street, but no one came outdoors to make small talk with a brain-damaged slaughterhouse machinist.

Mark strolled up the street, staggered. "This must have cost a fortune. I must be under massive observation. I only wish I knew why I've become so important."

Bonnie took his arm. Karin expected her to say something religious, about how God kept even the sparrows under massive observation. But she surprised Karin with her intelligence by saying nothing.

Mark spun a full circle. "I'd like to know where exactly we are."

Karin held her temples. "You saw how we came from town."

"Well, I was kind of keeping an eye on the rear window." He smiled, a little sheepish.

"South on County, and a straight shot west, eight miles down Greyser. Same as always. You saw everybody's farms."

He grabbed at her, stiffening. "Time out. Are you telling me that the *whole town* . . . ?"

Karin tittered. She felt herself losing it. The stress of daily life in her brother's newfound land was pulling her under. Kearney, Nebraska: a colossal fake, a life-sized, hollow replica. She'd thought as much herself, all the while growing up. And again, each time she returned during their mother's final illness. *Prairie World*. Her giggles came harder. She wheeled and looked at Bonnie, a paralyzed, shit-eating grin plastered on her face. The girl looked back, spooked, and not by Mark. "Help me," Karin managed, before breaking into more little laughs.

Something in the other woman rose to the challenge. Bonnie guided Mark back to the Homestar, leaning into him and tracing large ovals in his back as if practicing her cursive. "That's not what she's saying, Marker. She's saying this is it. Right here. Where you really live. And I'm telling you I will personally see to it that we get your nest exactly the way you want it."

"Serious? Would that include you moving in? Oh yeah, a woman's touch. The finer things in life. But I forget: you probably still want to hold out for the paperwork. Fully legal, and all that noise? No playing house?"

Bonnie blushed and steered him homeward. All back down the street, Mark pointed out little anomalies: a missing tree, the wrong car in a driveway. Every desperate feat of memory fed him a little. A neighbor's tool shed fifteen feet too far west left him exultant. His visual recall floored Karin. Damage had somehow unblocked him, removing the mental categories that interfered with truly seeing. Assumption no longer smoothed out observation. Every glance now produced its own new landscape.

Back at the house, Blackie had broken free from her backyard tether and was pacing the front steps, panting wildly. She held back, yipping, remembering her abuse at her master's hands at their last meeting. But longer memories got the better of her. As the humans approached, she bounded across the lawn, joyous and suffering, leaping forward but feinting sideways, ready to flee at the first confusion. Mark stood still, which emboldened the beast until she was all over him, throwing her paws against his torso, almost knocking him over. The lower the brain, the slower the fade. Love, in an earthworm, might never extinguish at all.

Mark took his pet's paws and danced her, a waltz with little conviction. "Look at this pathetic thing! It doesn't even know who it isn't. Somebody trained it to be my dog, and now it doesn't even know what else to be. I guess I'm going to have to take care of you, aren't I, girl? Who else will, if I don't?"

By the time the four of them got back inside, Mark was issuing a stream of authoritative commands to the ecstatic dog.

"So what the hell am I supposed to call you? Huh? What am I gonna call you? How about Blackie Two?"

The brute thing barked in ecstasy.

They're after Mark Schluter's ass: this much is obvious. A man would have to be a vegetable to miss that much. Setting him up in some kind of experiment, some of it so hokey that even a

251

child still stuck on Santa would snicker. But some of it so complex he can't even start figuring it.

Okay: something happened in the hospital, that night they operated. Some mistake they had to cover up. Or, no: the weirdness must have started hours before that. With the accident. Which clearly couldn't have been an accident. Great driver flips a fantastic-handling vehicle on a razor-straight road in the middle of nowhere? Sure; you might believe that, if you're brain dead.

But that's when it started, the switchings and impostors, all the medical crap to get Mark Schluter to think that he isn't who he thinks. He needs a witness, but nobody was there. Rupp, Cain: they swear they were nowhere. And the doctors surgically removed his memory of that night while he was on the operating table. The secret is out there, in the empty fields. But the fields are growing over, this summer's crop covering up the evidence. He needs a witness, but nobody saw what happened that night except the birds. Catch himself one of those cranes, one that was there, alongside the river. Find him a sandhill, and swear it in. Scan its brain.

Because it all started with the accident. Now everyone's all *Mark, Mark, he's different, he's losing his grip.* As if that's the issue. As if he's the one who's changed. The real deal is hidden behind doubles. He has only one clue. One solid thing beyond doubt: the note. The words from the person who found him, the one spectator to that night's events, before the weirdness set in. The note they tried to keep from him.

His only clue, so he's got to be careful. Can't act too eager. Take the days as they come. Rupp and Cain promise to take him truck shopping. Work is sending him checks for doing nothing. But that won't last forever; he's got to get back, eventually. For now, though, he sits tight and works his plan.

He asks Bonnie Travis to take him to church. The girl belongs to one of those renegade Protestant splinter cells called The Waiters in the Upper Room, a so-called religion that, in one of the screwed-uppedest things he's ever heard, actually has not-for-profit status. They meet early Sunday for marathon two-hour services in a converted real-estate office above the Second Life hobby shop. Bonnie has begged him for years to come to a service, to compensate for the assorted commandments they smashed together on Saturday nights.

He himself swore off religion the minute he turned sixteen and his father pronounced him fit for the damnation of his own choosing. Nobody's going to be comfortable with the whole Left Behind thing after growing up with a mother on a first-name basis with the Big Smiter Himself. It bugs the crap out of Bonnie when Mark busts Jesus' chops, so over the years they've gotten pretty good at ignoring the topic. It could be raining frogs and blood, and they'd be, like: *You bring your umbrella?* That's why, when Mark asks her to take him to the Upper Room, the woman acts like all the seven seals have just started barking.

Of course, Mark! Just say the word.

Like, what word do I need to say? *Methuselah? Vouchsafe?*

She laughs, at least. Sure; we can go anytime. This Sunday! And all the while, her face is going, *Is this a joke? I've been praying for this for years.*

She comes to get him in her car on Sunday morning. She's looking quite deluxe, in a short, sky-blue dress with white collar, like a chrome woman singer in an MTV video fantasy about a 1950 cornhusker girl's first communion. Really: he could pop himself off just looking at her, although that might not be entirely appropriate, given the circumstances. By the look she shoots him, he's made some miscalculation. Can't be his clothes: his fancy khakis—his wedding pants, Rupp calls them—a pretty clean denim shirt, and his best bolo tie. It's something else that he can't figure. Bonnie drives them to the Upper Room, all quiet. And she stays that way during the whole two-hour show, twitching her head side to side, just looking at him, like he's got a spider crawling out of his nose. Afterward, back in the car, tugging at the hem of her dress like she suddenly doesn't want it to be all that short, she's pissed.

You didn't hardly listen to one single word that Reverend Billy had to say.

I did. The whole bit about the repopulation of Palestine and the fulfillment of prophecy and whatnot.

And you wouldn't break bread with us.

Well, you can't be sure where that stuff has been.

Why did you bother coming? You spent the whole time just eyeing the congregation and waving that little note around like some kind of summons.

How can he tell her? If there's really some Guardian Angel hiding out, refusing to identify himself, claiming *God led me to you*, he's probably hanging somewhere like the Upper Room.

Bonnie comes back later that afternoon with his wannabe sister, while he's going through churches in the Kearney yellow pages. It hurts his head to look at the list, and maybe he's bitching a bit.

Jesus H. Crimmeny! Look at them all. They're breeding like bugs. What's a town this size need with so many churches? We've got more of these denomination things than we have people.

Bonnie slips behind him and rubs his back. This could become comforting. But counterfeit Karin sits down next to him and gets up in his face.

254

What is it, Mark? What do you want? We can help you.

He makes himself a stone. He tells them: I can do a couple every Sunday.

I can go with you, says Bonnie, pressing his shoulders.

But . . . how? These aren't your churches.

She jerks back and laughs, like he's being funny. They aren't yours, either, Mark!

He runs his hand down the yellow-page list. You know what I'm saying. These things are all—whatever. Baptist. Methodist, and such. You're an Upstairs Roommate.

So? They're not going to stop me at the door.

They might. Homo sapiens can be very territorial.

If they stop me, why wouldn't they stop you?

Because I'm nothing. Nobody stops a nothing from slipping in anywhere. They can still get to a nobody; convert him.

Pseudo-Sister reaches out to touch him, but stops. Mark. Honey. You want to know who wrote that note?

Like she's graduating to mind reading.

Maybe we can take an ad out in the newspaper or something.

No ads! He probably yells a bit. Freaks even himself out, a little. But it's just that whoever wrote the note might also know what happened to his sister. And if the people who got to his sister get to the note-writer first . . .

This upsets the sister stand-in. For some reason, it's more than an act. Pulling her hair, like Karin always does. Bugs the hell out of him.

What can I do, Mark? Okay, so whoever left you the note believes in God. In guardian angels. Everyone in Nebraska believes in guardian angels! I'd believe in them myself, if . . .

She stops, like she almost gives the game away. If what? he says. If *what*?

She won't answer, so he gets a scrap of paper and starts copying down addresses: *Alpha and Omega Church of Jesus Christ. Antioch Bible . . .*

Mark, I'm telling you. This is crazy. It's a total crapshoot.

Not as big a crapshoot as this guardian finding me out there in the dark, clear off the road. In the middle of winter. The middle of nowhere. What are the odds of that?

Bonnie, at least, is as good as her word. She thinks she's going to save Mark's soul. Maybe she is. They dress up every Sunday and go churchgoing, like a courting couple out of some pioneer schoolbook. Sex afterward and he'd be in heaven. But the best he can hope for after the service is a good buffet. They go to Phil's or the Hearth Stone, places with high old-folk turnover. It must be an old person, given the spidery scrawl. At both the churches and the restaurants, he keeps the note out in plain view. Even walks around with it, waving it under strangers' noses. But nobody even nibbles. And they're not faking ignorance. He'd know faking, blindfolded.

He overhears the Special Sister Agent talking to Bonnie, when they come back. She wants all the details. What's in it for B-Baby, to be filing reports on him? Distinctly possible that she's his leash, that she's helping set up the whole charade. But he can't confront her. Not just yet.

The Woman Who Would Be Karin keeps coming by, pretty much every day. She brings him groceries, and doesn't want cash for them. All very suspicious, but the food is mostly sealed, and by and large it tastes pretty great. Sometimes she cooks for him. Go figure. But it seems like a sweet deal, at least until he learns what it's going to cost him.

She corners him one afternoon when he's home alone,

digging a new post hole for his mailbox. He's gotten nothing but junk since leaving Dead Man's Glands. They put the mailbox in the wrong place. Throws the mailman off. His sister might have been writing him this whole time, and no one would know.

It's not where it was, before, he tells her.

She pretends to be horrified. Where was it before?

Hard to say, exactly. You can't measure against anything. What can you use as a baseline? Everything's a few feet off.

He looks out toward the few scattered trees fringing River Run Estates. Beyond the stand of houses, a single, green cornfield ripples out to the horizon. For a minute, the ground liquefies, like he and his real sister used to make it do when they were kids, spinning like tops, then slamming to a standstill. He looks at Karin's substitute; she, too, looks wobbly.

Mark, we need to talk. About the note.

His whole body surges up out of the post hole. You *know* something?

I . . . wish I did. Now, Mark. Mark! Stop it. Listen to me. If whoever wrote this note hasn't gotten in touch by now, it's because they want to be . . . selfless. Nameless. They don't want to be a hero or take credit. They don't want you to know who they are. They just want you to live your life.

He spreads the post hole digger and drives it into the parched dirt. Then what fucking good is leaving a note? Why bother leaving one at all?

They wanted you to feel protected. Connected.

Connected? Connected to what? He slams the shovel to the ground and kicks it, his arms twisting like bull snakes. Mr. Invisible Nameless Angel? That's supposed to make me feel safe? Connected?

Why do you need to—?

He almost jabs her. Whoever wrote this note saved my life. If I could find him, then I might find out what . . .

It gets to him: stupid, stupid. But he doesn't even care if she sees him kind of cry. She joins in. Whatever. Monkey see.

I know. I know what you're feeling, she says. And it's almost like she does. She says: Do you really need to put a face to this note? Would it matter if you found out that they . . . ? Mark, stop. No! Just tell me what you're thinking. Do you just want to thank them? Do you want . . . I don't know. Are you thinking you might get to know them? Make friends?

It's like she's just materialized out of nowhere. Suddenly trying to be the person she was just imitating.

I don't give a good flying leap who the guy really is. He could be a ninety-year-old Lithuanian girl-groper.

So why are you trying so hard to find him?

Mark Schluter grabs his head in both hands and rattles it. Guardian devils, everywhere. His muddy work boots kick at the earth, trying to destroy the fresh hole.

Read the note. Just read the goddamn note. He squeezes two fingers into the pocket of his overalls and pulls out the folded-up scrap. It's always with him now, next to his body. She doesn't take the paper. She won't touch it.

So you could live, he recites, holding the sheet up in her face. *And bring back someone else.*

She sits down in the dirt next to him, an inch away. Weird calm comes over the both of them.

Bring back someone? she asks. Like she might want to, herself.

He yanks forward, out of the hole. She falls back, her arms up to block him. But all he wants is to take her face between his hands.

You have to help me. I'm begging you. I'll do anything you want. I have to find this person.

But why, Mark? What can he give you that I . . . ?

This guy *knows*. Knows why I'm still alive. Something I'd like to learn.

Karin wrote Gerald Weber. He'd told her to write if Mark's status changed. She didn't mention seeing him on television. She said nothing about buying his new book or finding it cold and tired, filled with recycled pronouncements about the human brain and empty of the human soul. She wrote: "Mark is clearly getting worse."

She described the new symptoms: Mark's obsessive theories about the note. His doubling places now, along with people. His rejecting the house, the subdivision, maybe even the whole town. His drifting into territory so weird it left her shaky. She asked Dr. Weber if the accident could have given Mark false memories. Could something have happened to his inner, generalizing map? Every small change was making Mark split each now into a unique world.

She mentioned a case in Weber's first book, an elderly woman called Adele who'd assured Dr. Weber that she wasn't lying in a hospital in Stony Brook but was in fact in her cozy saltbox home in Old Field. When Dr. Weber pointed out all the expensive medical devices in the room, Adele had laughed. "Oh, those are just props, to make me feel better. I could never afford the real things."

Reduplicative paramnesia. She copied the words from his book into her e-mail. Could Mark actually be suffering from that? Could he be seeing details he'd never seen before? Did brain damage ever *help* memory? She cited Dr. Weber's second book, page 287: the man he referred to as Nathan. Damage to the man's frontal lobes somehow destroyed his internal censor and freed up long-suppressed recollections. Nathan, at fifty-six, suddenly realized that at nineteen he had killed another man. Could Mark be remembering old things about himself—or even about her—that he could not accept?

She knew her theories were crazy, even as she suggested them. But no crazier than Capgras. Weber's own books claimed that the human brain was not only wilder than thought, but wilder than thought could think. She quoted from *The Country of Surprise*: "Even baseline normality has about it something hallucinatory." Nothing in Dr. Weber's examination of Mark had anticipated these new symptoms. Either Mark needed a whole new diagnosis, or *she* was hallucinating.

She got back a cheerful reply from Weber's secretary. Dr. Weber's new book required him to travel to seventeen cities in four countries over the next three months. He'd be largely out of e-mail contact, except for emergencies, until the fall. The secretary promised to alert Dr. Weber to Karin's note at the earliest opportunity. And she encouraged Karin to be in touch if things with her brother became more serious.

The response enraged Karin. "The man's ducking me," she told Daniel. "He's taken what he wants, and now he's blowing us off."

Daniel tried to hide his embarrassment. "I doubt he even has time to duck you. Things must be nuts for him right now. Television, radio, and newspapers every day."

"I knew, all the time he was out here. He thinks I'm a problem patient. A problem relative. He read my e-mail and told his staff to cover for him. Maybe it wasn't even his secretary. Maybe it was him, just pretending . . ."

"Karin? K. ?" Daniel had grown older than the neuro-scientist. "We don't know . . ."

"Don't patronize me! I don't *care* about what we know or don't."

"Shh. It's okay. You're angry. You should be. With all the professionals. At this whole business. Maybe even angry with Mark."

"Are you analyzing me?"

"I'm not analyzing. I just see that . . ."

"Who the fuck . . . ?" *Do you think you are?*

The words, even stifled, knocked them both silent. Her hands started shaking and she sat down, numb.

"My God, Daniel. What's happening? Listen to me. I'm him. Worse than him."

He crossed to her and rubbed the life back into her upper arm. "Anger is natural," he said. "Everything gets angry."

Everything except the saint she lived with.

She made an appointment to see Dr. Hayes. Pulling into the garage at Good Samaritan for the appointment, she reverted to the night of the accident. She had to sit in the parked vehicle for ten minutes before her legs would support her weight.

She greeted Dr. Hayes professionally. The appointment meter was ticking. She listed Mark's new symptoms, which the neurologist copied into Mark's chart.

"Why don't you bring him in? I'd better have another look at him."

"He won't come," Karin said. "He won't listen to me, now that he's back living by himself."

"Have you considered taking steps to assume legal guardianship?"

"How . . . what does that involve? Would I have to declare him mentally unfit?"

Hayes gave her a contact. Karin jotted it down, the ugly hope washing over her. *Use the law against your brother. Protect him against himself.*

"How sure is your brother that his home is a fake?" Hayes asked, fascinated.

"Out of ten? I'd say he's a seven."

"How does he explain the switch?"

"He thinks he's been under observation since the accident."

"Well, he's right, isn't he? It's too bad our author isn't here to see this. This one could have come straight out of his cases."

"But it didn't," she said, brittle.

"No. I'm sorry. It didn't." He set down his pen and fingered a thick, green-bound medical text on the shelf behind him. But he didn't remove it. "Studies show a high incidence of overlap for the various misidentification syndromes. In fact, they may not be entirely distinct disorders. A quarter or more of Capgras patients go on to develop other delusional symptoms. When you consider the different causes of Capgras . . ."

"You're saying he could get worse? He might start thinking anything? Why didn't anyone tell me this before?"

He shot her a maddeningly composed look. "It hadn't happened before."

Dr. Hayes wanted more observation. Mark was scheduled for his first outpatient CBT session in a week. The therapist, Dr. Jill Tower, had already gone over the file. Dr. Hayes would do his own follow-up assessment. Meanwhile, neither the diagnosis nor the indicated treatment would change.

They'd reached minute seventeen; she was already overdrawn. "I also wanted to get your opinion," she started. "I understand that Dr. Weber is an acknowledged expert. But I've been reading about this kind of therapy. It just sounds to me like, I don't know. Like glorified conditioning. They try to weaken the delusion just by training and . . . modification. Do you think that such therapy is appropriate in Mark's situation? The scan shows damage. What good is mental habit-changing going to do against a physical injury?"

She hit a sore spot: clear by the way the neurologist started hedging. "We need to explore a variety of approaches. Cognitive behavioral therapy will certainly not hurt your brother as he learns to adjust to his new self. Confusion, anger, anxiety . . ."

She grimaced. "Does it have any chance of helping his Capgras?"

He swung back around to his shelf of books, but again removed none. "A small body of literature shows some melioration of misidentification delusions in psychiatric disorders. Whether CBT can do anything for Capgras caused by closed-head trauma, we'll have to wait and see."

"We're the guinea pigs?"

"Medicine often involves some degree of experimentation."

"Every time I show Mark how crazy he's being, he comes up with another more elaborate theory to explain himself. How can a therapist reason him out of this?"

"Cognitive behavioral therapy is not about reasoning. It's about emotional adjustment. Training patients to explore their belief systems. Helping them work on their sense of self. Giving them exercises to change . . ."

"Help Mark explore why he thinks I'm not who I am?" Whoever that was.

"We need to determine the strength of his delusion. It may be no more resistant to modification than any belief. Some people change political parties. People fall in and out of love. Religious persecutors get converted. We don't know what goes on in a misidentification syndrome. We can't cause it and we can't make it go away. But we might be able to make it easier to live with."

"Easier for . . . ?" She modified. "So 'easier' is the best we can hope for?"

"That might be a lot."

"Does Dr. Weber prescribe cognitive therapy for all his untreatable cases?"

His eyes flickered, a little glint that almost forgot its code of ethics. A glint that admitted: *Well, you know, physicians often prescribe antibiotics for colds.* "We wouldn't recommend this referral if it had no chance of helping."

The professional, closing ranks. But she might flush him out. "Would you have made this referral if Dr. Weber hadn't visited?"

His smile darkened. "I have no trouble backing his recommendation."

"But behavioral therapy for a lesion? That's like talking somebody out of going blind."

"A newly blind person could use help adjusting to blindness."

"So this is just help adjusting? There's nothing, then? Nothing medical? Even when he's clearly getting worse?"

Dr. Hayes folded his index fingers to his lips. "Nothing else advisable. Remember, this isn't for us. It's for your brother."

She stood and shook the neurologist's hand, thinking, *Whose brother?* She confirmed Mark's schedule with Dr. Tower's scheduling nurse on her way out.

She reached a truce with Rupp and Cain. Whatever their sins against her brother, she couldn't afford to go to war. She had no one else to draw on. Someone had to help watch Mark, especially at night, when things got rough. She'd lost the right to come and go. One bad evening, she volunteered to stay in his spare bedroom. He'd studied her so wildly it scared her back to Daniel's. The next day, Karin called Tommy Rupp, the brains, for want of a better term, of the Muskrateers. She could deal with Rupp over the phone. Anything, so long as she didn't have to look at him.

He was surprisingly decent, improvising a rotation that would keep constant tabs on Mark. The prospect of caretaking pleased him. "Just like the old days," he told her. "He won't think twice about us staying over."

"That's what I'm afraid of. Please don't make him do any drugs. Not when he's like this."

Tommy chuckled. "Make? What do you take us for? We're not monsters."

"According to current neurological theory, everybody's a monster."

Humiliating memory lay between them, untouched. Years ago, Karin and Rupp had done each other, just for grins, late one September night on the front porch of her family's house, while Mark, Joan, and Cappy Schluter were upstairs sleeping. Her senior year of college, with Rupp just out of high school. Almost like corrupting a minor. And she did corrupt him that night, drawing muffled squeals of disbelief from the boy that threatened to wake the whole house and get them both killed. She never knew why she'd initiated the one-shot entertainment. Curiosity. Simple thrill: the worst possible transgression. Maybe it gave her some leverage, dragging her brother's friend behind the porch swing on a dry, brisk, pitch-black September night and doing the animal deed. Tom Rupp exercised an unnatural influence over Mark. Even at eighteen: too cool to show the slightest desire. Just along for the ride. Well, she gave him one. Not until afterward did Karin realize how much leverage she'd given the boy.

But he never told Mark. She would have known; Mark would have disowned her, nine years sooner. Rupp never mentioned the occasion again. He'd gladly have taken second helpings anytime, but he was way above asking. She could feel his question in the way he skulked around her, the same nagging question banging around the back of her own head every time she crossed Tom Rupp's path: *That girl still in there?*

She'd had a thing for danger back then. And in the danger department, Tom Rupp was the Kearney High Bearcats' Great White Hope. At the age of thirteen, he hitchhiked the 130 miles to Lincoln and smuggled himself into Farm Aid III, bringing back to his dumbfounded friends John Mellencamp's fingerprints on a bottle of Myers's Rum. At fifteen, he stole the four flags that flew outside the Twenty-second Street Municipal Building—city, state, nation, and POW-MIA—and used them to decorate his room. Everyone in town knew who'd taken them except the police. He'd been a wrestler, placing fifth in state in the 152-pound class his sophomore year before dropping out of organized sports, proclaiming them "a training camp for prospective gays." Mark, who'd struggled for years to make a name as a hustling but flatfooted guard with a mediocre outside jumper, gratefully dropped out with him.

Rupp trained Mark, quoting ominously from the classics he fed himself in strict, autodidact regimen. "Be on your guard against the good and the just! They would fain crucify those who devise their own virtue. They hate the lonesome ones." Mark couldn't always follow the man, but the diction always pumped him.

They picked up Duane Cain as their all-purpose sidekick in senior year. Cain had already succeeded in earning an eighteen-month suspended sentence for believing himself to be the first person ever to come up with an insurance fraud scheme. The three of them grew inseparable. They spent weeks rebuilding any internal-combustion engine that stood still long enough for them to strip it. They were at perpetual war with every other clique in school. Duane led them on nighttime raids involving that old Native American gesture of contempt, leaving a warm, coiled calling card on prominent display in the enemy's front yard.

They enrolled together at U of N Kearney, Rupp finishing in four years, Mark and Duane managing a total of four between them. Rupp took a "telecommunications opening" in Omaha, abandoning Duane and Mark to lives of moving furniture and reading gas meters. Eight months later, Rupp was back in town, without explanations, but with a long-term plan to advance all three of their professional fates. He talked his way into a start at the Lexington packing plant, where he migrated from postprocessing over to the slaughter side, which paid three dollars more per hour. As soon as he amassed some seniority, he got jobs for his two friends. Duane joined One-shot Rupp on the zapping side, but Mark hadn't the stomach for it, let alone the nose. Mark gladly stayed behind in machine maintenance and repair, saving enough money over three years for a down payment on the Homestar.

Alone of the trio, Tommy Rupp was ambitious. The Nebraska National Guard offered him a supplemental paycheck and even promised three-quarters of his tuition if he went back to school. All that, for only one weekend a month. It was a no-brainer. He tried to get the other Muskrateers to join up together. Free money, and gender-integrated patriotic service: the best legal deal anyone was going to hand the likes of them. But Duane and Mark chose to wait and see.

Rupp enlisted in July 2001 as an MOS 63B: Light-Wheel Vehicle Mechanic, the same stuff he loved to do all weekend, anyway. The 167th Cavalry. They tried to poison him in basic, and he had the souvenir commemorative videotape to prove it: stumbling from the qualification gas chamber, crawling out of the sealed room full of chlorobenzalmalononitrile where he and twenty-five other recruits had been ordered to remove their gas masks. Duane Cain took one look at the tape—Rupp the Ironman, falling to his knees in the dirt, choking and puking—and decided that national service was not in his foreseeable future. The video freaked Mark, too. He'd never been especially big on inhaling poisons.

September came, and then the attacks. Alongside the rest of the world, the trio hung on the endlessly looping, slow-motion, cinematic insanity. From the Central Plains, New York was a black plume on the farthest horizon. Troops were securing the Golden Gate Bridge. Anthrax started turning up in the nation's sugar bowls. Then the bombs began to fall in Afghanistan. A broadcaster in Omaha declared, *It's payback time*, and all along the river came stony, unanimous assent.

Rupp called it simple self-defense. Early and often, he explained that America couldn't afford to sit and wait for some new fanatical operative dreaming of seventy-two virgins to smallpox the country in its sleep. The terrorists weren't going to stop until everyone looked just like them. Duane fretted over Tommy's future. But Rupp was philosophical. Freedom wasn't free. Besides, the army had no targets to send the Guard after.

By winter, America rose up striking at targets everywhere. Rupp's duty time increased, and a few guys he served with were dragged off to Fort Riley, Kansas. On the third of February, just after the president delivered his hunt-them-down State of the Union address and Washington lost track of bin Laden, Mark came to Rupp and said he'd changed his mind. He wanted to serve, despite the chlorobenzalmalononitrile. Rupp welcomed the news like an Amway distributor entitled to a cut. They hit the recruitment center together, and Mark went shopping. MOS 63G: Fuel and Electrical Systems Repairer. He wasn't sure he could pass the qualifying test, but figured it couldn't be much harder than what he did for IBP. He signed a letter of intent, and he and Rupp celebrated by going out and shooting .22s at pop cans out on country fence posts for a couple of hours. He called Karin late that night, his words slurred and swirling. He told her the whole story. He sounded different, his voice prouder, more serene then she'd heard him in a while. Like he was already a soldier. A credit to the country.

She told him not to go through with it. He laughed at her fears. "Who's going to protect your way of life, if not me? I just wish I'd gone with it sooner. So obvious. I can do this. Remember Dad and Mom?" She said she did. "They both passed, convinced I was a slacker. You don't think I'm a slacker, do you?"

He'd enlisted for her. Karin told him to quit, to invoke the forty-eight-hour escape clause. But hearing herself destroying her brother's one bid for self-esteem, she backed down. And maybe he was right. Maybe she, too, needed to pay for privilege. Two weeks later, he was lying upside down in a frozen roadside ditch, his tour of patriotic duty over.

Karin dealt with the Guard's recruiting officers while Mark was still in Good Samaritan. She tried to exempt Mark from the agreement altogether. But the best she could manage was a temporary medical waiver, subject to review. One more dangling uncertainty to live under. After a while, the whole idea of security felt like a sucker punch. The Guard would claim Mark, if they deemed him fit to serve. Meanwhile, Rupp drilled for all of them. Duane lent his moral support by sporting a T-shirt that read, *The Marines Are Looking for a Few Good Women*, complete with appropriate field-guide illustration.

But Duane did help Rupp and Bonnie guard the Homestar. Karin watched, from as close as Mark would allow. Mark basked in the company, never wondering why his homecoming festivities went on for weeks. So long as the guests hung around and the refrigerator kept replenishing itself, he seemed ready to live for the moment.

Karin hovered on the sidelines, appealing to Rupp's peculiar sense of duty. "Will you watch him when he smokes? He hasn't smoked for months. I'm terrified he's going to forget what he's doing and burn the house down."

"Hey. Lighten up. Except for a few bizarre theories, the man is basically back to normal."

She couldn't argue. She no longer knew what normal meant. "Can you at least go easy on the beer?"

"This? This piss can't hurt anybody. It's low-carb."

When she drove by the Homestar at night, the lights were always on. That meant raunchy martial-arts film festivals followed by all-night video-game binges. She abided them now. Even the insane NASCAR game couldn't be any worse than cognitive therapy, for bringing him back to life. The screen was the only place he could be happy now, racing without thinking, free from the suspicion that things didn't add up. But the game made him crazy, too. Before his spinout, his thumbs had been faster than his eyes. Now, he remembered all that he once could do, but not how to do it. That enraged him. Then she was glad for Rupp and Cain. No one else could protect her from his outbursts. Now that his body had healed, he might maim her before he even knew it. She was a government agent, a robot. He might take her head off in a minute, to find the wires. One bout of confused fury and she'd be no one.

Cain and Rupp contained his rage. They learned how to handle him: let him blow up, then stick the game controller back in his hands. The routine became part of the general festivities.

On Independence Day, everyone gathered to watch the fireworks. The boys got an early start, filling an oil drum with iced beer and grilling a quarter of a calf from the plant over an open pit. When Karin showed up, they were listening to the Mormon Tabernacle Choir singing patriotic lyrics grafted onto Sousa marches. The sound waves battered her as she pulled into the subdivision. Duane was working to tame an ice-cream maker, reasoning with the unruly gear. Mark laughed at him, more naturally than he'd laughed since the accident. "Your machine has diarrhea."

"I'll beat this bastard. And I'll fix the tape deck afterward. Show me a machine I can't whup. I think it's a polarity problem. You familiar with those?"

The whole show amused Mark so much he didn't even challenge Karin's arrival. "Look who's here! It's okay—you're a citizen, too. Nice little touch, anyway. The Fourth of July is my sister's all-time favorite. Let's dedicate this one to her, wherever she is. Her, and all the missing Americans."

She hadn't had a good thing to say about the holiday since

271

she was ten. But maybe he meant that ten-year-old Karin. Those two small children, their eyes gold sparklers, sick with fear and thrill when their father detonated an artillery barrage of illegal Class B fireworks in the north forty.

"She's gotta be abroad," Mark said, a cloud passing over him. "Abroad or in prison. I'd have heard from her if she was in the States. Today of all days. I'm telling you: maybe there's things to her life that I just didn't know about."

Bonnie showed up straight from work at the River Road Archway, still in her pioneer's bonnet and ankle-length cotton dress. She was about to duck into Mark's bathroom and change into her civvies when Mark stopped her. "Hey! Why don't you stay this way? I like you this way." He waved at her calico-printed bodice. "Nobody does that stuff anymore. I miss all that shit."

She stood, a giggling museum diorama. "What do you mean, 'miss'?"

"You know: olden days. Americana. Sort of sexy. It relaxes me."

Despite the salacious abuse she took from Rupp and Cain, she stayed in costume, fussing in the kitchen to prepare the impromptu feast alongside Karin in her cutoffs and bare midriff. Denim, duck-hunting camouflage, legible tees, and a fake calico bonnet: America at two and a quarter centuries.

"Where's your friend?" Bonnie asked Karin.

"What friend?" Mark called from the patio.

Karin considered snapping that frilly, calico neck. "He's at home. He's . . ." She waved her hand vaguely at the stereo system, the massed choral Sousa marches. "He hates military displays. He can't take the explosions."

"Invite him anyway," Bonnie suggested. "He can leave when the fun starts."

"What friend?" Mark, outside the kitchen window, pressed his nose to the screen. "Who are you talking about?"

"You banging somebody?" Rupp asked, with polite interest.

Duane savored his rare informational advantage. "Old news, Gus. She's shacking up with Riegel. What country have you dudes been living in?"

"Danny Riegel? Bird Boy? *Again?*" Rupp toasted Karin with a beer can wrapped in a foam Koozie. "That's priceless. Why didn't I see that coming? I mean, coming *back*? The annual migration."

Duane snickered. "That dude is going to save the planet someday."

"More than you'll ever do," Bonnie chided.

Karin scoped Mark through the kitchen screen. He sat back down on his patio chair, holding a piece of ice to his forehead. He wrestled with the name, fitting the long past into the five seconds of fleeting present where he now lived. Someone pretending to be his sister, shacking up with a boy who, in another life, had once been his inseparable companion. Who'd once shacked up with his actual sister. Impossible to assemble. How many lives was one person supposed to dope out in this life?

Over the cookout, the boys decided where America would strike next. Duane and Mark proposed various countries, and Tommy rated how hard each one would be to take out. Bonnie—a tinted daguerreotype with half a pound of steak on a paper plate balancing on her knee—listened, as if to a speech she had to memorize for her job at the Archway. "Don't you just feel sorry for them sometimes? Foreigners?"

"Well," Rupp said, doubtfully. "It's not like they're just being naïve."

"Reverend Billy says this thing with Iraq is actually predicted in the Bible," Bonnie contributed. "Something that has to happen, before the end."

Karin suggested that every dropped bomb might be creating more terrorists.

"Jesus." Mark shook his head. "You're a bigger traitor than my sister. I'm beginning to think you're not affiliated with the government at all!"

The Mormon Tabernacle Choir collapsed in exhaustion and was replaced by deeply affirmative Christian country rock. Groups of neighbors, camped over their own scattered cookouts, called out holiday greetings. The sun set and the bugs came out and the first tentative sprigs of fireworks tested the dark. The first Independence Day celebrations since the attacks, and the indolently exploding colored missiles felt both helpless and defiant. Tommy Rupp shot off a dozen "Exploding Terror Heads" he'd picked up at a roadside tent near Plattsmouth: colorful figures of Hussein and bin Laden that whistled skyward and burst into streamers.

Karin watched her brother in the shooting light. His eyes swung toward heaven, flinched at each explosion, then cackled at the flinching. His face, now green, now blue, now red, mouthed the same astonishment as all of Farview at this barrage of light they could no longer afford but couldn't do without. She saw him look around, trying to catch the attention of his friends, searching for confirmation none of them could give. Under the fall of a massive chrysanthemum, he turned and caught her staring at him. And brief as that flash, his eyes finding hers, the slightest sign of kinship issued from him: *You're lost here, too, aren't you?*

Weber's life began veering in late July. When plaintive chirps issued from a pile of his clothes, he thought it an animal. First Sylvie's struggles to evict the raccoon family from the attic, now a plague of locusts in the living quarters. Only the chirps' regularity made him recall the cell phone. He dug up the burrowing thing and stuck it to his face. "Weber."

"Big Daddy. Calling to wish you your day in the sun."

"Hey, Jess. It's you!"

His daughter, in her astronomical aerie in Southern California, wishing him a happy fifty-sixth. Whatever the awkwardness between them, Jessica always observed the forms. She flew back east for three or four days every Christmas. She sent them trinkets on Mother's and Father's Days—films and music, vain attempts to educate her parents in popular culture. She even remembered their anniversary, a thing no self-respecting child ever did. And she called them without fail on their birthdays, however halting the calls.

"You sound surprised. You know there's caller ID on the screen of your phone."

"Get thee behind me. Besides, how do you know which phone I'm on?"

"Daddy? Brain fart."

"Oh. Right. Forget that. How come you're calling on this cell thing, anyway?" Wrong foot, as usual, out of the gate.

"I thought you might enjoy birthday greetings from your daughter."

"I guess I'm not used to this ring-tone yet."

"You're not using it? You're sorry I got it for you?"

"I'm using it. I use it to call your mother, when I'm on the road."

"If you don't like it, Father, you can bring it back."

"Who said I don't like it?"

"Get Mom to return it for you. She knows how to move about freely in the retail world."

"I like it. It's handy."

"Fine. Listen, I'm telling you this now so you won't spin out when it happens. I'm thinking about getting you a DVD player for Christmas."

"What's wrong with tapes?"

His daughter snickered. "So, what birthday is this, anyway?"

"Sorry. We've stopped counting." The mere sound of each other's voices returned him to his thirties and her to thirteen.

Jess had never been big with words. She preferred figures. But she liked the phone, an unimpeachably clean technology. As a teen, she went through the obligatory phone stage—long, near-silent sessions with her friend Gayle while she played Tetris and Gayle watched cable, a medium the Webers managed to duck. The girls would breathe at each other for hours at a shot, punctuated only by Jess's occasional reports of high scores or interrogations of Gayle's plot synopses: "He's *kissing* her? Where? *Why?*" Sylvie would sweep through every half-hour, insisting, "You girls start talking or give it up."

Her phone behavior was much the same now, only Tetris had given way to Hubble scans. Weber could hear her computing on the other end; the furtive clacking of keys. Applying for grants or querying enormous online astronomical databases. She said nothing for some seconds. At last, he asked, "How's the planet hunting?"

"Fine," she clicked. "I've got Keck time in August. We're looking to supplement the radial-velocity method with . . . You aren't really interested, are you?"

"Of course I am. You found anything small, warm, and water-bearing yet?"

"No. But I promise your choice of half a dozen before I come up for tenure."

"You're filling in all the required promotion forms?"

She sighed. "Yes, Parental Unit." One of the rising stars among young cosmologists, and he was fretting about her paperwork.

"How's the new insulin pump working?"

"Oh my God. Best two months' salary I've ever spent. Absolutely life-changing. I feel like a new person."

"Really? That's fantastic. So it's keeping you from crashing?"

"Not entirely. Zuul still inhabits me from time to time. Capricious little fiend. Came and took me over in the middle of the night last week. First time in a long time. Scared the crap out of both of us."

Say her name, Weber willed Jess. But she didn't. "So how is . . . Cleo?"

"Father!" She sounded almost amused. He blessed the screens of distracting data on her end. "Don't you think it's strange that you would ask about my dog before you asked about my mate?"

"Well," he said. "How is . . . your mate?"

Deep silence from California. "You've forgotten her name, haven't you?"

"Not 'forgotten.' I've just mislaid it, for the moment. Ask me anything about her. Brookline, Massachusetts. Holy Cross, Stanford, dissertation on the French colonial adventure in sub-Saharan . . ."

"It's called 'blocking,' Father. It happens when you're anxious or uncomfortable. You've never really gotten used to it, have you?"

"Gotten used to what?" Stupid time-buying.

Jessica stopped clicking. She was enjoying this. "You know. Never gotten used to your daughter sleeping with someone from the humanities."

"Some of my best friends are humanists."

"Name one."

"Your mother is a humanist."

"My mother is the last of the pagan saints. How soul-strengthening you've been for her, all these years."

"You know, Jess. It's really starting to worry me. It's not just common names anymore. I'm surprised by entries in my agenda, in my own handwriting."

"Daddy, remember what you said in one of your own books. 'If you forget where you put your car keys, don't sweat. If you forget what car keys *are*, see a physician.' "

"Did I say that?"

Jess laughed, the same goofy, distracted, bucktoothed laugh she'd laughed at eight years old. It cut right through him. "Besides, if it gets really bad, you can get your hands on the latest and greatest drugs. You guys have all sorts of things you're not telling us public about yet, don't you? Memory, concentration, speed, intelligence: a pill for everything, I bet. Irks the crap out of me that you won't cut your own flesh and blood into any of this stuff."

"Treat me nice," he said. "You never know."

"Speaking of your book, Shawna showed me the *Harper's* review." Shawna. No wonder he could never remember. "I say to hell with him," his daughter said. "Obviously jealous, pure and simple. I wouldn't think twice about it."

A flash of disconnect. *Harper's*? They'd jumped pub date. His publishers must have known about the review days ago. No one had mentioned anything to him. "I won't," he said.

"And have yourself a happy little birthday? Can you do that much for me?"

"I will."

"Which I suppose means writing four thousand words and discovering a couple of heretofore unknown states of altered consciousness. I mean, in other people."

He said goodbye, folded and pocketed the cricket, then hopped on the bike and pedaled up to Setauket Common and the Clark Library. He ran the gauntlet of news-magazine headlines: U.S. bombs obliterate Afghan wedding. Cabinet-level Security Department rushed through. Where had he been while this was happening? Handling the new *Harper's* in its hardened red plastic folder, he felt vaguely criminal. Obscene, looking up a review of his work. Like Googling his own name. Scanning down the table of contents, he felt ridiculous. He'd been writing for years, with more success than he'd ever dared imagine. He wrote for the insight of the phrase, to locate, in some strange chain, its surprise truth. The way a reader received his stories said as much about the reader's story as about the story itself. In fact, his books explored that very fact: there was no story *itself*. No final judgment. Anything this reviewer might say was just part of the distributed network, signals cascading through the fragile ecosystem. What could a pan or praise matter to him? He cared only what his daughter thought. His daughter's mate. *Shawna. Shawna.* They'd read this piece, but not yet seen the book. If Jess got around to *The Country of Surprise* — and he imagined she would, someday — she'd be reading, inescapably, the book this review created, in her mind. Best to know what other volumes were now floating around, spun from the one he wrote.

The title of the review jumped off the page with a sickening thrill: "Neurologist in a Vat." The reviewer's name meant nothing to him. The article started out respectfully enough. But within a paragraph, it turned brittle. He began to scan, lingering on evaluative dismissals. The thesis, at the end of the second paragraph, was more damning than Jess had let on:

> Driven by medical imaging and new molecular-level experimental technologies, brain research has surged ahead phenomenally in the last few years; Gerald Weber's increasingly slender, anecdotal approach has not. He returns here with his familiar and slightly cartoonish tales, hiding behind an entirely predictable if irrefutable plea for tolerance of diverse mental conditions, even as his stories border on privacy violations and sideshow exploitation . . . Seeing such a respected figure capitalize on unacknowledged research and unfelt suffering borders on the embarrassing.

Weber read on, from out-of-context quotes to gross generalizations, from factual errors to ad hominem attacks. How could Jess have been so matter-of-fact about this? The piece made his book out to be both inaccurate science and irresponsible journalism, the pseudoempirical equivalent of reality television, profiting from fad and pain. He dealt in generalities with no particulars, facts with no understanding, cases with no individual feeling.

He did not read the review through to the end. He held the magazine open in front of him, a score to sight-sing. Around him in the bright, snug library sat four or five retirees and as many schoolchildren. None of them looked at him. The looks would start tomorrow, when he showed up on campus: the

280

nonchalant gaze of colleagues, the pretense of business as usual, behind masked excitement.

He thought to research the reviewer, get a character sketch of the character assassin. Pointless. As Jess said: to hell with him. Any explanation Weber might construct for the attack would be just a story against this story. Jealousy, ideological conflict, personal advancement: explanations were endless. In the field of public reviewing, one scored zero for appreciating an already appreciated figure. With a target as large as Gerald Weber, one earned points only for a kill.

Even as he rehearsed these rationalizations, they sickened him. Nothing in the review was out of bounds. His book was fair game. Some other public writer found him exploitative: fair enough. He had often worried about that very possibility himself. Weber stared out the picture window, across the Common at the two Colonial churches, their harsh, believing beauty. Reading the worst left him almost relieved. *No such thing as bad press*, he heard Bob Cavanaugh whisper.

The book was what it was; no further evaluation would change its contents. A dozen people in shattered worlds, putting themselves back together—what was there in such a project that merited public attack? If *he* hadn't authored the book, *Harper's* wouldn't have reviewed it at all. The review gave itself away: it didn't aim to destroy the book. It aimed at him. Anyone who read the review would see this. And yet, if Weber had learned anything about the species, after a lifetime of study, it was that people flocked. Already, the core of the intelligentsia, wet forefingers in the air, were gauging the change in the prevailing winds. The science of consciousness now needed protection from Gerald Weber's slender, anecdotal, exploitative approach. And oddly, as Weber slipped the plastic-bound issue back onto the shelf, he felt vindicated.

Something in him had half-expected this moment, for as long as he'd been celebrated.

He strolled past the circulation desk, hung a left out the main doors, and followed the familiar stone path a hundred paces down the slope before freezing. He stood at the path's end, the intersection of Bates, Main, and Dyke. He would telephone Cavanaugh, on the cell phone in his pocket, even at home, on Sunday, to ask how the man could think to hide this attack from Weber. He pulled out the shiny silver device. It looked like a remote detonator in a thriller film.

He was overreacting. The first sign of reasoned objection and he wanted to circle the wagons. He'd enjoyed public respect for so long—twelve years—that he assumed it; he no longer knew how to expect anything else. The book could stand on its own, in the face of any charges. Still: he did the math. For every twenty people who read the review, one, with luck, might read the book, while the others would describe it to friends in dismissive terms, without the inconvenience of having to look at it.

He slipped the phone into its pocket and doubled back up the path toward the bike rack. He would tell Sylvie, when he got home. She would be impervious, mildly amused. Smile and ask him: *What would Famous Gerald do?*

The bike ride back to Strong's Neck was all downhill. The tide was out and July tasted brackish in his lungs. He'd wanted to get back to pure science, away from the fuzzy, mass-marketed world of science popularization. Here was a further motive. The hard left whip of Dyke Road brought him along the reedy estuary. Gravity slung him along the rill where George Washington's Setauket spy ring had hung their lanterns at night, signaling over the sound to Connecticut, back when the terrorists were the heroes. The bike sped dangerously down the tidal embankment. In what world could the book he'd written be as evil as the book he'd just read about?

He looked back across his right shoulder. Setauket Harbor gleamed, brilliant in the midday sun. Across the blue-jade inlet, the spread wings of small sailboats skimmed. On such a day as this, anything might happen. The Bridgeport–Port Jefferson ferry lowed in the distance, a great migratory thing calling its way back to harbor. He loved his life here. A happy little birthday. He could still do that much.

Tour Director got them as far as Italy. Weber stood on the Ponte Vecchio, scanning the boutiques that had lined the bridge for centuries. A brief history of capitalism: butcher shops giving way to blacksmiths and tanners, giving way to silversmiths and goldsmiths, giving way to coral jewelry and neckties that would set you back weeks of salary. In the middle of a plume of people chattering scores of languages, he watched Sylvie, giddy with new euros and Florentine sun, nose around a window full of Nardin watches, just for play. Just pretending, happy to be away, someplace fully imaginary.

They had been all over the Duomo the day before. Already, Weber failed to form a detailed picture of the church's interior in his mind. That morning, she had picked out the night's entertainment, a performance of Monteverdi's *Il ritorno d'Ulisse in patria*.

"Serious?" he'd asked her.

"You kidding? I love Renaissance opera. You know that."

He didn't ask how long she'd loved it. He couldn't afford the answer. He studied her now, in the flowing crowd. When the light was right, at a distance, she could pass for a Japanese tourist. A holiday in this country, her favorite spot on earth, took decades off her. She looked as she had before they married, the girl for whom, a million years ago, he'd once performed a campy Schubert chorale, words by that rhymester Willie the Shake, sung to her with his friends over the phone as a Valentine, as if it were a collegiate glee number from 1928:

Who is Sylvia? What is she,
That all our swains commend her?
Holy, fair, and wise is she,
The heaven such grace did lend her,
That she might admired be.

Young Sylvie, when she stopped laughing at the rendition, scolded them all for singing without her. "Hey! Start again. Give me a part."

Still her, still his traveling companion, despite the years. But how they'd gotten from that year to this, Weber couldn't say. He could still name most of the cities they'd vacationed in, if not when, or what they'd seen. Now Florence in high summer: madness, he knew, even when they'd planned the trip. But July was the only time they both could get away, and the hot, dry press of crowds just made Sylvie happier. She turned and smiled at him, a little embarrassed at her window shopping. He smiled back as best he could, unable to take a step toward her through the stream of sightseers on the old bridge. *Love doth to her eyes repair, to help him of his blindness.*

The *Times* review had appeared just before they left the States. He'd read it at the breakfast table, as Sylvie tried to pull him out of the house to the airport. "Take it with," she said. "It doesn't weigh anything."

He didn't want to bring it. They were going to Italy.

Reviews not welcome. By the time they got to LaGuardia, he'd rewritten it in his head. He could no longer tell what he actually remembered from the evaluation and what he was fabricating. He did know that whole phrases in the *Times* were lifted from the *Harper's* piece. Surely any reader who read both would see the duplication.

He called Cavanaugh from the airport. "I wouldn't let it worry you, Ger," his editor said. "Strange days in America. We're looking for something to lash out at. The book is selling fine. And you know we're there for you with the new contract, whatever happens to this one."

By arrival in Rome, Weber was ready to expatriate. Resentment had given way to doubt: perhaps the *Times* review wasn't cribbed, but was merely independent corroboration. The idea ruined him for sightseeing. Their second night, in Siena, he and Sylvie argued. Not argued; struggled. Sylvie was being way too supportive. She refused to credit any of his qualms. "They might have one point," Weber had suggested. "Looked at the wrong way, these books could indeed be seen as milking others' disabilities for personal gain."

"Piffle. You've been telling the story of people whose stories don't get told. Letting the normals know that the tent is much bigger than they thought."

Just what he'd told her he was doing, all these years.

"You're tired. Jet-lagged. Bouncing around in a foreign country. Of course this whole thing makes you feel a little shaky. Hey! It could be worse. You could have some Medici hit man knifing you in the back for your art. C'mon. *Abbastanza.* What do you want to do tomorrow?"

Exactly the question that worried him. What to do tomorrow, and the day after. Another popular book was out of the question. Even lab work felt shaky. His research team already treated him differently—a new impatience with his low-tech, folksy anecdotal style, a hunger for more penetrating research—the sexy stuff with Big Imaging that was cracking the brain wide open. He was just a popularizer. An exploitative popularizer, at that.

After a week of anhedonia, he discovered a surprise weakness for Italian liqueurs with exotic nineteenth-century labels, as if he were some second-generation nostalgic lush returning to the fatherland. He couldn't concentrate on the old buildings, even his beloved Romanesque. Sylvie felt him soldiering through the ancient towns, but she never scolded him. Siena, Florence, San Gimignano: he took more than five hundred pictures, mostly of Sylvie in front of world-famous landmarks, dozens of them from the same angle, as if both woman and monuments were in danger of disappearing. He was cramping her holiday, and he worked to lighten up. But finally his militant gaiety made her sit him down in a dusty trattoria across from the Palazzo Pretorio in Prato and lecture him.

"I know you're gearing up for an ordeal when we get back. But there's no ordeal. No one to fight. Nothing's changed. This book is as good as anything you've ever written." Exactly his worst fear. "People will read it and do what they can with it, and you'll write something else. My God! Most writers would kill for the kind of attention you're getting."

"I'm not a writer," he answered. But perhaps he'd inadvertently given up the day job, as well.

Back in Rome on their last evening, he lost control. They were sitting at a café on the Via Cavour. She reminded him that they were having drinks that night with a Flemish couple she had met.

"When did you tell me this?"

"Which time?" She sighed. "Male pattern deafness." What other wives might have called self-absorption. "Come on, Man. Where are you?"

Against his better judgment, he told her. He hadn't mentioned the reviews for days. "I'm wondering if they might actually be right."

She threw her hands into the air like a ninja cheerleader. "Oh, stop! They're *not* right. They're just professional climbers." Her composure maddened him. He found himself saying absurd things in increasingly incomprehensible fragments. Finally he got up and left. Idiot, fool: he wandered at random through the Roman web, as the sun sank and the twisting streets disoriented him. He got back to the hotel after eleven. The Flemish couple had long since left. Even then, she did not rebuke him as he deserved. He'd married a woman who simply didn't understand drama. That night and on the plane the next day, she extended the same professional cool she gave her most erratic Wayfinder clients.

They made it back home intact. Sylvie was right: no ordeal awaited. Cavanaugh called with a few reassuring reviews, figures, and translation offers. But Weber still had book promotion to get through before summer's end. Readings, print interviews, radio: more proof, if his research team needed any, that a man couldn't serve two masters.

At a reading at Cody's in Berkeley, a member of the otherwise respectful audience asked how he responded to the press's suggestion that his personalized case histories violated professional ethics. The audience hissed at the question, but with a disguised thrill. He stumbled through an answer that had once been automatic: The brain was not a machine, not a car engine, not a computer. Purely functional descriptions hid as much as they revealed. You couldn't grasp any individual brain without addressing private history, circumstance, personality—the whole person, beyond the sum of mechanical modules and localized deficits.

A second listener wanted to know if all his patients always gave full approval. He said *of course*. Yes, but with their deficits, did they always fully understand that approval? Brain research, Weber said, suggested that no one could ever second-guess another's understanding. Even as he spoke it, it sounded incriminating. Even he could hear the blatant contradiction.

Weber looked out into the standing-room-only crowd. One attractive middle-aged woman in a madras dress held a miniature video camera. Others had audio recorders. "This is starting to feel a little like a feeding frenzy," he laughed. Something off with the timing. The audience hushed, nonplussed. He caught a rhythm at last, limiting the damage. But fewer people waited in line for signed copies than the last time he'd come through town.

The ordinary colors of his day took on a new cast: all too much like a case he'd once detailed. He knew Edward only from the literature, but in *Wider Than the Sky*, Weber made Edward his own, describing him, perhaps, as if he'd discovered him. Edward was born partly color-blind, like ten percent of all men, many of whom never discover their condition. A lack of color receptors in Edward's eyes left him unable to distinguish reds and greens. Color blindness was itself uncanny: the unsettling suggestion that any two people might disagree about exactly what hue a given object actually had.

But Edward's color vision was stranger still. Like far fewer people—one in tens of thousands—Edward was also synesthetic. Edward's inherited synesthesia was consistent and stable throughout his lifetime. His took a standard form: seeing numbers as colors. For Edward, numbers and hues actually *fused*, the way that smoothness usually fuses with comfort and sharpness with pain. He complained as a child that the colors on his number blocks were all wrong. His mother understood; she had the same fused wiring, too.

Those with the condition often tasted shapes or felt, in their skin, the texture of spoken words. These were no simple associations, no flights of poetic fancy. Weber had come to see synesthesia as something as durable as the smell of strawberries or the chill of ice: a left-hemisphere function, somehow buried beneath the cortex, a signal-crossing that every brain produced but that only a select few brains presented to consciousness, something not quite shed in evolution, or perhaps the advance scouts of mutation's next reel.

Edward, both color-blind and synesthetic, was his own story. The look, sound, or thought of the numeral one caused him to see white. Twos were bathed in fields of blue. Every number *was* a color, the way that honey was sweet or the interval of a minor second was dissonant. The problem came with fives, and nines. Edward called them "Martian colors," hues unlike any that he'd ever seen.

It puzzled the doctors at first. After some testing, the truth came out: those numbers were red and green. Not the "red" and "green" that his eyes saw and his mind had learned to translate. But red and green as they registered in the brains of the color-sighted—pure mental hues for which Edward had no visual equivalents. Colors that his eyes could not detect still registered in his undamaged visual cortex, triggered by numbers. He could perceive the shades by synesthesia; he just couldn't *see* them.

Weber had told the story years ago, concluding with a few thoughts about the locked room of personal experience. The senses were a metaphor at best. Neuroscience had revived Democritus: we speak of bitter and sweet, of hot and cold, but we come no closer to actual qualities than a rough thumbnail. All we could exchange were pointers—*purple, sharp, acrid*—to our private sensations.

But years ago, these ideas had been for Weber just writing, without aroma or tone. Now the words came back, rasping and clanging, springing up everywhere he looked: Martian colors, hues his eyes could not see, flooding his brain . . .

In August, he flew to Sydney, an invited speaker at an international conference on "The Origins of Human Consciousness." He had his problems with the evolutionary psychology crowd. The discipline was too fond of explaining everything in terms of Pleistocene modules, identifying gross, falsely universal characteristics of human behavior, then explaining, with ex post facto tautology, why they were inevitable adaptations. Why were males polygamous and females monogamous? It all came down to the relative economics of sperm versus egg. Not exactly *science*; but then, neither was his writing.

To Weber, much conscious behavior was less adaptation than exaptation. Pleiotropy—one gene giving rise to several unrelated effects—complicated attempts to explain characteristics in terms of independent selection. He had serious doubts about walking into a room full of evolutionary psychologists. But the meeting gave him a chance to try out a talk that he didn't dare present anywhere else: a theory about why patients who suffered from finger agnosia—the inability to name which finger was being touched or pointed to—often also suffered from dyscalculia—mathematical disability. He wasn't expected to break new ground with his speech. He was simply supposed to play himself, tell some good stories, and shake lots of hands.

The flight from New York to Los Angeles began badly, when his shoes triggered the security detectors and they found a nail-care kit he'd stupidly packed in his carry-on. It took a while to prove to the guards that he was who he claimed to be. In L.A., he transferred to the Sydney plane, which sat at the gate for an hour before being canceled. The pilot blamed a hairline crack in the windshield. Forty people on the plane: doubtless the crack would have looked smaller had there been four hundred.

He disembarked and sat in LAX for eight hours, waiting for his rebooked flight. By the time he boarded, he'd lost all sense of time. Somewhere out over the middle of the Pacific, he developed mild gaze tinnitus. When he looked to the left, he heard ringing in his ears. When he looked straight, the ringing went away. He thought about canceling his speech and returning to New York. The problem worsened throughout the in-flight dinner and movie. But after the forgettable film, the symptoms vanished.

He was so late clearing passport control in Sydney that he had to head straight to his first interviews, even before checking into his hotel. The first interview turned into a banal personality profile. The second was one of those disasters where the uninformed interviewer wanted Weber to comment on everything except his work. Could classical music actually make your baby smarter? How close were we to cognition-enhancing drugs? Weber was so jet-lagged he practically hallucinated. He heard his sentences growing longer and less grammatical. By the time the Australian journalist asked whether America could really hope to win the war on terrorism, he was saying injudicious things.

He was too tired to sleep that night. The next day was the conference. He walked about the cavernous convention center, bumping into chairs and office tables. Everyone recognized him, but most attendees looked away when he caught their eyes. For his part, he fought the urge to assign a five-digit *Diagnostic and Statistical Manual* code to everyone who came up to shake his hand. The crowd flowed through the conference rooms, whispering and laughing, displaying, preening, praising and faulting, flocking, forming factions, picking fights, plotting overthrows. He watched a middle-aged man and woman shriek upon seeing each other, embrace, and chatter in tandem. He waited to see them comb bugs out of each other's scalps and eat them. The evolutionary psychologists had that much right, at least. Older creatures still inhabited us, and would never vacate.

A morning of panels confirmed his impression that the field was paying undue respect to a handful of skilled showmen, some no older than his daughter. This, too, was science: fashions came and went; theories rose and vanished for all sorts of reasons, not all of them scientific. He had no more appetite for following the latest craze than he had for sitting through an entire baseball game. For one, few of the new theories could be tested. But the field was fundable and in a hurry, and they asked only that he give an entertaining keynote. A cartoonish tale-teller could do that much.

By mid-afternoon, he was seeing double. He sat through a baggy discussion of the phenomenology of synesthesia. He listened to a sensorimotor account of the origin of reading. He heard a fierce debate between cognitivists and new behaviorists on orbitofrontal damage and emotional processes. The one lecture of use to him examined the neurochemistry of the trait that truly separated humans from other creatures: boredom.

There followed an excruciating mass dinner during which his table mates—three American researchers he knew by reputation—baited him about the shaky reviews. Was it a statistical fluke, or some more significant shift in popular taste? Even the word *popular* sounded pointed. Pushed, he replied, "I suppose I have enjoyed the kind of attention that inevitably produces a backlash." He heard how self-serving the words were, even as they left his mouth, words these three researchers would now broadcast. The whole conference would hear them, by the time he gave his speech.

One of the conference organizers, a "holistic psychotherapist" from Washington, gave him an introduction so luminous it sounded mocking. Only when Weber stood behind the podium, at a moment that Sydney insisted was 8:00 p.m., did he realize the whole invitation might have been a setup. He looked out across a grassland peppered with the smiling, expectant faces of a species that hunted in packs.

He hated to read talks. Usually, he spoke from an outline, delivering freewheeling, campfire performances. But when he wandered from the script that night, vertigo hit him. He stood high on a towering cliff, water pounding over it. What was acrophobia anyway, if not the half-acknowledged desire to jump? He stayed close to the printed word, but with the stage lights on him and his eyes playing tricks, he kept losing his place. As he read aloud, he realized he'd pitched the talk too low. These were scientists, researchers. He was feeding them armchair descriptions, waiting-room stuff. He scrambled to add technical detail that got away from him even as he added it.

The speech wasn't a total disaster. He'd sat through worse. But it was no keynote, not worth the honorarium they paid. He took questions, mostly slow, fat lobs over the plate. The group felt sorry for him, seeing that the kill had already been made.

293

Someone asked if he thought that the narrative impulse might actually have preceded language. The question had nothing to do with the talk he'd just delivered. It seemed to refer, if anything, to the *Harper's* accusation that he'd missed his true calling, that Gerald Weber was, deep down, a fabulist.

He made it through the reception without further humiliation. The ordeal left him ravenous, just hours after dinner, but the reception offered nothing but Shiraz and greasy herring squares on crackers. The entire room developed Klüver-Bucy: popping things in their mouths like babies, carrying on a little too manically, mewling nonsense syllables to each other, propositioning anything that moved.

He didn't get back to the hotel until after midnight. He wasn't sure if he could call Sylvie. He couldn't even calculate the time difference. He lay awake, thinking of the answers he should have given, seeing the cracks in his ceiling as frozen synapses. Sometime after 3:00 a.m., it occurred to him that he himself might be an extremely detailed case history, a description of personality so minutely realized that it only thought it was autonomous . . .

At night, the brain grows strange to itself. He knew the precise biochemistry behind "sundowner syndrome"—the intense exaggeration of medical symptoms, during hours of darkness. But knowing the biochemistry didn't reverse it. Eventually, he must have fallen asleep, because he woke up from a dream in which people were plunging like missiles into a large body of water and emerging in molten proto-forms. Dreaming: that compromise solution for accommodating the vestigial brain stem. He woke to the phone, a wakeup call he'd forgotten asking for. It was still dark. He had thirty minutes to shower, eat, and cross town to the television studios for a live appearance on a morning news show. Five minutes on breakfast television, something he'd done half a dozen times before. He arrived at the studios with his mind still back at the hotel. They took him into Makeup and powdered him. He removed his glasses. Not vanity, really. Glasses under television lights became mirrors. He met with the show editor, who briefed him from photocopied notes and Internet printouts. The *Harper's* review peeked out of the stack. The editor seemed to be discussing a book written by someone else.

Weber sat in the cramped green room, watching a tiny monitor as the guest before him struggled to look natural. Then his turn came. They led him onto a tech-encircled set filled with glowing living room furniture. Around the couch, a small artillery unit of cameras dollied in and out. Without his glasses, the world was a Monet. They sat him next to the commentator, who looked down into what seemed to be a coffee table but was in fact a prompter. Next to this man, a woman: symbolic wife. The woman introduced him, garbling several facts. The first question came from nowhere.

"Gerald Weber. You've written about so many people suffering from so many extraordinary conditions. People who think that hot is cold and black is white. People who think they can see when they can't. People for whom time has stopped. People who think their body parts belong to someone else. Can you tell us the strangest case you've ever witnessed?"

A freak show, unrolling live in front of millions of breakfasters. Just like the reviews accused. He wanted to ask her to start again. The seconds clicked off, each as large, white, and frozen as Greenland. He opened his mouth to answer and discovered that his tongue was super-glued to the back of his front teeth. He could not salivate or moisten the freeze-dried hollow of his throat. Every Australian on earth would think he was sucking on a lug nut.

Words came out, but in chunks, as if he'd just suffered a stroke. He mumbled something about his books countering the idea of "suffering." Every mental state was simply a new and different way of being, different from ours only in degree.

"A person who has amnesia or experiences hallucinations isn't suffering?" the man asked in a journalistic voice, ready for instruction. Yet his tone bore just a tinge of sarcasm about to flower.

"Well, let's take hallucinations," Weber said. The *take* came out closer to *taste*. He described Charles Bonnet syndrome, patients with damage to the visual pathway that left them at least partially blind. Bonnet patients often experienced vivid hallucinations. "I know a woman who often finds herself surrounded by animated cartoons. But Bonnet's is common. Millions of people experience it. Yes, suffering is involved. Yet everyday, baseline consciousness involves suffering. We need to start seeing all these ways of being as continuous rather than discontinuous. Quantitatively rather than qualitatively different from us. They *are* us. Aspects of the same apparatus."

The woman commentator tilted her head at him and smiled, a megadose of gorgeous skepticism. "You're saying we're all a little out there?" Her companion laughed antiseptically. Television.

He said he was saying delusional thinking was similar to ordinary thinking. Brains of any flavor produced reasonable explanations for unusual perceptions.

"That's what lets you enter into mental states so different from your own?"

Like the worst traps, this one felt innocent. They steered toward the accusations about his work they'd found on the Internet. Do you really care about your patients, or are you just using them for scientific ends? Good controversy; better television. He felt the ambush develop. But he couldn't see, his mouth was dry, and he hadn't slept in days. He started to speak, sentences that sounded peculiar even before he formed them. He meant to say, simply, that everyone experienced passing moments of delusion, like when you look at the sunset and wonder, for an instant, where the sun goes. Such moments gave everyone the ability to understand others' mental deficits. The words came out sounding as if he were confessing to intermittent insanity. Both hosts smiled and thanked him for coming on the show that morning. They segued seamlessly into a teaser about a Brisbane man who had a piece of coral the size of a cricket-ball crash through his bedroom roof. Then a commercial break, and assistants hustled him off the set, his debacle taped forever and soon replayable on the Web, at any time, by anyone, from any-where on earth.

He called Bob Cavanaugh from the hotel. "I thought you'd want to know, before you heard from other quarters. Not good. There may be some fallout."

After the maddening satellite uplink delay, Cavanaugh sounded only bemused. "It's Australia, Gerald. Who's going to know?"

How much had Mark changed? The question dogged Karin, in that hot summer, a third of a year on. She measured him constantly, comparing him against an image of him before the accident that changed with each day she spent with the new Mark. Her sense of him was just a running average, weighted in favor of the latest person who stood in front of her. She no longer trusted her memory.

He was certainly slower. Before the accident, even deciding how to handle their mother's estate had taken him only twenty minutes. Now choosing whether to draw the blinds was like resolving the Middle East. A day became just long enough to sit down and figure out what he absolutely needed to do tomorrow, followed by a little necessary down time.

He was more forgetful. He could pour a bowl of cereal right next to the one he had left half-eaten. She told him several times a week that he was on disability, but he refused to believe it. His word blurs seemed almost playful to her. "Got to get back to work," he declared. "Bring home the bankin'." Seeing the president on the news, he groaned, "Not him again—Mr. Taxes of Evil." He complained about his clock radio readout. "I can't tell if it's 10:00 a.m. or 10:00 FM." Maybe this was still what all the books called *aphasia*. Or maybe Mark was goofing on purpose. She couldn't remember if he'd ever *been* funny, before.

He was often childlike now; she could no longer deny it. Yet she'd spent years before the accident badgering him to grow up. The whole country was juvenile. The *age* was childlike. And when she watched him alongside Rupp and Cain, Mark did not always suffer by comparison.

The slightest trigger set him raging. But anger, too, was an old familiar. Back in first grade, when Mark's teacher affectionately called him "an oddball" in front of the class, for bringing his lunch in a paper sack and not a metal lunch box, he'd cursed her in furious tears. Years later, when his father mocked him in a Christmas-dinner argument, the boy of fourteen sprang up from the table, ran up the stairs shrieking *Happy damn Holidays*, and put his fist through the maple-paneled bedroom door, winding up in the emergency room with three broken bones in his hand. And then there was the time a hysterical Joan Schluter tried to take shears to her son's locks after Mark and Cappy fought over his bangs. The seventeen-year-old had exploded, kicking in the oven and threatening to sue both parents for abuse.

In fact, even the Capgras had some precedent. For three years before puberty, Mark had refined Mr. Thurman, his imaginary friend. Mr. Thurman confided to Mark, in top secret, that Mark had been adopted. Mr. Thurman knew Mark's real family, and promised to introduce Mark when he was older. Sometimes Mr. Thurman made allowance for Karin, saying they were both foundlings, but related. Other times, they were drawn from different orphan lots. At those times, Mark consoled her, insisting they'd be better friends when they didn't have to carry on in that sham family anymore. Karin had hated Mr. Thurman with a passion, often threatening to gas him while Mark slept.

The Capgras was changing her, too. She fought against her habituation. For a little while longer, she still saw it: his laughter, eerily mechanical. His bouts of sadness, just statements of fact. Even his anger, mere colorful ritual. He'd burst out with some seven-year-old's declaration of love for Barbara, apropos of nothing. He'd go fishing with his buddies, mimic all the patter, sit in the boat casting and cursing his luck like the robot host of some television fishing show, going through the motions with fearful, flattened intensity, desperate to prove that he was still intact, inside the wrappings. For a little while longer, she knew the accident had blown them both away, and all the selfless attention from her in the world would never get them back. There was no *back* to get them to. For each new day, her own integrating memory increasingly proved that *my brother was always like that*.

Visiting the Homestar one early July afternoon, Karin found Mark watching a travel documentary featuring a gentle, anemic priest stumbling around Tuscany. Mark sat entranced, as if he'd just chanced upon the most extraordinary reality TV. He greeted Karin, excited. "Hey, guy. Look at this place! Unbelievable. People living there for millions of years. And stones even older than that."

Karin watched with him. He abided her now, a habit as upsetting as earlier hostilities. The travelogue ended, and Mark surfed the other channels. He buzzed his old favorites— motor and contact sports, music videos, manic comedies. But he flinched at the noise and speed. He could no longer open up the pipe that connected him to the outside world without overflowing. After five minutes of a rerun of his favorite syndicated farce, he asked, "Could that accident have made me psychic?"

She faked calm. "What do you mean?"

"It's like I can tell every joke before they even crack it."

He settled on a nature show about the three species of primitive egg-laying mammals, something he would not have been caught dead watching before the accident. "Jesus. What are those things? Somebody really screwed up on the design specs. Birds with hair!"

This was the Mark she remembered from childhood. Curious and tender, with no sudden moves. He'd grown baffled enough to want her there, sitting next to him on the narrow sofa. She had him just as she wanted. She could make tea for him, might even extend her arm across the sofa and touch his shoulder, and he'd bear it. The thought traumatized her. She stood and paced the room. Unthinkable: Tuscany, echidnas, and her brother. She stared at him where he sat on the couch, knitting his brows at the backward mammals, a charade of excitement. "Just look at that thing! Abandoned by evolution. Left behind. That's the saddest thing I've ever seen." He looked up and saw her pacing. "Hey. Would you sit down a minute? You're making me nervous."

She sat back on the couch next to him. He leaned toward her, turning on his idea of charm. He rested a hand on her thigh and launched into his daily litany. "How about driving me over to Thompson Motors? I can get a used F-150 for nothing. Trick it out. You gotta help me, though, because they stole my checkbook. Left me my address thingie, but the names and numbers are messed up."

"I don't know, Mark. That's probably not such a great idea yet."

"No?" He scowled and raised his helpless hands. "Whatever." He picked up a week-old copy of the *Kearney Hub* left on the coffee table as a place mat and flipped through the used-truck listings that he'd already penned up. She reached forward and pressed the power on the remote. He whirled on her. "Would you mind? I'm watching that. You don't really care about the egg mammals, do you? You don't care much about any species except yourself."

"Mark, the egg mammals are over."

"The hell they are. Living fossils. Greatest survival story in vertebrate history. Over? No way. Look! What is . . . that's . . . some kind of a sea unicorn or something."

"That's a new show, Mark."

"What the fuck do you know? It's all the same show." By way of proof, he flipped the clicker back around the channels. "Hey. Look at this one. Based on a true story. Doesn't anyone make movies based on fake stories, anymore?" He clicked some more, landing on Court TV. "All right? Satisfied? Jeez. Not from around here, are you?"

While Mark read his newspaper, she watched two neighbors sue each other over a garden plot they'd purchased together. After a while, she asked, "Would you like to go for a walk?"

He jerked up, alarmed. "Walk where?"

"I don't know. Down to Scudder's meadow? We could shoot for the river. Get out of the subdivision, anyway."

He looked at her with pity, that she'd think this possible. "I don't think so. Maybe tomorrow."

They sat for a long time, reading to a background of televised litigation. She fixed him a tuna melt for dinner. He walked her to the door when she left. "Damn it! Look at that. Night again. I don't know how I had time to work all day, when I was working. That reminds me: Infernal Beef. I should call the plant, shouldn't I? Gotta get back to the workaday, know what I'm saying? Can't live on free money forever."

He started cognitive behavioral therapy with Dr. Tower. Karin drove him to Kearney, in what Mark called "the little Jap car." He'd given up the idea that she might try to crash and kill him. Or perhaps he'd just reconciled himself to fate.

The treatment called for six weekly assessments followed by twelve "adjustment sessions," with as many follow-ups as necessary, through the next year. Karin drove him to Good Samaritan for the appointments, then walked around town for the hour. The hospital staff asked her not to talk with Mark about the therapy until they had her join the later sessions. She swore she wouldn't. After the second session, the question slipped out before she heard herself asking. "So how is it, talking to Dr. Tower?"

He turned clinical. "Okay, I guess. Doesn't hurt to look at her. Little slow on the uptake, though. Man, you have to tell the woman everything a hundred times. She thinks you might be real. Maddening."

Barbara came by, three times a week. She would drop in unannounced, always an event. Out of her hospital clothes, in gray shorts and burgundy tee, she was summer personified. Karin admired her bare arms and legs, wondering again about the woman's age. Barbara turned Mark into a water-drinking duck toy, constantly bobbing, game for anything she asked. And all the things she asked for felt like games. She took him to the grocery store and made him shop for himself. That course had never occurred to Karin, who stocked Mark's kitchen each week, keeping him both fed and dependent. Barbara, though, was merciless. She'd make no decisions for him, however much he appealed to her. "Hey, Barbie. Which of these do I really like better? You remember, from all those years in our little health hotel? Am I a sausage guy or a bacon guy?"

"I'll tell you how you can find out. Just watch yourself, and see which one you pick." She turned him loose, condemned to freedom in all the terror of American abundance, mounting interventions only in the matter of sprayable cheese and chocolate marshmallow cereal.

Barbara played video games with him, even the racing program. Mark loved it: a fish on wheels he could beat every time, even with one thumb tied behind his back. She got him on cribbage. Mark loved the epic contests, which often left him begging for mercy. "Is this how you get your kicks? A grown woman, beating up on beginners?"

Karin overheard. "Beginner? You don't remember playing this forever, with your mother, as a child?"

303

He scoffed at the idiocy. "Playing *forever*? My mother as a *child*?"

"You know what I'm saying. Using sheets of worthless Green Stamps as stakes."

Mark lifted his head from the cards, to sneer. "My mother did not play cribbage. Playing cards were the increments of the Devil."

"That was later, Mark. When we were little, she was still a card addict. Don't you remember? Hey. Don't ignore me."

"Playing cards. With my mother. My mother as a *child*."

Three months—no; thirty years—of frustration thickened the air around her. "Oh, for God's sake! Don't be such a gnat-skull." She listened to the echo, horrified at herself. Her eyes sought Barbara's, pleading temporary insanity. Barbara checked Mark. But Mark just tipped his head back and snorted.

"Gnat-skull. Where'd you learn that? My sister used to call me that, too."

Nothing rattled him, so long as Barbara was there. In small steps, she got him reading again. She tricked him into picking up a book he'd refused to crack when required back in high school. *My Antonia*. "Very sexy story," she assured him. "About a young Nebraska country boy who has the hots for an older woman."

He got fifty pages in, although it took him two weeks. He confronted Barbara with the evidence, betrayed. "It's not about what you said at all. It's about immigrants and farming and drought and shit."

"That, too," she admitted.

He stuck with the story, to protect his investment, throwing good hours after bad. The book's ending confused him. "You mean he goes back, after they're both married and she has all those fucking kids, just to hang out? Just to, like, be her *friend*, or something? Just because of what happened when they were little?"

Barbara nodded, her eyes filmy. Mark put out his hand to comfort her.

"Best obsolete book I ever read. Not that I got it all, exactly."

She took him on long walks under the summer sun. They wandered, parched yet sticky, July threatening to rasp on without end, with nothing they could do but endure and keep walking. They spent hours touring the ignited wheat fields, like local farm agents responsible for monitoring the region's harvest. They took the dog, Blackie Two. "This cur is almost as good as mine," Mark declared. "Just a little less obedient." Now and then he let Karin tag along, if she kept quiet.

Barbara could listen to Mark go on about modding vehicles long after Karin numbed. "I can never leave a car stock," Mark declared. He launched an extended anatomy of the vehicle he was building in his head: Rams, Bigfoots, and Broncos all spliced together into a monster hybrid. Ignored and invisible, tagging along fifty yards back, Karin studied the older woman's technique. Barbara absorbed and deflected him, drawing him out. She listened, rapt, to Mark's recited parts lists, then lifted her finger, as if in passing. "Did you hear that? What was that sound?" Without his realizing, she'd have Mark listening to the cicada choruses that he hadn't heard since fifteen. Barbara Gillespie had the lightest touch known to man, a self-possession that Karin could dissect and even imitate for short stretches, but could never hope to embody. It saddened her to see, in Barbara, what she finally wanted to be when she grew up. But she had no more chance of becoming Barbara than a lightning bug had, through diligence, of becoming a lighthouse. The other woman now belonged here more than she did.

Mark would do anything for his Barbie Doll. Karin came on them late one afternoon at his kitchen table, heads bowed over an art book, looking for all the world like Joan Schluter and her final pastor poring over Scripture. The book was called *A Guide to Unseeing: 100 Artists Who Gave Us New Eyes*. Some volume from Barbara's secret, surprise shelf. Karin drew behind them where they sat, afraid Mark might flare up and banish her. But he didn't even notice her. He was hypnotized by Cezanne's *House and Trees*. Barbara's fingers draped across the image, twining with the tree trunks. Mark had his face up to the page, following the scrape of the palette knife. He struggled with the picture, something forcing up from inside him. Karin saw at once what he wrestled with: their old farmhouse, the lean-to against the precarious years of their childhood, the house whose mortgage their father tried to pay by dusting crops in an ancient Grumman AgCat. She couldn't stop herself. "You know where that is, don't you?"

Mark turned on her, like a bear surprised while foraging. "It's nowhere." He pointed wildly at his own skull. "It's fucking fantasy, is where it is." She shrank back. He might have stood and struck her, except for the graze of Barbara's fingers on his arm. The touch threw a circuit breaker, and he turned back to the print, rage dissolving. He grabbed the pages and thumbed them, flip-book style, five hundred years of painted master-pieces in five seconds. "Who's been making all this stuff? I mean, look at this! How long has this been going on? Where have I been all my life?"

Minutes passed before Karin stopped shaking. Once, eight years ago, he'd split her lip with a backhand when she'd called him an unreliable asshole. Now he might truly hurt her, without even knowing. He'd be stuck like this for good, even farther gone than their father was, unable to hold down jobs, watching nature shows and browsing art books, reacting to the smallest impediment with cloudbursts of fury. Then turning away, puzzled, as if not quite believing what he'd just done.

It wrecked her: he'd be dependent on her forever. And still she would fail him, as she had failed to protect her parents from their own worst instincts. Her ministrations were making Mark even worse. She needed him to be a way he would never be again, a way that she was no longer sure that he had ever been. She hadn't the strength to cope with his crushing new innocence. She lowered herself into a folding chair. The arc of her own life no longer led anywhere. The years ahead collapsed, burying her under their dead weight. Then the graze of fingertips on her forearm took her out of herself.

She looked up into Barbara, a face whose gaze seemed equal to any behavior. Barbara retrieved her hand from Karin's arm and continued to walk Mark through the calming book. She seemed to know all the painters' names, without even looking at the captions. Did she extend this care to all her discharged patients? Why the Schluters? Karin didn't dare ask. The visits couldn't last much longer. But there Barbara was at Mark's kitchen table, keeping him company in his unseeing.

The two women left together that evening. Karin walked Barbara to her car. "Listen. I don't know how to say this. I am in your debt. I'll never be able to thank you for this. Never."

Barbara wrinkled her nose. "Pff. Hardly. Thanks for letting me drop in."

"Serious. He'd be lost without you. I'd be . . . worse."

Too much: the woman cringed, ready to flee. "It's nothing. It's completely for me."

"If there's ever anything—anything at all—please, please . . ."

Barbara held her eye: *There might be, one day.* To Karin's surprise, she rushed out, "Who knows when we'll need someone looking out for us?"

Not even the Muskrateers rattled Barbara. When their visits overlapped, Rupp and Cain enlisted Barbara in rounds of five-card stud or two-hand touch. Whatever game the boys were playing, Barbara joined. Mark came out of his maze for as long as she was nearby. Cain couldn't resist drawing her into running debates—the war on terror, the necessary curtailment of civil liberties, the invulnerable yet somehow infinitely threatened American way of life. He was one of those stubby, apoplectic debaters who jabbed out statistics, richly detailed and constantly mutating. Barbara pummeled him. Unsportsmanlike, even letting Duane into the same ring with her. Once, he cited some newly upholstered article from the Bill of Rights, and she countered with the entire document, memorized. He fled the room at peak decibel, shouting, "Maybe in *your* Constitution!"

Rupp hit on the woman conscientiously, duty-bound, resorting to increasingly desperate supplications: help with his pet ferret. A model rocketry excursion. Licking envelopes for a mass fund-raiser. Her job was the cheerful slam. Muzzle it. Try a solo lift-off. Get stuffed. Everyone waited for the next escalation. Everyone except Mark, who begged them, eyes wet, to quit.

Karin gave what he let her give. She loved to run the taxi service to the hour-long cognitive therapy sessions that Mark increasingly resisted. Taking him home after the third appointment, so casually she wasn't really breaking the hospital's orders, she sounded him out again. "How are things going with you and Dr. Tower?"

"Pretty good," Mark said, eyes, as always, glued to the road. "I think all this therapy is starting to make her feel a little better."

Before the fourth session, Mark demanded to visit Intensive Care. He picked a floor nurse at random, told her the story and showed the note. The startled woman promised to pass along anything she heard.

"See that?" he asked, as Karin steered him toward Dr. Tower's floor. "She was stonewalling. Claiming they didn't let anyone in to see me that first night except my next of kin. But you told me they let *you* in. It doesn't add up, does it?"

She shook her head, surrendering to the laws of his world. "No, Mark. It really doesn't."

She spent the hour of his session sitting in the hospital cafeteria, calculating the degree of her self-delusion. Therapy was doing nothing for him. She was clinging to medical science the same way her mother clung to Revelation. Weber's scientific assurances had seemed so rational. But then, Mark seemed rational to himself. And increasingly clearer-eyed than she.

When he came out of the session, Karin suggested dinner. "How about Grand Island, the Farmer's Daughter Café?"

"Holy crap!" Pleasure and fear struggled over his face. "That's my favorite place to eat in this whole forsaken life. How did you know that? You talk to the guys?"

She felt ashamed for everything human. "I know you. I know what you like."

He shrugged. "Hey! Maybe you have weird powers you don't know about. We should run some tests."

Mark and his friends loved to drive forty-five miles for the same bloody beef they could get anywhere in half a dozen places in Kearney. Karin had never understood the Farmer's

Daughter's appeal, but she was glad now for the ride. Mark, hostage, sat next to her, thoughtful, for most of an hour. Riding shotgun—*the death seat*, he called it—he scanned the fields of wheat, beans, and corn, scouring the landscape for the slightest thing that didn't fit. He read the road signs out loud: "Adopt-a-highway. Adopt a *highway*! Who would've thought so many of our nation's roads were orphaned?"

She waited until the sleepy stretch between Shelton and Wood River to question him. Medicine had betrayed her; she could betray medicine. "So what's the worst thing about Dr. Tower?"

His head was nearly on the dash, peering up at a raptor circling above them. "She's getting on my nerves. She wants to know all this crap that happened twenty million years ago. What's different, what's the same. I tell her: You want ancient history? Go buy an ancient history book." The hawk fell away behind them. Mark straightened and leaned over toward her. " 'What did you do when you were little and your sister made you angry?' What's the point? I mean, it's weird, don't you think? Trying to find out so much about me. Change the way I look at things."

Her pulse quickened at his conspiratorial tone. She remembered their covert adolescent resistance, surviving their parents' worst certainties. Now he offered a new alliance. She could join him, however crazy. They'd both have what they needed. She sucked air, dizzy to toady to him. "First of all, Mark. No one is *making* you do anything."

"Whew. That's a relief."

"Dr. Tower just wants to understand what's on your mind now."

"Why don't they just stick me back inside one of those scanners? Damn, they've got to work the kinks out of those things. You ever been inside one of those tubes? Damn racket. Like having your skull worked on in a body shop. And you can't move. Chin all strapped in. Mess you up good, if you're not messed up already. Computerized mind reading."

She let it drop until Grand Island. Summer along the Platte: the shimmering mirage, the burnt-green wall of flattening heat that made the Plains everyone else's model of godforsaken barrenness released Karin. The surging, Lego grid of Chicago had oppressed her. The Rockies left her edgy. L.A.'s wraparound glitz felt like hysterical blindness. This place, at least, she knew. This place alone was open and empty enough to disappear in.

The Farmer's Daughter occupied an old 1880s storefront with cherry wood wainscoting and bits of rusting farm implements hanging on the walls. Nebraska playing itself. The grandmotherly hostess greeted them as long-lost friends, and Karin replied with like effusion. "They've changed this place around," Mark insisted, in their booth. "I don't know. Rehabbed. It used to be newer." And when they ordered: "The menu's the same, but the food's relapsed." He ate with resolve, but little joy.

"Dr. Tower just wants to get a sense of your thoughts," Karin insisted. "That way, she can, you know, kind of put things back together."

"I see. I see. You think I'm coming apart?"

"Well." She knew *she* was. "How do you feel?"

"That's what that damn doctor keeps asking. I never felt better. Felt a whole lot worse, I'll tell you that much."

"No question. You're worlds better than you were, this time five months ago."

He laughed at her. "How can you have 'this time' five months ago?"

311

She waved her hands, flustered. Every word her mind fingered melted into meaningless figures of speech. "Mark, for days after they cut you out of that truck, you couldn't see, you couldn't move, you couldn't talk. You were barely human. You've worked a miracle since then. That's the word the doctors use: miracle."

"Yep. Me and Jesus."

"So now, with all the ground you've gained, Dr. Tower can help you even more. She might find some things that could make you feel better."

"Not having had that accident would make me feel better. You going to finish those potatoes?"

"Mark, this is for real. You want to feel more like yourself again, don't you?"

"What are you talking about?" He giggled again, approximately. "I feel exactly like myself. Who else am I supposed to feel like?"

More than she could claim. She let the matter fall. When the modest meal check came, she reached to take it. He snatched her hand. "What are you doing? You can't pay for this. You're the woman."

"It was my idea."

"True." Mark toyed with the pepper shaker, figuring. "You want to pay for *my* dinner? I don't get it." His voice searched for a teasing tone. "Is this some kind of date? Oh, no. Wait. I forgot. Incest."

The waitress came and took Karin's credit card. Soon it would be maxed out and she'd have to start another. In another five months, her mother's life insurance, the sum that Karin hadn't wanted to dip into, the money she was supposed to use to do good things, would be wiped out, too.

"This absolutely proves you can't be my sister. My sister is the cheapest person I've ever met. Except for maybe my father."

She jerked back, wounded. But his blank face stopped her. He was probably right. Her whole life she'd clutched, panicked, at anything buoyant enough to float her free from the maelstrom of Cappy and Joan. And all her hoarding had depleted her. So it went, with safety: the more you guarded, the less you had. She would make up for it, now. Mark would cost her no less than everything. She would spend what life she'd had, to pay for the life he couldn't even see he'd lost. Did it count as generosity, if you had no choice?

"Next one's on you," she said. "Come on, let's go home."

By the time they left Grand Island, night was falling. Ten miles out of town, Mark took off his seat belt. It shouldn't have unnerved her. Just the opposite: the old Mark never wore his belt. Here he was, coming back to normal, trusting her again. But she panicked. "Mark," she shouted. "Buckle up." She reached to help, and he slapped her hand. Shaking, Karin pulled over onto Highway 30's dark shoulder. She refused to continue until he fastened. He seemed perfectly happy to sit there in the dark, enjoying their Mexican standoff.

At last he said, "I'll put the belt on. But you have to take me."

"Where?" she said, knowing.

"I want to see where it happened."

"Mark. You don't, really."

He stared straight ahead, into his own universe. He spun his hand around his head, the sign for *gone*. "I might as well never have been there."

"We can't. Not tonight. It'll be pitch-black. You won't be able to see a thing."

"I can't even see that much, now."

313

"Let me take you home. I promise you, we'll go first thing in the morning."

He turned on her. "That would be convenient, wouldn't it? Take me back 'home,' call your people, and then go and smooth out everything, while I'm sleeping. And I wouldn't ever know the difference."

Solid shapes, artfully altered in the night, data manipulated while their backs were turned. Everything certain, carried away downstream.

"Tampering with the scene of the crime," he said. He flipped the glove compartment of her Corolla up and down.

"Crime? What do you mean? What crime?"

"You know what I'm talking about. Going through the ditch and removing the evidence. Laying down false tracks."

"Mark, anybody who wanted to tamper with the evidence has had almost half a year. There's no evidence *left*. Why would they wait until now?"

"Because I didn't want a look, until now."

His jiggling accelerated, and she reached out and stopped his hand. "There's nothing left to see. It's all been washed away or grown over."

He sat up, excited. "You agree with me, then? Somebody's altering every clue I might have to crack this thing?"

This thing. His life. "Nature, Mark." Overgrowing all that ever happened. "Put your seat belt back on. Let's go."

He did as instructed, but on the condition that she stay the night in the Homestar where he could keep an eye on her. "I have this hide-a-backache thing in my front room you can sleep on." They rode back to Farview in silence. Mark wouldn't let her play the radio, not even KQKY, which he claimed no longer played the kind of music it used to. At his house, Mark asked for her car keys, to put under his pillow.

314

"I've been sleeping kind of hard. I probably wouldn't hear you if you snuck off during the night."

While her brother showered, Karin called Daniel. She tore him out of deep meditation. She told him about the evening and said she was staying at Mark's. "See you tomorrow?" she said, wanting off the phone. For just an instant, he failed to respond. He didn't believe her. She closed her eyes and teetered. History under the floorboards, waiting to flame up.

Daniel grew solicitous. "Is everything all right? Would you like me to come over?"

"Who's that?" Mark demanded, materializing in the living room doorway, dangling a towel in front of him and dripping on the gold pile carpeting. "I told you not to contact anyone."

"I'll see you tomorrow," Karin said into her cell, then powered off.

"Who was that? Damn it. I can't turn my back on you for a second."

"That was Daniel Riegel." Mark cocked a forearm in front of him, warding off the name. "We've been seeing each other for, for a little while. I guess I'm living with him, you could say. It's good with him, Mark. After all the crap we dumped on each other. Finally good between us." She didn't add: *because of you.*

"Danny Riegel? Mother Naked boy?" He sat, still damp, on the arm of his Naugahyde recliner, abstractedly toweling his chest. A little late, Karin looked away. "So you two really are an item?"

"He came to see you in the hospital." Stupid, forced, irrelevant.

"He did? Danny Riegel. Well, he can't hurt me. He wouldn't hurt an amoeba. He can't be in on any big doings.

Not Danny Riegel. But, shit. How did you know to get involved with him? That's really eerie. My sister and him were, like, some tape loop. They must have programmed you in advance, put it in your DNA, or something."

She turned back to him, past fatigue, slipping back into what she would have to do every day for the rest of her life, if she stayed on nursing him. "Mark, go for the easy solution, for once. The obvious."

"Ha! In this life? You've lost it."

He wrapped the towel around his waist and helped her open the sofa bed. Later, after midnight, she lay on that mat of shifting ball bearings and razor springs, listening in the dark for movement. Everything was alive: air conditioning cutting on and shuddering off, lightweight creatures scuffling in the walls, warm-blooded branches tapping the window, something the size of a subcompact reconnoitering the azaleas, insects excavating her ear, their beating wings like dentist's drills drawing near her eardrum. And every creak sounded like her brother, whoever he was, slipping into the living room.

After a habitual, puffed-sugar breakfast, Karin brought him out to North Line Road. The early-morning air was already asbestos, ready to break one hundred humid degrees before noon. Yet Mark wore his long black jeans. He couldn't get used to the scars on his legs and didn't want anyone thinking that was how he looked. The stretch of shimmering road seemed almost featureless: sedge-lined pasture and grassy fields, the rare road sign and scrub tree, and crossroads named only with numbers. But Karin pulled over within thirty feet of the accident.

"This is it? You sure this is where I rolled it?"

Wordless, she left the car. He followed. They combed the deserted road in opposite directions. They might have been a vacationing couple, stopping to search for a map that had blown out of their car window. The scene offered even less than when she'd come with Daniel, nothing except the brute business of nature, the base of the whole pyramid, too small and sprawling to bother with: a green, ground-hugging cover running all the way to the horizon, with a trickle of melting asphalt burned through it.

Mark drifted across the road, as baffled as the herd of Simmental on the hillock three hundred yards to his right. Only, the drifting cows didn't shake their heads.

"Which way was I going?" She pointed west, back toward town. Whatever evidence he sought had long ago been whisked away by forces intent on erasing his life. "See? Nothing here. Told you. It's all been moved out." He squatted and brushed the asphalt with one palm. At length, he dropped to the ground and sat on the drooping road edge, his arms around his knees. She came over to him, to beg him to move off onto the shoulder. Instead, she dropped down beside him, both of them targets for any passing vehicle faster than a combine. He didn't look up. He held his arms in the air, lifting the emptiness. "We were at the Bullet. I remember that."

"Who?" she whispered, trying to sound as blank as he.

"Me, Tommy, Duane. Couple guys from the plant. Music, the band, I think. It was cold. I was arm-wrestling somebody. And that's it. Total blank. I don't even remember getting in the truck. Nothing, until I'm sitting up in a hospital bed drooling on myself. How long was that? Weeks? Months? Like I'm locked away somewhere and somebody else is living my life." The monotone came out of him, in poor computer speech.

She rested her arm on his shoulder and he didn't pull away. "Don't worry about it," she said. "Just try to . . ."

317

He tapped her arm and pointed. An ancient Pontiac wagon lumbered in from the east. They rose to their feet and moved a yard off the road. The car slowed to a stop in front of them, its windows open. The seats were piled high with gear—boxes full of clothing, stacks of dishes, books, tools, even a corsage of plastic flowers. In the back, an air mattress lay covered with a ratty cotton blanket. A thick-featured, crimson-faced man of seventy, unmistakably Winnebago, leaned across the front seat. "Car trouble?"

"Kind of," Mark said.

"You need a lift?"

"I need something."

The Winnebago man opened his passenger door. Karin pushed forward. "We're okay. We're good." The man looked through them both and stared a long time before closing the door and driving away, slower than a riding mower.

"That reminds me," Mark said, no faster than the vehicle. She waited, but patience produced nothing. "Of what?"

"It just reminds me." He strayed from the roadside to the center line. She tagged behind. He held out his hands, re-creating the imagined path. "I know I rolled the truck. I know they operated on me."

"They didn't really operate on you, Mark."

"I had a damn metal spigot coming out of my skull."

"That wasn't exactly brain surgery."

He flashed a palm to silence her. "I'll tell you what else. That car reminded me. There was someone else out here. I wasn't alone."

Insects burrowed in her skin. "What do you mean?"

"What do you think I mean? In the damn truck. I wasn't the only one in there."

"I think you were, Mark. You know, if you can't remember being in the truck yourself . . ."

318

"Well, *you* were not fucking there, either! I'm telling you what I know. Somebody was sitting there talking to me. I remember talking. I distinctly remember another voice. Maybe I picked up a hitchhiker somewhere."

"There was no one else anywhere near your truck."

"Then whoever it was just picked up their death bed and walked away!"

"If the investigators found any prints, they would have—"

"Judas Christ! Do you want to know what I remember or not? I'm telling you what this thing's about. People appearing and disappearing, like that!" He snapped his finger, a vicious crack. "First they're right there, then they're not. In the truck, out on the road, gone. Maybe I dropped them off somewhere. Anybody can disappear on you, at any point. One day, they're your blood relations, the next day, they're plants." He scrambled into his pocket and pulled out the crushed scrap of paper, his sole anchor. The gift that kept on taking. His eyes welled up, blinding him. "First they're angels, then they're not even animals. Guardians that won't even admit they exist." He threw the scrap of paper on the pavement. The crosswind raked it over the road into the ditch, where it snagged on a stand of switchgrass.

Karin cried out and tore after it as if chasing a straying baby. She ran headlong into the ditch, scraping her bare legs on a patch of prickle-weed. She leaned down and snatched the scrap, sniffling. She turned to face him, triumphant. Mark stood frozen in the road, looking east. She called him, but he didn't hear. He didn't break his gaze, even as she came back to him.

"Something was right there." He swung around in a half-circle. "I was coming this way, just over the rise." He turned back east again, nodding. "Something in the road. Just here."

319

Her spine ignited. "Yes," she whispered. "That's right. Another car? Swerving over the center line. Coming at you, in your lane."

He shook his head. "No. Not that. Like a column of white."

"Yes. Headlights—"

"No car, damn it! A ghost, or something. Just floating up, things flying. Then gone." His neck caved forward and his eyes widened, pulling himself from the wreck.

She guided him back to the car and got him into the passenger side. He ran the same continuous calculation, all the way back to Farview. A mile before town, he demanded the note. She almost had to stand up behind the wheel to extract it from her too-tight shorts. He read it again, nodding.

"I'm a killer," he said, as she pulled into the Homestar's empty driveway. "Some kind of guiding spirit in the road, and I tried to kill it."

So the note writer's not a churchgoer. Fine. He's proved that much, at least. Visited all the non-illegal churches, shown the note to every believer in town, and nobody's claimed it. Time to head out among the heathens. People don't generally know this about Nebraska, but it's filled with heathens. He takes Bonnie-baby with him. Old missionary trick: send out the youngest, sexiest girl you've got. The core cults are all over this. People are nicer to foxes. Send a fox to somebody's front door, and a woman will assume that you can't possibly be a serial killer, while a man will stand there melting, emptying his pockets for the charity of your choice. Even read the Book of Mormon, if she smiles at him right.

The two of them set out together, the fox and the grapes. Like they're married or husband and wife or something, which he personally would have no problem with, if it meant getting your claws painted and your ashes hauled on a regular basis. Sometimes they even take the dog—one big happy family. Bonnie's not crazy about the idea at first, but she gets into it. They go on a door-to-door campaign, note in hand. House-to-house fighting, to flush out the messenger hiding behind the message.

A lot of people are familiar with Mark Schluter, or say they are. He recognizes some of them, but you never can tell, with people. Maybe he went to school with them, or worked with them out at IBP or at his prior not-so-gainful employment. Small-town life: worse than having your picture up at the post office. A lot of people say they know him, although they don't really mean *know*. They just mean: *Oh, the dumbass we read about in the* Hub *who flipped his truck and had to work his way back from a vegetative condition.* It's pretty easy to read their real thoughts, just by how nice they are to him when he and Bonnie ring the bell. At least, when they sit him and Bonnie down and serve them the fizzy drinks, he can check their handwriting. Maybe they've left some letters out to be mailed. Maybe a shopping list stuck on the refrigerator with the little *Star Wars* magnet. Or they'll make some pathetic suggestion— some number to call or book to read—and he can go, *Hey, great idea. Can you write that down?*

But nobody writes like the note. That handwriting died out a hundred years ago, in the Old Country. Everyone he shows it to gets all quiet, like they know that those twisting letters could only have come from beyond the grave.

The note is disintegrating, turning back to dust. He gets Duane-o to laminate it, up at the plant. Make it perpetual, for however long he needs to haul it around. But in early August, something strange starts happening. They've been knocking on doors for weeks. No one in Farview will admit to anything. Farview's pretty much eliminated, checked off his list. He wants to tackle Kearney. They could stand out at the Speedway station pumps, or alongside the Sino-Mart greeter. At worst, they get thrown out of the store. But Bonnie gets weird about the whole thing. Then he picks up on it.

Have you noticed anything out of the ordinary? he asks her.

Ordinary how, Marker?

She's in a white sleeveless blouse and cut-off jeans, like *way* cut off, and that straight black hair of hers and that navel that just won't quit. She really is maximally adorable, and it's kind of a mystery that Mark was never onto that fact in any systematic way before this whole accident.

Unordinary. Extraordinary. Notice any peculiar . . . well, let's just say, *patterns*?

She shakes her pretty head. He wants to trust her. She's a little too close to the Pseudo-Sister for comfort's sake, but that woman has everyone fooled, even Barbara.

You're saying that nobody we've talked to . . . seems at all odd to you?

The little laugh, like a music box. Odd, how?

He has to make it sound like something that won't scare her. Nobody's going to believe something that endangers their whole worldview. Okay, he tells her. A lot of those people who've been answering the doors when we knock? I'm not saying all of them. I'm just saying . . . some, some of them are like the same person.

The same . . . ? The same person as what?

What do you mean, *same as what*? Same as each other.

You're saying . . . you're saying they're . . . the same as themselves?

Well, it's not rocket science; not even brain surgery. Kind of a simple concept, actually: somebody's been following them around. They shouldn't have been going up and down the streets so obviously. They should have mixed things up, randomized. They've been suckers, predictable. Walked right into this.

Listen. I know this is going to sound a little out there. But there's . . . one guy who keeps coming back.

Coming back? Back where?

You know what I'm saying. Following us. One house to the other. And I think I know who this person is.

This prompts her to say a number of fairly dopey things. Understandable: she's freaked. Him, too, but he's had a little more time to think about it. Bonnie is still back in beginner's denial: How can anybody be following us? How could they get into the next house, put on a disguise, etcetera, all before we get there?

Pretty lame objections, that dissolve the minute you examine them. But Bonnie's upset; she doesn't want to make the rounds anymore. He should have guessed this would happen. She probably thinks her life is in danger. He tries to explain: the disguise artist is interested in one person and one person only: Mark Schluter. But Mark can't convince her to stay with the search. Maybe that's best, after all. The hunt has produced nothing, and who can say when this little cat-and-mouse game might turn violent? After all, there's been violence already. Last February 20, to be precise.

He carries on alone. He works the Public Library and Moraine Assisted Living. But interestingly, few people are willing to give him handwriting samples, and every third person who does pretends they're someone they aren't. The disguise artist keeps trailing him. Someone he hasn't seen in many years. There's a sad droop about the eyes that gives it away every time. Like we're all hosed and this lone, wise face is the only one to fully understand the fact. Danny boy. Riegel, the birdman of Kearney.

It occurs to Mark: his accident happened right at the very start of bird season. Sure, that could be just coincidence. But now that Mr. Migration has taken to following him around, it lends more than a little weight to a larger theory. What's more: Riegel and his fake sister are rubbing genitals. It's all too much. Mark doesn't know exactly what to make of it, but he's got to make something soon, or it's going to make him.

He confronts the artificial Karin. Nothing to lose. He's in the crosshairs already. He waits until she shows up at the would-be Homestar with her latest bag of unrequested groceries. Then he asks her point-blank, before she can confuse him. Just tell me, honestly. What is your friend the nature man up to? Don't lie to me; we've known each other a while now, right? Been through some rough times.

She gets all shy, holds her elbows and studies her shoes like they just jumped onto her feet. I don't know, exactly, she claims. Strange, isn't it? How he keeps coming back into my life at different crises? First when Cappy died, then Mom, and now—

Kind of strange how he keeps coming back into *my* life. Every time I try to talk to anyone about my little message from heaven?

She stares at him, like at a firing squad. Guilty, as charged. But then she goes into a major stall routine. Following you around? What are you talking about? She starts to cry, one step away from an admission of guilt. But then she turns worse than worthless. She gets on her cell phone and calls Bonnie, trying to synchronize their stories. Ten minutes later, it's two against one, with both of the women carrying on about the most irrelevant shit, handing him the phone and telling him it's Daniel on the other end, just say a few words to Daniel . . .

He's got to get out of this place, someplace he can think. He's got a little spot down by the river where he can just sit in the flats and let those hundreds of muddy, liquid miles wash over him. He starts south, on foot. He hasn't been on the Platte since last fall. He's been afraid to discover that somebody's jacking with the river as well. He leaves the house without his hat, and the sun scalds him. Birds track him from tree to tree. A pack of grackles, animal spies. They make an entirely uncalled-for racket, like they've got a problem with him. Their so-called songs echo in his head, going *gaw, gaw, go, goat-head, goat-head, goat-head* . . .

And then the words are already there: the words he was saying, just before his truck took to the air. *Goat-head* may be the Ram, like he was saying the truck's name. But no. *Goat-head*: something more, if his life means anything. He gets to the edge of River Run Estates, slips through the fringe of sycamores. He reaches the long cut, a mile and a half of headland thick with black flies and pollen, nothing to protect him from the elements. The river recedes as he walks toward it. The grackles get on his case. *Goat-head, goat-head.*

Go ahead.

The force of it sits him down smack in a patch of prickleweed. He was saying, *Go ahead*. Or someone was saying it to him, in the cab of the truck. He'd picked up some angel hitchhiker, someone who survived the flipped truck, walked away from the wreck back to town, to call in the disaster. And afterward, followed him to the hospital, to leave the note, instructions for Mark Schluter's future. An angel hitchhiker, telling him, *Go ahead*. Go where? Toward the wreck; through the wreck. Here.

He stands up, shaky with insight. In the singed green of this field, black spots rise and his vision tunnels. His body wants to go down, but he fights upright. He turns back toward Farview, jogging. His brain spurts like a hot coal stabbed with a poker. He reaches the fake Homestar, doubled over by a stitch in his side. How did he get so out of shape? He bursts in the front door, eager to tell anyone, even people he probably shouldn't tell. A manic Blackie Two almost knocks him down, already knowing, with animal telepathy, about this breakthrough. The woman is still there, sitting at his desk, at his computer, like she owns the place. She swings around, guilty, caught by his return. Even redder than usual, pushing the hair back, like: *Oh, nothing*. Trying to hack his credit card cookies or such. She logs off quickly and turns toward him. Mark? Mark, are you okay?

Unbelievable question. Who in the whole godforsaken world is okay? It may be death, to tell her what he's discovered. She might be anyone. He still has no idea whose side she's on. But they've grown close over these months, in adversity. She feels *something* for him, he's sure of that. Sympathy or pity, seeing what he's up against. Maybe enough to make her break ranks and join him. Or maybe not. Telling her may be the stupidest thing he's ever done, since whatever he did to lose his real sister. But finally, he wants to tell her. He needs to tell her. Logic's got nothing to do with it. It's about survival.

Listen, he says, excited. Your fiancé? Boyfriend, whatever. See if you can find out what he was doing the night of my accident. Ask him if the words *go ahead* mean anything to him.

For a moment, Weber couldn't find his left arm or shoulder. No sense of whether his hand was underneath him or above him, palm up or down, flung out or drawn in. He panicked, and the alarm congealed him, bringing him almost alert enough to identify the mechanism: awareness before the full return of the somatosensory cortex from sleep. But only when he forced his paralyzed side to move could he locate all his parts again.

An anonymous hotel, in another country. Another hemisphere. Singapore. Bangkok. A slightly more spacious version of those Tokyo morgue hotels, with businessmen filed away in drawers, rented by the night. Even when he remembered where he was, he couldn't credit it. *Why* he was there lay beyond answer. He read the clock: an arbitrary number that might have meant either day or night. He flipped on the diffident bedside light and headed to the bathroom. A hot shower would help to disperse his lingering displacement. But his body came back only tentatively. None of the bizarre neurological insights acquired over the course of his professional life unsettled him more than this simplest one: baseline experience was simply wrong. Our sense of physical embodiment did not come from the body itself. Several layers of brain stood in between, cobbling up from raw signals the reassuring illusion of solidity.

Scalding water streamed over his neck and down his chest. He felt his shoulders relax, but he did not place too much faith in the feeling. The cortex's body maps were fluid at best, and easily dismantled. He could alarm any undergraduate by having her slide her arms into two boxes with a window in the end of the right one. The student's hand appeared in the window. Only: the hand in the window wasn't her right one, but a cleverly superimposed reflection of her left. Asked to flex her right hand, the student saw, through the window, a hand that wouldn't move. Instead of reaching the only logical conclusion—a trick of mirrors—the student would almost always feel a surge of terror, believing her hand to be somehow paralyzed.

Worse still: a subject who watched a rubber hand being stroked in synchrony with his own hidden hand would continue to feel the strokes, even when the stroking of his real hand stopped. The dummy hand didn't even have to be lifelike, or even a hand. It could be a cardboard box or the corner of a table, and still the brain would absorb it as part of its body. A subject with a dowel strapped to the tip of one finger would gradually incorporate the dowel into his body image, extending his sense of finger inches too far.

The smallest warping could distort the map. Each fall, Weber asked his lecture full of undergrads to roll their tongue tips upside down, then run a pencil from the right to the left across their tongue's bottom, now uppermost in their mouths. Every subject felt the pencil as if from underneath, running from left to right. He made other students don prismatic glasses until they normalized the image of an inverted world. When they removed the glasses and looked out again with their unaided eyes, the real, unfiltered landscape now presented itself, upside down.

Soapy rivulets ran over the apron of his belly and down his knobby legs. They reminded him of Jeffrey L., a man whose spine was crushed in a motorcycle accident. The wreck had sprawled Jeffrey upside down on an embankment, with his legs in the air, at the moment that his spinal cord was severed. He lost all use of his body below his neck, and should have lost all feeling as well. But Jeffrey still felt his inverted body, his feet

328

hovering forever above his head. Another of Weber's patients, Rita V., had been sitting with her wrists crossed when thrown from a horse. Ever afterward she lived in agony, wanting only to straighten her arms, which, in fact, lay perpetually extended at her sides. Still other quadriplegics reported no bodily sensation at all, simply the sense of existing as a floating head.

More disconcerting still were the phantom limbs. Nothing worse than excruciating pain in a limb that no longer existed, pain dismissed by the rest of the world as purely imaginary— *all in your head*—as if there were another kind. A person could suffer persistent tenderness in any removed part—lips, nose, ears, and especially breasts. One man continued to experience erections in his amputated penis. Another told Weber that he now enjoyed vastly intensified orgasms that reverberated through his missing foot.

Then there were the border wars, the brain maps of the amputated part invaded by nearby maps. Somewhere—God only knew in which book—Weber described discovering a largely intact and responsive hand blossoming across the face of an amputee, Lionel D. Touched high up on the cheekbone, Lionel felt it in his missing thumb. Grazed on the chin, he felt it in his pinkie. Splashing his face with water, he felt liquid trickle down his vanished hand.

Weber shut off the shower and closed his eyes. For a few more seconds, warm tributaries continued to stream down his back. Even the intact body was itself a phantom, rigged up by neurons as a ready scaffold. The body was the only home we had, and even it was more a postcard than a place. We did not live in muscles and joints and sinews; we lived in the thought and image and memory of them. No direct sensation, only rumors and unreliable reports. Weber's tinnitus—just an auditory map, rearranged to produce phantom sounds in an undamaged ear. He would end up like one of his stroke patients, an extra left arm, three necks, a candelabrum full of fingers, each discreetly sensed, hiding under a hospital blanket.

And yet the ghost was real. People with lost feet, asked to tap their toes, lit up that part of their motor cortex responsible for walking. Even the motor cortex of intact people flashed, when they simply imagined walking. Seeing himself running from something, Weber felt his pulse shoot up, even as he stood immobile in the tub. Sensing and moving, imagining and doing: phantoms bleeding, one into the other. He could not, for a moment, decide which was worse: to be sealed in a solid room, thinking yourself outside; or to be freed to pass through the porous walls, into the protean blue . . .

Without reaching for a towel, he flipped off the bathroom light and moved back toward the dimly lit bed. He sat dripping on an upholstered chair. He had humiliated himself abroad. Back home, hundreds of subjects awaited him, real people he'd used as mere thought experiments. Every one of them throbbed in him and could not be cut out. The world had no place left, real or imagined, where he might put down.

She found a description online, at Mark's house, in something called *The People's Free Encyclopedia*. The site looked reputable, with footnotes and citations, but assembled in public, by community vote, leaving her as uncertain as ever.

FREGOLI SYNDROME: one of a rare group of delusional misidentification syndromes in which the sufferer is convinced that several different people are in fact all a single person of changing appearance. The syndrome takes its name from Leopoldo Fregoli (1867–1936), an Italian stage magician and mimic whose lightning ability to change his face and voice into any character astonished audiences . . .

Like Capgras Syndrome, Fregoli involves some disruption of the ability to categorize faces. Some researchers suggest that all misidentification delusions may exist along a spectrum of familiar anomalies shared by ordinary, nonpathological consciousness . . .

She told Daniel, over Chinese dinner. She'd pushed him into a night out, needing to escape his monk's cell and talk in public. She'd dressed up, even used scent. But she'd forgotten about the logistical problems, which started as soon as Daniel got the menu. Daniel dining out: like a Calvinist minister at a rave. He wagged his head, whistling. "Eight dollars for a plate of beef and broccoli? Can you imagine, K. ?"

The entrée was the restaurant's loss leader. She battened down and waited.

"Eight dollars is a lot of money to the Crane Refuge."

With matching grants and good management, they could buy and retire a square inch of marginal farmland. The waitress came to tell them the specials. The list of slaughtered fish, flesh, and fowl crucified Daniel.

"This 'Chinese eggplant,' " he asked the blameless woman. "Would you know, offhand, how that's prepared?"

"Vegetarian," the waitress assured him, like the menu said.

"But is the eggplant fried in butter? Do they use milk fat in the preparation?"

"I could find out?" the waitress bleated.

"Would it be possible just to get a plateful of sliced vegetables? Raw carrots, cucumbers? That sort of thing?"

Karin had been crazy to suggest the outing, and he'd been crazy to agree. The beef and broccoli sounded like a dream, a cure to her growing whole-foods anemia. Weeks of living with Daniel had left her wasted. She peeked at him, the waitress hovering. His face was placid, like something being led up a ramp to the waiting stun gun. She ordered the tofu and bean threads.

She'd forgotten what he was like in these places, places the rest of the civilized world depended on. When the waitress brought his sliced cucumbers, he just slid them around the plate with his fork, quibbling with them.

"It doesn't seem possible for him to suffer both conditions at once," she said. "I mean, Capgras is about underidentifying. Fregoli sounds like the exact opposite."

"K.? We probably want to be careful with the self-diagnosis."

"Self . . . ? What do you mean, '*self* . . .'?"

"Lay person's. You and I aren't qualified to diagnose him. We need to go back to Good Samaritan."

"To Hayes? He practically insulted me, the last time. Daniel, I have to say, I'm a little surprised. Since when have you defended organized medicine? I thought they were all faith healers. 'Native Americans have forgotten more medicine than Western technology has yet discovered.' "

"Well, that's basically true. But they didn't have many car accidents, back when the First Nations discovered their medicine. If I knew a Native American with experience in closed-head trauma, I'd recommend him above anyone you've talked to."

He didn't mention Gerald Weber by name. He didn't have to. Daniel had taken an irrational dislike to the man without having met him.

"I have to tell Dr. Weber," Karin said. She meant she'd already written him.

"Do you?" Daniel grew blissfully calm. Like he was meditating.

"Well, he is one of the leading . . ." But then, maybe he wasn't. Maybe he was just famous. Not quite the same thing. "I promised I'd let him know if Mark changed." Daniel had changed; so had Mark's friends. She herself had altered, more than any of them.

Daniel studied his fingertips. "Is there any downside to contacting him?"

"Aside from more humiliation and disappointment?"

The waitress came to ask how everything was. "Wonderful," Daniel said, smiling.

After she left, Karin asked, "Did we go to school with her?"

Daniel grinned out the side of his mouth. "She's a decade younger than us."

"No way! You think?" They ate in silence. At last she said, "Daniel, I'm making him worse."

He objected nobly; that was his job. But all the evidence was against him.

"Really. I think the strain of seeing me every day, of not being able to recognize—it's breaking him apart. I haven't been able to do much of anything for him. And now he's getting new symptoms. It's me. The sight of me is messing him up. I'm making him . . ."

Daniel trained his full calm on her, but his alpha state was wavering. "We don't know what he would've been like, if you hadn't been here all this time."

"Your life certainly would have been simpler, wouldn't it?"

He grinned again, as if she'd just cracked a joke. "Emptier."

333

Empty as she felt. Empty as all her gestures turned out to be. She ran her fork through her bean curds, like a scythe. "You know the strangest part? He doesn't think I'm her; and he's never going to think I'm her. So if I just took off—stopped torturing him, got a job, started to work my way back out of debt—it wouldn't be like *she* was abandoning him at all. His sister. He'd never hold it against me. He'd celebrate!"

She saw the flash in his eye before he could suppress it. She was spooking him. She would pull him down, too. She was doing to Daniel what Mark was doing to her. Soon she would be a stranger to him. Then to herself. Better for Daniel, too, her exit.

He shook his head, marvelously certain. "*He* wouldn't be the casualty."

"What? Stay for myself?" The worst imaginable reason. The words pushed her a million miles away from him, off on an airless planet. "You're preoccupied," she said.

He shook his head, a little sadly.

"Y'are," she accused, trying to clown. "I read in one of my brain books that women are ten times more sensitive at detecting another's internal states than men."

Daniel stopped badgering a split bell pepper and set down his fork. "But we're talking about you," he said. "About Mark . . ."

"I'd love to discuss something else for a while."

"Well, I've been thinking . . . Strange days at the Crane Refuge. But I feel funny talking about anything so . . . while we're facing . . ."

"Talk," she said. And to her vague sense of betrayal, he did.

The Refuge, he told her, was heading for a shootout. For years, combined environmental groups had kept the river's management honest by threatening to invoke the Endangered

Species Act if demands on the Central Platte dropped the flow below levels needed to sustain wildlife. They'd surrendered that threat after the establishment of environmental accounts—guaranteed levels of flow set aside for wildlife by the three states that lived off the river.

But now the precarious scheme of water-rights trading was teetering. The system of winter recharge basins no longer accommodated all the groups that wanted to drink from the stream. In the most recent round of negotiations, the Refuge had alienated everybody but the cranes. "They're coming after us from all sides. I was down by the river yesterday, just west of the old wagon bridge, cutting across the rise. I've been walking those fields since I was six. All of a sudden, this farmer comes down a row toward me. Jeans, big mud boots, work shirt, and a shotgun draped over his forearm like a tennis racket. He just rolls up to me, all smiles, and says, 'You're with the people trying to save those damn birds, aren't you? You have any idea how much damage those birds do?' I walk faster, to avoid trouble, and he starts shouting: 'It took Americans hundreds of years to turn this swampland into beautiful farms. And you people want to turn it back into swamps again. Better get yourself some protection. Watch your back. It's in your own best interests.' Can you believe it? He actually threatened me!"

"I believe it," she said. "I've been warning you for years."

He giggled, the clicks of a squirrel. "*Watch my back?*"

"Not everyone here believes in putting birds ahead of people."

"Those birds are the best thing this place has going. You'd think people would realize that. But no: all the local agreements that took us a decade to hammer out are breaking down. Kingsley Dam, relicensed for forty years. Insane! You should come work for us, K. We need a fighter. We need everyone we can get."

"Yes," she said, and almost meant it now.

"I'm telling you, greed has run amok. The Development Council, whoring itself for this new consortium of builders. They promised there wouldn't be any new building. That's what we'd fought for, and won. A freeze on large-scale development for ten years. They're selling us out, like we're the new Pawnee."

"Consortium?" She stacked her tofu into pyramids on her plate. She knew who he meant, without his saying. And he knew her question, before she asked.

"A wolf pack of local wheelers and dealers. You wouldn't happen to know . . . ? You haven't heard anything about this, have you?" He scanned her, his face uncertain.

"Nothing." Karsh. "Should I have?"

He shrugged and shook his head, apologetic. "We know which developers are involved, but we don't know what they're after. They have their eye on some parcels of land for a new project. Some open tract, near the river. We blocked them two years ago. Snatched four dozen acres out from underneath them. They're gearing up for war again, now that they know we're broke. They're convening the Development Council after the November elections."

"What are they after?" She brushed at the tablecloth.

"They're holding their cards pretty tight. They'll need to address the water use first before they tip their hand on the properties they want."

"What do you know about them?" Almost offhand, but the question caught him in the face. "I mean, how many are there? How deep are their pockets?"

"It seems to be three different outfits. Two from Kearney

and one from Grand Island. Whatever they're up to, it's on a big scale."

"Big enough to be a problem?"

"They're looking at riverfront. And whatever they build will increase usage. Every cup that comes out of that river reduces flow and encourages vegetative encroachment. The birds—"

"Yes," she preempted. She couldn't bear the whole story again, just then. "So how will the Refuge counter?"

"We have to prepare a strategy, more or less in the dark." He gauged her, and for an awful moment, she felt him calculate her trustworthiness. As close to an accusation as he could make, without accusing. "We're forming a loose consortium of our own: the Environmental Defense Fund, the Refuge, and the Sanctuary. If we can build up a shared war chest, we can grab strategic bits of land and try to block any large acquisitions by the other side. We'd never beat them in any open auction, of course. But if we secure a couple of keystones, a little strip in the most probable areas, before the bidding wars begin. It has to be Farview. Somewhere around Farview. The best undeveloped land outside of Kearney."

The name of Mark's town jerked her back from her reverie.

"As usual, it's the birds who suffer," Daniel declared. "In myths, gods are always screwing birds. Why stop now?"

The waitress came by, too soon. "How's everything here?"

"Everything's just fine," Karin intoned.

"How are your vegetables?" the waitress quizzed Daniel.

"Terrific," he answered. "Fresh."

"Are you *sure* I can't get you anything else? Something a little more . . . ?"

Daniel smiled. "Thanks. I'm good."

His eyes followed the waitress as she left. When the server came to refill their waters, Daniel said *sorry* for *thank you*.

A great dam of humiliation broke, and waves of old current washed over Karin. Her spine became a willow. Her fists sat in her lap like stones. "Which do you like better?" she asked.

"Which who?"

"You know. The server or the waitress?"

He smiled at her and shook his head, the model of evasive innocence.

She stared off in the middle distance, her face a copper to match her hair. "Would you rather be somewhere else?"

He tried to keep smiling, even now. "What do you mean?"

She admired his nerve, however transparent the denial. She smiled back, full wattage. "You can do better out there, can't you?"

The words crushed him. He looked down at his plate, the strewn slices. "Karin. Please, let's not . . . I thought we weren't going to do this anymore."

"I thought so, too." Until he'd doubted.

"K. I don't know what . . . what you think you saw . . ."

"Think? *Think* I saw?"

"I swear to you, the thought never crossed my mind."

"What thought?"

He bowed his head again, like one of those fairy creatures who gathered more life force from simply cowering and taking the hits. "Any thought."

She might still do anything: laugh it off, grow up. Get over herself. Or plunge them back into their worst nightmare. A dizzy thrill coursed through her. "She's a cute little cucumber herself. 'Fresh.' And the water-pourer, too. Both delicious. Your lucky night. Two-for-one sale."

"I wasn't shopping." He tried to hold her eye, but the sick spark of it got to him, too. All their history.

She matched his calm. "Just window gazing?"

He raised his palms in the air. "I wasn't looking. What did I do? Did I do something wrong? Say something to hurt you? If so, I am sincerely—"

"It's okay, Danny. I can accept the fact that males are genetically programmed for variety. Every man has to inspect the wares, out in the marketplace. That doesn't bother me. I just wish—don't! please, just *don't!*—wish you would come to terms with it."

He pushed his plate forward and folded his hands in front of his face, a guidance counselor or a priest. He rested his forehead on the steeple of his fingers. "Listen. I'm sorry. Whatever I did to upset you just now, I'm sorry for it."

"Just now? You can't say it, can you? You can't say that you were simply enjoying her. Both of them. I don't even want you to be sorry about it. It would just be nice if you could admit for once that you were simply imagining . . ."

His head snapped back. Old words came out of him, as old as the ones she struck him with. "I would say that, if that's what I was doing. I didn't even see her. I can't even tell you what she looks like."

Pointlessness flooded her, the futility of all exchange. Nobody really cared how the world looked to anyone else. She felt a deep need to break everything that pretended to connection. To live in this hollowness, where loyalty always led. Love was not the antidote to Capgras. Love was a form of it, making and denying others, at random. "Forgotten already? Have another look!"

His words came through his teeth. "I am not that kind of man. I told you as much eight years ago. I told you that five

339

years ago. You didn't believe me then. But I was waiting for you when you came back. I'm with *you*. I've always been, and I always will be. With you, and no one else. Not looking. Found already."

He reached out across the table to take her hand. She flinched, flipping her fork and scattering tofu. "With *me*? With your eyes still everywhere? Which 'me' do you mean?" She looked around, embarrassed by herself. The whole restaurant was avoiding looking at them. She turned back to him and chirped, "It's okay, Daniel. I'm not judging you. You are who you are. If you would just agree to tell me . . . "

He withdrew his hand. "We should never have come out to eat. We should have remembered what always . . ." She arched her eyebrows at the admission. He inhaled, trying to regain his scattered possession. "Someday you'll know what I'm looking at. Always. Trust me, K. . . ."

He sounded so scared it stung her. At that moment she felt the deep appeal of Robert Karsh, a man without a tenth of Daniel's idealism. Karsh, of all the men she'd ever been with, at least had the decency to say which women he was looking at. No illusions. At least Karsh never once deceived himself about being all hers. Karsh, always on the lookout. Karsh, the relentless developer.

They sat and stirred their plates, hot with shame. More words would only clarify. People at nearby tables wolfed their food, paid, and left. She ached to change the subject, to pretend she'd said nothing. Doubt formed a little scab over the wound, which she picked at. She wanted only to tear down everything, clear the landscape, escape somewhere empty and true. But no true place existed; only brief mirage, followed by long, humiliating self-justification. She would return with this man to his monk's cell tonight. He was her lover, her mate.

This year's current, eternal promise. She had no other bed, no other place to go back to, and still be near her brother, the brother she probably shouldn't be near. "I'm sorry," she said. "I think I'm losing it."

"It's nothing," he said. "It doesn't matter."

Everything mattered. The waitress came back around, still smiling, but wary. Everyone knew them, now. "Can I get this out of your way, or are you still working . . . ?"

Daniel held up his half-empty plate, eyes averted from the Medusa. The contortion only confirmed her, made things sadder. When the girl left, he turned the full force of his will on Karin, desperate to show a decency even she would have to affirm.

"We need to tell Weber about Mark. We're in new territory here."

Karin nodded, but could not look at him. Everything old, new again.

Back at last in his corner of the globe, his aerie on the shores of Conscience Bay, Weber touched ground. Sylvie was stalwart, of course, truly indifferent to what anyone aside from their daughter thought of them. Public judgment meant no more to her than spam. As far as Sylvie was concerned, consensus was the delusion. "We can't think clearly alone, let alone in groups of two or three. And you want me to trust *the marketplace*? Let's see what they say about you in twenty years."

The fate of Famous Gerald concerned her less than the epidemic of corporate scandals: Enron, WorldCom—the mega-billion-dollar fraud of the month. She read him the latest outrages over breakfast.

"Leaping lizards, Man. Can you believe what's happening? We're living in the age of mass hypnotism. As long as we keep clapping our hands and believing, the captains of industry will take care of us."

He was grateful for the distraction, her righteous anger at corporate deception. She was right not to humor his private jitters. And yet a part of him resented her indifference, resented being upstaged by corporate crooks. Resented that she temperamentally could not be shaken by the sudden, summary judgment against him.

He began to check his Amazon ratings, each time he logged online. Cavanaugh had shown him the feature, back in the good times. He wanted a reality check. Public reviewers had a vested professional interest; the private reader did not. But the private ratings were all over the map. One star: Who Does This Guy Think He Is? Five stars: Ignore the Naysayers; Gerald Weber Does It Again. The praise was worse than the poison. Responses multiplied, like the snakes writhing in his family's basement in the one recurring nightmare of his childhood. Scores more, each time he looked. Somehow, when he wasn't looking, private thought gave way to perpetual group ratings. The age of personal reflection was over. From now on, everything would be haggled out in public feedback brawls. Call-in radio, focus groups every time anyone moved. Leo Tolstoy: 4.1. Charles Darwin: 3.0.

And yet, every time he logged off, nauseated by the relentless assessments, he found himself immediately wanting to check again, to see if the next response might erase the last mindless dismissal. He compared his numbers to those of other writers he was lumped with. Was he alone in this backlash? Who was the moment's darling? Which of his

342

colleagues had also fallen? How did the public manage to bank and wheel in such perfect synchrony, as if on signal?

He'd done nothing this time that he hadn't done at least twice before. Perhaps that was the problem: he'd failed the endless collective appetite for novelty. No one wanted to be reminded of bygone enthusiasms. He'd become an icon of a former decade. Now he'd have to pay for all his previous acclaim.

And that was the ugly irony. When he'd started out, back in his thirties, his evening writing had been for no one. Pure reflection, a letter to Sylvie. Words to little Jess, for when she grew up. Just a way to understand his field a little more humanely, with a few more connections, those soft speculations forbidden by empiricism, the stuff science was really after but didn't dare admit. Just something to refresh his sensibilities each evening. The human brain musing on itself.

Only the enthusiasm of a few close friends to whom he'd shown excerpts convinced him there might be an audience for such essays. Public approval meant nothing, until he had it. Now the thought of losing his audience shamed him. What started as a sideline had grown defining, a definition that vanished the moment he accredited it. He was only fifty-five. Fifty-six. How would he fill the next twenty years? There was the lab, of course. But he'd been little more than an administrator there for a long time. The curse of successful science: senior researchers inevitably became chief fund-raisers. He could not spend the next two decades raising funds.

Most of neuroscience had been discovered since Weber began research. The knowledge base was doubling every decade. One might reasonably guess that everything knowable about brain function would be known by the time his current graduate students retired. Cognition was heading toward its prime collective achievement: grasping itself. What self-image would be left to us, in light of the full facts? The mind might not endure its self-discovery. Might never be ready to know. What would the race do, with full knowledge? What new creature would the human brain build, to take its place? Some new, more efficient structure, stripped of its ancient ballast . . .

He went for long walks around the mill pond, until he began running into pleasant neighbors. He took the boat out onto Conscience Bay. The dinghy had lain upside down in the yard for so long that an opossum was nesting under it. Befuddled by daylight, the creature hissed at him as he uncovered it. Out along the Neck, drifting with the tide, he felt the wind twist the boat at will. He had embarrassed his wife and daughter in public. He'd become a matter of easy mockery.

He'd done nothing wrong, committed no conscious deception or serious error. He could still point to thirty years of reputable research, a tiny corner of the species' crowning enterprise. Only his attempt to popularize that science had somehow gone wrong. To his surprise, he realized how he felt: *seedy*, caught in some infidelity.

September came, that bleak, first anniversary. What did private setback matter in the shadow of that shared trauma? He tried to recall the public dread of the year before, turning on the radio to find the world blown away. The force was intact, though the details were gone. His memory was surely worsening. Even simple stuff: the names of graduate students. A tune he'd known since childhood. The opening words of the Declaration of Independence. He obsessed over retrieval, proving to himself there was nothing wrong, which only made the blocking worse. He didn't tell Sylvie. She would have just scoffed. Nor did he mention the bouts of depression. She would only have made excuses for him. Perhaps something was wrong with his HPA system, something that might account for all this emotional oversteering. He thought of self-prescribing a low dosage of deprenyl, but principle and pride prevented him.

In the last days of the month, when even Bob Cavanaugh had given up on the book and stopped calling, a short story came out in *The New Yorker*, where Weber had sometimes published his own meditations. The author was a woman still in her mid-twenties, apparently well-known, and well beyond whatever came after hip. A two-page humorous vignette, "From the Files of Dr. Frontalobe" took the form of a series of first-person case histories as told by their examining neuroscientist. The woman who used her husband as a tea cozy. The man who awakened from a forty-year coma with the urge to believe his elected officials. The man who turned multiple-personality in order to use the HOV lane. Sylvie laughed at the piece. "It's affectionate. And anyway, it's not about you, Man."

"Who is it about?"

She flared her nostrils. "It's about people. Infinitely peculiar packages of walking symptoms. The whole lot of us."

"It's laughing at people with cognitive deficits?" He sounded ludicrous, even to himself. He would have suggested they take a vacation, except that they just had.

"You know what it's laughing at. What comedy always laughs at. Whistling past the graveyard. Nobody wants to believe that we're what you people are saying we are."

"Us *people*?"

"You know who I mean. You brain guys."

"And what exactly are we saying that no one wants to hear? We brain guys?"

345

"Oh, the works. Objects may be closer than they appear. Equipment may give unexpected results. No warranty written or implied. Everything you know is wrong."

That night, he got another e-mail from Nebraska. It came in alongside messages from friends and colleagues who wanted, with all the deniable aggression of good humor, to rub his nose in the *New Yorker* piece. He skipped to Karin Schluter's note, again remembering not yet having responded to her notes earlier that summer. The critics were right. Mark Schluter had stopped existing once he could do nothing more for Weber.

Karin's news electrified him. Her brother believed that someone was following him, in a variety of disguises. Mark was assembling a list of documented details proving that his entire town of Farview had been replaced between the night of his accident and the day he came out of his coma, for the express purpose of misleading him.

Weber had just come across a case in the clinical literature, from Greece of all mythic places, describing co-existence of Capgras and Fregoli in a single patient. Something truly remarkable was happening to Mark Schluter. A new, systematic workup might shed light on mental processes that weren't even poorly understood, processes that only this devastating deficit could reveal. *All the things nobody wants to hear.*

But even as this thought took form, he had another. Gerald Weber, neurological opportunist. Violator of privacy and sideshow exploiter. He could not decide which would be worse: to follow up these new complications or to let this repeat appeal drop. These people had asked for help, and he had entered their story. Then he had forgotten them. They were still in distress, still looking to him. His one prescription—cognitive behavioral therapy—seemed to be making things worse. Even if Weber could do nothing more, he was obliged at least to listen and attend.

Karin Schluter's note made no overt requests. "I don't mean to push again, especially after hearing nothing back since July. But I heard your Public Radio interview, and given what you said about the brain's plasticity, I somehow thought you would at least want to know what's happening to Mark." He looked up from his screen, out his window, onto the ancient maple that—when?—had broken out in the color of a May goldfinch. Nebraska at harvest: the last place on earth he wanted to go. What was the word again, for unreasonable fear of rolling, empty spaces?

Only more writing could save him. One concentrated report, published or not. One that might redeem whatever he'd botched with the last one. Not a case history: a life. He could secure, in advance, the goodwill of everyone involved. He could re-create Mark Schluter, no composites, no pseudonyms, no glossed-over detail, no hiding behind the clinical. Just the story of invented shelter, the scared struggle to build a theory big enough for wetware to live in.

He told Sylvie, after dinner the next night, while he was washing dishes. The whole transaction thickened with déjà vu. But he never imagined the announcement would upset her. "Back to Nebraska! Are you serious? You couldn't get home fast enough the last time."

"Just for a couple of weeks or so."

"Two weeks! I don't understand this. It's sounds like . . . a complete reversal."

"I think Tour Director wants me to do this."

She was hefting the clean glasses out of the strainer, wiping them slowly, and putting them away in all the wrong places. "You'd tell me if anything was happening to you, wouldn't you?"

He killed the spray of hot water. "Happening? What do you mean?" What could still happen, in his life?

"Anything . . . Any big rearrangements. If anything was, you know, truly messing with you? Or with Famous Gerald. You'd tell me?"

Weeks now. He put down the sponge, took the dish towel from her hands, folded it neatly in half, and hung it lengthwise on the handle of the stove. "Of course. Always. Everything. You know that." He crossed back to her, placed three fingers on her temporal lobe. A mind scan; a scout's kiss. "It's only when I tell you things that I understand them myself."

PART FOUR

SO YOU MIGHT LIVE

What was full was not my creel, but my memory. Like the white-throats, I had forgotten it would ever again be aught but morning on the Fork.

—Aldo Leopold, *A Sand County Almanac*

They find their way back down from the Arctic. The family of three now fly with scores of others. In mid-morning, with the sun cooking the air into wide, rising columns, the birds lift up a mile or more above the earth. They float in growing flocks, dropping to the next thermal to the south, where they rise again. They reach fifty miles an hour, make five hundred miles a day, with little beating of wings. In the evenings, they glide to the surface and roost in shallow, open waters remembered from previous years. They sail in over harvested fields, feathered dinosaurs bugling, a last great reminder of life before the self.

The fledged crane colt follows his parents back to a home he must learn to come from. He must see the loop once, to memorize its markers. This route is a tradition, a ritual that changes only slightly, passed down through generations. Even small ripples—left down that valley, on past that outcrop—are preserved. Something in their eyes must match symbols. But how it's done, no person knows and no bird can say.

They wing back down across the western states. Each day graces them with a tailwind. In the first week of October, the family roosts on the eastern prairies of Colorado. After daybreak, as they graze the fields, waiting for the ground to heat and the air to rise, the space around the fledged crane colt explodes. His father is hit. He sees his parent sprayed across the nearby earth. Birds scream into the shattered air, their brain

351

stems pumping panic. This chaos, too, lays down a permanent trace, remembered forever: *open season*.

When the world sets again from the rush of blood, the young bird locates his mother. He hears her calling, half a mile off, circling traumatized. They wait two more days, searching, sounding some ghost of the unison call. Nothing can tell them; no way they can know. There is only circling and calling, waiting, a kind of religion, for the dead one to show. When he doesn't, there is only yesterday, last year, the sixty million years before that, the route itself, the blind, self-organizing return.

The sandhills do not gather in Nebraska now. The Platte hosts no great fall staging. The cranes stop only briefly, in small groups. The mother brings her fledgling through, priming him. She leads him within ten yards of the spot where, late last February, she and her mate huddled themselves, yards from where the truck flipped over. She wades in the flat of the autumn river, ready to meet her mate again back here in the river's loops, in opened, animal time, the standing now, the map whose edges wrap back on themselves.

But her mate is not in this place, either. She grows jittery again, remembering that ancient incident, the trauma of last spring. Something bad once happened here, as loud and deadly as the new, fatal wrong. A kind of forecast, that grainy irritant in the widow crane's mind is all that remains of what happened that night. All eyewitness accounts have disappeared into the present of animals. No one can say what a bird might have seen, what a bird might remember.

Her edginess rubs off on this year's colt. Contagious distress lifts him into a leap. He kicks out at the surrounding emptiness. His primaries spread like splayed fingers. His neck curls back and calls, curdling the air. He tosses leaves up over his arcing back, cowling his wings. And for the first of a thousand times in his life, he dances. In the falling dark, other species might mistake it for ecstasy.

He quits the so-called cognitive therapy. He should have quit long ago. Anything that Kopy Karin pushes so hard can't possibly be in his best interests. It's just a trick to distract him, get him to think about everything except what's happening all around him. A kind of brainwashing to trick him into taking all these fakes at face value. He only hopes it hasn't yet messed him up for good.

Dr. Tower freaks. She practically pleads with him: *But we haven't even gotten out of assessment.* Well, he's ready to give her a full assessment, if she's interested. But she just rags on. Is he sure he's ready to leave? Doesn't he want to feel better about things, before . . . ? All pretty pitiful and self-serving. He tells her to get professional help.

But he needs to talk to someone, someone who can help put all the facts together. Bonnie's out. Okay: she's still his Bonnie-baby. Call it love, whatever. But Kopy Karin has gotten to her, turned her, as the federales say. Convinced her there's something wrong with him. Even when he lays out all the accumulated evidence—his missing sister, the fake Homestar, nobody admitting to the note, the new Karin hooking up with the old Daniel, the disguised Daniel following them around, training animals to watch them—she says she's not sure.

He could ask Rupp and Cain. He might have, a long time ago, but for that little seed of doubt. Where were they, after all, on the night he rolled the Ram? He's held back, waiting for an explanation that never quite materializes. But now it occurs to him: Who planted that doubt? Karbon Karin again, trying to do to *him* what she's managed to do to Bonnie. Convince him his friends are foes, and vice versa. The whole three-car theory: all the impostor's idea. He's crazy to give it a second thought.

He looks for a chance to enlist the guys. He gets it, one chilly afternoon, when they come by to take him on a squirrel dump. One of Ruppie's specialties: all summer long he picks off gray squirrels in his yard with a pellet gun, then stashes them in his freezer until he has enough to justify a disposal run out of town. Then the three of them take binoculars, a couple of sixes, some brats, and a Hefty Bag full of the thawed rodents and head out to a little strip of uncultivated prairie along the South Loup. Build a little squirrel pyramid in the open field, set up camp a hundred yards away, and wait for the turkey vultures. Rupp loves those things, could watch them all day. *Cathartes aura*, he calls out when they start circling overhead. *Ave, Cathartes aura*, like they're something out of the Bible, and the squirrels are their burnt offering. And it is kind of biblical, in fact: the swarming cloud of them.

Mark and Duane are in jeans and sweats. Rupp is in shorts and a black tee; unfreezable. They set up camp and kick back. Talk turns to desirable women. Want to know who's hot? Cain says. That Cokie Roberts is hot.

Seven, Rupp says. Seven and a half. Great face, but the superabundance of ideas lowers the property value. So what's up with that Christiane Amanpour? I mean, what's *her* angle? Is she even American, or what?

Talking in code. The one says: You know what would look good around Britney's neck? And the other answers: Her ankles? It gets on Mark's nerves after a while. He watches the squirrel pile. Why do you kill those things, anyway? he asks Rupp.

Because they kill my best and brightest tomatoes.

That's their job description, Duane-o says. Your basic yard rat is supposed to wreak havoc on your typical tomato. Were you aware that the tomato is a fruit?

I have long had my suspicions, Rupp says. I wouldn't mind if the rodents actually ate the things. But they like to just pull them off the vine and play polo. No reasoning with them, short of the deep freeze.

Killing is a sin, man.

I am aware. I wrestled with my conscience and beat the bastard, two out of three falls.

The three of them sit, drink, cook up some brats on the little hibachi. The vultures arrive, and it's two kindred species, fraternizing over a little shared picnic.

Ah, Labor Day, Duane says. You gotta love it.

Rupp agrees. *Vita* doesn't get any *dolcier* than this. Day like this calls for some poetry. Recite some poetry for us, will you, Cain?

I'd rather yank a fart out of a cow's ass, Cain says.

Rupp shrugs. There's a herd over that hill. It's your America. Knock yourself out.

Duane suggests they take some target practice, but Rupp just slaps him upside of the head. You don't shoot at *Cathartes aura*. It's nobility. The finest we have. You wouldn't take potshots at the president, would you?

Not unless he wings me first. Speaking of which: You hear anything more about your unit? Orders to mobilize, or what have you? Rupp just laughs. But Duane-o is all: It's gonna be any minute now. You know America is going on a tear before the year's out, and nobody better get in her way. Afghanistan's going to look like a training bike with streamers. The big one's coming. Armor get-on. Direct flight from Fort Riley to Riyadh. You're going on the hajj, bud. One weekend a month, my ass.

If it be not now, yet it will come, Rupp says. We have to do *something*. Can't just sit here, burning. But it's going to be cruise missiles against camel jockeys, all over again. All I personally have to do is keep the wheels greased. Home by Veterans Day. He shoves Duane's shoulder: Come on, dipstick. Join up. No knowledge without suffering.

Get shot at? I'd sooner be anally savaged by Hastings escapees.

Hey. Who says you can't have it all?

Got a letter from the National Guard, Mark says.

What? Rupp shouts. Like he's upset. What did it say?

Mark waves his hand around his head, swatting gnats. Just a letter; friendly and personal, in a legal sort of way. Not something you can just sit down and read through.

When was this, Rupp wants to know. Like it's an issue.

Who knows? A while back. No biggie. They're the damn army, man. It's not like they're in any hurry.

But Rupp is all upset, ball-busting him. We'll get on that puppy instantly, soon as we take you home. Remind me.

Sure, sure. But just chill for a minute. Listen. It's possible that the government has other plans for us, altogether.

This gets their attention. But Mark has to take it slow. The big picture is a little hard to grasp, and he doesn't want them to overload. He starts with the stuff they're already familiar with. The substitutions: sister, dog, house. Then the note, given to him, he now believes, by somebody who was there, in the truck with him.

That's impossible, both fellow Muskrats say at once.

He gives them a hard look: I know what you're going to say. There was nobody there. Nobody in the wreck when the medics came. Except me. He walked away. He called in the accident.

356

Rupp shakes his head, holding a cold beer to it. No, no man. If you had seen . . .

Duane jumps in. Dude, your truck looked like a big old Angus on the other end of the cutters. Picture in the paper. Nobody was walking away from that. It's a miracle you . . .

Mark Schluter gets a little upset. He flips over the hibachi. A rolling coal burns a brown spot in the tops of his Chuck Taylors.

Okay, okay, Rupp says. Let's assume. For point of argument. What makes you think this guy was . . . ? Who was he? What was he doing in your truck?

Mark holds up his hands. Everybody just relax. Regroup. I know he was there because I remember him.

It's like the moment in a thriller when the guy reaches underneath his chin and pulls off the latex face.

You remember? Who . . . ? What are you saying?

All right: so Mark doesn't remember the hitchhiker himself. But he remembers talking to him. As plain as this conversation. Must have picked him up a while earlier, because they were in the middle of some kind of interview guessing game. Questions the hitchhiker wasn't directly answering, except with hints. Warmer, colder kind of thing. Guess the secret.

Rupp is upset, which doesn't happen often. He's all: Hang on. What *exactly* do you remember?

But the details aren't worrying Mark right now. He's after the full jigsaw. Which is exactly what everybody wants to keep him from seeing. Some kind of systematic cover-up, to keep him from finding out too much about what he's stumbled into. Look at the facts: A few minutes after he picks up this angel hitchhiker in the middle of nowhere and starts in on this whole Twenty Questions thing, he has an accident. Then, in the hospital, something happens to him on the operating table. Something that conveniently erases his memory. And when he does come back to himself, they've swapped out his sister, who might help him remember, and replaced her with a fake who keeps him under 24/7 surveillance. That's a lot to call coincidence. And then they set him up in a parallel Farview. A whole live-in experiment, with Mark as the lab monkey.

What about us? Duane wants to know. How come they didn't swap us out? He sounds offended. Left out.

Isn't that obvious? You two don't know anything.

This pisses Duane off. But Mark doesn't have time to make every little point. He's got to get them to see how big this must be, in order for the government to throw around that kind of money, replacing a whole town.

Jesus, Duane says, starting to grasp the scale. What do you think they're up to?

That's just the thing. That must have been what the hitchhiker was hinting at. Warmer. Colder. They're using this place for some project. Either they need some big old empty spot with nobody in it. Or there's something specific they need—something special about life out here.

Rupp snorts. Something *special*? About life out *here*?

Mark pushes them. Think: something so close we don't even see it anymore. Something we do that nobody else does.

Duane almost chokes on a bratwurst. Wheat. Meatpacking. Migrating birds.

Good Christ, Mark says. *The birds*. How could we have missed it? Don't you two remember? When did I have my accident?

Nobody says anything, it's so obvious. The few weeks of the year when their godforsaken nowhere becomes world famous.

And I haven't even told you the key: when I was going door

to door with the note? There was somebody . . . Somebody kept popping up, although never exactly . . .

It's like Rupp isn't even listening. Doesn't even follow the logic. Just asks: How do you know it's the government?

This is exactly what Mark is trying to tell him. He's been followed around for weeks by someone who can only be Daniel Riegel. The Bird Man. Plus, the guy has conveniently gotten involved with the fake Karin. And you know exactly who he works for, don't you?

Daniel? Danny Riegel? He doesn't work for the government. He works for the damn Crane Refuge.

Which is a government . . . which gets most of its money from . . .

You know, I think it might actually be a government operation, Cain says. Come to think.

You are totally whacked. Rupp tries to laugh, but it comes out small-caliber.

Public outfit, anyway, Duane says. Public sanctuary.

It's not public. It's a foundation. A privately funded . . .

It's definitely got some kind of state affiliation . . .

Everybody shut up for a second? You're missing the point. Suppose this guy I picked up was a terrorist. Months after. Trying to strike at something really . . . American. And suppose the government . . .

You never picked anyone up, Rupp says. There was no hitchhiker.

How do you know? You told me you *weren't fucking there*.

Maybe Mark Schluter yells a bit. Rupp and Cain, too. It's a little distressing, truth be told. They all chill for a minute, just sit and watch the turkey vultures pick at the squirrel pile. But the picnic is basically over.

We should get back to your place, Rupp says. Check out that Guard letter.

Don't do me any favors, Mark tells him.

But they pack up and pile into Rupp's '88 Chevy 454. Rupp drives, Duane rides shotgun, and Mark takes one of the jumps, like old times. Only he's beginning to see there are no more old times, if there ever were any. Rupp has the new Cattle Call CD on the player, *Hand Rolled*. A song called "I've Had Amnesia for as Long as I Can Remember." It sounds like gelded goslings, the same old crap CC has been singing since the band got paroled. But Duane gets all jumpy and Rupp punches the player to skip the track, like it embarrasses him. Which only makes Mark want to go back and listen closer.

They're coming back Route 40, just before the Odessa turnoff, when a big buck breaks from a copse and leaps across the road in front of them. It's dead for the truck, a missile aimed at the hood. Not even time to scream. But just as the creature reaches them, Rupp twists into a power skid that takes them over the center line and back twice. The deer stops, on the far shoulder, baffled. It so badly expected to be dead that it doesn't know what to do with the changed itinerary. Only when the thing shakes itself and runs off into the trees do the three humans revive.

Jesus *fuck*.

Both friends look at Mark. Rupp grabs his knee, Duane his shoulder. You all right, man? Damn it, we were gone. Finished.

But nothing's happened, really. The truck isn't even scratched, and the deer will get over it. He's not sure why they want him to be so upset.

God damn, Duane keeps jabbering, cranked. We were done. Life insurance payout time. How the hell did you do that? Turning before I even saw the thing.

Rupp is shaking. Duane and Mark try not to look, but there it is. Mr. Natural Guardsman, quivering like a Parkinson's guy on stilts in an earthquake. Deer tried to kill us, he says. Faking his old self. But they see now, see him. I'm telling you, that maniac tried to jump through our windshield. The fucking video game saved our life. He looks at his hands, which are triggering. If I hadn't played hundreds of hours of that video game, we'd all be toast.

Rupp restarts the truck and pulls back into the right lane. Cain howls like a coyote. He can't believe he's gotten lucky, for once in his life. He punches the air. Jesus, Jesus. What a trip. He punches the glove compartment, which pops open. He pulls out a little black communicator, something Mark's seen before. Duane presses it up to his face, chewing into it like some kind of cop. Yo, there, Saint Peter, good buddy? Cancel those three reservations you were holding for this evening? Goat-head.

At the word, Mark is up out of the jump seat, grabbing at the communicator. Give me that. But he doesn't really need to hold it. He's held it before. Or one just like it.

Put it away, Rupp commands. Cain scrambles with the glove compartment, keeping the communicator from Mark. But there's no putting it away again.

Mark's finger swings between the two of them, a waving pistol. You? I was talking to you two? *You two* were the hitchhiker? I don't get . . . how am I supposed to . . . ?

Rupp lays into Cain. You stupid shit-for-brains. He's driving with one hand, grabbing at the communicator with the other. In the scrimmage, he comes up with it. He chucks it out the driver's-side window, like that's the answer to all questions. He glares at Cain, ready to kill him. You pointless gamete. What were you thinking?

What? I was just . . . *what*? How was I supposed to know?

You told me you weren't there, Mark says. You lied to me.

We weren't *there*, they say, together. Rupp silences Cain with a look. He turns to Mark, begging. You had one in your truck. We were just . . . we'd just bought the things.

That was the game? Your little walkie-talkie speak? That was you? *Goat-head?*

You invented it, man. It made you laugh. We were just doing the CB thing, yakking at each other at a distance, when you . . .

Mark Schluter is a statue. Pure sandstone. You, *too*. You're *in* on this whole thing. They start talking at once, trying to explain, clouding the facts. Mark puts his hands over his ears. Let me out. Stop this truck. Let me out right here.

Marker. Don't be crazy, man. We're two miles from Farview.

They argue, but he's not listening. I'm walking. I'm out of this thing.

He gets violent, so finally they have to drop him. But for a long time they trail alongside him in the truck, at walking speed, trying to talk him back in. Trying, as always, to further confuse him, before the Chevy pulls off in an angry squeal.

They didn't touch each other, the night of the restaurant fight. The next day, they talked in kind, obliging monosyllables. They slunk through the house, doing small favors for each other. All the next week, Daniel was self-effacing, patient, devoted, pretending they still inhabited that sunlit upland safe from their old nightmare. He acted as if she were the one who had slipped, and he, selfless, were forgiving her. She let him, encouraged him, even as it enraged her. That's who she was.

Obviously, he had no idea what was best for him or what

he needed. He had only that maddening mask of selflessness. She wanted to scream: Go, sample, taste. Find yourself. I know I'm not good enough; you tell me as much, in every patient acquiescence. Instead, she said nothing. The truth would only have incensed him. She understood him now. Saint Daniel: needing to transcend the rest of the race. Needing to prove that a human could be better than humans, could be as pure as an instinctive animal. But he needed her confirmation. Some part of her was willing to grant that he might be as good a man as she had any chance of meeting in this world. She loved his sad insistence that any bruise might be healed. But his glance of doubt, of vague disappointment, that constant *looking* for something a little more worthy and shining . . . Virtuous, sacrificial, long-suffering: and slowly choking her.

Her smallest suggestion that Daniel might be as frail as anyone threw him into a tailspin. Panicked, he worked to please her, labored for the relationship as if it were endangered. He cleaned and cooked, splurged on delicacies—morels and macadamias. He found her articles on Fregoli syndrome and indulged her every fear. At night, he rubbed her back with tiger balm, finally pressing her almost as hard as she asked.

She made love to him, imagining herself the woman whom he was imagining. Afterward, she was seized by frantic tenderness, a last-ditch effort to catch herself and fix them. "Daniel," she whispered in his ear, in the dark. "Danny? Maybe we need to think about something small. Something new. Something a little of both of us."

She touched his mouth and saw him smile in a sliver of moonlight. Ready to go almost anywhere she needed him. He spoke no objection aloud, but one, minute muscle in his upper lip was wrong, saying: *No babies. No more humans. You see what they do.*

She saw, at least, what he thought of her chances as a mother. Saw, at bottom, how he really imagined her.

At week's end, Mark told her he was quitting therapy. The news blindsided her. She felt as she had at eight, the first time Cappy Schluter went bankrupt and the repossessors came to auction off their living room. Her last hope for rehabilitating Mark vanished. She pleaded with him, so drained from prolonged lack of sleep that she actually wept. Her tears bewildered Mark. But finally, he shook his head. "This is mental health? What we're shooting for, here? Not for me, brother. Last thing I want is health that good."

She drove out to Dedham Glen to consult Barbara. Months had passed since Mark's stay, but Karin half-expected him to come shuffling down the hall, berating her. She sat on the plasticized couch across from the receptionist's, primping anxiously, waiting for Barbara. When Barbara did walk by, her face clenched at the ambush. She had always told Karin to come to her for anything. Perhaps she'd been lying. But she rallied fast and managed a game smile. "Hey, friend! Is everything okay?"

They sat and talked in the community television room, surrounded by the dazed and incontinent. "I'm no lawyer," Barbara told her. "I'm crazy even to think about advising you. I'm guessing you could force the issue, if you wanted. You're his legal guardian now, right? But what good would that do you? Forced therapy isn't likely to help. It would only convince Mark that you were persecuting him."

"Maybe I *am* persecuting him. Just by not being who he thinks. Everything I do just makes him worse."

Barbara covered Karin's hand in the shell of hers. Her touch did more for Karin than Daniel's. Yet even Barbara's care kept its counsel. "It must feel that way, at times."

"It feels that way always. How can I know the right thing to do, if I can't trust how things feel?"

"You've written to Gerald Weber? That's the right thing."

Karin felt the urge to open completely to her, to tell Barbara the simple and defensible truth that she'd never felt so helpless in her life. But she knew enough about human brains now, damaged or otherwise, not even to think of going there. She needed a woman, someone to confirm her, to remind her of the worth of casual warmth, to save her from endless male dismissal. A girl's crush. No, more: she loved this woman, for everything Barbara had done for them. But her first word would drive Barbara away. She listened to herself drop into a tone of pure invitation. "Do you have children, Barbara?" Ready, if rebuked, to deny all attempted intimacy.

Barbara's "No" gave nothing away.

"But you are married?"

This time, *no* meant *not anymore*. Something in Karin leapt up at the admission, as if she might yet be able to give this woman something back. But she couldn't be sure what she was allowed to ask. "You're alone?"

Impulse broke across the woman's face before she could suppress it. *Someone isn't?* Her face softened. "Not really. I have this." She shrugged, her upward palms taking in the television room. "I have my work."

Karin snorted, before she could stop herself. She felt the real question she'd long needed to ask. "What do you get from this place?"

Barbara smiled. The Mona Lisa might have been a bouncing contestant on tell-all television, next to her. "Connection. Solidity. My . . . friends. New ones all the time."

Her eyes said *Mark*. Karin flashed on something illicit, ready to suspect even Christian charity. If Barbara had been a

365

man, the police would have been all over the situation. Mark, her *friend*? Connection, with these patients, trapped in their own collapsing bodies, people who couldn't hold a spoon or pick one up off the floor where it fell? One harsh thought opened onto another, and she slipped into resentment. Resentment that this woman wouldn't give her a tenth of what she happily gave a brain-damaged man fifteen years younger than herself. Resentment that Barbara had Mark and she did not. The thought pinched shut her eyes and twisted her face. Resentment: the family name for need. Couldn't this woman see how close the two of them were?

"Barbara . . . How do you do it? How do you stay loyal, when everyone's so . . . ?" She would lose control, disgust the woman. She looked at the aide, trying not to beg.

But Barbara's face showed only surprise. Her mouth opened in refusal. "I'm not the one . . ." Not crushed, not stroked out, no lesion. "It's not me . . ."

Could anyone really have so mastered herself? How did she find such maturity? What had she been like, at Karin's age? The questions piled up, none of them permissible. The conversation stalled. Barbara grew nervous and needed to get back to work. Karin felt that this might be the last time they would talk like this. She grabbed and hugged Barbara before leaving. But whatever *connection* was, that embrace held none of it.

That evening when Daniel came home, she was sitting on top of her three packed suitcases, five feet down his front walk. She had been sitting there for half an hour. She'd planned to be long gone well before he returned from work. Instead, she was camped out, twenty-five feet away from her parked car, unable to move in either direction. Daniel sprang off his bicycle, thinking she was hurt. But ten feet from where she sat, he figured out everything.

366

He was relentlessly noble, even in being abandoned. All the questions that he didn't ask—*Why are you doing this? Are you sure this is what you want? What about Mark? What about me?*—burned into her as she sat, paralyzed. He didn't even try to guilt her with talk or stroking. He said nothing at all for a long time, just stood two feet away from her, taking things in, thinking. He hunted for her eyes, trying to determine what she needed of him. She couldn't meet his gaze. When he did speak, it was almost without accusation. Pure practical concern for her: exactly what she couldn't bear. "But where will you go? All your stuff is in storage. Your place has just sold."

She said what she had been rehearsing in her head for weeks. "Daniel, I'm breaking. I can't do this anymore. For every little thing I do to help, I hurt him in three other ways. The sight of me makes him worse. He wants me gone. I'm sick and broke and in your way, light-headed and I haven't slept well in six weeks. He makes me think I'm invisible, a virus, a nothing. I'm falling apart, Danny. I'm floating and buzzing. Like little spiders on my skin, all the time. I'm a mess. I'm disgusting. You just don't, can't, you have absolutely no . . ."

He put his hand on her shoulder to slow her. He did not say, *I know*. Only nodded.

Something like excitement propelled her. "The condo doesn't close for another ten days. I can camp out on my floor. It'll be so simple—just the essentials. I can use the money from the sale to line up a rental. I can get my job back, start reimbursing you for everything that you've paid for, all these . . ."

He shushed her. He cast a quick glance over his shoulder at the row of picture windows, through which the neighborhood now watched this piece of September-evening street theater. Now, on top of everything, she was making a scene, embarrassing him. She lunged up and grabbed at one of the suitcases, to drag it to the car. Her sudden speed pitched her over, into him. He grabbed her shoulders and steadied her. He reached down to take the bag. "Here. Let me help you."

His stupid, brute charity made her lose it. She curled away from him, pressed two fists to her jaw, and began to hyperventilate. He stepped back toward her, to give what comfort he could. She fought him off with both hands. "Leave me alone. Don't touch me. These aren't real tears. Don't you see, yet? I'm not her. I'm just a simulation. Something you invented in your head." She could not make out her own wet and rubbery words. It crossed her mind, in a seed of bright, spreading fear, that she was having that thing that she and Mark used to speculate about, in the terror of childhood: a *breakdown*.

But just as suddenly, all her wildness stopped, and she stood on the curb, becalmed. Something in her must have known all along: she could never get farther than going through these motions. Leaving would prove Mark right. Would strip her of every account she might give of herself. A great curiosity came over her, an impatience to learn what she might yet become, in staying here. Who she might still be, if she could no longer be the other. She sat back down on the toppled case. Daniel sat down on the lawn next to her, now indifferent to what any other human being saw or thought of them. "I can't leave yet," she announced. "I forgot. The note from Dr. Weber. He's coming back next week."

"Yes," Daniel said. "True." He made no show of even trying to follow her. And even that, in a way she could not name, was a small relief. They sat together on her packed clothes until the first fat drops of a sparse autumn rain began to plash around them. Then he helped her carry the luggage back inside.

The next day, Karin saw Karsh. She strolled down Central

in front of his office, a stretch she'd avoided for months. The morning was glorious, one of those crystalline, dry, blue, fall days when the temperature hovers right at anticipation. She knew she would end up coming here, the moment Daniel had spoken those words during their disastrous dinner. Almost like he was daring her, flushing out all unfinished business into the open. New developer consortium. *Local wheelers and dealers.* You wouldn't happen to know . . . ? Well, she didn't know. Didn't know the first thing about anyone.

But about herself, there were things she could find out. She looped down the block in front of Platteland Associates, pretending to window-shop those few stores—hospital supplies, Salvation Army, used books—that hadn't yet been euthanized since the Wal-Mart landed. He would emerge for lunch at ten to twelve and head for the Home Style Cafe. Four years would have changed nothing. Robert Karsh was habit incarnate. *A first-rate mind knows what it wants.* Everything else was chaos.

He came from the office with two colleagues. Flawless gray coat and burgundy tie, Brooks black slacks: over-compensating businessman, pretending Kearney was the next Denver. She turned to inspect the window of a locksmith shop, a carousel of key blanks. He saw her from two blocks away. She lifted an arm to her hair, then dropped it instantly. He gave his partners a vague meet-you-later wave. Then he was standing in front of her, not touching, but taking her in, consuming her all over again. A tourist back when travel was still hard.

"You," he said. Voice a little deeper. "It's you. I can't believe it's you."

For the first time in months, she knew herself. The last half a year took its fingers from her throat. Her shoulders dropped. Her head lifted. "Believe," she said, her voice like God's own phone receptionist.

He winced, hands waving. "What did you do to yourself?" Her haircut: the one meant to trick Mark into thinking she was her. "Damn. You look amazing. Like a manufacturer-refurbished virgin. College all over again."

She scowled, trying not to giggle. "You mean high school."

"Right. Like I said. You've lost weight?" He'd called her a failed anorectic once.

She stood almost posing, savoring the payback. "How're your kids?" She could almost do this. Capable, no-nonsense. "Your wife?"

He grinned, raking his fingers through his hair. "Good, good! Well . . . long story."

Her heart, that stupid holdover, spun like a pigeon in a Skinner box. For this man, she'd once bought a book called *How to Elope*, even while browsing for wedding dresses. At least she'd confined herself to apricot and peach.

He kept looking at her, shaking his head in disbelief. "How's . . . your brother?"

"Mark," she said. She expected him to flinch apology. She'd been with Daniel that long.

"Right. I read about him in the *Hub*. Nightmare."

In remarkably few words, they maneuvered to the bench in front of the war memorial. He sat next to her, in broad day, center of town. Caution to the wind. He kept asking if she wanted something—a sandwich, maybe something fancy. She kept shaking her head. "You eat," she said. It would be a while before she ate again. He waved off the idea of food, insisting that this was even bigger than nutrition. He asked for details about Mark and sat still for a surprising amount of them, compared to the Robert Karsh of four years ago. He shook his head and said things like *Twilight Zone* or *Invasion of the Body Snatchers*. Crude, crass, banal. But words like home.

As easy as breathing, she unloaded. She told him everything, making her collapse seem almost comical. "He's been my entire life for the last six months. But he's decided I'm never going to be me again. And after half a year? He's right."

"Oh, you're still you, let me tell you. A few new wrinkles, maybe." Robert's motto: *The asshole of truth*. The more brutally truthful, the better. He had ten times the self-knowledge Daniel had. He'd always almost relished admitting all the women he lusted after. *I'm a man, Rabbit*. We're programmed to *look. Everything worth looking at*. Brutal truth was why she was sitting with him now, in the center of town, in front of the war memorial, in plain view of everyone.

His voice chilled her—the sound of time starting up again. His hair had the slightest rime of frost now, over his ears. His shirt stretched over his belt, rather than bunching. Otherwise unchanged: a slightly squashed, forgotten Baldwin brother, just a little too wide-faced to make it into the movies, and so, suppressed by the rest of the clan. Something nagged at her, some small difference. Maybe just a matter of pacing. He'd grown just two clicks slower, more open, peaceful. A touch of the acid, neutralized. Less slick, less aggressive, less self-satisfied. Or maybe he was just on his best behavior. Anyone could be anything, for an hour.

He took her elbow, like she was blind and he was helping her cross the street. She didn't pull away. "Why did you take so long?"

The catch in his voice shocked her. "What do you mean?"

"To look me up?"

"I didn't look you up, Robert. I was walking downtown. You found me."

He grinned, warmed by her transparent lie. "You called me last spring."

"Me? I don't think so." Then she remembered the curse of caller ID.

"Well, it was your brother's number. But he was still in the hospital." The smirk, more teasing than sadistic. "Somehow, I just assumed it was you."

She closed her eyes. "I got your daughter. Ashley? I realized, the second I heard her . . . I'm sorry. Stupid. Wrong." She recalled her mother's words, the day before she died: *Even mice don't spring the same trap twice*.

"Well," he said. "I've seen worse crimes against humanity." He pulled out a small black agenda from his coat pocket, flipping back to spring. He showed her the note, in his icy, clean handwriting: *Rabbit, phone*. Her brother's pet name for her, from childhood. The name she never should have told Karsh. The name she thought she'd never hear herself called again. "I wish you'd stayed on the line. I might have helped."

Not a sentiment the old Robert Karsh could even have faked. Their meeting might end here; she might never see him again and still feel vindicated, a thousand times better about herself than he'd last made her feel. "You're helping now," she said.

Robert returned the talk to Mark. The symptoms fascinated him, the prognosis depressed him, and the medical response outraged him. "Let me know when Dr. Author gets back. I'd like to run a few tests on him."

She did not describe Barbara to Karsh. She didn't want those two meeting, even in imagination. "Tell me about you," she asked. "What have you been doing?"

He waved at the surrounding buildings. "All this! When were you through last? The town must look pretty different to you."

The town looked like Brigadoon. The Land That Time

Forgot. She tittered. "I was thinking that nothing has changed since Roosevelt. Teddy."

He grimaced as if she'd kneed him. "You're kidding, right?" He looked around, through three compass points, as if he himself might be hallucinating. "The fastest growing non-metro city in Nebraska. Maybe the eastern Plains!"

She swallowed her laughter into hiccups. "I'm sorry. Really . . . I have noticed a few new . . . things. Especially out near the interstate."

"I can't believe you. This place is undergoing a renaissance. Improvements under way everywhere."

"Closing in on perfection, Bob-o." The name slipped out of her. The one she'd sworn never to use again.

He looked ready to inflict full frontal assault, like the old days. Instead, he buffed his skull with his knuckles, a little hangdog. "You know, Rabbit? You were right about me. We built a lot of shit. Nothing substandard, but still. A lot of strip mall and cinder-block apartment complexes I have to atone for, come Judgment. Fortunately, most of it will blow away in the next high wind." He hummed a high-pitched rendition of the tornado music from *The Wizard of Oz*. She laughed, despite herself. "But we're different now. We've brought in two new partners, and we're lots more ambitious."

"Robert. Ambition was never your problem."

"No, I mean good ambition. We were involved with the Arch!"

She hiccupped again. But he glowed with an Eagle Scout pride that stunned her. Inconceivable that she'd ever been afraid of this man. She'd simply mistaken him, never understood what he was really after.

"It took me a while to realize, but good conscience actually sells. You just have to teach people how to recognize their own best interests. We pushed through the paper recycling plant. Have you been out to see that? State of the art. I call it *Mea Pulpa* . . ."

She asked him about new projects. As soon as was safe, she fished. Something big and new, out near Farview? Bluntness was best with him. He didn't try to hide; he never had. He stared at her question, his surprise threatening to become desire. "Where on earth did you hear that? You're talking about a top-secret business deal there, missy!"

"Small town." Why she'd spent her adult life trying to leave it. Why she'd never be able to.

He wanted to know how much she knew. But he refused to ask. Instead, he just gazed, a look as intimate as an arm around her waist. "Wait a minute. You haven't been talking to the Druid again? How is the world of sacred ecoterrorism these days?"

"Don't be spiteful, Bob-o."

He beamed. "You're right. Anyway, he and I are practically in the same business now. Building a better future. From each according to his abilities."

She looked up at him, disgusted, delighted. The four blocks of downtown that she could see did feel somehow revived. Maybe Kearney really was resurrecting, back to its glory days of a hundred years earlier, when buoyant Gilded Age residents actually lobbied to move the capital from Washington to their miracle city at the nation's center. That bubble had burst so badly it took Kearney a century to recover. But to hear Karsh go on about broadband, the access grid, satellite streams, and digital radio: geography was dead, and imagination was once again the only limit to growth.

Half an hour, and already she was thinking like him. She waved at a renovated bank across the street, big arm movements, like a magician's assistant or an actress selling appliances on the Home Shopping Network. "Are you responsible for this one?"

"Maybe." He rubbed his wide Baldwin face in his hand, amused by his own zeal. "But this new . . . development. It's something different. This one's a good thing, Karin."

"And big," she said, neutral.

"I don't know what you've heard, but this is a beautiful project. I always wanted to do at least one thing in my life that would make you proud of me."

She spun to face him. His words came out of nowhere, out of her own head, so wholly unearned that she teared up. She'd always dreamed that a few years of absence might make him like her more. She steadied herself with one arm, sucking air and pressing the other palm into an eye. Too much display: she had to stop. He placed his hand on her neck, and half a year of extinction lifted from her. Broad daylight. Not caring who saw. The old Robert Karsh could never have done that.

They sat still until her tears stopped and he removed his hand. "Miss you, Rabbit. Miss the side by side." She didn't reply. He mumbled something about maybe being able to get away for half an hour or something, next Tuesday night. She nodded, twitching like an awn of soft wheat on a windless day.

To make her proud of him. No one on the planet was who you thought he was. She got control of her face, staring down the street to the left. *The town must look pretty different to you.* She swung back toward him, a solid, sardonic look all prepared. But he was looking off at a clump of four office workers in their twenties, three of them women, heading back into the Municipal Building after their hour away.

"You probably have to get back to work," she said.

He turned, grinned, and shook his boyish head. Her misguided mammal heart slammed again.

"Go," she told him. The word sounded light, nonchalant. "Go ahead. You must be starving."

"Maybe I will just . . . grab a little something?" She waved him away, dismissal, benediction. He needed something more. "Tuesday?"

She just looked at him, a minute tightening around her eyes: *What do you think?*

She said nothing to Daniel that evening. Not really deception; telling him—inviting the wrong conclusion—would have been deceptive. Even now, he was keen to prove that he could love her largest anxiety, remain as devoted to her as he was to the blameless birds. And she did love that core of his that didn't know how to be tainted. Her brother—Mark *before*—had been right: Daniel was a tree. A decades-long trunk, tilting toward the sun. No victory or defeat, only constant bending. Every time she hurt him, he grew a little. That night, he seemed almost fully grown.

Over dinner—couscous with currants—the claustrophobia of recent days caught up with them. Daniel sat across from her at the old farmhouse table, his elbows on the oak, the steeple of his fingers pressed together against his lips. He threatened to disappear into reflection. He stood and stacked the dirty dishes. His quiet care as he took them to the sink betrayed the fact: she was defeating him. Breaking down his green ideals.

He placed the dishes in the basin and began to scrub them with a cup of lukewarm water. As always, when he did the dishes, he leaned his head on the cabinets protruding above the sink. Over years, the paint on the cabinet had worn away in a small oval, from the oils in his hair. She did love him.

"Daniel?" she asked. Almost like real small talk. "I've been thinking."

"Yes? Tell me." He still sounded ready to go anywhere. His old pagan Christianity: *Do animals hold grudges?* He was a good man, the kind of good man that only a truly insecure person could find contemptible.

"I've been a leech on you. A parasite, really."

He spoke to the basin. "Not at all."

"I have been. I've been so preoccupied with Mark. Out with him all the time. Afraid to get a job with real hours, in the event . . . in case . . ."

"Of course," Daniel said.

"I need work. I'm making us both nuts."

"Not at all."

"I was thinking . . . that I could help," she whispered. "If it were still available . . . the job that you talked about, at the Refuge?" She would die a fund raiser.

He set down the dish rag and faced her. His eyes bored into her, ready to shine. One offer of help and his wariness fell away. The worst no longer occurred to him, and the best seemed already half-confirmed. How badly he needed to believe in her. "If you just need money . . ."

"This wouldn't be just money." Not just water; not just air. Not, she told herself, *just* anything.

"Because we couldn't pay much, right away. Tight times, at the moment." He was so sure she would rise to what was best in her that she almost backed out. "But, man, do we need you right now."

And shouldn't need be enough? Something needed her more than Mark ever would. She studied Daniel for hints of unaffordable charity. Would he cook books, risk his professional standing, just to keep her straight? Could anyone trust anyone who trusted anyone so much? She held his eyes; he didn't look away. He needed her absolutely, but not for herself. For something larger. Once, that had been all she'd ever wanted. She rose and crossed to where he stood. She kissed him. Sealed, then. What Mark wouldn't take from her, she would give elsewhere. The Refuge would be amazed at her energies.

The following Tuesday, she met Robert Karsh again.

Four months on, and the place was another country. The shin-high fields of green he'd driven through last June now waved gold and brown. Identical route from the Lincoln airport westward, in an interchangeable rental, yet everything around him had altered. Not just the simple turn of a season: more roll now, more tangled range, drumlins and pitches, rifts and concealed copses disturbing the perfect expanse of agribiz, surprise features where Weber had seen only the peak of emptiness. He'd missed everything, the first time through.

So why, in the final twenty miles before Kearney, did it feel so familiar? Like returning to the sealed summer house to retrieve some article of clothing mistakenly left behind. He needed no map, just drove from the exit ramp to the MotoRest on inner compass. The marquee out front still read "Welcome Crane Peepers," already ready for next spring's migration, now only four and a half months away.

He felt he was on a spiritual retreat, recharging his cells, wiping the slate clean. Signs in his room still asked him to spare a towel and save the earth. He did, and went to bed oddly tranquil. He woke refreshed. At the breakfast buffet—healthy midwestern spread, with three kinds of sausage—it struck him that his writing should never have become anything more than private meditation, a daily devotion for himself and a few friends. He could start again, with the extraordinary Mark

Schluter. He had come back not so much to document Mark as to help his story forward into the total unknown. Neuroscience might finally be powerless to settle this desperately improvising mind. But he might help Mark improvise.

He followed Karin's directions out to Farview, River Run Estates, on numbered roads as right-angled as rationality pretended to be. He found the house, in a subdivision cowering in the middle of an enormous harvested field, bounded on one side by the snaking line of cottonwoods and willows that declared the hidden river. He sat in his rental for a moment, gazing at the house: mail-order, springform, something that hadn't been there yesterday and certainly wouldn't be there tomorrow. Walking up to the wood-laminated door, he had the passing feeling, not of déjà vu, but of déjà ecrit, of a passage he'd written long before that was only now coming true.

The man who opened the door to Weber was some foreigner. All Mark's scars had healed and his hair had grown out. He stood like a fledgling god, somewhere between Loki and Bacchus. He seemed only mildly surprised to see Weber.

"Shrinky! Am I glad it's you. Where the hell have you been? You won't believe what's been going on around here." He scouted the yard behind Weber before ushering him in. He shut the door and leaned against it, excited. "Before I say anything: What have you heard?"

All clinical interviews should take place in the subject's home. Weber learned more about Mark in five minutes in his living room than in all their previous encounters. Mark sat him in the overstuffed chair and brought him a bottle of Mexican beer with some honey-roasted peanuts. He shushed Weber and went to root around in the bedroom. He returned with a pad of paper and a pen. He gestured to Weber to start his recorder, the two of them old collaborators. "Okay, let's tackle this thing, once and for all."

Mark was remarkably animated, spinning a story that smoothed out all the breaks. He raced through the answers before Weber even asked the questions. He traced a single, clean line of thought: all his friends were conspiring to hide what had happened that night. Cain and Rupp knew; they'd been talking to him on the walkie-talkie just as he flipped over. But they'd lied to him about it. His sister knew, so she'd been replaced, to keep her from telling. Like the guardian note-writer, she was probably locked up somewhere. Daniel Riegel was somehow trailing him, for reasons unknown. "Like I'm some creature or something. He's a big tracker, you know. He can find wild things invisible to the naked eye. Things you and I don't even know are there."

Your fake sister's boyfriend following you around in disguise: Freud might do more than the MRI. Surely the phenomenon had to be something more than a dissociation between ventral and dorsal recognition pathways. But what did *psychological* mean anymore, except a process that did not yet have a known neurobiological substrate? Weber made no theories about Mark's new belief. His job now was just to help this new mental state adjust to itself. He would never again leave himself open to charges of failed compassion. He would let Mark write the book.

What did it feel like to be Mark Schluter? To live in this town, work in a slaughterhouse, then have the world fracture from one moment to the next. The raw chaos, the absolute bewilderment of the Capgras state twisted Weber's gut. To see the person closest to you in this world, and feel nothing. But that was the astonishment: nothing *inside* Mark felt changed. Improvising consciousness saw to that. *Mark* still felt familiar; only the world had gone strange. He needed his delusions, in order to close that gap. The self's whole end was self-continuation.

Mark, at least, was still himself—more than Gerald Weber could claim. Method-acting, Weber tried to inhabit the man who sat in front of him, weaving theories. Weber might more easily have channeled Karin, her frightened research, her desperate, self-effacing e-mails. How could he inhabit Mark Schluter, the oblivious Capgras sufferer, when he couldn't even inhabit Mark Schluter, the healthy truck customizer and slaughterhouse technician? He could no longer even imagine what it felt like to be Gerald Weber, that confident researcher from last spring . . .

"Everyone born around here is in on the cover-up. You and Barbie Doll are the last two people I can trust."

What did Mark suppose was being covered up? Worse: What made him think he could trust Weber? As a rule, Weber never humored patients' delusions. Yet he humored everyone else, every day of the week. The Pakistani cabbie on the way to LaGuardia, with his theories about Al Qaeda links to the White House. The security agent at the airport, making him remove his belt and shoes. The woman in the plane seat next to him who grabbed his arm at takeoff, sure the cabin would explode at fifteen hundred feet. Humoring Mark was status quo.

"So I was apparently talking to the guys on these communicators. Them in Rupp's truck, me in mine. We were on to something, chasing. And one of us had to be stopped. Funny thing? This woman playing Karin? She kept hinting those two were there, and I didn't listen."

Something *had* happened to Mark, the night of his accident. And his friends *had* lied to him. Weber himself couldn't account for the guardian's note or interpret the swerving sets of tire tracks. His own explanation for why the world now felt different to Mark wasn't even partially satisfying. Mark had been thinking about his internal state longer and deeper than anyone. Weber could afford to humor his theories. Maybe humoring was empathy by another name.

Slumping on his couch with his shoulder on the armrest and a throw pillow between his knees, Mark launched his best hypothesis. He leaned toward a secret biological project. "Experimental breakthrough. Like the kind of thing my father was always trying to hit on. But big, on the scale only the government could swing. And it's got to do with birds. Otherwise, why would Birdman Danny be after me?"

For that, too, Weber had no explanation.

"The whole thing must be pretty hush-hush. Otherwise, we'd have heard about it, right? So here's what I'm thinking. All this stuff started the minute I came out of the hospital. They did something to me when I was under the knife. Okay, so K2 says I wasn't 'under the knife,' in so many words. But I had a bolt coming out the head, right? A little spigot? They could inject crap, draw it out. I could be dreaming this whole situation, right now. They could have implanted this whole meeting with you, right into my cere-beanie."

"Then they injected me, too. Because I am convinced that I'm here, too."

Mark squinted at Weber. "Really? Are you saying . . . ? Wait a minute. Get the hell out of here! It doesn't mean that at all."

He scribbled on his notepad. He leaned back on the sofa and put his feet up on the coffee table, staring across the room. He jerked up, raising his arm and pointing his shaking finger. He stood unsteadily and walked over to his computer. He tapped his monitor repeatedly with his index-finger nail. "It never occurred to me. Simply never dawned . . . You think it's possible that the last several months of Mark Schluter's life have been programmed in a government machine?"

Weber could not say that it wasn't possible.

"That would go a long way toward explaining why I feel like I've been living in a video game. One where I can't beat the level and advance to the next."

Weber suggested they go outside and stroll down toward the river. A little nervously, Mark agreed. The brisk air worked on Mark. The longer they talked, the more adamant Mark became. It struck Weber that maybe he'd been helping the man create this illness. Iatrogenic. Collaboration between doctor and patient.

"So I'm on the walkie-talkie to my buds. We're communicating, we're chasing this thing down. All of a sudden, I see something on the road. I flip the truck. So the question is: What did I see? What was out there in the middle of the road that night? There just aren't too many choices."

Weber conceded the point.

"Someone who wasn't supposed to be out there. I'm not saying terrorists, necessarily. Could be working for either side."

They walked back along a dusty gravel road through two walls of russet corn days away from harvesting. Autumn, the season that always crippled Weber with anticipation. The cool, dry, alerting breeze got to Weber as it hadn't for years. His pulse quickened, tricked by the perfect day into thinking something was about to happen. At his side, Mark walked, grim and resigned. His stride no longer showed any injury.

"Sometimes I think it was, you know: Mark Schluter. The other one. The guy who used to work for a living. The sure one, who could pass all your little trick tests without even thinking. That's who was out there, in the middle of nowhere. I ran that guy over. Killed him."

He'd begun to double himself. This boy-man might throw no end of light on consciousness. They came back through the fields to River Run, the Homestar. They sat side by side on the concrete front steps, Mark's legs spread too wide. The dog, Blackie Two, came up on its chain and stuck its muzzle into Mark's hands. Mark petted and ignored it at random. The dog whimpered, unable to decode human whim. Nor could Weber. He'd sworn off anything that could be accused of exploitation. Yet surely empathy with Mark didn't preclude a wider care. Perhaps science wasn't over yet. He said nothing for as long as he could. Then he asked, "Would you like to come to New York for a while?" A full workup at the Medical Center, state-of-the-art equipment, the luxury of time, lots of talented researchers, interpretations less vested than his own.

Mark leaned away from him, astonished. "New York? What, and have some airplane slam me?" Weber told him there would be no danger. Mark just scoffed, well past conning. "You guys are big on anthrax out there, too, right?"

Nothing mattered but trust. "I hear you," Weber said. "Probably safer to stick around here."

Mark shook his head. "I'm telling you, Doc. It's a weird world. They can hit you, wherever you are." He studied the horizon for the clue that had to appear there, eventually. "But I do appreciate the offer. I might've been dead by now without you, Shrinky. You and Barbara are the only ones who have truly cared what happens to me."

Weber flinched at the words, the most delusional Mark had spoken all afternoon.

Mark's arms began to shake, as if his body had gone terribly cold. "Doc, I've got a really bad feeling about my sister. It's been like, what? Half a year. Not even a word. Nobody willing to say what happened to her. You have to understand: she's been checking up on me weekly since I was old enough to wet the bed. God knows why, but she's always cared for me. She and this guardian both, disappearing without a trace. Even if they have her locked up, she'd have found some way to get a message to me by now. I'm beginning to think I've hosed my sister. Gotten her in trouble, maybe even killed, just for being related to me. You don't suppose . . . it couldn't have been her who . . . ? She must be . . . let's face it. I think she's probably . . ."

"Tell me about her," Weber said, to keep him from worse speculation.

Mark sucked the air and a sharp syllable of laugh shot from him. "Don't ever tell her I said this, but there's nothing at all to her. Simplest person in the world. She just needs petting. Give her, like, three-fifths of a gold star and she'll go through fire for you. See, we had this mom? Nothing short of Jesus' starting five was good enough for her. She and my sister had what you might call issues. *You miserable thrill-seeking liberal ingrate*, yada yada. *Nine months of morning sickness followed by the most excruciating pain of my life, just so you can go and seduce your Physical Education teacher*, yada yada yada. So Karin? She decides she's going to be perfect. Find out what everyone expects of her, and serve it up to a T. Even a total stranger's disappointment just kills her. Simpler than a household pet, though. Just needs two things: Love me, and tell me I'm doing right. Don't call me a shiftless shit-kicker. Hey; maybe that's three things. How about you, Doc? You got any of the sibling thing going? Hey: don't take so long answering. It ain't a trick question or anything."

"A brother," Weber said. "Four years younger. He's a cook out in Nevada." If he was still out there. If he was still alive. Weber had last heard from Larry two years before, with too much detail about the Liberty Riders' annual "Lead, Follow or Get the Hell out of the Way Fest." Fanatical conservative national motorcycle organization: Lawrence Weber's whole life. Sylvie nagged Weber every few months to call, make some effort to stay in touch. "A good man," Weber claimed. "He reminds me a little of you."

"No shit?" The notion tickled Mark. "Your folks?"

"Gone," Weber said. More than half true. His father, dead of a stroke when three years younger than Weber was now. His mother with advanced Alzheimer's, in a Catholic assisted-care facility in Dayton where he visited once a season. He and Sylvie still conversed with her twice a month over the phone, dialogues out of Ionesco.

"Sorry to hear that," Mark said, and by way of consolation invited Weber in for dinner. The simple kindness stabbed at Weber. How many tiny mental courtesies persisted in their own obscure loops, oblivious to the disasters that hammered them? Dinner was beers out of the bottle and frozen lasagna reheated in a deep aluminum tin. "Something the surrogate sister brought over. Eat at your own risk."

"Are you okay?" Sylvie asked that night. "You sound different, somehow. Your voice is very . . . I don't know. Unfolded. Like a philosopher or something."

"Philosopher. Now there's a career future."

"Makes me nervous, Man."

In fact, he felt different, even to himself: pooled somewhere outside the realm of public judgment. "Strange, isn't it? Two round trips, four thousand miles each, just to see a man who really only wants me to be a detective."

"And they say doctors no longer make house calls."

"But what a case! Medicine needs to know about this."

"Medicine should know lots of things. I'm glad you're doing this. I know you, Man. This one's been preying on you."

"Wife? Remind me to call my brother when I get home."

After the call, he went out and walked into town, block after gingerbread block, under the amber globe of streetlights, as if on his way to some obscure assignation. Autumn thickened the air. The year was drawing into itself, dense with preparation. Massive maples flared up on their way to going dormant. A restless insect swarm blared its bandsaw death chorus. He stood at the corner of four white-wood A-frames, one flickering with nineteenth-century glow, two lit blue by television, and the fourth dark. He'd never felt more eager to find out. Find out *what*, he couldn't say. What was he doing back? Something that autumn promised to answer.

He was still walking at random when the street went dark. He took four full seconds to think: power failure. The thrill of thunderstorms and ambulances came over him. He looked up; the sky was deep in stars. He'd forgotten how many there could be. Washes of them, spilling in streams. He'd forgotten how rich darkness looked. He could see, but poorly, without color, plunged into achromatopsia. Both of the achromats he'd interviewed had raged against the very words, *red, yellow, blue.* They lived for the night world, where they were superior to the color-sighted and merely ordinary. Weber fumbled in the dark for blocks, his sense of direction failing. When the lights surged back on, he felt the banality of sight.

The next day, Mark took him fishing. "Nothing fancy, man. Crude stuff. Maybe previous Mark might have taught you how to tie kick-ass midges and sculpins. But we're talking commercial lures today. Scented rubber worms dragging around their lazy, fake-invertebrate barbed asses through the water until some loser crappie takes a hit. Anybody can handle it. Little kids. Neuroshrinkists. What have you."

The fishing spot was secret, as all fishing spots are. Weber had to swear a vow of silence before Mark would take him. Shelter Lake, on private land, turned out to be little more than a dew pond with delusions of grandeur.

"Here we are. The hidey-hole. Catch and release," Mark said. "Man with the most fish by 2:00 p.m. is the superior human being. Ready, set, go. Dude, you look like you've never baited a hook."

"Only in self defense," Weber said.

His father had taken him, every summer until he turned twelve — bluegill in a small stocked lake just over the Indiana line. His father told him the fish felt nothing, and he'd believed it, on no evidence at all. Nonsense; of course they felt pain. How could he not have seen it? He took Jess once, some nostalgic recreation, surf casting on Long Island's South Fork, when she was still small. The expedition ended in disaster when she hooked a bass through the eye. He could still picture her, running up and down the beach, shrieking. That was the last time.

"Are you sure this is legal?" he asked Mark.

Mark just laughed. "I'll take the rap for you, Shrink, if they bust us. I'll keep your sheet clean."

They fished from the shore, Mark cursing. "We should have stolen the damn boat from Rupp. It's part mine, anyway. He'd probably shoot me in the back if I tried to take it now. Can you believe they lied to me? Whoever we were hunting together that night must have gotten to them. Turned them. Now I'll never learn what went down."

They fished deliberately, casting and reeling without conviction. Weber caught nothing. Mark enjoyed harassing him. "No wonder you're wiping out. You cast like some girls' sixteen-inch softball pitcher."

Mark caught half a dozen midsized sunfish. Weber inspected the catch each time, before Mark threw it back. "Are you sure those are all different? I think you're catching the same fish, again and again."

"You must be shitting me! The first few were full of fight. This one's completely limp. Nothing to do with one another." Mark waded ankle deep in the water, shaking his head in amused disgust. "This look like any fish you know? You've finally lost it, Doc. Too much direct sunlight. Not good for someone in your line." He stood like a heron, leaning forward, frozen in the reeds. He fished the way that Weber typed: in a distracted rapture. He'd needed to get Weber away from town, someplace slow enough to think and talk, without any danger of being overheard. "Why do you suppose they're so worried about me, when I don't know anything? This whole elaborate fantasy, just to keep me in the dark. Why not just kill me? They could have done that easily, in Intensive Care. Slipped into the room, switched off the machines. Pffft."

"Maybe you know something that they want to find out."

The idea stunned Mark. It stunned Weber more, to hear it come out of his mouth.

"That must be it," Mark said. "Like the note says: kept alive, to bring back someone else. *Do* something with what I know. But I don't fucking *know* what I know."

"You know a lot," Weber insisted. "About some things you know more than anyone else alive."

Mark spun his neck, his eyes a barn owl's. "I do?"

"You know what it means to be you. Now. Here."

Mark looked back at the water, so defeated he couldn't even rouse a rage. "Fuck if I do. I'm not even sure that this *is* here."

He changed them both over to bass spinners, not in the hopes of catching anything on them in so small a pond, but for the simple pleasure of pulling them through the water. Weber marveled at his own ineptitude. Not just his failure to catch anything: his complete inability to sit still and enjoy himself. Wasting half a day, holding a stick with a string on it, while his whole career, all his professional duties, unraveled around him. But this *was* his professional duty now, his own self-selected job description. To sit still and watch, not some syndrome, but some improvising *being*. Without that, the reviewers were right and the rest of his life a lie.

Mark, meanwhile, had grown as placid as a bottom feeder. He tasted the air in large gulps. "You know, Shrink? I've been thinking. I think you and I might be related somehow. Aw, don't give me that neurological look. You know what I'm saying, Sherlock. I'm just saying: collision paths, and all. Listen." Mark dropped his voice, so none of the nearby chordates could pick him up. "You believe in guardian angels?"

It distressed Weber to remember: he had been the most devout of children. A kid who liked nothing better than to put on a white cassock and swing something brass and smoky. Even his parents had found him upsettingly spiritual. He'd considered it his personal responsibility, to tip the world toward ancient and reverent. His zeal for purity, some compulsive cleaning mania of the soul, had lasted, only mildly modified, all the way through adolescence, extending even to bouts of shame at failing to refrain from what he and his priest tacitly code-named *susceptibility*, the pleasure that diminished all grace, simply by being solitary. Even science had not wholly killed off his belief; his Jesuit teachers had kept faith and facts ingeniously harmonized. Then, in college, religion had died, overnight, unmarked and unmourned, simply in his meeting Sylvie, whose boundless faith in human sufficiency led him to put away childish things. After that, his whole childhood seemed to have belonged to another person. Nothing to do with him. Nothing remained of that boy but the adult's trust in the scalpel of science.

"No," he answered. No angels but what selection left standing.

"No," Mark echoed. "I didn't figure. Me neither, until I got this note." His face convulsed with thought. "You don't think my sister could have written . . . ? No, that's insane. She's like you. Realistic to a fault."

They stood and watched the ripples of their lines race time to a standstill. Weber's vision tunneled, tranced out on his lure. The air in all directions turned dark as the lake. He looked up into a ceiling of clouds like flour-flecked eggplant. Only then did he feel the drops of rain.

"Yep," Mark confirmed. "T-storms. Saw it coming on the Weather Channel."

"You *saw* this?" Water began to slap down all around them. "Then why on earth did you take us fishing?"

"Aw, come on. Grow up. Three-quarters of what they say on that show is paid for by some sponsor."

Weber fluttered, but Mark would not be rushed getting the gear back into his tackle box. They made for the car, through pillars of falling water, Mark fatalistic, cackling strangely, and Weber running.

"What's your hurry?" Mark yelled, above the pounding sluice. Lightning tore a seam in the sky, followed by so violent a crack that Mark fell back onto the ground. He sat there, laughing. "Knocked me on my literal ass!" Weber wavered between helping Mark up and saving his own life. He did neither, but stood in the middle of a grassy field, watching Mark struggle to his feet. Mark looked up, giggling into the torrent. "Try that again! I dare you!" The sky cracked open and he fell back to the ground.

By the time the two of them waded to the car, hail was pelting them. They slipped soaking into the front seat. A sheet of mothball stones blew up, slamming the rental hard enough to pockmark it.

Mark craned his head, gazing straight up through the windshield. "What do we still need, here? Locusts. Frogs. Firstborn." He fell silent, inside the pounded gray cocoon. "Well, maybe we've had that one already." The hail turned back to electrified rain, light enough to brave. Still, Weber did not start the car. At last Mark said, "So tell me something about yourself. When you were a kid or something. Doesn't have to be the so-help-me-God or anything. Just a throwaway. Make it up if you want. How else am I supposed to know who you are?"

Weber could think of nothing. He'd worked his entire life to efface his past, no biography except what would fit on the flaps of a book. He looked at Mark, trying to think of some story. "I liked to adore girls from a distance, without telling them."

Mark curled his lip and shook his head. "Done that. Very little ROI. How'd you ever get married, Romeo?"

"My friends mounted an intervention. They set me up on a blind date. I was supposed to go to a coffee shop on a Sunday afternoon and find a woman who looked exactly like Leslie Caron. I got there, and nobody in the place even remotely fit the description. It turns out the woman got cold feet. But I didn't know, so I just stood there in a haze, analyzing every female in the place, thinking: *Well, could be, maybe . . .* You know: brown hair, bilateral symmetry . . . A waitress asked if she could help me. I told her I was hoping to find a woman who looked like Leslie Caron. She mistook me for a brash young man with a sense of humor. Three years later we were married."

"You're shitting me. You married a total accident? You're a maniac."

"I was pretty young."

"And did *she* look anything like . . . Lindsay Whozit?"

"Nothing at all. Maybe a tiny Natalie Wood thing. But more like . . . the woman I was going to marry."

Mark looked out through the wraparound waterfall, his glee collapsing. "You're saying fate? Two inches to the left, and your life is somebody else's. She's just standing there, making a living, and bang: your lifelong companion. I'd say somebody was looking out for you." Weber started the engine. Mark stayed his arm. "Only—we don't believe in that angel shit, do we? Guys like us?"

Weber now saw how badly he'd failed the man and his sister. He wouldn't do so again. He made calls, tapping his network of colleagues. To a person, they were discomfited to hear from him, assuming he'd gone off somewhere to die of public disgrace. But Mark's story fascinated them. None had ever worked with anything like it. And no two of them proposed the same course of action, except the pair who suggested leaving a nonthreatening condition alone. Most sounded grateful when Weber said goodbye.

He worked the broadband connection in his hotel lobby, late into the night. He logged into all the medical indexes, exploring every clinical reference in the literature. He'd done as much before, but cursorily. The patient had been Dr. Hayes's; Weber was just a visiting interviewer. He'd looked at the literature, enough to conclude that no real literature existed. What few cases he had found bore no direct bearing.

On a second trip through the most current databases, a single abstract jumped out at him. Butler, P. V. Seventeen-year-old man with Capgras delusions following traumatic brain injury. Treatment and outcome: Delusional ideation fully resolved within 14 days of commencement of olanzapine 5 mg daily.

He checked the date: August 2000. Two years old, in the *Australian and New Zealand Journal of Psychiatry*. No excuse for having missed it on first look, not with electronic search. But he hadn't really been looking, the first time. The sister had begged him for some treatment, but Weber hadn't *wanted* Capgras to be treatable with yet one more newly marketed miracle pill. Psychopharmacology: hit or miss, hard to tune, ripe with side effects, symptom-masking, and once begun, difficult to tail off of. Medicine's next generation would surely remember Weber's as sadly as Weber remembered his father's. The general level of barbarism receded, but never as quickly or completely as thought. Or maybe *he* was the last barbarian. Months of unnecessary suffering, because of Weber's eyes-averted Puritanism. Because he'd never considered Mark anything but a good story.

Karin came to meet him at the hotel. She even came up to his room, bringing her boyfriend for protection. For no reason, Daniel Riegel, a perfectly decent man, made Weber acutely uncomfortable. Spontaneous unease, hidden in some association: the goatee, the loose-fitting collarless shirt, the aura of calm self-acceptance. Karin was understandably anxious. He'd hurt her with his quick departure the first time, and baffled her by agreeing to a second. Her lips moved as Weber spoke, struggling against the hope that he might still help. How she'd gone on hoping that, Weber could only dimly imagine. How hope itself got selected for, over the eons, Weber had no clue.

He had straightened his room before their arrival, squirreling his possessions away in closets and drawers. He'd missed a pair of socks, a milkshake cup, and his bedside reading—*The Seven Pillars of Wisdom*—and couldn't now retrieve them without calling attention. The room gave no real place to sit, and he lost the rhythm of a real office visit. For their part, Karin and her Daniel walked into the meeting as if dragging into court. And Weber hadn't even presented them with options yet.

He described his follow-up visit with Mark. Mark's condition definitely had grown more pronounced. Spontaneous improvement no longer seemed likely. Behavioral therapy had failed. "I do still believe that Mark is in no danger of harming anyone," he pronounced. Karin gasped, which irked him. "I think it's time to try something more aggressive. I recommend that Mark be started on a low-dosage regimen of olanzapine."

Karin sat blinking at the word. "Is this something new?" *New since June?*

Daniel challenged him. "What kind of drug is that, exactly?"

Weber felt like pulling rank. Instead, he just raised his eyebrows.

"I mean . . . is it a . . . what category? Is it an antidepressant?"

"It's an antipsychotic." Weber found the exact tone of professional assurance. But reflex fear struck both listeners. Karin reddened. "Mark isn't psychotic. He's not even . . ."

Weber was ready with the necessary reassurances. "Mark isn't schizophrenic, but he's developed complicated symptoms. This drug is effective in countering those symptoms. It was very successful in a similar case . . . elsewhere."

Daniel bridled. "We wouldn't want to dope him or put him in some kind of chemical straitjacket." He checked with Karin, who did not back him up.

"He wouldn't be in a chemical straitjacket." No more than everyone, always. "A small number of people experience lethargy, and some put on some weight. Olanzapine adjusts levels of various neurotransmitters, including serotonin and dopamine. If it works for Mark, it will reduce his agitation and confusion. With luck, there's a chance it could leave him more lucid, less susceptible to extraordinary explanations."

"Luck?" Karin asked.

Weber smiled and spread his hands. "It's medicine's great ally."

"He would recognize me again?" Ready to try anything.

"No guarantees. But there does seem to be a precedent."

Daniel geared up for moral battle. "Don't these drugs lead to dependency?"

"Olanzapine is not addictive." Weber didn't say how long Mark would have to take it, for the simple reason that he didn't know.

Daniel persisted. He'd heard stories. Antipsychotics producing social withdrawal, flattened affect. Weber gently pointed out the obvious: Mark was already worse. Daniel began a list of every side effect known to medication. Weber nodded, fighting his irritation. He wanted to see the man in distress, repenting. "This is a newer drug, one of the so-called atypical antipsychotics. It has notably fewer side effects than most."

Karin sat on the lip of the purple hotel chair, her leg pumping. Postural hypotension and akathisia: two of olanzapine's side effects. Sympathetic suffering, in advance. "Daniel means . . . we're just afraid the medicine might turn Mark into someone else."

Exactly the result she was asking Weber to produce. Weber wavered, then gave in to saying, "But he's someone else now."

The consultation broke up with all three of them ruffled.

Weber felt stymied. Daniel Riegel withdrew in dignified dismay. Karin was all over the emotional highway. She badly wanted the magic bullet, but couldn't move without failing someone. *Love me, and tell me I'm doing right.* "If you're sure it will lessen his symptoms," she fished, but Weber would promise nothing. "I need to think about this. Weigh things."

"Take all the time you need," Weber told her. All the time in the world.

He called Sylvie, went out for dinner, showered, read, even wrote a little, although not well. When he checked his e-mail, there was already a letter from Daniel. He'd been frightened by information he found online, a site announcing, "Olanzapine is used to treat schizophrenia. It works by decreasing unusually high levels of brain activity." The letter overflowed with links to malpractice sites, lists of known and suspected side effects of the drug. The note itself was infuriatingly careful. Did Weber know that olanzapine produced drastic changes in blood-sugar levels? A pending suit even claimed that olanzapine had "turned some people into diabetics." Daniel disclaimed his own role in the decision-making. "But I'd like to help Karin make the right choice."

The blessing of endless information: the Internet, democratizing even health care. Suppose we gave all pharmaceuticals an Amazon rating. The wisdom of crowds. Do away with experts altogether. Weber inhaled and began his reply. Here was precisely why the medical profession erected multiple barriers between its practitioners and their clients. A mistake, even to answer this e-mail. But he did, as caringly as possible. A debt to pay off. He was aware of the drug's possible side effects, and he'd mentioned them at their meeting. His own daughter was a diabetic, and he had no desire to induce the condition in anyone. He didn't want to suggest any course of action that

Karin wasn't completely comfortable with. Daniel was doing the right thing by informing her in every way possible. The decision was entirely Karin's to make, but Weber stood ready to assist in any way possible. He copied the message to her.

He fell asleep to questions of his own, for which he had no higher appeal. What had triggered such continuous surprise in him, this sense of awakening from a long sham? Why had *this* case unsettled him and not the hundreds before it? Not since puberty had he so doubted his impulses. When would he feel discharged, paid up, ready again to trust himself? He had become a matter of intense clinical fascination, the subject of his own open experiment . . .

The next morning, he walked through town, searching for the diner where he'd breakfasted once, months before. The air was crisp and bracing, readying him for anything. Clear and unbroken, robin's-egg blue to all four compass points, however far he walked. The buildings, houses, cars, grass, and tree trunks all shone forth, supersaturated. He might have been inside some Kodachrome harvest festival. Dirt and dried cornstalk in his nose: he couldn't remember the last time he'd smelled anything so baldly. He felt as he had at seventeen, when, as a Dayton Chaminade senior, he'd set himself the task of writing one Persian-style ghazal a day. Back then, he knew he would become a poet. Now he filled with this sense of awful fraudulence, new lyric possibilities.

He'd let his critics convince him. Something had eroded, the core pleasure in his accomplishment. All three books now seemed uniformly shallow, vain, and self-serving. The braver Sylvie had been in the face of his unnerving, the more certain he was that he'd let her down, that she'd lost some basic faith in him and was too scared to admit it. Who knew how Karin Schluter must see him?

After much random turning, he stumbled upon the diner. Inescapable grid: no town for getting lost in. Ready to push through the door and challenge the waitress's memory, he glanced up through the glass. Karin Schluter sat in a corner booth across from a man distinctly not Daniel Riegel. This man, in a thin teal tie and charcoal suit, looked as if he could buy the conservationist with the loose change that had fallen through his pocket into his jacket lining. The couple held hands across the breakfast-strewn table. Weber backed away from the door, turned, and kept walking. Perhaps she'd seen him. He turned and headed down the street. Over his shoulder, he glanced at the storefronts across the way: trim law offices, a dark, cluttered music shop with a cracked front window, a video store flying a white pennant whose festive letters read "Wednesday is Dollar Day." Behind the bright aluminum siding and plastic signage poked bits of brick and corbels from the 1890s. The whole town lived in continuous retrograde amnesia.

No one could ask him to do more than he'd now done. He'd spent more time with Mark than any clinician could afford. He'd found the best available treatment. He'd made himself available to Karin, in her decision. He would not profit from the visit in any way. In fact, the whole trip had cost him considerable time and money. But he didn't yet feel like leaving. He was not yet square with Mark. He walked back to the hotel, grabbed a breakfast-like-object from the buffet, got in the rental, and drove out to Farview.

In a field two miles out of town, he passed a boxy green brontosaur combine that was ravaging the rows of standing corn. The fields gained a stark, minimal beauty in dying. Nothing could ever sneak up on you, here in these blank horizons. The winters would be the hardest, of course. He should like to try a February here. Weeks of snow-crusted, subzero air, the winds pouring down from the Dakotas with nothing to slow them for hundreds of miles. He looked out over a grain-fringed rise at an old farm just one upgrade beyond sod house. He pictured himself in one of these gray-white clapboards, connected to humanity by no medium more advanced than radio. It seemed to him, as he drove, one of the last places left in the country where you would have to face down the contents of your own soul, stripped of all packaging.

A few years before, River Run Estates had been a single field of wheat or soy. And just decades before that, a dozen kinds of grasses for which Weber had no name. Twenty years on, twenty hundred, it would devolve into grasses again, no memory at all of this brief human interlude. Another car sat in Mark's driveway; he guessed whose. Weber's pulse shot up, surprised fight-or-flight. He checked his face in his rearview mirror: he looked like a bleached garden gnome. He arrived at the front door with no plausible reason, either professional or personal, but Mark opened as if expecting him. Weber saw her over Mark's shoulder, seated at the kitchen table. She was smiling at him, sheepish, familiar. He still couldn't say who she reminded him of. A first hint of awareness broke over him, and he ignored it. She welcomed him, an old confidant. He winced back, the guilty grin you use, clearing customs with contraband in your bag.

Mark shook him by the shoulders in dull delight. "So you're both here, the last two people I can trust. That's pretty interesting all by itself. Don't you think that's interesting? The only people still with me are the ones I've met since the accident. Come on in. Sit down. We were just going over possible plans. Ways to flush the guilty parties out of the underbrush."

Barbara sucked in her cheeks and raised her eyebrows.

"That wasn't quite what we were talking about, Mark."

Weber admired her deadpan. It seemed impossible that she'd never had children.

"Give or take," Mark said. "Don't bust me on a technicality."

"So what *were* you talking about?" Weber asked Barbara. Exposed, off balance, drowning in the shallow end of the pool.

Her smile hinted at private communications. "I was just suggesting to young Mark here . . ."

"A.k.a. me . . ."

". . . that it's time for a new approach. If he wants to know what Karin wants . . ."

"She's means the Pseudo-Sib—"

"If he wants to 'get to the bottom of her,' then the best plan is just to talk to her. Sit down and ask her everything. Who she thinks she is. Who she thinks he is. What she remembers about her past. Listen for any . . ."

"Kind of a sting operation, see? Draw her out. Really push the alibis and the briefings. Trip her up somewhere. Get something to pop out."

"Mr. Schluter."

Mark saluted. "Present and accounted for."

"That's hardly the spirit that we . . ."

"Hang on. All too exciting. I gotta pee. Seems like I have to pee all the time these days. Doc? How old do you need to be before you can reasonably be working on a prostate thing?" He didn't wait for an answer.

Weber looked at Barbara, admiring. Her plan possessed a simple beauty, out of reach of neurological theory. No one— not the brain-as-computer people, not the Cartesians or neo-Cartesians, not the disguised revived behaviorists, not the pharmacologists or the functionalists or the Lesionnaires— none but some civilian would have suggested it. And it seemed no more destructive or helpless than anything science could come up with. It might accomplish nothing at all, and still be useful.

She avoided his eyes and murmured a question. He answered, "Mostly New York."

She looked up, smiling in alarm. "I'm sorry! Did I say 'Where?' I meant 'How?' "

"Oh," he said. "Then the answer is, 'Mostly shaky.' "

The words seemed to come from someone else. But they surprised him less than their instant comfort. Out from hiding, after months: he might say anything to her, this unlikely caretaker, this unreadable woman.

Barbara took his confession in stride. "Of course you've been. If you weren't shaky, there'd be something wrong with you. Open season on you, right now." Laying down her hand for him to see. A nurse's aide, up on the latest *New Yorker* satire. But the most natural shared feeling imaginable. She looked up, the pupils of her hazel eyes as large as the spots on a masquerading moth. They knew him. "It's all still about pecking order with humans, isn't it? Even when the ranking is imaginary."

"Not a contest I have much interest in."

She reared back, that same look of amused skepticism she'd just given Mark. "Of course you have interest. This book is you. The hunters are circling. Nothing imaginary there. What are you going to do, roll over and die?"

The gentlest reprimand, a chide based on total loyalty. Utter confidence in him, but on what authority? An hour and a half of shared time, and reading his books. Yet she saw what Sylvie didn't. The woman unsettled him; why? What was she doing reading book reviews? What was she doing here, at a former patient's? Could these two be involved? The idea was

402

mad. A private visit, months after Mark's discharge: even less a part of her job description than of his. Yet here *he* was, too. She studied him, suspicious of his own hidden motives, and what answer could he give the return question? He stood and said nothing, ready to roll over and die.

Mark came out of the bathroom, still zipping. His head swung, as animated as Weber had ever seen him. "Okay, here's the plan. Here's what I'm going to do."

His words sounded tinny and far away. Weber couldn't make them out, over the nearer din. Barbara Gillespie's face, that open oval, still regarded him, the simplest interrogation. His insides, airborne, answered for him.

The two of them ended up at a restaurant back in Kearney, one of those chains drawn up in Minneapolis or Atlanta and faxed around the nation. Historic, vanished America, reincarnated as comforting franchises. This one was supposed to be a silver mine from the 1880s, about four hundred miles out of place. But then, Weber had been to an identical one in Queens.

The ease of their conversation confused him. They spoke in the compressed, comic shorthand of people who'd known each other from childhood. Idioglossia, as shared as any. They picked at a deep-fat-fried onion, chatting without having to explain themselves. Of course they had Mark's brain to talk about, a topic of inexhaustible interest to them both. "So how do you feel, personally, about his going on this medication?" Barbara's voice gave away nothing, no hint of her own inclination.

Her interest in Mark nagged at him, indicting his own. Why should she be so intimate with the boy, when she shared even less with Mark than Weber did? He shook his head and combed his hand through the idea of his hair. "Hesitant, at best. I'm ordinarily conservative, when it comes to something

403

so powerful. Every roll of the neurochemical dice is a bit of a crapshoot. Like trying to fix a ship in a bottle by shaking it. I'm not even a fan of serotonin reuptake inhibitors, before exhausting other possibilities."

"Really? You must not suffer from depression."

He was no longer sure. "Half the people who respond to them will respond to placebos. I've seen studies suggesting that fifteen minutes of exercise and twenty minutes of reading a day can do as much for depression as most popular medications."

She blinked and tilted her head. "I read for three or four hours a day, and it doesn't keep me particularly safe."

A woman who read more than he did, who suffered her own dark bouts: he would have guessed neither fact. Now both seemed self-evident. "Yeah?" He twisted his mouth. "Try cutting back to twenty minutes."

She grinned and flicked her forehead. "Yes, Doctor."

"But this may be the right thing for him. The only path with any chance of helping." Two different things, he knew. But he didn't point out the difference.

She asked many questions, avid for the topic of Mark. Seamlessly, they drifted to Capgras, then reduplicative paramnesia, then intermetamorphosis. She couldn't get enough of anosagnosia: patients unable to see their symptoms, even when shown. "I can't wrap my head around it. Do you think this man Ramachandran can be right? That there's a little 'devil's advocate' brain subsystem that goes on the blink?"

She'd read far more than just Weber's books. And she was far too eager to talk about what she'd read. He listed hard, looking at her, ear almost on his shoulder, a gesture vaguely canine. He wanted to ask, *So who are you, when you're not yourself?* He asked, "So how long have you been in nursing?"

She dipped her head. "I'm not really a nurse. You know

that. I'm a nurse's aide. A care attendant." Furtive, she stole a fried ring from the onion bloom.

"And you never felt like getting licensed? You never thought of training as a therapist?" He began to form a theory: something had left her as panicked by the arena of public judgment as he was fast becoming. Another thing that linked them.

"Well, I haven't been in the health business for very long."

"What did you do before?"

Her eyes sparked. "Why do I feel like I'm the next case history?"

"I'm sorry. That was a bit pushy."

"Oh, don't apologize. I'm flattered, really. It's been so long since anyone gave me the full interrogation."

"I promise to quit prying."

"No need. To tell the truth, it feels good to talk about . . . real things. I don't get much chance . . ." Her eyes wandered off. He caught a glimpse of her, starved for any scrap of intellectual connection, here in a place where she had chosen exile, a place that distrusted intellect and resented words. Perhaps the only reason she responded to him.

"You're . . . by yourself? No friends? You're not married?"

She laughed. "The proper question these days is: 'How many times?' "

"I'm sorry! Crass of me."

"You say 'sorry' a lot. One might almost think you meant it. Anyway: twice. The first time was a twenty-something temporary insanity. No-fault. The second one left when I took too long deciding on the kid thing."

"Hang on. He divorced you for not having children?"

"He needed an heir."

"What was he, the king of England?"

"A lot of men are."

He studied her face, needing neuroscience to immunize him against beauty. He saw her as she would look in her late seventies, plagued by Alzheimer's and sitting vacant at an empty window. "And you didn't want children?"

"About these neural subsystems," she said. "Just how many of them are there? I'm getting a ramshackle, electoral-college feel."

She was using him. And not even *him*, but just an available, crowded brain, something to bounce herself off of. "Ah! Politics. I should probably go home now."

He didn't go home. They sat talking until the waitress cut off their coffee refills. Even in the parking lot, leaning against his car in the leaf-crackling air, they kept talking. They returned to Mark, to retrograde amnesia, to whether the memory of that night was still inside, theoretically retrievable, if not by him.

"He talks about being at a bar," Weber said. "Some roadside dance house."

She smiled, the most solitary smile he'd ever seen. "Want to see the place?"

Only then did Weber see he'd been fishing.

"Call your wife first," she instructed.

"How did you . . . ?"

"Please. You've been with me all evening. I told you I've been married. I know the drill."

So Weber stood in the parking lot, checking in with Sylvie for the night, while the unreadable woman walked in loops under a streetlight fifty yards away, giving him privacy, hugging herself in her too-thin suede coat.

They took his rental to the Silver Bullet. When he started the engine, the radio roared to life—the classical station he'd found, coming in from Lincoln. He flicked it off. "Wait!" she told him. "Go back."

He flipped it on again and nosed out of the parking lot, onto the deserted road. High unaccompanied voices wove through each other, borne up by a curtain of brass. Music from another planet, antiphony, a lost way of thought.

"My God," she said. She sounded ill. He glanced over at her. In the darkness, her face was taut and her eyes wet. She held up an objecting palm and looked away. "Sorry." Her voice was damp. "Listen to me! 'Sorry.' I sound like you. *Sorry*. It's nothing. Don't mind me."

"Monteverdi," he guessed. "Something you know?"

She shook her head, hard. "I've never heard anything like it." She listened as if to an old crystal set broadcasting news of a foreign invasion. After half a chorus, she reached and turned off the radio. They drove out of town along dark country roads, in silence, Barbara navigating with only hand gestures. When she spoke again, her voice was casual. "This is the road. This is Mark's stretch."

He studied it, but could see nothing. Utterly featureless. They might have been anywhere between South Dakota and Oklahoma. They rode along in the autumn dark, the head-lights just bright enough to push them ahead forever through total ignorance.

The dance house was deafening, music so loud it trampolined on his eardrums. "At least it's not topless night," Barbara yelled. "That's the band that was playing the night of the accident. Mark's favorite."

He wanted to say that he knew all about the band, that he knew as much about Mark's musical tastes as she did. It angered him, that her care for Mark was so spontaneous, while his was full of motives.

They found a booth in the corner. She went to the bar and brought back two pale beers in ribbed plastic cups. She leaned across the table and shouted into his ear, " '*You may ask yourself: How did I get here?*' "

"How's that?"

She looked at him, checking if he was serious. "Nothing. Talkin' 'bout my generation."

He spread his arms out in a fan. "Are these people all regulars?" She shrugged: *Most of them*. "Some of them were here, the night that Mark and his friends . . . ?" The music swallowed his words.

She leaned into him, elbows on the table. "The police have talked to everyone. Nobody knows anything. Nobody ever does."

They sat in the confined booth and drank, each periscoping the room. He measured her. Up close, her face was like some child's, counting the days to its birthday. The woman's inexplicable isolation disturbed him. Something had happened to seal her inside a pose, some bizarre collapse of confidence that left her eking out a life far beneath her ability. She had lost something of herself, or thrown it away, refusing to compete, declining to take part in that collective enterprise that every day grew more unstoppable. Could damage to the prefrontal cortex have turned her into a hermit? No damage necessary. He recognized her, her withdrawal. Something bound them together. Something more than the unthinkable weirdness of Capgras—the orphan in their shared custody—had estranged them both. She had been through a crisis much like the one that now eroded him.

She caught his eye, probing. She reached across the narrow booth and took his wrist. "So this is what you mean by 'Mostly shaky'?"

Even as she held it, he could not control the palsied limb. His whole body: tremoring as if he'd just tried to lift something many times his own weight over his head.

She leaned in and lifted his chin. "Listen to me. They're no one. They have no power over you."

It took him a moment to identify *them*: the court of public opinion. "Clearly they do," he said. More power over him than he had over himself. The human cortex had first evolved by way of navigating intricate social rank. Half of cognition, the chief selection pressure now in play: the herd in the head.

And shaped for it by the power of *them*, her brain read his. "What do you care about that monkey-troop stuff? Grooming and jockeying. Nothing matters but your own sense of work."

All sense of his work was gone. Only the summary judgment remained. She tilted her head at him, searching. And at that one helpless gesture, the words flowed out of him. "That's the problem. Everything the reviewers say is perfectly true. My work is highly suspect."

Almost elating, to admit as much to this woman. She narrowed her eyes and shook her head. "Why are you saying that?"

"I didn't come out here to help the man. Not originally." The music battered away; all around him, people were at work making other people. He could bear to look at nothing more complex than the foam on his beer. "Simple narcissism, to think I could help him in the first place. What more can I do but hand him some chemical shotgun—'Here, take this, and let's cross our fingers and hope for the best'?"

She stroked his knuckles with the back of her thumb, as if she had been doing it forever.

"What good is all the brain science in the world to him? Arrogance, really. A kind of charlatanism. What am I even doing out here?"

She kept a steady pressure on his fingers and said nothing. Her spine curved forward. Something in her shared his sense of deception, took it into her own body. Only her eyes assured him: empathy meant vertigo. She shook his wrist in the air. It had almost stopped quivering. "*Basta*. Enough flagellation. Let's dance."

He shrank back against the back of the booth, stunned. "I don't dance."

"What are you talking about? Everything alive dances." She laughed at his look of terror. "Just get out there and wiggle. Like you're catching bugs."

He was too spent to object. She towed him out to the middle of the dance floor, a tug pulling a wounded freighter. He scrambled along in her wake, looking for instructions, but none were forthcoming. Dancing in a bar with a woman he didn't know: he felt queasy, the way he felt when going a day without work. But this was just simple, improvised, mutual shelter. The idea of anything illicit felt almost comical—*assault with a dead weapon*, he always joked with Sylvie. Weber and Barbara stirred and unfolded. All around them, people moved. Salsa and boogie. Box step and rhythmic stumble. Odd writhings to match the house band's even odder Appalachian fiddling and thrashing guitars. Next to them, a younger couple stared at each other and vigorously kicked shit. Farther away, a Ponca descendant did a variation of the ground-stomp-and-scan, his partner soaring to full flight. Everywhere, knees kicking forward, shoulders flapping. The woman was right: everything alive shook itself under the pull of the moon.

She laughed at him. "You look great!"

He looked like a fool. A clumsy, autumn-honking fledgling. But his body pulsed with the beat of things. The music stopped, stranding them. Weber stood in a pool of shame, needing to fill the emptiness. "Do you suppose that Mark and his friends were dancing that night?"

She squinted at the possibility. "Bonnie said she wasn't here. Not that there weren't women involved. There certainly was drinking, as well as other substances. Mark has told me as much."

The music started up again: heavy bluegrass metal. A wave came over Weber, light, omniscient. Even dancing felt too full to bear. "Come on," he said. "We should go. Nothing to learn here."

She felt it, too: he was sure of that. All the thrill of collapse. They might have been anyone, in any life, hiding from discovery. Her face, as unsteady as his, pretended to carelessness. She found the exit and they fell out of the cloud of smoke and noise into a star-filled sky. He felt the most improbable calm, the placidity of helplessness, and knew that she, too, had spilled into that silence with him. The air was dense and dry with harvest. His feet scuffed the gravel as he crossed toward the car. She grabbed his elbow, stopping him. "Shh. Listen!"

He heard it again, in the night's version. Storms of insects, and the screeches of insect hunters. Now and then owls—*Who cooks for you? Who looks for you?*—and the antiphonal call of what could only be coyotes. Creatures, all of whom heard *humans* and knew them as just part of the wider network of sounds. Living things of every gauge for whom the roadside bar was just another mound in the continuous test of the landscape, just another swarming node in the biome to exploit.

She looked up at him, the loneliest woman he'd ever met, desperate for connection, for some proof that she hadn't created this whole existence out of her own mind. He listened to the night, to the sound of her seclusion. But like Mark's note-writing secret witness, he held dead still, hoping to be passed over. He broke from her questioning gaze and walked

411

toward the car. By the time they reached the rental, he could no longer defend himself, even *to* himself, that easiest of audiences. Yes, he'd made himself return to right things with the Schluters, to square things with himself again. But here, in the sounds of the inhabited night, in the light graze of wind on his arm, in the look of this recluse woman, so burrowed outside life, he recognized the vanishing that he, too, was after.

Karin went to Karsh for advice. All of Daniel's advice was clouded in morality. Medication, Daniel said, would cause more problems than it solved. But Daniel wasn't Mark's brother. Working for the cause was one thing. Sacrificing her blood relation to it was another.

She'd seen Karsh twice. Drinks, catch-up. Nothing criminal, nothing she couldn't handle. She'd been pleasureless for so long that a few quick jolts barely reset the system. She got in touch, through his old secret e-mail alias. He suggested breakfast. "Kind of a switch, no? Post-game show, with no game."

It used to madden her. All she wanted was to sit together, once, like civilized people, over a breakfast table, instead of slinking off like felons. She met him at Mary Ann's, just down the street from his office. When she entered the diner, he jumped up and pecked her on the cheek. She flinched at the sudden move.

But just breakfast: she sat and ordered. The man's mind was just what she needed, as brisk and brutal as an audit. She laid out Dr. Weber's proposed medication. "Antipsychotic," she whispered. Robert just nodded. She tried him on Daniel's most frightening objections. "I'm afraid of leaving my brother doped up on mood-altering substances."

Karsh shook his head and waved at their breakfast. "A cup of coffee is a mood-altering substance. A Spanish omelet. I

412

seem to remember a little addiction of yours—that Swiss triangular chocolate? Don't tell me a few tabs of that stuff never buzzed you."

"This isn't a chocolate bar, Robert. This is psychoactive."

He shrugged and flapped his palms. "You're behind the times, Rabbit. Half the people in the U.S. are on something psychoactive. Look around. See those people over there?" He waved somewhere between a table of four seniors in jogging suits and a family of Mennonites. "Almost even odds. Forty-five percent of America, on something behavior-modifying. Antianxieties. Antidepressants. Name your brew. Couldn't function otherwise. The world is just too wired. I'm on a couple things myself, in fact."

She looked at him, reeling. His fresh ease, that newfound comfort and humility: maybe just something he was taking. The softening of his features, the added layer of baby fat. All just chemical. But then, the brain itself was a wash of one mood-altering substance or another. So said every book she'd read since Mark's accident. It sickened her. She wanted the real Karsh, not this tolerant philosopher, squidding all over the place. "But antipsychotic . . ."

He did this thing: his right hand perpetually checking his left wrist's pulse. It used to make her nuts. Now it just scared her. Robert held his index finger in the air, turning preacher. " 'A gram is better than a damn.' "

"What's that?"

"You don't remember?" he gloated. "We had to read it in high school. You do remember high school, don't you? Maybe you need some memory enhancers."

"I remember taking you to the Sadie Hawkins Dance, and finding you out behind the levee, rooting around in that bitch Cricket Harkness like a truffle hound."

"I thought we were talking literature here."

"We were talking about my brother's future."

He bowed his head. "I'm sorry. Tell me what worries you. Best and worst cases."

It felt good, just to be heard, without the perpetual, silent judgment. To smoke in front of a man—no hiding—felt even better. She told him all her fears for Mark: that he might hurt himself. That he might hurt someone else. That some new, uncanny symptom would crop up, leaving him one more step less human. That the medication might make him even less recognizable. "It's tearing me up, Robert. I was packed and ready to go. And I couldn't even do that. Mark is exactly right about me. I'm a stand-in. Look at my life. I'm a joke. One of those chameleon people. Nothing, at the core. Everybody's girl Friday. He says I'm an impostor? He's right. I've never done anything but go through the motions. Never wanted anything but what I thought someone else might want me to . . ."

"Hey," Robert scolded. "Easy. Maybe we need to get *you* some of this stuff."

She succumbed to bleary laughter. She told Robert about the olanzapine lawsuit Daniel had discovered, pretending she'd found it herself. Karsh made notes in his agenda.

"We keep a stable of lawyers. I'll have somebody see what they can find out."

Just talking to Karsh reassured her, more than it should have. Of course, he was every bit as biased as Daniel. None of them knew what was best for Mark. But just hearing his counterarguments was liberating. A wrong decision would no longer come down on her head alone.

Karsh took his pulse. "You know, if you do go this route, there's still a problem."

"Namely?"

"Getting Mark to comply."

"Get Mark to take pills? A problem?" She snorted in pain.

"Getting him to stay on it. Or to tail off properly. He wouldn't be the most reliable of patients. If he gets it into his head to stop suddenly . . ."

She nodded, one more thing for her to stress about. Each had reached their coffee limit. It was time to leave. Neither moved.

"I should head to work," she said.

"So you're really a volunteer Sandhill Helper now?"

She returned his smile, slash for slash. "Believe it or not, they're actually paying me." She still couldn't quite believe it herself. Over a few weeks, racing to make herself worthy of being hired, she'd read every report the Refuge had issued. And right out of the gate, the Refuge had entrusted her with genuine responsibilities. In some incriminating way, her new duties lifted her from the trough of helplessness she'd lived in since Mark's accident. Some place that actually needed her energies; some useful definition to her days. Like Daniel, she now worked at least fifty hours a week. Mark couldn't blame her: impostors owed him no loyalty. She now knew more about the effort to protect the river than any trainee should know. Information Karsh would kill to learn.

"Really?" he said, eyebrows up. "Paying, as in cash, American? That's great. So what exactly are you doing for them?"

She did everything: stacked boxes. Proofed copy. Made cold calls to local politicians and prospective donors, employing that rich, mezzo, reassuring, consumer-relations voice that was her greatest asset. "Robert. You know? I'm not supposed to say."

"I see." Those aqua eyes glinted with hurt innocence. The

old Robert. The one who could dismantle her without an owner's manual. The Karsh she could no more evade than she could escape herself. "Closely held secrets of the wetlands protectors. I understand completely. What's our personal history, compared to preserving the four-billion-year march of evolution?"

Two years ago that month, she'd lain with this man in the pouring rain, naked in the sloppy riverbanks, licking his armpits like a kitten. "Jesus, Karsh. What can I say? It's the most fulfilling work I've ever done. Bigger than myself? How about bigger than anyone. I'm working through some papers . . . Did you know that we've changed that river more in one hundred years than in all the ten thousand years prior . . . ?"

"Sorry . . . papers? What kind of papers?"

"Photocopies from the County Office, if you must know." Already too much. But surely he'd guessed. She watched him faking calm. She'd often seen that look, but had never before been able to cause it. The sight was nothing short of mood-altering.

"You're right, you probably shouldn't tell me anything." Pouring on the charm, charm more weirdly boyish now that he was graying. "But you'll tell me if I guess, right?"

"Depends."

"On?"

"On what you tell me in return."

Hands spread on the table. "Go ahead. Ask me anything."

"Anything?" She snickered. "How's family life?"

He sat back against the booth and surrendered, too quickly. "The kids are . . . really great. I'm just so glad I got into this whole father thing. Something different every week. Skate-boarding, amateur theatrics, industrial-scale software piracy. No, really: they're fantastic. Wendy and I are another story."

"Another story than . . . ?"

"Listen. I don't want to lay this on your doorstep, Rabbit. This has absolutely nothing to do with your coming back home. It'd been in the works for months before I saw you."

Not, apparently, another story than the one he'd told her for years. But it couldn't hurt her now. Like one of those pieces of junk mail stamped *Urgent: Dated Material. Please Respond.* "I'm sure, Robert. My comings and goings would never affect you."

"You know that's not what I mean. But I'm going to show great psychological acuity by letting you attack me." Retaliating, she salted the half strip of bacon left on his plate. He popped it in his mouth, contrition. "This is exactly what I'm saying." He waved his arms, beaming. "Do you know the last time I felt this free? Wendy and I drag through that disinfected Colonial, appraising each other like insurance-fraud investigators after a fire. We are so over each other. We're at the point where we have to split up for the sake of the kids." He gazed out the plate-glass window, onto Central.

"Anything you like out there? Good morning talent?"

He just nodded. "I like everything I see a little bit more. When you are around."

Most dangerous pitch of all. Someone who made others happier to be who they were: that was all she'd ever dreamed of being. And this man alone knew her fatal weak spot. She listened and indulged him, nodding at his details—the escape apartment he'd lined up, the lawyer who promised reasonable protection. She let him go on about his emerging future. At least he had the decency not to ask whether she was interested in filling it. And all that this brief escape cost her was a peck on the cheek and the surrender of her breakfast tab.

He grabbed her by both elbows as he said goodbye. "I think

your brother might be right. You *have* changed." Before she could cry out, he added, "You're better," and disappeared down Kearney's recently renovated main drag.

That evening, Dr. Weber called. "How are you holding up?" he asked. He sounded genuinely solicitous. But she would not be analyzed. She did not need his help: only her brother. She scrambled to find her list of new questions about the proposed treatment and began to ask them. He gently cut her off. "I'm going back to New York tomorrow morning."

The words silenced her. She started two confused objections before she understood. He was signing off again, even faster than last time. She would not see him anymore, whichever option she chose.

"I'll be in touch with Dr. Hayes at Good Samaritan. He'll have my full write-up. I'll give him all the material I've found, bring him up to speed on where you are."

"That's . . . I don't . . . I still have questions . . ." Searching through a pile of paperwork for the Refuge, she tipped the stack and knocked it to the floor. She cursed brutally, then covered the receiver.

"Please," Weber said. "Ask anything. Now, or any time after I get back home."

"But I thought we were going . . . I thought we'd have another chance to talk about choices. This is a big decision, and I don't have . . ."

"We can talk. And you have Dr. Hayes. The hospital staff."

She felt her control slip and didn't care. "So this is doctor–patient compassion," she said out loud. Things needed letting out, for her own and everyone's good. The man's professional composure enraged her. Why bother coming back at all if this was what he planned? Going home to his family, his wife.

418

Suppose he walked in his front door and his wife wouldn't recognize him? Threatened to call the police if he didn't leave. Antipsychotic. "You don't know what this is doing to me."

"I can imagine," Weber said.

"No you can't. You haven't the slightest idea." She was sick of people imagining they could imagine. She was ready to tell him exactly what he was. But for Mark's sake, she calmed herself. "I'm sorry," she said. "That was inexcusable. I'm not quite together these days." She reassured him that she understood his choice, and that she'd be fine on her own. Then she thanked him for all his help and said goodbye to him for good.

She all but threw it in his face: *You haven't the slightest idea.* Like she deliberately meant to confirm the worst of public accusations. Cold, functionalist opportunist. Not interested in people at all. All that interests you is theories.

The woman's nerve boggled his mind. He'd handed her a treatment where there was none, an option that had cost him some time and effort to find. Tens of thousands of dollars of care, delivered to her doorstep for free. Two pro bono cross-country trips by a researcher with an international reputation, when she might have been knocking on doors, begging for appointments, dragging her brother around the continent, clinic after unproven clinic, in search of anyone who even knew what he was looking at.

Weber had stayed surprisingly composed, at least in memory. He didn't, in any case, say what he was feeling. Too much training for that. To the best of his recollection, he'd never lost his temper in a professional capacity. He'd wanted to explain: *My leaving is not what you think.* But then he would have to tell her what his leaving *was*.

419

She was right in one silent accusation: he was no psychologist. Human behavior, so opaque when he'd started his studies, now struck him as worse than religious mystery. He understood no one. He couldn't begin to grasp *her*. She'd gone from gratitude to entitlement, on no grounds at all. Vulnerability wheeling to attack, even as she begged for mercy. He'd studied the absurdities of behavior his whole life, and he hadn't come close to predicting the words she threw at him.

Yes, the damage he'd made a career of studying fell along a spectrum continuous with baseline psychology. But the things he labored to explain in deficits he couldn't excuse in this healthy person. No medical court would have convicted him had he hung up on her. Instead, he hung on, feeling everything, from far off. He'd seen the same condition in a young woman patient once. Pain asymbolia: damage to the dominant parietal lobe's supramarginal gyrus. *Doctor, I know the pain is there; I feel it. It's excruciating. But it just doesn't bother me anymore.* Pain everywhere, but just not distressing.

Maybe he'd suffered a lesion and was in full-fledged compensation. But on the phone, he could do nothing but go through the motions: What would Gerald Weber do? He let Karin Schluter abuse him, saying nothing in his own defense. He answered her questions as honestly as possible. He hung up feeling worse than humiliated. But the humiliation did not concern him. The thing dismantling him also exhilarated, lifted him so bodily he hovered above himself. On the brink of sixty, and tomorrow threatened to reveal the mystery his whole life had struggled to unlock. A rush of anticipation flooded through him, worse than something pharmaceutical. He'd fallen in love with a total cipher, a woman he didn't know from Eve.

He called Christopher Hayes at Good Samaritan, who greeted him warmly. "I'm in the middle of your new book. I haven't finished it yet, but I just can't understand the press's pile-on. It's no different than anything you've ever written."

Weber had reached the same annihilating conclusion. Everything he'd written now only added to his vague disgrace. He told Hayes that he'd been in town examining Mark. The news silenced Hayes. Weber described Mark's further deterioration, mentioned the article he found in the *ANZJP*, and conveyed the case for olanzapine.

Dr. Hayes concurred with everything. "Of course you remember that I thought we should explore this direction, back in June."

Weber did not remember. Acutely aware of how he appeared to the other man, he nudged the conversation to a close, finally euthanizing it. He drove back to Lincoln that night, waiting on standby until he could get a flight. He called Mark from the airport to say goodbye.

Mark was stoic. "I figured you might be bailing. You tore out of here kinda fast. When you coming back through?"

Weber said he didn't know.

"Never, huh? Can't say I blame you. I'd get back to the real deal myself, if I knew how."

Mark's not good for squat these days except for failing people's tests. First, he lets Shrinky down. He's not sure why—something to do with his less-than-optimal performance in their latest Q and A—but the man tears out of town like he's taken a fire hose of sweat bees up the ass. No sooner does he drive Shrinky away than the Guard is after him. Some kind of agreement that young Mark signed, and apparently his country is now in desperate need of his services.

You-Know-Who—at least she's dependable—runs him up to the recruiting office in Kearney. Same place that Rupp and the aforementioned Mark turned up worlds ago, to talk about doing Mark's bit for Homeland Security. He tries to work it out, on the ride up: the same Specialist Rupp who has finally admitted to communicating with him just after Mark supposedly signs some official papers, and just before somebody runs Mark off the road. As usual, it doesn't add up, except to implicate the government. But government involvement is generally a no-brainer.

At the Guard office, there's a heavy conference that he's not privy to, between the Karin-like person and the Top Guardsman. She's trying to bust up the deal, whipping out files from the hospital, brother obviously impaired, etc. But the army sees through her, of course. And Mark Schluter is asked to answer a few questions for his country. He does his best; he honestly does. If America is under siege and has to go whip some serious foreign butt to break free again, Mark needs to go, just like everybody else. But he has to laugh out loud at some of the questions. True or false: *I believe that meeting people with different backgrounds can improve me as a person.* Well, that all depends. Is "people" some Arab waving a gun and trying to crash my airline? *I sometimes get angered by repetitive or monotonous situations.* You mean, like answering these questions? He asks the recruiting doctor whether we are, in fact, preparing to take the Saddamizer out at last, finish the job, after ten years. But Mr. Ramrod is unbelievably uptight. I couldn't say, sir. Just answer the questions, sir. Apparently we're dealing with some heavily classified dope.

Karbon Karin expresses her own opinions on the way home, opinions suspiciously close to his own sister's. *Family is our country* kind of noise. Mark forgets about the whole thing until a week later, when he gets a letter from NEARNG, with the little Patriot head logo in the circle of stars on it. Basically: don't call us, we'll call you.

Then he whiffs a third time. Pseudo Sib lets slip that the checks he's been getting from Infernal may dry up after the accident's anniversary. You can tell she's sorry as soon as she says it, like he's not supposed to hear, which of course gets his attention. There's absolutely no reason why *she* should be so freaked. So, needless to say, her whole little secretive song and dance freaks *him* something serious.

He calls the plant. After about a million minutes on hold listening to Surprising Beef Processing Facts while being bounced from one clueless personnel officer to another, they put him through to somebody who seems to know all about his situation. Not a good sign, and it makes him think that Rupp or Cain has gotten to them first and given them the other side of the story, the side that everyone is keeping from Mark. The personnel officer tells him that he'll need a whole new round of tests—clean bill of health from Good Samaritan—before they'll consider rehiring him. What the hell do they mean, rehire? He already works there. The desk man says something rude, and Mark counters with something about: Do you want me to tell the feds about the thirty Hispanic illegals you have working the cutting floors? An idle threat, really, since Mark and the feds aren't on great terms at the moment. The guy hangs up on him, so there's nothing to do but take the hospital tests. He's sure he can do pretty well on these, having had his fair share of practice. But the hospital is pissed at him, apparently, for quitting Thera-Play, and they give him some truly bizarre questions, which he bombs out on again.

So that's three strikes, and by the rules of the game, he's out of there. Only, Mark is still in the thick of shit. He's looking at real unemployment. The whole thing is a life-and-death video game, on a countdown timer to detonation. He's got until the anniversary of his accident to figure out what they did to him on the operating table. His one hope is to find his finder, the note-writer, his guardian angel, the only one who knows everything.

A plan comes to Mark, something he should have thought of a while ago. Would have, too, if it hadn't been for all the craziness around these parts. Simple enough, and the beauty of the plan lies in how it forces the hand of the authorities. He'll go public. He'll put the note on *Crime Solvers*. Everybody in four counties will see the plastic-laminated thing pressed up against their TV screens. *I am No One, but Tonight on North Line Road* . . . If any real, unbrainwashed people who know what happened that night are left alive, they'll have to come forward. And if the Powers That Be try to snag and silence them, all of central Nebraska will know.

A year ago, he'd never have considered stooping so low. The show is just too pathetic: the worst kind of local television brain-scrambler. A female reporter and a male policeman run all over the Big Bend region, pretending to be interested in everybody's so-called unsolved mysteries, while all they really want to do, obviously, is run off into the wheat fields somewhere off camera and drill each other silly. And the tangled, baffling cases they go after? Three-quarters of them are clueless women bleating about how they haven't seen their husbands for weeks. Lady, have you tried your teenage Mexican housekeeper's apartment? Once in a blue moon they show some interesting stuff, like the two applicator tanks full of anhydrous ammonia stolen off a siding in Holdrege that turned up in this big old subterranean meth facility in Hartwell. Or the Prairie Bigfoot, this sasquatch thing spotted at night rooting through people's trash barrels in North Platte, and subsequently reported all over the place from Ogallala to Litchfield, which turned out to be this telco wire guy's illegal escaped pet sun bear: one very confused creature, whacked out by a few hundred hysterical, hallucinating humans.

But *Crime Solvers* is his last hope. He does a phone interview with their "story hunter," also known as unpaid student intern. They're interested, and they send the famous Tracey Barr over in person, along with a camera guy, to film him. The Homestar, on the idiot box. Or at least the fake Homestar. Tracey Barr herself, in his living room. He wants to call the guys, get them over to gawk, maybe even get them on camera. Then he remembers he can't really call the guys anymore.

The statuesque Miss Barr is a bit older and not quite as sexual in person. Not as sexual, shall we say, as a certain Bonita Baby, in her homestead garb. Nevertheless, Tracey—she asks him to call her Tracey, believe it or don't—is impressive, in a kind of black tube skirt and backward ruby blouse kind of way. Fortunately, Mark remembers to dress up, too: his fancy green long-sleeve Izod. Present from Bonnie Before.

Tracey wants the whole story. Of course, Mark Schluter doesn't *have* the whole story. That's the point of dragging in the Grime Patrol in the first place. And he's learned that when he does tell everything he knows, people go weird on him. He doesn't want to trip any more mines than he has to. The less the station knows about the big picture, the better. He gives her the basic package: accident, tire tracks, hospital, sealed ICU, and the note on the bedside table, waiting for him when he comes back to himself weeks later. She eats it up. They film all over the yard and house: Mark alone, gazing off into fields. Mark with photo of truck. Mark with

Blackie Two, because who's going to know the difference? Mark holding note, showing note to Tracey. Tracey reading note out loud. And most important: full-screen close-up of note, so everyone at home can see the handwriting and read every word.

Tracey drags him out to North Line, to film him at the scene of the crime. They're joined by this week's Cop on the Case, Sergeant Ron Fagan, who, it turns out, knows Karin from high school, perhaps even in the Old Testament sense. He keeps asking Mark about his sister. Like "the police" don't know about the switch. How's that sister of yours? She's real nice. She still in town? She dating anyone? Quite creepy: this big guy in a uniform, probing to see how much Mark suspects. Mark ducks the questions without, he hopes, getting in any deeper than he's already in.

But Officer Fagan is masterful with Tracey, going on about the accident-scene evidence: the tracks that cut Mark off and the ones that ran off the road behind him. You mean like a squeeze? Tracey asks. And with a straight face, the cop says he doesn't want to leap to conclusions. Leap, after almost a year. Says they have no match on the treads, no leads on the vehicles . . .

Unfortunately, he also mentions the speed Mark was going when he flipped. It's a figure that isn't going to endear him to any potentially watching guardians. Mark had no idea he'd been going so fast. It dawns on him that the car behind him must have been pursuing. He was evading, and he blasted right into the ambush.

They set up the accident-scene camera at the wrong spot. Right road, wrong stretch. Mark objects, but they blow him off. They claim the backdrop looks better here; more picturesque or something. The cop waves his hands like a conductor, pointing out what happened where, but it's all wrong. All fake.

Mark tells them, maybe a little too loud. Tracey commands him to shut up. He yells back: How the hell is the person who found him going to recognize the place and come forward, if the show doesn't even show the right spot?

Well, they all look at him like he's just escaped from Floor Five. But they relocate to the real spot, rather than push it. They film him walking along his little stretch, which is nuts when you think about it, since he wasn't exactly in walking shape that night. But hey: Hollywood. It's mild and dry—light jacket weather, with a teasing wind and all the fields taken in. But he's absolutely freezing, cold at his core, so cold he might as well be lying there, pinned in a ditch, in February, his face pressed through the broken windshield in a slurry of ice.

Another prairie winter, the thing Karin Schluter had fled her whole adult life. She'd been raised on stories of the killer of '36, with its month of unbroken subzeros, or '49, with its forty-foot drifts of snow, or the Schoolchildren's Blizzard of 1888, with its one-day drop of eighty degrees dotting the landscape with frozen statues. This one was nothing. And still, she feared for her survival.

The cardboard browns and gunmetal grays took over. The last of the squashes and pumpkins dried off their vines, and everything sane went south or underground. Longer nights settled in, hooding the town early. Most nights, the wind kept her up; few places on the globe had air so loud. She suffered her traditional November break, that sense that she'd crashed through the world's guard rail and now lay under the unbroken gauze of Nebraska sky, unable to do anything but wait for spring and someone to discover her.

She'd have diagnosed herself with seasonal affective disorder, but she refused to believe in recently invented diseases. Riegel tried to get her to sit under his plant grow lights. "It's all about sun. Your number of hours of sunlight per day."

"You want to trick my body with fluorescent lights? That doesn't seem very natural to me." She felt herself sniping at him more as the days shortened, but couldn't stop herself. He suffered in noble silence, which only made things worse. She rushed to apologize with small kindnesses, telling him again how grateful she was for the work, the most meaningful work she'd ever put her hand to. The next day, she'd snipe again.

She called Barbara for advice. "I don't know what to do. I can change him with this drug, into God knows what. I can leave him who he is now. It's too much power."

She recited Daniel's problems with pharmaceuticals. The nurse's aide listened carefully. "I understand your friend's fears, and I'm speaking to you as someone who has, in her life, given up cigarettes, caffeine, and processed sugar. I know you're scared of anything that might make things worse. I can't tell you what to do. But you need to look into this olanzapine as carefully as . . ."

"I've done that," Karin snapped. "And the man who dumped this in my lap is gone. Barbara! Please?"

"I can't advise. I'm not qualified. If I could make this choice for you, I would."

Karin, who'd dreamed once of becoming this woman's friend, even her confidante, hung up the phone hating her.

She increased her hours at the Refuge. If she'd had this work from the beginning—a river to give herself to—she might have become a different creature. They had her preparing pamphlets. Copy for fund raising and lobbying. Small-arms fire in the increasingly desperate war over water. The pros did the real work, of course. But even her gopher efforts contributed. Daniel, almost afraid to look at her growing wildness, walked her through the research materials, laying out the goals. "We need something to wake sleepwalkers," he instructed her. "To make the world strange and real again."

She was seeing Robert, too, every several days, when he could get away. They'd done nothing, at least nothing Wendy could use in court. They squeezed each other's heads. There were certain lines on the skull Daniel had taught her about, and she showed Robert. Meridians. Powerful stuff, if you could find them. They spent hours outside, at Cottonmill Lake, under the skeletal trees, looking for them: pressure above the eye ridges, a track leading up and back to the crown of the head that, pressed hard, could absolutely pickle your senses. When she tapped into Robert's lines, he'd lean back, shout "Wasabi!" and take his pulse.

The nights grew too cold to stay out of doors. But they had no place to go. They ended up steaming up her car, pulled over on the shoulders of dark country roads or in the far corners of abandoned box-store parking lots. They couldn't use his car, because of Wendy's acute sense of smell. The woman was, by her husband's account, as olfactorially acute as a badger.

"It's worse than being a teenager," Karin groaned. "Damn it, Robert. I'm going to explode."

Then they'd stop and turn back to touchless talk. They had reached the age when frustration offered more than delivery. It meant something, this holding on to technical fidelity. Cheating came later, when they returned to their respective mates.

It surprised her to discover: if she had to choose between fooling around and talk, she'd choose talk. That's what she needed most from him, these days. His mind was so brutally *other* than Daniel's, or her own. She thought faster around Robert. He was a huge, calculating extension of that PDA he was forever poking at. He could sit behind the steering wheel of the parked Corolla, fiddling with the handheld device like a newborn exploring a Playskool Activity Center. To her anxiety over starting Mark on drugs, he said, "Figure the costs. Count up the benefits. See which is bigger."

"Listen to you. If only it were that easy."

"It *is* that easy. Unless you want to make it harder. Come on! What else is there? The plus column and the minus column. Then the math."

His clarity maddened her, but it kept her going.

"Really," he told her. His voice was so calming—Peter Jennings visiting a junior high social studies class. "What's to keep you from starting him on these antipsychotics and seeing what happens?"

"They're hard to tail off of, once you start."

"Hard on you, or hard for him?"

She slugged him, which he enjoyed. "What do I do if they work?"

He twisted in his seat to face her. He didn't understand. How could he? She wasn't sure she did. He shook his head. But his eyes were more amused than exasperated. She was his brainteaser, his handheld puzzle box.

She took his palm and stroked it with her thumb, their most dangerous transaction to date. "What would he be like, if he . . . came back?"

Robert sniffed. "Like he was. Your brother."

"Right. But which one? Don't look at me like that. You

430

know what I'm saying. He could be such an aggressive prick. Always riding me."

Karsh shrugged, the guilt of all mankind. "I've been known to, you know, be a bit that way myself."

"It's just that I can't really . . . When I try to picture him, before? I can't be sure I . . . He was really hairy, sometimes. Raging about my going off and saving myself, condemning him to the faith healer and the entrepreneur. Calling me a . . . Sometimes he really hated me."

"He didn't hate you."

"How would you know?" His palms flew up, a bull's-eye for her rage. "I'm sorry," she rushed. "I'm just not sure I can do all that again." They sat in silence. He checked his watch, then cranked the ignition. She did not have much time to ask it. "Robert? Do you think I ever resented him, back then? You know. Some kind of hidden . . . ?"

Robert drummed the wheel. "Truth? Nothing hidden about it."

She flared up, then hung her head. "But see? That's part . . . I don't really resent him now, like this. I . . . don't really mind, anymore. His being who . . ."

"Don't mind?" Karsh downshifted. "You mean you like him better this way?"

"No! Of course not. It's just . . . I like his new idea of me, better than his old one. Well, not of me; you know: of 'the real Karin.' I like who he thinks I was. He defends the old me now, against everyone. Two years ago, the real Karin was a constant source of disappointment. I was forever letting him down. A tramp, a sell-out, a money-grubber, a pretentious middle-class wannabe, too good for my roots. Now the real Karin is some kind of victim of history. The sister I never quite managed to be."

Karsh drove in silence. He looked as if he needed to flip open his pocket PC and start a spreadsheet ledger. Karin Schluter upgrade. *Costs. Benefits.*

"I can't believe I'm telling you all this. Am I totally disgusting?"

Eyes on the road, he smiled, taunting. "Not totally."

"I can't believe that I told anyone. That I even admitted it to myself, out loud."

They pulled up four blocks from his house, where he always got out and walked. He opened the driver's-side door. "You told me because you love me," he said.

She passed a hand over her face. "No," she said. "Not totally."

He called her at times, when his office was empty. They talked in stolen installments, whispering about nothing. Once they got past the essentials—what did he have for lunch? what was she wearing?—everything else devolved into current events. Was the Washington sniper a terrorist or just a self-made, rugged individual? Why weren't the UN weapons inspectors in Iraq turning up anything? Should the Enron and ImClone executives be given their own reality television network? As good as outright phone sex to both of them.

She held out for fairness, and he for freedom. Each thought they might convert the other: that had always been their fatal attraction. Both agreed that the government was out of control. Only, she wanted to put it to decent use at last, while he wanted to put it down once and for all. A chance encounter with *The Fountainhead* had turned a sunny, self-effacing high school swimming champion into a Libertarian, although Karsh found even that name way too restricting. "Every competent person on earth is a kind of god, babe.

432

Together, we're unstoppable. Human ingenuity might accomplish anything. Name a material constraint, and we're halfway to transcending it. Get out of our way and watch the miracles roll in."

"Oh my God, Robert. I can't believe you're saying that. Look around! We've trashed the place."

"What are you talking about? The ordinary rez teenager lives better than royalty used to. I'd rather live now than at any other moment. Except the future."

"That's because you're an animal. I mean: that's because you're not an animal."

"Since when did *you* get such convictions?"

Since she realized how little she could do to change Mark. She had to put her energies elsewhere, or die. This river might need her, more than her brother ever had.

They'd get onto thin ice within minutes, then stay out there, spinning arm in arm, a whole pairs freedance routine. Each needed to rout the other: pointless yet irresistible. She preferred screaming in horror at Karsh's outrages to murmuring in agreement at Riegel's pieties. Robert knew the truth that would forever elude Daniel, all the way to the grave: we love only what we can see ourselves in.

Invariably, Karsh would pump her. "How are things at the Save-a-Bird store? Tell me about this shiny new fund drive. You folks planning on buying up some wetlands?"

"First tell me about your consortium's new shopping center."

"Not a shopping center!"

"What the hell is it, then?"

"You know I can't tell you that."

"While I'm supposed to shout my little secrets from the rooftops?"

"So you do have a secret? You people *are* up to something?"

Heady, his begging. She had some power over him. The taste of it made up for no end of past humiliations. "There aren't that many contestable spots of value along the river left, you know." Something Daniel had said at breakfast, a couple of mornings earlier. She repeated it as if she'd just thought of it herself.

"We only want to stay out of your way," Karsh claimed. "We wouldn't want to develop in any areas that the Refuge sees as essential to preserve."

"Then you ought to sit down with the trustees and work this out, acre by acre."

He chuckled. "Have I told you that you are really adorable?"

"Not in this lifetime."

"Well, if you and I were in charge, that's what we'd be doing. Seriously. All this corporate cloak-and-dagger stuff gets on my nerves. Let's talk once this thing is public. You'll be a whole lot prouder of me then."

The word *proud* went right through her. Something in her did admire him. He could point to things and claim paternity. Mostly horrible things, granted, but solid and finished. At least Karsh had left a scar on the landscape. She could point to nothing except a series of service jobs, all lost, and a condo, now sold. She hadn't even procreated, something all her old high school acquaintances did more easily than Karin cleaned house. Even her own brother said she was nothing. At thirty-one, she had stumbled at last into work of consequence. She ached to tell him how worthwhile. "Proud?" she asked, ready to be lost. "How proud?"

"You'll see, if we get our Development Council approval.

If we don't, the whole thing is moot. Come to the public hearing and find out."

"I have to," she said, a sultry tease. "For my *job*."

She went to the hearing with Daniel. He drove, and she judged mercilessly the whole way. "If you get to the stop sign first, you're supposed to go through it first. Don't sit there and wave other people through."

"It's basic politeness," he said. "If everyone . . ."

"It's not politeness," she shouted. "It just screws people up."

He shrunk back. "Evidently." All the cruelty he could muster, and it mortified her. By the time they got to the hearing, she was contrite. She took his arm as they walked through the Municipal Building parking lot.

She dropped it in the foyer, seeing Karsh and his Platteland colleagues. She kept her eyes down on the peach-colored marble as Daniel led her to the hearing room. They hunted for seats in the filling chamber. Daniel scoped the room. She followed his eyes, over the mostly geriatric crowd. Two kids from the university community cable channel manned a video camera halfway down the right-hand aisle. Other than them, most of the room was drawing Social Security. Why did people wait until they had one foot in the grave before caring about their future?

"Not a bad house," she told Daniel.

"You think? How many, would you say?"

"I don't know. You know me and numbers. Fifty? Sixty?"

"So . . . roughly one-tenth of one percent of people directly impacted?"

They joined the Refuge contingent. Daniel came alive and Karin dragged behind him, a cowbird in the nest. The group fell into plan and counterplan, Karin serving up her prepared research. She watched Daniel at work, energized by the forces deployed against them. Long odds made him more attractive than he'd been in weeks.

Just behind the student cable crew, on a chair pulled deliberately off-camera, sat Barbara Gillespie. The sight of her rattled Karin: incompatible worlds. "That's Barbara," she told Daniel. "Mark's Barbara. What do you think?"

"Ah!" Daniel flinched.

"Doesn't she have something? Some kind of aura? It's okay; just the truth."

"She looks very . . . self-possessed." Afraid to look, confirming her.

The Platteland contingent chose that moment for their entrance, striding as a group up to the other developers in the front row, just in front of the council tables. She and Daniel both looked away. After a minute, she sneaked another look. If Karsh had acknowledged her, the moment had passed. He was waist deep in presentation materials, the art of consequence. Dizzy, Karin glanced back at Barbara, who lifted one palm in a covert wave. *Danger*, the flicker of greeting said. *Humans everywhere*.

The hearing came to order. The mayor addressed the council and established the procedures. A spokeswoman from the development group took the podium, darkened the room, and fired up an LCD projector. The screen behind the council tables flashed a title slide, the ubiquitous *Nature* template. The slide, in Mistral font, read: *New Migrants on Our Ancient Waterway*.

Karin twisted around to Daniel, incredulous. But he and the Refuge braced for the show, jaws clenched. The slides flipped through their paces, meandering like the river in question. The pitch aimed at the last target Karin had expected: what the Development Council called the "Hospitality Sector."

A bar graph showed the number of visitors to the spring migration over the last ten years. Numbers were an eternal mystery to her, but she could gauge lengths. The bars were doubling every three years. By the time she died, much of the country would be traipsing through every March.

The speaker metamorphosed into Joanne Woodward before Karin's eyes. "The concentrated staging of almost every migratory sandhill crane on earth has become one of the most breathtaking wildlife spectacles available on earth."

"Available?" she whispered. But deep in mental battle, Daniel couldn't hear. A panoramic photo followed—a stretch of the Platte not far from Mark's. An overlay faded in, an artist's rendition of a rustic settlement complete with old homesteads and sod houses. The speaker christened it the Central Platte Scenic Natural Outpost, and was deep into listing its environmental principles of construction—low-impact setting, passive solar, simulated split-rail fences made from millions of recycled milk cartons—when Karin saw: the consortium wanted to build a sprawling tourist village for crane peepers.

The battle unfolded in glacial pantomime, with developers and conservationists charging and counter-charging. Daniel waded into the fray, landing a couple of stinging blows. The birds were spectacular, he pointed out, precisely because the river had drained away beneath them, concentrating them in a few remaining havens. Drawing even one more cup of water out of an already breaking biome was unconscionable. Karin had been over the facts, facts she'd helped research. Every word Daniel spoke was gospel. But he preached with such messianic passion that she felt the room discount him as yet another finger-pointing Jeremiah.

Robert, smiling like an innocent bystander, rose to defend. The Outpost wasn't in a roosting area, but only nearby. The visitors would come, one way or another. Didn't it make sense to absorb them as ecologically as possible, in buildings that preserved an historical awareness, integrated into the natural landscape? Visitors would leave more aware of the need to conserve wildness. Wasn't the whole point of conservation to protect nature for our appreciation? Or did the Refuge believe that only a select few should enjoy the birds?

This last point was met by room-wide approval. Student council all over again. The Karshes of this world always crush the Riegels, in any open poll. The Karshes had humor, style, unlimited budgets, sophistication, subliminal seduction, neuromarketing . . . The Riegels had only guilt and facts.

Robert sat back in his seat. He glanced at Karin, a look that lingered like a stalker. *How was that?* For a weird, fleeting fugue moment, she felt privately responsible for the whole contest.

The Refuge countered: the developers were requesting ten times more water shares than their Natural Outpost would consume. The developers explained their own cautious projections and promised that the Outpost would sell all unused water shares back into the public kitty at cost.

Democracy flailed on, the most cumbersome form of deciding known to man. Breath-powered sailboat. Every village eccentric and homeless aluminum-can collector had his say. How could so blind a process ever reach a right decision? A developer in a pale-green suit and a Refugee in stringy denim, what little hair remaining to him pulled in a ponytail, sparred, their arms ceremonial swords, their voices rising and falling in spectral Kabuki wails. A gauzy filter settled over the gathering, as if Karin had stood up too quickly. The whole room shimmered, like a bean field in an August wind. These people had been gathering here since before development was even an issue. For as long as there were prairies open enough to blind and madden, men had met here to argue, just to prove to themselves that they weren't alone.

The public was as conflicted as her brother. Worse: as her. The debaters circled, doubling each other, doubling themselves, squaring off against phantom combatants . . . She sat in the middle of the fray, a double agent, selling herself to both sides. She took the combat inside herself, all possible positions banging around the loose democracy in her skull. How many brain parts had Weber's books described? A riot of free agents; five dozen specialties in the prefrontal bit itself. All those Latin-named life-forms: the olive, the lentil, the almond. Seahorse and shell, spiderweb, snail, and worm. Enough spare body parts to make another creature: breasts, buttocks, knees, teeth, tails. Too many parts for her brain to remember. Even a part named the *unnamed substance*. And they all had a mind of their own, each haggling to be heard above the others. Of course she was a frenzied mess; everyone was.

A wave moved through her, a thought on a scale she'd never felt. No one had a clue what our brains were after, or how they meant to get it. If we could detach for a moment, break free of all doubling, look upon water itself and not some brain-made mirror . . . For an instant, as the hearing turned into instinctive ritual, it hit her: the whole race suffered from Capgras. Those birds danced like our next of kin, looked like our next of kin, called and willed and parented and taught and navigated all just like our blood relations. Half their parts were still ours. Yet humans waved them off: *impostors*. At most, a strange spectacle to gaze at from a blind. Long after everyone in this room was dead, this camp meeting would rage on, debating the decline in life's quality, hammering out the urgent details of a vast new development. The river would dry up, go elsewhere. Three or four surviving decimated species would drag here annually, not knowing why they returned to this arid wasteland. And still we'd be trapped in delusion. But before Karin could fix the thought taking shape in her, it turned unrecognizable.

The hearing ended without a resolution. She clutched Daniel, confused. "Don't they have to come to some decision?"

He gauged her with pity. "No. They'll sit on the proposal for a few months, then slip out a ruling when no one is looking. Well, at least we know what we're up against now."

"I thought it was going to be a lot worse. Some kind of factory outlet megaplex. Thank God it's just this. You know. Something that doesn't spew poison. Something that's at least pro-bird."

She might as well have stabbed him. He'd been drifting to the exits at the back of the room. He stopped in the middle of the milling pack and grasped her upper arm. "Pro-bird? This? Have you lost your fucking mind?"

Heads turned. Robert Karsh, deep in numbers with two Development Council members, looked up from across the room. Daniel reddened. He leaned in to Karin and apologized in a hot whisper. "I'm sorry. Unforgivable. It's been a sick few hours."

She stepped forward to hush him. A hand petted her shoulder. She wheeled to see Barbara Gillespie. "You! What are you doing here?"

That single, arch Gillespie eyebrow. "Being a good citizen. I do live here!"

Caught, Karin made introductions. "I want you to meet my friend Daniel. Daniel, this is Barbara, the . . . woman I told you about."

Riegel turned toward her, a stiff, grinning Pinocchio. He couldn't even stammer. Karin caught sight of Karsh as he left the room, leering at Barbara.

"I liked what you said," Barbara told Daniel. "But tell me something. What do you suppose these people plan to do with this facility during the five-sixths of the year when there isn't a crane to be seen?"

Daniel stood gaping at the environmentalists' combined failure to raise the question during the hearing. "Maybe a conference facility?"

Barbara considered. "That's possible. Why not?" Then, so briskly it spun Karin, she added, "Well, great to see you, my dear! And good to meet you, Daniel." Daniel nodded, limp. "Fingers crossed on this one!" Barbara backed away with a crooked smile and a paralyzed prom-queen wave, then stumbled out of the room through the thinning crowd. A part of Karin cursed her exit.

Daniel was suffering. "I'm sorry. I wouldn't have lost my temper if things hadn't gone so . . . I don't know where that came from. You know I'm not . . ."

"Drop it. It doesn't matter." Nothing mattered but getting free, reaching the real water. "So I've lost my fucking mind. We both knew that already."

But Daniel couldn't drop it. On the car ride home, he came up with three more theories explaining his verbal assault. And he wanted her to ratify all of them. She did, in the interests of peace. This wasn't good enough for him. "Don't say you believe me if you don't."

"I agree with you, Daniel. Really."

441

It got them home, at least, and into bed. But the postmortem went on, in the dark. He spoke to the plaster cracks in the ceiling. "The whole hearing was a total disaster, wasn't it?" She couldn't tell if she was supposed to agree or object. "We didn't know what hit us. We went into the hedgehog defense right away. Fighting it like it was the usual commercial-strip land grab. We failed to discredit this thing. The Council probably left that room thinking what you did: that this Nature-rama is somehow beneficial."

She still thought so. Done right, it could even be a populist equivalent of the Refuge, managing the impact of tourists, whose numbers would just keep swelling, anyway.

"They're obviously up to something. This is just stage one. Look at the water they're asking for. And your friend is right. They can't possibly make money if the place is only filled two months out of the year."

She rubbed his back, big gentle circles. Weber's book said that made endorphins. It worked for a minute or two, before he flipped over.

"We blew it. We should have exposed them, and instead . . ."

"Shh. You did the best you could. I'm sorry; I don't mean that. I mean, you did the best that anyone could have, under the circumstances."

Daniel was up all night. Sometime after one, he started tossing so badly she came out of her own fitful sleep enough to rest a hand on his shoulder. "Don't worry about it," she mumbled, still half dreaming. "It was only a word."

Around three, she woke to an empty bed. She heard him out in the kitchen, pacing like a zoo creature. When he at last crawled back into bed, she pretended to be asleep. He lay still, an all-hearing ear, out in a field, tracking something big. *Bring your sphere of sound inside your sphere of sight.* Fully motionless, even his lungs. By five-thirty, neither could pretend any longer. "You okay?" she asked.

"Thoughtful," he whispered.

"I gathered."

They should have just risen and had breakfast, pioneer style, in the dark. But neither moved. At last, he said, "Your friend seems very sharp. She's right. These birder houses are just the tip of something."

She crushed the pillow. "I *knew* you were thinking about her. Is *that* why you—?"

He ignored her. "Did you already introduce me to her somewhere?"

"Look at me. Do I look like I've lost my fucking mind?"

He blinked at her, his head dipping. "I told you I was sorry. It was unforgivable. I don't know what else to say."

She had: she *had* lost it. Ground down by failed caretaking. "Forget it. It's nothing. I'm insane. What are you saying about Barbara?"

"I have the weirdest sense that I know her voice." He stood and crossed naked to the window. He pulled back the curtain and stared into the dark yard. "She sounds like someone I know."

Winter on Long Island: Why did they persist in staying? Surely not for the few breathtaking postcard moments: rime on the water mill, the duck pond frozen over, Conscience Bay whited out, with nothing but the invader mute swans and a single confused heron holding tight before the snow turned sooty and the real season of lifelessness settled in. Not for their health, certainly: pelted for days at a shot by tiny, sleet hypodermics. Not out of any economic necessity. Only some fathomless expiation, clinging to the former fresh, green breast of the new world.

"Dug in, in that vast obscurity beyond the city," he told Sylvie, over a ruthlessly administered breakfast regimen of muesli and soy milk. "Where the dark fields of the republic roll on under the night."

"Yes, dear. Whatever you say. How 'bout them Rangers?"

"I could be teaching in Arizona. Or guest-lecturing in California, just down the street from Jess. Better yet, we could both be retired. Living in some ramshackle farmhouse in Umbria."

She knew her job. "Or we could both be completely dead. Then we'd have everything handled and out of the way already." She rinsed their breakfast bowls, for the ten thousand nine hundredth time in their shared life. "Lecturing at the Medical Center in seventeen minutes."

He watched her walk into the bedroom to dress. What did she look like to strangers? Still slim for her age, hips and waist still echoing the past, her body still waving the advertisement of vigor, long after it had any right. She'd become almost unendurably dear to him in recent weeks, the result of his Nebraskan near-derailment.

The night he'd returned, he told her why he'd rushed home. Say everything: their marriage contract from the beginning, and to salvage anything real with this realest of women, he could not hide now. He'd always believed in Blake's "Poison Tree": bury a fantasy if you want to nurture it. Kill it by exposure to the open air.

The dank Long Island air did not kill his fantasy. Rather, describing his awful discovery to his wife the night of his homecoming killed something else. Lying in bed alongside

444

her, he laid it out. He felt some sick frisson of collapse, just gearing up to speak. "Sylvie? I need to tell you something."

"Uh-oh. Real first name. Big trouble." She grinned, turned on her side, head on an elbowed arm. "Let me guess. You've fallen in love."

He squeezed shut his eyes, and she sucked air. "I wouldn't say . . . ," he started. "It seems I may have gone back to Kearney, at least in part, for another look at a woman around whom, without any awareness, I've fabricated an entire hypothetical life."

She lay there, the grin still poised, as if he'd just said, *So this neuro-scientist walks into a bar* . . . "Syntax getting all fancy, Ger."

"Please. This is ruining me."

Her grin stiffened. She rolled onto her belly, regarding him as if he'd just confessed a love for donning women's underthings. Second by second, she grew more professional. Sylvie Weber, Wayfinder. Supportive; always, horribly supportive. "Did you sleep with her?"

"It isn't that. I don't think I even touched her."

"Ah. Then I'm really in trouble, aren't I?"

He deserved the slap, even wanted it. But he shrank and said nothing.

"I know you, Man. The Weber Nobility. I know that idealist's mind of yours."

"This is not something . . . I want. That's why I came back so fast."

She lashed out. "Fleeing?" Then soft again, ashamed. "You didn't know, when we talked about your making another trip out there?"

"I . . . still don't *know*. This is not . . ." He meant to say *lust*, but that seemed evasive. As shifty as something Famous Gerald

445

might write. More desperate scramble to make a continuous story out of chaos. "In retrospect, perhaps some part of me was looking forward to another look."

"You weren't aware of being attracted to her, on your first visit?"

He thought before answering. When he spoke, it was from up near their bedroom ceiling. "I'm not sure that what I felt yesterday is best called attraction."

She drew her hands in and shaded her eyes. "How serious is this?"

How serious could it be? Three days versus thirty years. A total cipher versus a woman he knew like breathing. "I don't want it to mean anything at all."

Underneath her cupped hands, Sylvie cried. Her crying, so rare over the years, had always puzzled him. Detached, almost abstract. Too civil to count as real weeping. Maybe calm grief was genuine maturity, the thing that mental health demanded. But only now did Weber realize how much her vague dispassion in distress had always bothered him. The crisis that their bedrock certainty always mocked—all their binding kindnesses and silly games, *Man* and *Woman*—the estrangement they'd never understood in others was now theirs. And she was crying, without sound. "Then why the hell are you telling me this?"

"Because I can't let it mean anything."

She pressed her temples. "You aren't just throwing this in my face? My punishment for . . . ?" For what? For finding herself, finding steady fulfillment in mid-life, while his abandoned him. Something animal flared in her face, ready to hurt back. And he felt how cruelly he loved her.

He tried to say. "I'm giving you . . . I'm trying . . ."

Then she was up and out of her crouch, game again, too

446

quickly. She sat up and exhaled, as if she'd just been exercising. She patted the bed with a palm. "Okay. So tell me what you like about this babe." Improvement project. Life's next step to self-mastery.

"How can I . . . like anything about her? I don't *know* anything about her."

"Unknown commodity. Mystery? Lock and key thing? How old is she?"

He wanted to stop talking for good. But talking was his penance. "Pushing fifty," he said, lying by a decade. A pointless lie—forty hardly qualified as a younger woman—after the harder truth. Barbara *was* younger. But youth was irrelevant.

"She remind you of someone?"

And it came to him. "Yes." That aura of having evaded life. One step outside and above it. The same angelic pretense as the author of those three books. And yet, that private frenzy, just beneath the surface of her flawless act. "Yes. I seem to be linked to her. She reminds me of me."

He might as well have slapped Sylvie. "I don't understand."

The two of us. He pressed his palms into his eye sockets until his lids splashed green and red. "There's something to her that connects. That I need to understand."

"You're saying it's not physical? That it's more . . . ?"

And then, what he'd tried to tell Karin Schluter, a thing he could not entirely bring himself to believe: "Everything's physical." Chemical, electrical. Synapses. Fire or not.

She fell back on the bed, next to him. "Come on," she grinned, grappling the sheets for safety. "What does this floozy have that I don't?"

He covered his bald spot with both hands. "Nothing. Except for being a totally unreadable story."

"I see." Between brave and bitter. Either one would kill him. "No real chance of competing with that, is there?"

At last he roused himself and encircled her, drew her shaking head into his chest. "Competition's over. No contest. You have . . . all my knowledge. All my history."

"But not all your mystery."

"I don't need mystery," he claimed. Mystery and love could not survive each other. "I just need to get a hold of myself."

"Gerald. Gerald. Is this the best midlife crisis you can manage?" Her spine collapsed and she burst into tears. She let him hold her. After some time, she surfaced, wiping her damp, red face. "Do I have to buy complicated underwear from the Internet, or something?"

They broke out in choked laughs, scalded with compassion.

The encounter shook them, worse than Weber imagined. Sylvie was still heartbreakingly herself, and he kicked himself for his idiocy every time she smiled gamely at him. After thirty years, she should have taken the news with wry fatigue, realized that he was hers by default, buried under the fossil record of experience. Should have patted him on the head and said, *Dream on, my little man; the world is still your proving ground.* Should have known he was going nowhere, except in symbols.

But a life of neuroscience had proved that symbols were real. No place else to live. They passed each other in the den and embraced. They touched each other's forearms in the laundry room. They sat alongside each other on their stools at meals as they had always done, both of them brightened by danger, trading casual theories about UN weapons inspectors or harbor seal sightings in the Sound. Sylvie's face was clear and bright, but far away, like a color-enhanced nebula beamed back from the Hubble. She refused to ask how he was, the only question that mattered to her. It bruised his chest to look at her. All that unbearable care would crush him.

A few years back, Giacomo Rizzolati's group in Parma had been testing motor-control neurons in a macaque's premotor cortex. Every time the monkey moved its arm, the neurons fired. One day, between measurements, the monkey's arm-muscle neurons began firing like crazy, even though the monkey was perfectly still. More testing produced the mind-boggling conclusion: the motor neurons fired when one of the lab experimenters moved *his* arm. Neurons used to move a limb fired away simply because the monkey saw *another* creature moving, and moved its own imaginary arm in symbol-space sympathy.

A part of the brain that did physical things was being cannibalized for making imaginary representations. Science had at last laid bare the neurological basis of empathy: brain maps, mapping other mapping brains. One human wit quickly labeled the find the *monkey-see monkey-do* neurons, and all others followed suit. Imaging and EEG soon revealed that humans, too, were crawling with mirror neurons. Images of moving muscles made symbolic muscles move, and muscles in symbol moved muscle tissue.

Researchers rushed to flesh out the staggering find. The mirror-neuron system extended beyond the surveillance and performance of movement. It grew tendrils, snaking into all sorts of higher cognitive processes. It played roles in speech and learning, facial decoding, threat analysis, the understanding of intention, the perception of and response to emotions, social intelligence, and theory of mind.

Weber watched his wife moving about the house, going about her days. But his own mirror neurons failed to fire. Mark Schluter had gradually dismantled his most basic sense of acquaintance, and nothing would ever seem familiar or linked again.

Jess came home for three days at Christmas. She brought the mate. Sheena. Shawna. Jess noticed nothing wrong. In fact, her parents' closeness—*the lovebirds in winter*—became the running joke between Jess and her cultural studies scholar. "I warned you: disgusting displays of hetero-bourgeois devotion like you witness only in the bowels of Red America." The three women soon condensed into a trio, running out to vineyard tastings on the North Fork or over to Fire Island for frigid beachcombing, leaving him to solitary "testosterone musings." When the girls left, Sylvie settled into a post-holiday empty-nest funk. Only long hours of social-service referral at Wayfinders seemed to help.

He fantasized about treating his own holiday descent with piracetam, a nootropic with no known toxicity or addictive properties. For years, he'd read amazing claims about the drug's ability to enhance cognition by stimulating the flow of signals between the hemispheres. Several researchers he knew took it with small dosages of choline, a synergistic combination said to produce greater increases in memory and creativity than either drug taken alone. But he was too cowardly to experiment with a mind already so altered.

The Country of Surprise showed up on no end-of-year lists except the ones for dubious achievement. Its rapid disappearance almost relieved Weber—no lasting evidence. Sylvie ministered to him with studied indifference, which only made him sad. They were sitting in front of a fire on Sunday evening after New Year's when he made some crack about Famous Gerald forgetting to come down the chimney this year. She laughed. "You know what? To hell with Famous Gerald. I could kiss Famous Gerald goodbye right now and never miss him. A postcard once a year from Club Med Maldives would do."

"That strikes me as unnecessarily cruel," he said.

"Cruel?" She smacked the brick mantel with real force. Her hands stabbed out at the pent-up weeks when she'd said nothing. "Jesus, Man. Can you tell me when this is going to be over?"

Her eyes burned, and he saw the size of her fear. Of course: having to sit by and watch his private deterioration, unsure where or whether it would ever end. "You're right. I'm sorry. I've not been . . ."

She took a series of deep breaths, willing herself down. She came to the couch where he sat and pressed her hand into his chest. "What are you doing to yourself? What's this about? Reputation? Public judgment is nothing but shared schizophrenia."

He shook his head, pressed two fingers into his neck. "No. Not reputation. You're right: reputation is . . . beside the point."

"What then, Gerald? What *is* the point?"

No one saw his own symptoms. No one knew who others knew him to be.

Sylvie twisted his shirt, wincing at his silence. "Listen to me. I would gladly trade every recognition you have ever managed to have my husband back and working for himself again."

But her husband, stripped of recognitions, was no one Sylvie would recognize. He was a breath from telling her what he now felt certain of: the basic immorality of his books. Two

451

words that would have finished them faster than any infidelity, imagined or real.

Lecturing at the Medical Center in seventeen minutes. All she wanted, finally, was for him to master his own life again, as he had for decades, ever since they'd met as Columbus undergrads. Her Man. The man who threw himself into every activity, not because of where it might lead, but for the innate strangeness of raw engagement. The man who had taught her that any life one came across was infinitely nuanced and irreproducible. Go teach. Go learn. How much more flavor do you want? How much bigger could you hope to make yourself?

As he toyed with his grapefruit, something struck the window of the breakfast nook with a sickening thump. He knew before he turned around. When he did turn, he saw the bird struggling away, broken: a large male cardinal who, for the last two weeks, had been attacking his reflection in the nook window, thinking himself an intruder on his own territory.

He stood in front of the quarter-bowl of students, fiddling with his wireless mic and fighting that sense of deceit that hit him before every lecture now. The students were the same as any year: upper-middle white kids from Ronkonkoma and Comack, trying on every identity from Prison Yard Tattoo to LaCoste alligator. But their manner had changed this semester, turned sardonic. They had passed around the public indictments of him by e-mail and instant messenger. They still wrote down every word he said, but more now to catch him out, to root out charlatanism, their pens angled in challenge. They wanted science, not stories. Weber could no longer tell the difference.

He tested the mic and focused the projector. He looked up

into the Greek theater filled with college seniors. Feral facial hair was making a comeback. And the piercings, of course, the heavy hardware: he would never adjust to that. The grandchildren of Levittown, with rods through their eyebrows and noses. As a plump tattooed girl in the fourth row made her last legal cell call before the bell—*Hey, I'm in my neuro lecture*—he watched her tongue stud glisten in the sheen of saliva, a surprising little freshwater pearl.

Looking into this bowl of world-weary twenty-one-year-olds, he couldn't help assigning them case histories. Since his last curtailed visit to see Mark Schluter, the world had broken out in Dickens and Dostoyevsky. The feverish anarchist, Bhloitov, stretched out sideways on a bank of three chairs in the back row. The high-strung stickler, Miss Nurfraddle, in the aisle seat two rows from the podium, fussed over her perfectly aligned texts. From the center of the auditorium, a slim man with slick black hair, Slavic or Greek, glared at Weber when the lecture failed to begin at the stroke of the hour. What was there in life worth such anger?

Every soul in this room would look upon itself in time with amused disgust. *I never dressed like that. Never scribbled notes so earnestly. I couldn't have thought such things. Who was that pathetic creature?* The self was a mob, a drifting, improvised posse. That was the subject of today's lecture, all the lectures he had given, since meeting his ruined Nebraska meatpacker. No self without self-delusion.

Two seats down from the slick-haired Greek sat the woman in this semester's class that he avoided looking at. They came and went every year, growing eternally younger. They were not all beautiful. But each played at being older than her age, eyebrows raised a nanometer too high. This one, eight rows up, right in his fovea, in a clinging peach turtleneck, smiled at him, her round face flushed, eager for anything he might say.

The sister, Karin, had said something, the first time they met for lunch. An accusation. *I can't believe it. You do it, too. I just thought that someone with your accomplishments . . .* He thought he hadn't known what she was talking about. But he had. And he did—did do it, too.

He cast a last look at his notes: organized ignorance. Next to the brain, all human knowledge was like a lemon drop next to the sun. "Today I want to tell you the stories of two very different people." His disembodied voice came out of speakers high up on the walls, full of amplified authority. The last fragments of nattering conversation fell away. The word *stories* drew a suppressed snicker. Bhloitov stared at Weber's first slide, a coronal cross section, with open skepticism. Miss Nurfraddle pleaded with a digital voice recorder. The turtlenecked woman gazed at Weber with pliant curiosity. The others betrayed no emotion beyond mild boredom.

"The first is the account of H.M., the most famous patient in the literature of neurology. One summer day half a century ago, just across the Sound from here, an ignorant and overzealous surgeon, trying to cure H.M.'s worsening epilepsy, inserted a narrow silver pipette into H.M.'s hippocampus—this gray-pink area right here—and sucked it out, along with most of his parahippocampal gyrus, amygdala, and entorhinal and perirhinal cortexes—here, here, and here. The young man, roughly your age, was awake through the entire procedure."

So, suddenly, was this entire room.

"Those of you with functioning hippocampi who attended last week's lecture will not be surprised to learn that, along with all the tissue evacuated through the pipette, came H.M.'s ability to form new memories . . ."

Weber heard his florid showmanship, and it made him ill. But he'd told the story so many times over the years, in lectures as well as in his own neurological novelistic books, that he could tell it no other way. He clicked through the slides, recounting the outcome by heart: H.M. returning halfway to the land of the living, his personality intact, but unable to tag new experience.

"You've read Dr. Cohen's account of H.M. Four days of tests, and each time the examiner left the room and came back, he had to introduce himself all over again. Decades had passed since his surgery. H.M. felt them as if they were days."

A doctor's first duty is to ask forgiveness. Where did that come from? A film he and Sylvie had seen together, in grad school. Film and line had shaken them as only couples in their early twenties can be shaken. Not long after that night, he committed to his future career. And around the same time, Sylvie must have committed to him for life. *A doctor's first duty is to ask forgiveness.* He should have spent a moment every evening, begging forgiveness from everyone he'd inadvertently harmed that day.

"H.M.'s memory of the past was intact, even impressive. When shown a picture of Muhammad Ali, he said, 'That's Joe Louis.' Asked again, two hours later, he responded identically, as if for the first time. He was trapped in a vault, frozen at the moment just before his operation. He couldn't even learn that he was locked in an eternal present. He had no idea what had happened to him. Or rather: the part of him that knew couldn't convey the fact to his conscious recollection. Several times an hour he would repeat, 'I'm having a little argument with myself.' He was plagued by a perpetual fear that he'd done something wrong and was being punished for it."

Weber looked up past a row of horror-thrilled faces and

455

saw her. He stopped speaking, disoriented. She had slipped into the hall, a secret auditor. Sylvie. Sylvie at twenty-one, in Ohio. She sat a quarter of the way up the slope, just inside the left-hand aisle, gazing at the slides, a spiral notebook on her crossed legs, her pen touching her top lip. On her folding desktop sat all the course's texts. Here they were, at term's end, and he'd never noticed her.

"Over the decades, H.M. became one of the most studied subjects in medical history. Through massive daily repetition, he managed to learn that he was under observation. His constant testing became a source of painful pride. A hundred times a day, he would repeat, 'At least I can help someone. At least I can help people understand.' But he still had to be constantly reminded where he was and told, after decades, that he wouldn't be going home to his mother and father that day."

He watched the waterfall of curly hair overwhelm the woman's earnest face. She looked very little like Sylvie, in fact. She just *was* her. The gentle, inward intensity. The game curiosity, ready for anything that study might throw her way. Weber snapped back to his restive audience, the seconds ticking. He elaborated the case's details without having to think them. His students scribbled away. This is what they wanted: just the facts, solid and repeatable.

"Now, alongside H.M., I would like you to consider the story of David, a thirty-eight-year-old Illinois insurance agent, married with two young children, in perfect health, who displayed no unusual neurological conditions aside from the persistent belief that the Chicago Cubs were just a season away from a pennant."

Polite laughter rippled through the auditorium, more diffident than last year. He looked up. Young Sylvie bit her lip, eyes on her notebook. Perhaps she pitied him.

"The first sign that something was amiss came when David, ordinarily an R.E.M. man, developed a passion for Pete Seeger."

No response from the audience. Nor had there been the year before. These names had passed into cultural amnesia. Seeger had never existed. R.E.M. was now not even a fever dream.

"His wife found this odd, but wasn't alarmed until a month later, when David started badmouthing his favorite author, J. D. Salinger, denouncing him as a public menace. He began to collect, although never to read, what he called 'real books,' which were limited to western and naval adventures. David's style of dress began to change—*regress*, his wife called it. He wore a pair of bib overalls to the office. His wife tried to get him to see a doctor, but he insisted that he was fine. He was so lucid his wife doubted her own distress. He spoke often about recovering the person he had once been. Over and over again, he told his wife, 'This is the way we all used to live.'

"He began to suffer from headaches and vomiting, lethargy and reduced alertness. One evening, David came home three hours later than usual. His wife was beside herself. He'd walked back from his office, twelve miles away, having sold the car to a colleague. His wife, frightened silly, shouted at him. He explained that cars were bad for the environment. He could bike to work, saving huge amounts of money that they could put away for the children's college. His wife suspected some stress-induced personality disorder, a thing that used to be called an acute identity crisis . . ."

Young Sylvie scribbled a note into the tablet balanced on her thigh. Something about the way the elbows flared, the dip of the neck, both tough and vulnerable. Sensations bombarded Weber, all their old keys, those million moments that had disappeared, one chord after the other: studying together in the library until closing; Tuesday-night European art films at the Cineclub; long debates about Sartre and Buber; more or less continuous sex. Blindfolding her and running various swatches of cloth over her bare belly, to test her claim that she could feel colors. Sylvie always guessed right.

Traces, still intact. Everything he'd been was still on file, archived somewhere. But he'd misplaced the sensations of recall until this living ghost sat down in front of him in the scooped amphitheater, scribbling all the wrong notes into her own accreting record.

"David's wife insisted that he call the person he sold the car to and buy it back the next day. He did. But a few weeks later, he failed to come home at all. Crossing the parking lot at his office, he grew so entranced by the changes of sky above him that he spent the night there, sitting on the asphalt, staring up into space. When the police found him the next morning, he was disoriented. His wife brought him to the hospital, where he was admitted to psychiatry, who quickly passed him to neurology. Without modern scanning technology, who knows how he might have been treated? But with a scan: look here at the caudal orbitofrontal cortex, where you will see a large, circumscribed neoplasm—a meningioma—growing for years, pressing into his frontal lobes and gradually incorporating itself into his personality . . ."

It struck Weber as he advanced the slide: his Nebraska waver was not the first blot on an otherwise perfect record. He'd never betrayed Sylvie, technically. But every so many years, Faithful Gerald nosed up to the brink. The year he turned fifty, he'd met a sculptress who lived in the Bay Area. They corresponded for a long time, maybe a year and a half, before she forced him to admit that she was nothing but his pure invention. Ten years ago, there had been a Japanese graduate research assistant, eager and expectant, just past thirty. A near-miss thing, by any measurement. She'd gone away when he turned cold. She, who could barely lift her eyes to his when speaking, left a note for him after her departure: *In Japan, researchers at least have a day of mourning for all the test animals they've sacrificed* . . . Each of these theoretical love affairs had been an exception: half a dozen exceptions, all told. He seemed to be a hit-and-run repeat offender. He told Sylvie each time, but after the fact, always downplaying the near disaster. Nothing went into the permanent record.

As the next slide clicked, he saw the truth: he wanted Barbara Gillespie. But why? The act she performed did not add up. Something in her life had gone as wrong as his. She already lived in the void he was entering. A huge thing, in hiding. She knew something he needed. Something in her could recall him.

But there was a more parsimonious explanation. How would these students diagnose it, given the facts? Banal midlife crisis? Pure biology, classic self-deception, or something more striking? Some deficit that would show up on a scan, some tumor, relentlessly pressing on his frontal lobes, imperceptibly recasting him . . .

He cleared his throat; the sound ruptured through the speakers above him. "David couldn't see how badly he was altered, and not just because the change had been so gradual. Remember my lecture on anosagnosia, two weeks ago. The job of consciousness is to make sure that all of the distributed modules of the brain seem integrated. That we always seem familiar to ourselves. David didn't want to be fixed. He thought he'd found his way back to something true, something that everyone else had abandoned."

459

Young Sylvie raised her head and studied him. He filled with self-loathing. He could forgive the man with the list of pathetic, halfway infidelities. But the man whose unblemished self-image had so completely erased that list: What could such a person deserve beyond a slow and agonizing public exposure? He bent his shoulders and hung on to the podium. He felt anemic, and countered with more structural analysis, more functional anatomy. He lost himself in lobes and lesions. A soft beep from his watch declared time to wrap things up.

"So we have the stories of two very different deficits, two very different men, one who could not become his next consecutive self and another who plunged into it without control. One who was locked out of new memories and the other who manufactured them too easily. We think we access our own states; everything in neurology tells us we do not. We think of ourselves as a unified, sovereign nation. Neurology suggests that we are a blind head of state, barricaded in the presidential suite, listening only to handpicked advisors as the country reels through ad hoc mobilizations . . ."

He looked out into the blunted audience. No good. Bhloitov was furious. The clinging turtleneck woman's eyes wandered. Miss Nurfraddle seemed ready to call the attorney general on her BlackBerry and arrest Weber for violations of the Patriot Act. He could not bear to look at young Sylvie. He saw himself reflected in their faces, a neurological freak show, a case.

How could he tell them? Energy fell on an ancient cell; the cell registered. Some prodding set off a chemical cascade that incised the cell and changed its structure, forming a cast of the signals that fell on it. Eons later, two cells clasped, signaling each other, squaring the number of states they might inscribe. The link between them altered. The cells fired easier with each fire, their changing connections remembering a trace of the outside. A few dozen such cells slung together in a lowly slug: already an infinitely reshaping machine, halfway to *knowing*. Matter that mapped other matter, a plastic record of light and sound, place and motion, change and resistance. Some billions of years and hundreds of billions of neurons later, and these webbed cells wired up a grammar—a notion of nouns and verbs and even prepositions. Those recording synapses, bent back onto themselves—brain piggy-backing and reading itself as it read the world—exploded into hopes and dreams, memories more elaborate than the experience that chiseled them, theories of other minds, invented places as real and detailed as anything material, themselves matter, microscopic electro-etched worlds within the world, a shape for every shape *out there*, with infinite shapes left over: all dimensions springing from this thing the universe floats in. But never hot or cold, solid or soft, left or right, high or low, but only the image, the store. Only the play of likeness cut by chemical cascades, always undoing the state that did the storing. Semaphores at night, cobbling up even the cliff they signaled from. As he once wrote: *Unsponsored, impossible, near-omnipotent, and infinitely fragile . . .*

No hope of showing them that. He could at best reveal the countless ways the signals got lost. Shattered at any joint: space without dimension, effect before cause, words cut loose from their reference. Show how anyone might vanish into spatial neglect, might swap up with down and before with after. Sight without knowing, recall without reason, tea parties of personalities fighting it out for control over the bewildered body, yet always continuous, whole to themselves. As consistent and complete as these bright and skeptical students now felt.

"One last case, in our few seconds left. Here is a lateral

cross section, showing damage to the anterior cingulate gyrus. Remember that this area takes input from many higher sensory regions and connects to areas controlling higher-level motor functions. Crick writes about a woman with just such damage, who lost her ability to act upon or even form intentions. Akinetic mutism: all desire to talk, think, act, or choose was gone. With forgivably human excitement, Crick declared that we had located the seat of the will."

The bell rang, saving and damning him. Students began evacuating, even as he scrambled to conclude. "So much for an introductory look at the enormously complex question of mental integration. We know a little about the parts. We know considerably less about how they cohere into a whole. For our last session, we'll look at the strongest candidates for an integrated model of consciousness. If you don't have the article on the binding problem, get one from your discussion leader before you leave."

With a bang of desks and slam of books, the students rose to go. What would he say the following week, to sum up a discipline drifting away from him? Long after his science delivered a comprehensive theory of self, no one would be a single step closer to knowing what it meant to be another. Neurology would never grasp from without a thing that existed only deep in the impenetrable inside.

Students emptied the hall, smoldering up the aisles in clumps of mutiny. A feeling came over Weber, a desire to supplement genuine neuroscience with half-baked literature, fiction that at least acknowledged its own blindness. He would make them read Freud, the prince of storytellers: *Hysterics suffer mainly from reminiscences.* He would give them Proust and Carroll. He would assign Borges's "Funes," the man paralyzed by perfect memory, destroyed by the fact that a dog seen in profile at three-fifteen had the same name as that dog seen from the front a minute later. *The present, almost intolerable, it was so rich and bright.* He would tell them the story of Mark Schluter. Describe what meeting the boy-man had done to him. Make some motion that their mirror neurons would be forced to mimic. Lose them in the maze of empathy.

The usual stragglers clustered around the podium. He tried to listen to each question, to give each observation his full attention. Four students, suffering end-of-semester anxieties. Just behind the first wave, four more waited. He scanned the hall, not knowing what he looked for. Then he saw her, hovering, halfway up the left-hand aisle. Young Sylvie, looking back at him. She stood, debating with herself. She had a message for him, for the boy he'd once been, but she couldn't wait. She had some future place to get to.

He tried to rush the questioners, each with a reassuring smile. The crowd began to thin, and he looked up, surprised, into the face of Bhloitov. This close, Weber saw that the anarchist's black hair was dyed. He had on a studded leather arm bracelet and, peeking below his left sleeve, a bright red and cyan Virgin of Guadalupe. His downy mustache was split by a faint scar—imperfectly repaired cleft lip. Weber glanced up into the hall. Young Sylvie, hesitant, started to drift away. He looked back at the anarchist, trying to master himself. "Sir. How can I help you?"

Bhloitov flinched, blinked, and backed away a little. "Your account of that, that meningioma. David?" His voice apologized. Weber nodded him on. "I'm wondering . . . I think that maybe my father . . ."

Weber looked up, desperate reflex. Sylvie had on her backpack and was marching upstairs to the auditorium exit. He watched her all the way up, as Bhloitov murmured and effaced himself. She never turned to look back. *Where are you going?* Weber called in symbol space. *Come back. It's me. Still here.*

It was time to retire. He could no longer trust himself in the classroom, let alone the lab. He could find some volunteer work, adult literacy or science tutoring. In the twenty years he had left, he could learn another foreign language or write a neurological novel. He had stories enough, anyway. He would never have to publish it.

He stayed on campus until early evening, submerged in invented labor, the steady swapping of letters of recommendation that comprised academic existence. It felt like atonement, scutwork. For a dose of phenylethylamine, he prescribed himself a dozen ounces of chocolate. Recently, it had helped lift the cloak of winter evenings.

The strange thing was, he felt almost no *desire* for Barbara Gillespie. Perhaps he found her attractive, in the abstract. But even now, his imagined transactions never involved anything more than harmless clasping. She was like—what? Neither family nor friend; certainly not mere lover. Some relation that hadn't yet been invented. He didn't want to possess her. He wanted only to investigate, with the usual battery of questionnaires, what had collapsed her, and why it felt so acquitting to be with her. He wanted to break her down, to draw her out. Get her history and vita. She'd said almost nothing in the few minutes they'd actually spent in each other's presence. Yet she knew something about Mark that he was blundering to find.

He saw her in green dungarees and white cotton shirt, climbing a wooden stepladder. The ladder was up against a white Cape Cod house, near the ocean. She was reaching up to the eaves. What did he know about her? Nothing at all. Nothing but what his prefrontal cortex might spin out of thin air and flotsam from the hippocampus. He saw her as a little girl with a black veil pulled down over her face, lighting a fifty-cent candle and placing it on an altar in an incense-choked church. What did he know about anyone? He saw her and Mark Schluter, in gray jumpsuits and yellow hardhats, inspecting a bouquet of gauges on a gleaming stainless-steel cylinder as tall as a house. He saw her hanging out of the passenger window of a trolling blue coupe driven by Karin Schluter, holding out a stuffed teddy bear to the winds. He saw himself, standing shoulder to shoulder with Barbara in a crowded courtroom somewhere like Kabul, trying to get legal custody of the Schluter brother and sister, but unable to make their request understood in any useful language.

It struck him that he'd invented Nebraska. The whole story: some foray into a mixed, experimental genre, a morality play masquerading as journalism. He had no reliable memory of anything that had happened there. He could accurately reconstruct exactly none of Barbara Gillespie's traits, let alone her features. Yet he could not stop summoning up recovered memories of her, all of them so detailed that he might have sworn they were documented data.

What did he know about his own wife's life? Who she was when she wasn't his wife. He drove home, through the snow-covered commons. The two colonial churches never failed to settle him. He made the long bend onto Strong's Neck, the brown-green harbor at low tide. He turned up Bob's Lane, that passage impossible for visitors to find unless they'd already been on it. The winter rains still swamped the front yard. A family of green-winged teal had, all fall, made a home alongside the temporary lake. But now that lake was frozen over, and the ducks had flown.

Sylvie had beaten him home. She tried to return from

Wayfinders early these days, ever since he'd dropped his bombshell. He hadn't asked her to. But neither did he have the courage to tell her it wasn't necessary. She was feeding something into the oven, egg-plant casserole. Twenty years ago, he'd told her that he would gladly eat it every night, and now she remembered that buried zeal. Her anxious smile when she looked up went right through him. "Good day?"

"Golden." Something they used to say.

"How did the lecture go?"

"If you're asking *me*, I believe there's a distinct possibility that I was brilliant." He took her in his arms too quickly, while she struggled to remove her oven mitt. "Have I told you that I'm absolutely mad about you?"

She giggled doubtfully and looked behind him. Who did she imagine might be coming? Who could he possibly be bringing home? "You have indeed. Yesterday, I believe."

The TV show airs. But it's strange. They've done something digital to Mark—run him through some kind of high-tech video filter. People who don't know him would never suspect. But his friends, what few friends Mark Schluter has left, will think he's some kind of stunt man stand-in.

The show gets the story mostly right, at least. They talk about the crash, the vehicle that cut in front of him, the one that ran off the road behind. And there's a great moment when the handwritten note comes up and fills the screen, and they even have subtitles, in case you can't read or something. *I am no one.* I am no one. Man, that could be anybody, these days. But there's a cash award, like five hundred bucks. With the economy down the toilet again and the whole state

466

on the dole, somebody's bound to come forward and collect.

He'd like to sit around and wait for the phone to ring with anonymous tips, but there's too much to do. The Kopy Karin comes by, all cranked because she heard about the show but missed it. *When did you do this? Why didn't you tell me?* It's a good performance; he pretty much believes she had no idea.

He's got a plan to test her, something he's been thinking about forever. He asks if she'd like to take a drive, out to Brome Road, the old abandoned farm his father once tried to run. The place he lived in from eight until almost fourteen. The place his sister always talked about like it was some kind of paradise lost. Her replacement seems to have been drilled on the routine. She's bouncing like a girl as soon as the invitation is out of his mouth. You'd think he was asking her to the prom or something.

They drive out together, in her little Jap car. It's weirdly warm, for two weeks before Christmas. He's in his light-blue jacket, October gear. Greenhouse ecological catastrophe, probably. Well, enjoy the short-term bennies. She's all stoked, like she hasn't seen the place forever. Funny thing is, she probably hasn't. They head up the long farmhouse driveway, and it's like somebody dropped a neutron bomb on the front porch. All the windows, black and curtainless. The yard, a sea of tall grass and weeds, like some kind of prairie restoration project. There's a black and orange NO TRESPASSING sign nailed to the porch, which is a joke. Nobody's lived in the place for years. Truth be told, the Schluter family kind of ran the place into the ground, and no subsequent resident has been able to bring it back. Abandoned since '99, but he's never come prowling until now.

The barn is leaning hard to the right, like it'll ditch if it gets hit by a little microwave radiation. But before they can pull up to it, Karin Two slams on the brakes. She's all: Where's the tree? The sycamore is gone. The one that you and Dad planted for my twelfth birthday. Well, it shakes him up, at first. She knows what they planted, when. But then, there's the stump sitting right there. And anybody in town could've told her. Those fool Schluter men, planting a big water-sucking tree, when they don't even have water table enough to keep their beans from getting singed.

He says: I heard they were taking it down, a while ago.

She turns on him, her eyes all hurt. Why didn't you tell me?

Tell you? I didn't even know you then.

She pulls over on the gravel and gets out. He follows her. She walks up to the stump and just stands there, in her baggy jeans, her hands in the pockets of her little brown leather jacket just like the one Karin One used to wear. She's not a bad human being. She's just gotten mixed up in bad business.

When did it go? she asks. Before or after Mom?

The question knocks him back a little. And not just her asking it. He's not sure.

She looks at him, going: I know. It's like she's still around, isn't it? Like she's going to come out that side door with a plateful of pigs-in-blankets and threaten us with a belt whipping if we don't say grace and eat.

Well, the words really creep him. But this is exactly why he's brought her out here. To probe the limits. What else do you remember about her? he asks. And she starts unloading all kinds of stuff. Stuff only his sister knows. Things from when they were young, when Joan Schluter still looked like the original Betty Crocker. She goes: You remember how proud she was, about that award her family won when she was little?

468

He can't help answering: Fitter Family Contest, Nebraska State Fair, 1951.

Run by some kind of national eugenics society, she says. Judging them on their teeth and hair, like they did the cows and pigs. And they got a gold medal!

Bronze, he corrects her.

Whatever. The point is, she spent the rest of her life pissed off at Cappy for polluting the gene pool and producing us.

She keeps reciting these amazing things, things that Mark himself has forgotten. Things from late childhood, before Joan was on a first-name basis with Mr. Omnipotent. Things from the bad years, when you couldn't say boo to her without her falling to her knees and belching minor spirits. You remember that book, Mark? The one she used to carry around that always made you hysterical? *Jesus Fills Your Hole?* And the day she finally figured out what you were laughing at?

The two of them stand there by the sycamore stump, giggling like teen stoners. A wind blows up, and it gets cold, fast. He wants to go up to the house, but her words now are like a snowmelt river. Things from the end, when his mother became a premature saint. You wouldn't have recognized her, she says, like Mark wasn't even there. You wouldn't have believed her, so agreeable and sweet. We were talking one afternoon, after she went on the drip, and out of the blue, she started telling me that the afterlife was probably a delusion. And yet, she'd sit there, more Christian than Christ, sucking down the cheddar cheese hospital soup that I was spooning into her mouth, and saying, *Oh, that's good! That's good!*

She's jumbled the facts a bit, but Mark's not going to argue. He's freezing out here, all of a sudden. He takes her arm and pulls her toward the house. She won't quit talking.

You know, I'm still getting her mail? I guess they don't

469

forward beyond the grave. Mostly charities and credit-card apps. Catalogs from the store where she used to order those frumpy cardigans.

They reach the front door. He tries it: locked, even though there's nothing inside but mouse shit and paint chips. He looks at her, not volunteering anything.

You don't remember? she says. And she goes right to the loose slat just to the left of the front picture window, jiggles it a little bit, rusty. Finally pops it open, and there's the spare key. The one they didn't even mention to the family who moved in after them. It's distinctly possible she's reading his brain waves. Wireless scans, some kind of new digital thing. He should have asked Shrinky, when he had the chance. She unlocks the door and they step into something right out of a horror film. The old living room is stripped, with a layer of gray dust and cobweb over everything. The sitting room has had the stuffing beat out of it. There's signs of infestation, mammals a lot larger than mice. Karin Two pulls her cheeks back with her palms.

Don't do that. It makes you look like one of those bank robbers with the nylon-stocking faces.

But she doesn't hear him. She just wanders from room to room in a coma, pointing at invisible things. The puke sofa, the TV with the rabbit ears, the parakeet cage. She knows everything, and she brings it all back with such hypnotic pain that she's either the greatest actress who ever lived, or there's truly something of his sister's brain transplanted in her. He's got to figure it out, before it drives him certifiable. She's walking around stunned, like one of those bomb victims on cable news. Here's where we ate. Here was the shoe pile. She's really upset. Meanwhile, he's wondering whether it's the original house or some scale model. She turns on him. You remember when Dad caught us playing doctor and locked us in the pantry?

That wasn't what we . . . But why start with her? She wasn't there.

Prisoners. For days, it seemed. And you started this whole Great Escape thing. Using a piece of uncooked spaghetti to push the skeleton key through the keyhole onto a square of wax paper that you pulled in under the crack of the door. What were you, six? Where did you learn that kind of stuff?

The movies, of course. Where else does anybody learn anything?

She stands at the kitchen window, looking out on the back forty. What do you remember about . . . your father?

And that's kind of funny, actually. Because that's what he and Karin One used to call the man. *Your* father. Blaming him on each other. Well, he tells her. The man was no farmer. That's for damn sure. Always a minimum of three weeks late or early. Beat the system. Defy conventional knowledge. Year he harvested anything at all was a golden era. We were lucky he got out, and into all those can't-miss bankruptcies.

She just shrugs, sticks her fists into the dry and dusty sink. You're right, she says; we were lucky. The Farm Crisis would have gotten him anyway. It got everybody else.

Ah, but rainmaking, Mark says. Nobody ever lost a buck rainmaking.

She snorts bitterly. Who knows why? It's only a job for her. But she's great at it. She shakes her head. I mean, can you remember his voice? The way he walked? Who *was* that guy? I mean, I'm now about as old as he was, when he locked us in the cellar. And I just can't . . . I remember he had a big scar on the lower inside of his right shin from some kind of accident he had when he was young.

Railroad tie, he tells her. It doesn't matter if she knows: they can't hurt him with ancient history. Dropped a railroad tie on himself, working for the Union Pacific.

That can't be right, Mark. How can you drop a railroad tie on your shin?

You don't know my father.

She starts to laugh, but then it freaks her. You're right, she says. She starts to cry. You're right. And he's got to hug her a little to get her to quit. She drags him out back, to the utility room, a little overhang above the tool rack. She says: When we moved out, to the Farview house? Mom and I, we found these videos . . .

What, you mean those self-employment things? *Cream Your Competitors*? *The Big Score*?

She shakes her head, shuddering. Horrible, she says. I can't even. I can't.

Oh, Mark says. The fisting stuff. Yeah, I knew about those.

And when Mom, in shock, brings them to him and starts screaming, he just stands there and says he's never seen them in his life. He doesn't know how they got there. Maybe the previous owners left them. Videos! Videos weren't even invented when we moved into this house. He just took them out back and poured gasoline on them. Bonfire.

Tell me about it, Mark says.

And Mom just took it all in. Points toward martyrdom. Believed he was well on the way to repentance.

Well, Mark says. Maybe not.

No. Okay. Maybe not.

They go upstairs, where the bedrooms were. He's getting used to it, to the devastation. Little scraps of crap line the hall: an old telephone bill, an empty cigarette lighter. Piece of a tarp and a couple of beer bottles. Thin carpet of plaster dust coating the floors. But a person could live here. No big deal. You get used to anything.

She stands in his old room, pointing with her finger, going,

472

Bed, dresser, shelves, toy chest. Her eyes check with him, seeing if she gets everything right. She does. They couldn't possibly have trained her in all this. There has to be some kind of direct synapse transfer. Which means that something of his sister is actually downloaded inside this woman. Something essential. Some part of her brain, her soul. A little bit of Karin, here. She points out the niche in the windowsill, the tiny house where Mr. Thurman lived, year after year. Mark's only reliable childhood friend. He winces, but nods.

That challenge look of hers, again. Mark? Can I ask you one thing?

I didn't go anywhere near those damn *Seventeen* magazines.

She laughs a little, like she's not sure if he's trying to be funny. But she presses on. Did Cappy . . . did he ever touch you?

What do you mean? Used to almost break my legs. I still have the bruises.

That's not . . . Never mind. Forget about it. Come do me. My bedroom.

Hang on, he says. *Do* you? You're not trying to seduce me, are you?

She slugs him in the shoulder. He follows her obediently, snickering. Always worth a laugh. They stand in the rotting gray room, playing more quiz. Bed. Wrong. Bed? Wrong! Dresser? Not quite.

Well, how the hell should I know? She was always changing it around.

Karin Two puts a hand on his wrist, stops his arms. She tries to look him in the eye. What was she like? Tell me what . . . she was like.

Who? You mean my sister? You're really interested in my sister?

473

Gone so long that she can't ever be coming back. And something must be wrong with Mark Schluter, something from the accident that not even the hospital knows about, because he stands there bawling like a goddamned child.

They stood alone together in the abandoned Brome house, reconstructing the past they no longer shared. There came a moment, amid the trashed rooms and shaky memories, when it struck Karin that they'd have that day, at least, that one sunlit afternoon of confusion in common, if nothing else. And when her brother started to cry and she moved to console him, he let her. A thing they'd never had, before.

They went outside, into the warm December. They walked the length of their father's old field, not knowing who farmed it now. In the crush of stubble under their feet, she felt those summer mornings, waking before daylight, going out to walk beans while the dew was still on them, hacking weeds with a hoe so sharp she once almost sliced off her big toe, right through the leather of her work boot.

Mark tagged alongside, head down. She felt him struggling and was afraid to say a word, afraid to be anyone, least of all Karin Schluter. Oddest of all, she was okay with holding back. She'd gotten used to the doubling, to being *this woman*. It let her start from scratch with him, even while the other Karin improved so drastically in his memory. A chance to rewrite the record: in fact, two chances at once.

They rolled over the stubbly black rise. She felt all over again, as she had as a child, the vicious treelessness of this place. Not a scrap of cover in sight. Do anything at all, and God would spy you out. Off on a slight crest in the middle distance, cars and trucks whipped back and forth on the interstate like scythes. She turned to look at the house. This time next year, it would be gone, collapsed or bulldozed, never to have existed. The open-book roof, the slanting cellar door propped up against the brick foundation, the square-shouldered white stump of a box, jutting up from the bare horizon. Protection from nothing.

"You remember when you and Dad tried to clean out that backed-up cistern?"

He pounded his head, as if the disaster had just happened. "Don't remind me about shit you can't know."

She didn't know how hard to push. "Remember when your sister ran away?"

He folded his hands over the crown of his head, to keep it from flying off. He started walking again, studying the rill in the soil that his feet followed. "She was a godsend, all those years growing up. She kept me out of a heap of death. Oh, she had her little quirks. Don't we all? But she just wanted to be loved."

"Don't we all?" Karin echoed.

"You two really are a lot alike. She used to sleep around a bit, too." She swung toward him, violent. He gaped back, mocking. "Hey, chill. I'm just bashing you. Man, you are even easier to get a rise out of than she was." She slapped him in the chest with the back of her hand. He just laughed that mirthless laugh. "But, hey, I have to ask you—that guy you're currently doing?"

She dropped her eyes and studied the plow cut. *Which one?*

"Why are you with him, anyway? Is he entirely sexually normal?"

She couldn't help snickering. "What's normal, Mark?"

"Normal? Man, woman, front door. Nothing that's going to get you arrested."

475

"He's . . . pretty normal."

Mark stopped and knelt down on the ground, over a dried carcass. He prodded it with his toe. "Pocket gopher," he declared. "Poor thing."

She pulled him away. "What do you have against Daniel, anyway? You were such deep friends, all those years. What happened?"

"What 'happened'?" Mark traced the quotes in the air. "I'll tell you what 'happened.' He tried to queer me. Out of the blue. Sexual harassment."

"Mark! Come on. I don't believe you. When did this happen?"

He spun around and raised his hands. "How am I supposed to know? Like, November 20, 1988, five o'clock in the afternoon?"

"Oh, Markie. What were you? Fourteen, fifteen?"

"You should have heard him. 'Something we could have, together. Just touch each other, there. Just you and me . . .' One sick puppy."

She lifted her hands and knelt to the dried mud. "You've got to be kidding. This is the big fight that neither of you would talk about, all these years?" He squatted next to her and combed the dirt with his fingers, avoiding her eye. "All growing boys do that kind of thing with each other, at least once."

"Huh. Not this growing boy."

"You threw away a friendship on that?" But she'd exiled best girlfriends for less.

Mark toyed with a root mass, his mouth twisted. "He went his bent way; I went mine."

She touched his shoulder. He didn't pull away. "Why didn't you tell me? I mean, why never mention it to your sister?"

"Why? You're both college-educated women. If you want to experiment with diddling a bisexual, what's it to me?" He squinted in resentment across the swollen, rolling field. "What do you think he'd say, if he saw the two of us out here, like this?"

She lay back against a furrow ridge, wanting to laugh. Horrible. Worst of all, this was their most honest, intimate conversation since they'd lived in this house.

"It wasn't just, you know. Petting my pecker. The guy really loved me or something."

His eyes caught the scudding clouds, and a sick feeling started in her. The scrape of explanations. *The guy really . . .* But it couldn't be true. Not in the way Mark meant it.

"I also think he may have had sex with animals."

"Jesus, Mark! Will you quit? Who told you that? Your friends? Biggest barnyard abusers there are."

He hung his hands around his neck, miserable with thought. "You know, you were right about Rupp and Cain. You were right and I was wrong. I didn't listen to you. I should listen to you more."

"I know," she told the dirt. "Same here." She listened now, Daniel changing as she heard. She pushed off the harvested earth with her scuffed palms and stood. "Come on. Let's head back, before we get arrested for trespassing."

"What do the two of you do together, anyway? For pleasure." He twisted his head to the side and screened it with his hands. She blinked at him, feeling ill. "Don't give me any messy details. I mean, you go to the opera? Hang out at the public library until they throw you out?"

What did they do together? Pleasure was not something they'd perfected. "We walk, sometimes. We work together. For the Refuge."

"Doing what?"

477

"Well, at the moment, trying to save the cranes from their admirers." She sketched out the details of her working day, surprising herself while she talked. She had been with the Refuge for a little more than a month, and she had all the fervor of a convert. She couldn't imagine herself now without the work. Sitting for hours at a table strewn with buttes of government pamphlets, trying to put them into language that would make an indifferent person come awake and see all the things that drank from the river. The work had populated some emptiness in her, taken up the slack Capgras had left. She'd been on hold for so long. She wanted to tell Mark her data. Humans consuming twenty percent more energy than the world can produce. Extinction at a thousand times the normal background rate. Instead, she settled for telling him about the fight for water rights, the land war unfolding outside Farview.

"Wait a minute. You're saying this Nature Outpost is bad for the birds?"

"That's what the numbers say. That's what Daniel thinks."

The name plunged Mark back into a funk. "So-called Daniel. He's the missing link, you know. Everything keeps pointing back to him."

Missing link. Coupler with animals. Champion of all creatures that could not compete with consciousness. They were almost back to the house. Mark had his hands in his back pockets, kicking a field stone down the furrow. He stopped short and bore around on her. "Where's this nature village supposed to go?"

She got her bearings and pointed southeast. "They want to put it in over there somewhere. Down on the river."

He snapped his head back, and his body jerked to attention. "Fuck. Look where you're pointing! What in God's name is going on?" A cry of pain came out of him. "You don't see it? Right where I had my accident." He fell back against the inclined cellar door. "Figure this out for me." For a second he seemed on the verge of a seizure. "Save the birds? Save the river? What about saving me? Where the hell is Shrinky? There's so much shit I have to ask him. The man bailed out of here so fast, you'd think *I* had tried to queer *him*."

His desperate chestnut eyes widened at her, and she had to say something. "It wasn't your fault, Mark. The man has problems of his own."

He leaned forward on the incline, ready to lunge. "What do you mean 'of his own'?"

She stepped backward. Checked the distance to the car. He was capable of anything. Something basic was in him, clawing to get out.

But he leaned back again and held up his palms. "Okay, bag it. Just listen. I asked you out here for a reason. Sorry about tricking you, but this is wartime. There's something I need to settle, once and for all. I'm not sure who you answer to, or whose side you're really on. But I do know you helped me out while I was down. I'm still not sure why, but I'll never forget it." He craned his neck and looked up at the eggshell sky. "Well, let's put it this way. So long as I remember anything, I'll remember that. I don't know how you know what you know, but it's clear you've got my sister's entire database, give or take. They downloaded her, imprinted you, or something. You know more crap about me than I know about myself. You're the only one who can answer me this. I have no choice but to trust you. So don't screw me on this, all right?" He stood and walked ten feet from the house, angle enough to point up at his old bedroom window. "You remember that guy?"

She managed to get her skull to bob.

"Something in your memory banks. Who he was, how he grew up, what became of him? What he became?"

She willed her head to nod again, but it would not. Mark didn't notice. He was staring up at his childhood window, waiting for the evidence to come crawling down on a long pillowcase-and-sheet rope.

He turned and took her by the shoulders like she was God's own messenger. "You have a strong memory of Mark Schluter, this time last year? Say, ten or twelve days before the accident? I need to know whether you think, given your sense of that guy they primed you with . . . whether you think he could have done it . . . on purpose."

Her brain made a muffled buzz. "What do you mean, Markie?"

"Don't call me that. You know what I'm asking. Was I trying to off myself?"

Her gut folded. She shook her head so hard her hair whipped her face.

He studied her for betrayal. "You're sure? You're absolutely sure? I didn't say anything beforehand? Wasn't depressed? Because here's what I'm thinking. Something was in the road in front of me. I'm remembering something in the road. White. Maybe that oncoming car, cutting me off. Then again, maybe it was, you know, my finder, that note-writer, changing the course of my life. Because maybe I was out there, you know: trying to roll it. Finish up the story. And somebody stopped me."

Objections appeared before she could think them. He'd shown no sign of depression. He had his job, his friends, and his new home. If he'd wanted to do something like that, she would have known . . . But she'd suspected the possibility herself. As early as the hospital, and as late as that morning.

"You're sure?" Mark said. "Nothing in the sisterly memories they fed you to suggest anything suicidal? All right. I have to believe you wouldn't lie to me about this. Let's go. Take me home." They walked back to the car. He got in the passenger side. She started the engine. "Just a minute," he said. He got out again, ran up to the rotting porch, and tore off the NO TRESPASSING sign. He ran back to the car and piled in, jerking his head toward the road.

She drove him home, a distance that expanded as they rode. She wavered again over the olanzapine decision. Mark liked her now, at least a little. Better, he liked what she'd been. She knew what a cure might return him to. Maybe Mark was better off like this. Maybe well-being meant more than official sanity. He—the old Mark—might have said as much himself. But succumbing to reason, she told him that they needed to go see Dr. Hayes again. "They've found something, Mark. Something they can give you that might help clear things up. Make you feel a little more . . . together."

"*Together* would be very helpful, right around now." But he wasn't really listening. He was peering off to his right, toward the river, the future Nature Outpost, his past accident. "Save the birds, you say?" He nodded stoically at the utter insanity of the race. "Save the birds and kill the people."

He flipped on the car radio. It was tuned to the frenzied conservative talk station that she listened to, for the pleasure of confirming her own worst fears. The president had ordered half a million servicemen vaccinated against smallpox. Now the home audience was calling in with advice about protecting yourself from the coming outbreak.

"Biological warfare," he chanted. He turned, his face plastered with absolute incomprehension. "I wish I'd been born sixty years earlier."

The words blindsided her. "What do you mean, Mark? Why?"

"Because if I'd been born sixty years earlier, I'd be dead by now."

She turned into River Run and crawled up in front of his house. "I'll make an appointment with Dr. Hayes, okay, Mark? Mark? Are you with me?"

He shook off his fog, hesitating, his right foot dangling out of the car door. "Whatever. Just do me one small favor. If my real sister ever does show up again?" He drummed his forehead with his first two fingers. "You think you could still save a little feeling for me?"

"The self presents itself as whole, willful, embodied, continuous, and aware." Or so Weber wrote once, in *The Three-Pound Infinity*. But even back then, before he knew anything, he knew how each of those prerequisites could fail.

Whole: Sperry and Gazzaniga's work with commissurotomy patients split that fiction down the middle. Epileptics who'd had their corpus callosum cut as a last-ditch method to treat their disease ended up inhabiting two separate brain hemispheres with no connection. Two severed minds in the same skull, intuitive right and patterning left, each hemisphere using its own percepts, ideas, and associations. Weber had watched the personalities of a subject's two half brains tested independently. The left claimed to believe in God; the right reported itself an atheist.

Willful: Libet laid that one to rest in 1983, even for the baseline brain. He asked subjects to watch a microsecond clock and note when they decided to lift a finger. Meanwhile, electrodes watched for a readiness potential, indicating muscle-initiating activity. The signal began a full third of a second before any decision to move the finger. The *we* that does the willing is not the *we* that we think we are. Our will was one of those classic comedy bit parts: the errand boy who thinks he's the CEO.

Embodied: consider autoscopy and out-of-body experience. Neuro-scientists in Geneva concluded that the events resulted from paroxysmal cerebral dysfunctions of the temporoparietal junction. A little electrical current to the proper spot in the right parietal cortex, and anyone could be made to float up to the ceiling and gaze back down on their abandoned body.

Continuous: that thread was ready to snap at the lightest pull. Derealization and depersonalization. Anxiety attacks and religious conversions. Misidentification—the whole continuum of Capgras-like phenomena, phenomena that Weber had witnessed his whole life without quite noticing. Eternal love retracted. Entire life philosophies abandoned in disgust. The concert pianist he'd interviewed who woke one morning after prolonged illness, no discernible pathology, still able to play, but unable to feel the music, or care about it . . .

Aware: here was his wife, asleep on the pillow next to him. This thought formed in him as he lay awake at dawn, listening to a mockingbird roll through its round of pilfered calls: of selves as the self describes itself, no one had one. Lying, denying, repressing, confabulating: these weren't pathologies. They were the signature of awareness, trying to stay intact. What was truth, compared to survival? Floating or broken or split or a third of a second behind, something still insisted: *Me*. Always the water changed, but the river stood still.

The self was a painting, traced on that liquid surface.

Some thought sent an action potential down an axon. A little glutamate jumped the gap, found a receptor on the target dendrite, and triggered an action potential in the second cell. But then came the *real* fire: the action potential in the receiver cell kicked out a magnesium block from another kind of receptor, calcium flowed in, and all chemical hell broke loose. Genes activated, producing new proteins, which flowed back to the synapse and remodeled it. And that made a new memory, the canyon down which thought flowed. Spirit from matter. Every burst of light, every sound, every coincidence, every random path through space changed the brain, altering synapses, even adding them, while others weakened or fell away from lack of activity. The brain was a set of changes for mirroring change. Use or lose. Use *and* lose. You chose, and the choice unmade you.

As with synapse, so went science. When long-term potentiation was discovered in the 1970s, perhaps a dozen articles appeared in half a decade. In the half-decade after that, almost one hundred. *Fire together, wire together.* In the early nineties, a thousand papers or more. Now more than twice that, and redoubling every five years. More articles than any researcher could hope to integrate. Science was loose, with the exposed synapse. The synapse was *already* science. Smallest imaginable machine for comparing and conjoining. Classical and operant conditioning, written in chemicals, able to learn the entire world, and float a *you* on top of it.

The mockingbird peeled off its bursts: fives, sevens, threes. Each burst mutated like the spins of a cycling car alarm. *Listen to the mockingbird. Listen to the mockingbird.* He'd sung that song with this same wife once, when they still sang. *A mockingbird is singing over her grave.*

This was the bird's hymn to plasticity, every glance of

rising sunlight off the rippled bay changing the shape of its brain. The brain that retrieved a memory was not the brain that had formed it. Even retrieving a memory mangled what was formerly there. Every thought, damaging and redamming. Even this mockingbird accompaniment, *this* one, changing Weber beyond recall.

The tangle thickened as he traced it: groups of wired neurons that modeled and memorized the changing light were themselves modeled, in other neuron groups. Whole chunks of circuitry reserved for sandboxing other circuits, the mind's eye cannibalizing the brain's eye, social intelligence stealing the circuitry of spatial orientation. What-if mimicking what-is; simulations simulating simulations. When his little Jess was not yet a month old, he could get her to stick out her tongue just by sticking out his tongue at her. No counting the miracles involved. She had to locate his tongue relative to his body, then somehow map his parts onto the feel of hers, find and order a tongue she could not even see, could not even know about. And she did all this at the mere sight of him, this infant who had been taught nothing. Where was the end of his self, the start of hers?

The self bled out, the work of mirror neurons, empathy circuits, selected for and preserved through many species for their obscure survival value. Baby Jess's supramarginal gyrus conjured up a fiction, an imaginary model of what her body would be like if it did what his was doing. Weber had seen people with damage to the area—ideomotor apraxia. Asked to hang a picture, they could. But asked to *pretend* to hang a picture, they slapped helplessly at the wall, no clasped hammer, no mimed nail.

When his girl, at four, looked through her picture books, her face would match the expressions painted there. A smile made her smile, inducing girlish happiness. A grimace gave her real pain. Weber, too, to witness: emotions moved the muscles, but merely moving the muscles made emotions. Those with damage to the insula could no longer do the imitative, integrated mapping of body-states necessary to read or adopt someone else's muscles. Then the community of self collapsed into one.

The bird mocked on from a branch up close to their bedroom window, bits of riff stolen from other species and stuffed into the growing melody. On the backs of his eyelids, using the same brain regions as real sight, Weber watched a little boy he did not recognize—it might have been Mark, or someone much like him—out in a frosty field watching birds taller than he. And seeing them arch and leap and curl their necks and beat their wings, the boy beat his.

To be awake and know: already awful. To be awake, know, and *remember*: unbearable. Against the triple curse, Weber could make out only one consolation. Some part of us could model some other modeler. And out of that simple loop came all love and culture, the ridiculous overflow of gifts, each one a frantic proof that *I* was not it . . . We had no home, no whole to come back to. The self spread thin on everything it looked at, changed by every ray of the changing light. But if nothing inside was ever fully us, at least some part of us was loose, in the run of others, trading in all else. Someone else's circuits circled through ours.

This was the dawn thought that formed in Weber's brain, his shifting synapses, all the insight that he ought ever to have needed. But it scattered at the arrival of new bursts, as Sylvie moaned and twisted awake, opened her eyes and smiled at him. "Did you?" she asked, fuzzily. Old code between them: *Sleep well?*

And, yes, he nodded his head, smiling back at her. All his life long, he had slept well.

Christmas came and went, and still no angel. Dozens of people called in after the broadcast, all of them with theories but none with useful information. When even *Crime Solvers* let him down, Mark hinted broadly to Karin that he now had a pretty good idea of what had really happened that night. Any ambitious business project for transforming the region would first require transforming the region's inhabitants. When she tried to get him to elaborate, he told her to use her head and figure it out herself.

Early in the evening of New Year's Day, Specialist Thomas Rupp, 167th Cavalry Regiment—the Prairie Soldiers— appeared on the doorstep of the Homestar. He was coatless in his three-color desert camouflage fatigues, having just returned to town after unit exercises. Mark looked out his dirty front window into the dark yard, thinking that paramilitary forces had arrived with the purpose of commandeering his house in conjunction with this new Nature Outpost development.

Specialist Rupp stood on Mark's doorstep, rapping triplets on the front door's simulated wood. The soundtrack from a public television antiques show seeped through the windows. "Gus. Wassup. Open up, Gus. You can't stay mad at us forever."

Mark stood on the other side of the door, brandishing a thirty-six-inch Ridgid pipe wrench. Realizing who it was, he called through the flimsy panel. "Go away. You're not welcome around these parts."

"Schluter, man. Open the door. It's getting ugly out here."

It was twenty degrees, with a visibility of ten feet. The wind whipped a fine-grained dry snow into a white sandstorm. Rupp was shivering, which only convinced Mark of a trap. Nothing ever froze Rupp.

"Stuff to clear up, buddy. Let me in and we'll talk."

By now, the dog was hysterical, snarling like a wolf and leaping three feet into the air, ready to plunge through the window and attack anything to protect its master. Mark couldn't hear himself think. "What stuff? Like the fact that you lied to me? Like the fact that you ran me off the road?"

"Let me in and we'll talk. Clear this crap up, once and for all."

Mark hit the front door with the wrench, hoping to scare off the intruder. The dog began to howl. Rupp screamed profanity, to shock Mark into stopping. The next-door neighbor, a retired data processor who served homeless people lunches at Kearney Catholic, threw open her window and threatened to firebomb them. Both men continued to yell at each other, Mark demanding explanations and Rupp demanding to be let in out of the cold. "Open the fuck up, Gus. I've got no time for this. I've been called up. Active duty. I'm going to Fort Riley the day after tomorrow, man. Then on to Saudi, soon as they pull my chain."

Mark stopped yelling and hushed the dog long enough to ask, "Saudi? What for?"

"The Crusades. Armageddon. George versus Saddam."

"You're so full of it. I knew you were full of it. What good is that going to do anyone?"

"Round two," Rupp said. "The real thing this time. Going after the bastards who brought down the Towers."

"They're dead," Mark said, more to the dog than to Rupp. "Died on impact in a flaming fireball."

"Speaking of death." Rupp stamped the ground and yelped with cold. "Dressed for a hundred and ten degrees, and it's Scott of the Antarctic out here, Gus. Are you going to let me in or do you want to kill me?"

Trick question. Mark said nothing.

"All right, man. I give up. You win. Talk to Duane about it. Or wait for me to get back. This showdown thing is going to be over fast. We're giving these goons a week at the outside. One-shot Rupp'll be back here slaughtering again, by Flag Day. Take you fishing for your birthday." Silence issued from the house. Rupp backed away, into the icy sandstorm. "Talk to Duane. He'll explain what happened. What do you want from Iraq, Gus? One of those little white skull caps? Some prayer beads? Miniature oil well? What can I bring you back? Just name it."

Rupp had vanished in his truck by the time Mark shouted, "What do I want? I want my friend back."

On Groundhog Day, a Sunday, Daniel Riegel called his boyhood friend. They'd had no contact for fifteen years, aside from deniable sightings at a distance and a supermarket run-in where they'd passed each other without a word. Daniel's hands shook as he dialed the number. He hung up once, then forced himself to start again.

Karin had told him all about that afternoon at the abandoned Schluter house, a house Daniel remembered as well as he remembered his own. She confronted him with Mark's disclosure, something broken in her. *You loved my brother, didn't you?* Of course he had. *I mean, you really* loved *him.* She had stood there rethinking everything, appraising Daniel as she would an alien.

He had no idea what he'd say if Mark Schluter picked up.

It no longer mattered what he said, so long as he said something. A voice at the other end shouted, "Yeah?" and Daniel said, "Mark? It's Danny." His voice slid like some pubescent's between soprano and bass. Mark said nothing, so Daniel filled, insanely matter-of-fact. "Your old friend. How are things going? What have you been up to? It's been a while."

At last Mark spoke. "You've been talking to her, haven't you? Of course you have. She's your wife. Lover. Whatever." Mark's voice wavered between bafflement and awe. Why should people discuss him behind his back? What difference in the world did he make to them? His words were swimming in mysteries, and ready to give up paddling and drown.

Daniel started in, faltering, about old misunderstandings, crossed wires, experiments gone wrong. Not what you think; should have said; should never have suggested. A long silence came from Mark. Fifteen years' worth. Then: "Look. I don't care if you're gay. It's a big trend these days. I don't even care that you like animals better than people. I would, too, if I weren't a human. Just watch your back. I know this is a college town, but get out into the surrounding areas and you'd be surprised."

"You're right about that," Daniel said. "But wrong about me."

"Fine. Whatever. It doesn't matter. Forget it. Burial. Little Danny; young Markie. You remember those guys?"

It took Daniel some moments to decide. "I think so," he answered.

"I sure as hell don't. No idea who those guys ever were. Two different worlds. Who cares?"

"You don't understand. I never meant for you to think . . ."

"Hey. Have sex with whatever you want. You only live once, for the most part."

And then, on nothing at all, they were back in the trivial now.

"But can I just ask you? Why *her*? Don't get me wrong. She's all right. At least, she hasn't hurt me yet. But . . . this doesn't have anything to do with me, does it?"

Daniel tried to say. Say why *her*. Because with her he didn't have to be anyone but who he'd always been. Because being with her made him feel familiar. Like coming home.

Mark crashed the explanation. "I thought so. You're using her for my sister! Sleeping with her because she reminds you of Karin. Old times. Man! Memory. It'll screw you up royal every time, huh?"

"It will," Daniel agreed. "It does."

"Well, okay. There you have it. Whatever gets you through the night. Just remember: this love thing comes and goes. You wake up one day, and wonder. I guess I don't have to tell you that. So what have you been doing with your life?" He chuckled like a belt-driven tool sharpener. "In the last fifteen years. In two hundred words or less."

Daniel recited the short résumé, marveling at how little had changed since childhood, and how little he'd really accomplished in so long a time. He could barely hear himself talk, over the noise of the past.

Mark wanted to hear about the Refuge. "Some kind of Dedham Glen for birds?"

"Yes, I suppose. Something like that."

"Well, can't hurt me with that. Karin Two says you're fighting this sandhill Disney World thing? Camp Crane Peeper?"

"Fighting, and losing. What did she tell you about it?"

"I've seen their real estate operatives out this way, sniffing around. Seems to me they have their eye on the Homestar. Going to requisition my house."

491

"Are you sure? How can you tell they're from . . . ?"

"Team of guys with one of those surveyor thingies? Guys out there, dynamiting fish?"

The idea coursed through Daniel, with a surge of sick thrill. The developers were running an environmental impact survey. The real capital outlay had started. "Listen," he said. "Can we meet? Can I swing by your place?"

"Whoa. Hang on, big fella. I told you a long time ago. I'm not like that."

"Neither am I," Daniel said.

"Hey. It's fine. It's a free country." Mark fell silent, but calm. "But tell me something. You know all that avian crap. Can you train one of those birds to spy on someone?"

Daniel weighed his words. "Birds will surprise you. Blue jays can lie. Ravens punish social cheaters. Crows fashion hooks out of straight wire and use them to lift cups out of holes. Not even chimps can do that."

"So following people would be no problem."

"Well, I'm not sure how you'd get them to report back to you."

"Dude. That's the easy part. Technology. Little wireless cameras and such."

"I don't know," Daniel said. "Not my strong suit. I've never been good at telling the possible from the impossible. That's why I ended up in preservation."

"The point is, they're not just—you know—bird brains?"

Daniel held still at the sound, the ten-year-old Mark, the love of his boyhood who'd always deferred to Daniel's bookish authority. They'd fallen back by instinct into the forgotten cadence. "It turns out that their brains are much more powerful than people ever thought. Much more cortex, just shaped differently from ours, so we couldn't see it. They can think, no question about it. See patterns. People have trained pigeons to tell Seurats from Monets."

"Gore-tex? Tell who from what?"

"The details aren't important. Why do you ask?"

"I had this idea, a few months back. I thought . . . you might be following me around. You and your birds. But that's crazy, isn't it?"

"Well," Daniel said. "I've heard crazier."

"Now I realize that if anyone's following me, it's the other side. These Nature Outpost people. And it's not really me they're after. Nobody gives a flying fart whether I live or die. They probably just want my real estate."

"I'd love to talk to you about this," Daniel said. Using a delusion to chase a delusion.

"Ah, man. Maybe I'm just scrambled. You have no idea what I've been through. A fuck of an accident, one year ago this month. It all started then."

"I know," Daniel told him.

"You saw the show?"

"Show? No. I saw you."

"Saw me? When was this? Don't jerk me around, Danny. I'm warning you."

Daniel explained: in the hospital. Early on. While Mark was still coming back.

"You came to see me? Why?"

"I was worried about you." All true.

"You saw me? And I didn't see you?"

"You were still in pretty bad shape. You saw me, but . . . I scared you. You thought I was . . . I don't know what you thought."

Mark took off, fragments of words scattering like pheasants from a gunshot. He knew who he'd thought Daniel was.

Someone else had come to see him in the hospital. Someone who left a note. Someone who'd been out there that night, on North Line. "You didn't see the TV show? *Television*, man. You *had* to see it."

"I'm sorry. I don't have a set."

"Jesus. I forgot. You live in the freaking animal kingdom. Never mind; it doesn't matter. If I could just get a look at what you look like now. Maybe it would come back to me. Who I thought you were. What this finder looks like."

"I'd love that. I'd . . . like that. Maybe if I came by sometime . . . ?"

"Now," Mark said. "You know where I live? What am I saying? The Crane Refuge probably wants to liberate my house, too."

Daniel knocked, and the prefab door opened on someone he might have passed on the street without identifying. Mark's hair was flowing and tangled, as he'd never worn it. He'd put on twenty pounds in the last few months, and the weight surprised Mark's small frame as much as it surprised Daniel. Strangest of all was his face, manned by some pilot baffled by the controls. Foreign thoughts now moved those muscles. The face stared out at Daniel on the icy February threshold. "Nature Boy," Mark said, a little skeptical. Trying to put his finger on a vast difference. At last, he figured it. "You got old."

He dragged Daniel inside and stood him in the center of the living room, inspecting. Brine spilled out of the corners of his eyes. Yet his face remained studious, like a shopper examining the ingredients on a strange brand's label. Daniel stood still, shaking. After a long time, Mark shook his head. "Nothing. I'm not getting anything."

Daniel's face curdled, until he realized. Mark didn't mean fifteen years ago; he meant ten months.

"It never comes back, does it?" Mark said. "Shit's never what it was. Probably wasn't what it was, even back when it *was* it." He laughed, cotton wrapped in barbed wire. "Doesn't matter. You were Nature Boy once, and that's good enough for me. Pleasure to meet you, Nature Man." He threw his arms around Daniel, like tying a horse's reins to a hitching post. The hug was over before Daniel could return it. "Sorry about the historical bullcrap, dude. A lot of wasted time and anxiety, and now I can't even remember what the big deal was. So I didn't want your hand working my front privates. That doesn't mean I had to beat you to a bloody pulp."

"No," Daniel said. "It was me. All me."

"Man, getting old is nothing but accumulating stupid shit we have to apologize for. What are we going to be like when we're seventy?" Daniel tried to reply, but Mark didn't really want an answer. He reached into the pocket of his corduroy overshirt and pulled out a piece of laminated paper full of chicken scratch. "Here's the deal. Does this mean anything to you?"

"Your . . . Karin Two told me about it."

Mark grabbed his wrist. "She doesn't know you're here, does she?"

Daniel shook his head.

"Maybe she's okay. You never know. So you're saying you're not my guardian angel? No idea who? Well, whatever happened back in the hospital, you aren't reminding me of anybody, now. Except a big, crusty, old version of Nature Boy. So what can I get you to drink? Some kind of wetlands whole-grain tea?"

"You have any beer?"

"Whoa. Little Danny R. comes of age."

They sat at the round vinyl dinette table, jittery with reunion. They did not know, yet, how to be anything but boys together. Daniel asked Mark to describe the surveyors. They sounded only slightly more solid than his guardian angel. Mark asked about the development, which, in Daniel's recounting, sounded like paranoid invention.

"I don't get it. You're saying this fight is all about *water*?"

"Nothing else is more worth fighting over."

The idea dazed Mark. "Water wars?"

"Water wars here, oil wars overseas."

"Oil? This new one? Man, what about revenge? Security? Religious showdown, and such?"

"Beliefs chase resources."

They talked and drank, Riegel exceeding his last two years' consumption. He was prepared to pass into unconsciousness, if need be, to stay with Mark.

Mark was flush with ideas. "You want to know how to steal this land right out from underneath these jokers? Danny, Danny. Let me show you something." With the closest thing to energy he'd shown, Mark stood and clomped into his bedroom. Daniel heard him moving things around, sounding like a backhoe in a trash dump. He returned triumphant, waving a book above his head. He held it up to Daniel: *Flat Water*. "Local history textbook from my first year in college. My last year in college, I should say." Mark flipped through the pages in a state almost like excitement. "Hold your horses. It's here, somewhere. Mr. Andy Jackson, if I'm not mistaken. Weird about the ancient past: how it keeps coming up. Here. Indian Removal Act, 1830. The Intercourse Act, 1834. Don't get excited; it's not as interesting as it sounds. All the lands west of the Mississippi that aren't already Missouri, Louisiana, or Arkansas. May I quote? 'Forever secure and guarantee.' 'Heirs or successors.' 'In perpetuity.' That means forever. We're talking a long time, buster. The *fucking law of the land*. And they say *I'm* delusional? This whole country's delusional! There's not a white person out here who's a legal property owner, including me. That's how you should handle this. Get your lawyers, get a few natives down from the rez on your side: you should be able to clear out the whole state. Get it back how it was."

"I'll . . . look into that."

"Give it back to the migratories. The birds can't mess it up any worse than we have."

Daniel smiled, despite himself. "You're right, there. To really finish things off, you need human-sized brains."

The word woke Mark up again. "Danny. Danny Boy. Speaking of brains and cranes? How come all their heads are red? You don't find that weird? It's like they've all been operated on. You should have seen me, man, with my bloody skull in a sling. Oh, wait: you *did* see me. *I'm* the one who didn't see me." He held that same battered head in his hands, split all over again. Riegel said nothing; he moved less than his little finger. The life-long expert tracker, reverting to form. Join yourself to where you are, and the creature will come to you, of its own accord.

Mark gathered himself for a leap of faith. "That woman you're doing? She wants me to take these pills. Dope me up, I guess. Well, not exactly dope. If only it were that interesting. No, this stuff's called Olestra. Ovaltine. Something like that. It's supposed to give me 'clarity.' Make me feel more like myself. I don't know who I've been feeling like, lately, but, man, it would be good to be off this ride." He looked up at Daniel, a flicker of false hope begging to be confirmed. "Thing is, this could be Stage Three of whatever they're trying to do to me. First, run me off the road. Second, take something out of my head while

I'm on the operating table. Third, feed me some chemical 'cure' that changes me forever. Danny, you're from the early days. The earliest. Okay, so we fucked up the friendship. Killed the past and wrecked fifteen years. But you never lied to me. I could always trust you—well, except for your impulses, which you couldn't really help. I need advice on this. It's tearing me apart. What would you do, man? Take this shit? See what happens? What would you do, if you were you?"

Daniel stared into his beer, drunk as a junior high schooler. Some other dizziness kicked in: What *would* he do, in Mark's place? He'd sat in Gerald Weber's hotel room with Karin, taking his predictable high moral stand. He might have changed tunes, had his own brother, just out of half a year of cocaine detox in Austin, suddenly refused to recognize *him*. Daniel Riegel: absurd with certainty. *He* might take this olanzapine, if the world turned strange on him, if he woke up, one day, sick of the river, blind to the birds, out of love with everything that had once been life. "It's possible," he mumbled. "You might want . . ."

A knock on the door saved him. Playful, familiar rhythm: *Shave and a haircut, two bits.* Daniel jumped, vaguely criminal.

"Now what?" Mark groaned, then shouted, "Come on in. It's always open. Rob me blind. Who gives a damn?"

A shivering figure pushed inside: the woman that Karin had introduced to Daniel at the public hearing. Daniel sprang up, knocking the table and spilling his beer down his pants. A facial tic proclaimed his innocence. Mark, too, was on his feet, rushing the woman. He grappled her in a bear hug, which she, to Daniel's amazement, returned.

"Barbie Doll! Where have you been? I was starting to panic about you."

"Mr. Schluter! I was just here four days ago."

"Oh, yeah. I guess. But that's a long time ago. And only a short visit."

"Stop whining. I could move in, and you'd still complain I was never around."

Mark shot a look at Daniel, licking the canary feathers off his lips. "Well, we could give it a try. Purely for health-research purposes."

She blew past him into the kitchen, struggling to remove her coat while holding out her hand to Daniel. "Hello, again."

"Ho, ho-hold on a minute. You're telling me the two of you know each other?"

She drew her chin back and frowned. "That's the usual sense of 'Hello, again.'"

"What in God's name is going on? Everybody knows everybody. When worlds collide!"

"Now just cool your little heart. There's an explanation for everything in this life, don't you know." She described the public hearing, how impressed she'd been with Daniel's performance. The explanation quieted Mark. Daniel alone was unconvinced.

"I should go," he said, flustered. "I didn't realize you were expecting company."

"Barbie? Barbie's not company."

"Don't run," Barbara said. "It's just a social call."

But something in Daniel was already running. On his way out the door, he told Mark, "Ask *her*. She's a health professional."

"Ask her what?" Mark said.

"Yeah," Barbara echoed. "Ask me what?"

"Olanzapine."

Mark grimaced. "She seems to think the decision is all mine." As Daniel slipped through the door, Mark called after him, "Hey! Don't be a stranger!"

Not until he got back to his apartment and checked his answering machine did Daniel Riegel, lifelong tracker, remember where he'd first heard Barbara Gillespie.

In the middle of February, the birds came back. Sylvie and Gerald Weber saw a late-night news feature on the cranes, lying in bed together in their snow-covered Setauket house on Chickadee Way. As the camera panned over the sandy banks of the Platte, husband and wife looked on in embarrassment. "That's your place?" Sylvie asked. She couldn't very well say nothing.

Weber grunted. His brain was wrestling with some blocked memory, some problem in identification that had been bothering him for eight months. But his thoughts pushed the near-solution farther away, the more he chased it. His wife misunderstood his preoccupation. She raised her knuckles to his upper arm and stroked. *It's all right. We two are past simplicity. Everyone's messy. We can be, too.*

The woman in front of the camera, a clumsily urbane New Yorker who seemed unnerved by so much emptiness, related the story as if it were news. "It's been called one of the most spectacular shows of nature anywhere, and it stars half a million sandhill cranes. They start to arrive on Valentine's Day, and most will be gone by St. Patrick's . . ."

"Smart birds," Sylvie said. "And great holiday observers." Her husband nodded, peering at the screen. "Everybody's Irish, huh?" Her husband said nothing. She clenched her jaw and rubbed his shoulder a little harder.

By Presidents' Day, saluting everyone goodbye, Mark began the medication. Dr. Hayes doubled the dosage of the

Australian case: a still-conservative 10 mg every night.

"So we should see some improvement in two weeks?" Karin suggested, as if any doctor's agreement would be legally binding.

Dr. Hayes told her, in Latin, that they'd see what they would see. "Remember what we talked about. There may be some chance of social withdrawal."

You can't withdraw, she told the doctor, in American, if you're not there to start with.

Four days later, at two in the morning, the phone tore Daniel and Karin out of a deep sleep. Naked, Daniel stumbled to the phone. He mumbled incoherently into the receiver. Or the incoherence was Karin's, listening from the bed. Daniel stumbled back to her, bewildered. "It's your brother. He wants to talk to you."

Karin squeezed her eyes and shook herself. "He called *here*? He *talked* to you?"

Daniel scrambled back under the covers. He turned the heat off at night, and now his naked body was going hypothermic. "I . . . we saw each other. We talked to each other, a little while ago."

Karin grappled with the lucid nightmare. "When?"

"It doesn't matter. A few days back." He flicked his fingers: the ticking clock, the waiting phone, the story too long. "He wants to talk to you."

"Doesn't *matter*?" She tore the gray army-surplus blanket off the bed. "It's true, isn't it? You loved him. I mean, *love*. He was the only reason you . . . I was never anything more than . . ." She wrapped the wool blanket around her shoulders and turned her back on him, fumbling for the phone in the dark. "Mark? Are you all right?"

"I know what happened to me during the operation."

"Tell me." Still drugged with sleep.

"I died. I passed away on the operating table, and none of the doctors noticed."

Her voice came out of her, thin, pleading. "Mark?"

"It clarifies a bunch of stuff that made no sense. Why everything has seemed so . . . *far*. I resisted the idea because, well, obviously, someone would realize, right? If you weren't alive? Then it hit me: *How would they know?* I mean, if nobody saw it happen . . . I mean, it just now occurred to *me*, and I'm the one who's in the middle of it!"

She talked with him for a long time, first reasoning, then irrational, just trying to comfort him. He was panicked; he didn't know how to "get properly dead." He spoke of messing up the transition—"I scattered the deck"—and now there seemed no way to get things back into the right sequence.

"I'm coming over right now, Mark. We can figure this out, together."

He laughed, as only the dead can laugh. "Don't worry. I'll keep overnight. Haven't started rotting yet."

"Are you sure?" she kept asking. "Are you sure you'll be okay?"

"You can't get worse than dead."

She was afraid to hang up. "How do you feel?"

"Okay, actually. Better than I felt when I thought I was still alive."

Back in the bedroom, Daniel held one of the neuroscience books that Karin had perpetually renewed from the library. "I've found it," he said. "Cotard's syndrome."

She threw the gray wool blanket back on the bed and crawled under it. She'd read all about it, had spent a year exploring every horror the brain allowed. Another misidentification delusion, perhaps an extreme form of

Capgras. Unrecognized death: the only possible explanation for feeling so cut off from everyone. "How can he get it *now*? After a year? Just when he's started the treatment."

Daniel killed the light and crawled in next to her. He put his hand on her side. She flinched. "Maybe it's the medication," he suggested. "Maybe he's having some kind of reaction."

She spun around to face him in the blackness. "Oh my God. Is that possible? We need to get him back under observation. First thing tomorrow."

Daniel agreed.

She froze in thought. "Shit. Jesus. How could I forget?"

"What? What is it?" He tried to rub her shoulders, but she pulled away.

"His wreck. One year ago today. It completely slipped my mind."

She lay down and pretended stillness for something like an hour. At last she got up. "I'm going to take something," she whispered.

"Not this late," he said.

She went into the bathroom and closed the door. She didn't come out for so long that he finally followed her. He knocked on the bathroom door, but there was no answer. He opened it. She sat on the closed toilet lid, glaring at him, even before he entered. "You saw him? You talked with him? And you never told me. It's him for you, isn't it? I'm nothing but his sister, am I?"

Dr. Hayes examined Mark, baffled, but fascinated. He listened as Mark announced, "I'm not saying it's a cover-up. I'm just saying that nobody noticed. You can see how it might happen. But I'm telling you, Doc, I never felt like this when alive."

He scheduled Mark for another scan, for the first week in

March. Mark, weirdly compliant, left to see the lab techs. "It can't be the medication," Hayes told Karin. "There's nothing like this in the literature."

"Literature," she repeated, everything fictional. She could feel the neurologist, already writing up this new wrinkle for publication.

The Cotard's diagnosis changed nothing substantial. Now that Mark had started the olanzapine, Dr. Hayes insisted that he continue without missing any doses. Could Karin vouch that he'd kept with the medication schedule, exactly as given? She could not, but did. Did she feel able to continue supervising her brother, or would she like to put Mark back into Dedham Glen? Continue supervising, Karin said. She had no choice. The insurance coverage would not pay for readmission.

She couldn't afford to increase her hours out at Farview. Already, there weren't enough hours in the week for the Refuge. What had begun as an invented job, the charity of a man who wanted to keep her nearby, had turned real. It was no longer even a question of meaningful work, of self-fulfillment. As absolutely delusional as it would have sounded to say aloud to anyone, she now knew: water wanted something from her.

Desperate, she called Barbara and asked for help in covering. "It's only for a few days, until the medication kicks in and he pulls out of this." The goals of care had changed. She no longer needed Mark to recognize her. She only needed him to believe he was alive.

"Of course," Barbara said. "Anything. For however long he might need it."

The woman's willingness stung her. "It's a crazy time at the Refuge," Karin explained. "Things are heating up with . . ."

"Of course," Barbara said. "Someone should probably be there at night. Nights are probably bad for him, right now."

Her voice hinted willingness, even that far. But that much Karin refused to ask of her. If the night shift couldn't be Karin, it wouldn't be Barbara, either.

Karin called Bonnie, the only real choice. She got the infectious answering machine—*I wish I was here to talk to you for real*—in that cheerful treble that sounded like the horn of a Ford Focus on mood elevators. Karin tried twice more, but couldn't bring herself to leave a message. *Would you mind spending nights at my brother's for a little while? He thinks he's a dead man.* Even by Kearney standards, something you'd want to ask in person. At last, Karin went out to the Arch, on Bonnie's shift. Karin hadn't yet bothered to take a look. Sixty-five million dollars to turn her great-grandparents into the Cartoon Channel and to trick people on their way to California in their Navigators into thinking there was something here worth stopping for.

She paid her $8.25, pushed past the life-size pioneer figures, and rode up the escalator through the covered wagon, surrounded by giant murals. She spotted Bonnie near the sod house exhibit, in her calico dress and poke bonnet, talking to a group of schoolchildren in a bizarre, old-fashiony voice—an MTV version of Ma Kettle. Seeing Karin, Bonnie broke into a big wave and, in the same fake-archaic voice, called out, "Hiya!" She picked clinging first-graders off her skirt and joined Karin in the Pawnee exhibit, calico alongside Tencel.

"He's convinced he died and no one noticed," Karin told her.

Thought soured Bonnie's nose. "You know? I felt that way myself, once."

"Bon? Do you think you could stay with him for a bit? At the Homestar? Just for the next few nights?"

The girl's eyes went wide as a lemur's. "With Marker? 'Course!" She answered as if the question were itself deranged. And last of anyone again, Karin saw how things were.

Arrangements firmed; the women each took a shift, with Mark indifferent to the measures all around him. "Whatever," Mark told Karin, when she described the arrangements. "Knock yourself out. Can't hurt me. I'm already gone."

But he assembled Karin and Bonnie in the Homestar living room on the first Monday evening in March, to see the latest edition of *Crime Solvers*. "Got a heads-up call today," he explained, refusing to say more. He moved methodically, forcing hot drinks and bags of corn nuts on them, making sure everyone used the facilities before the show started. Karin watched him, feeling the folly of all hope.

Then, as if on command, Tracey, the show's hostess, announced, "There's been a break in the story we brought to you some weeks ago about the Farview man who . . ."

On screen, a farmer out by Elm Creek pointed to a hole in the border of his front lawn. Five days before, his wife had discovered some bloodroot growing up inside the planter he'd fashioned for her out of an old tire he'd fished out of the river back in August, when the water was low. "Now, my wife and I are a couple old fans of your show, and as I stood there, looking at that tire, your television story came back to me, and it crossed my mind to ask myself . . ."

Police Sergeant Ron Fagan explained how the tires had been impounded and checked by forensics against the crime-scene evidence on file. "We believe we have a match," he told the world, a bit crestfallen to be describing computer database searches instead of high-speed chases. But he reported that the tire had been traced to a local man who had been brought in for questioning. The man worked at the Lexington packing plant and was named Duane Cain.

Karin shouted at the tube. "I *knew* it. That pond scum."

Bonnie, on the other side of Mark, shook her head. "That can't be right. They swore to me it was someone else."

Mark sat rigid, already a corpse. "They ran me off the road. Chicken goat-head. They left me for dead. At least I finally know I am."

Karin threw on her coat, slamming around in her bag for her keys. "I'll give him questioning." She fumbled for the door. In her haste, she sprang it open on her face and smashed her lip.

Mark lifted off the sofa. "I'm coming with you."

"No!" She wheeled, furious, scaring even herself. "No. You let me talk to him!" Blackie Two growled. Mark stepped back, hands raised. Then she was out in the dark, blundering toward her car.

She checked at the police station. Duane Cain had been released. Sergeant Fagan was not on duty, and no one would give her details. The night was as cold and the world as airless as any meteor. Her breath came frozen out of her nostrils and bathed her hands in flinty smoke. She beat her elbows against her sides to keep her lungs pumping. She got back into her Corolla and headed across town, making it to Cain's apartment in minutes. He opened the door to her assault in a purple sweatshirt reading: *What Would Beelzebub Do?* He was expecting someone else, and he shrank at the sight of her. "I take it you saw that show?"

She pushed into the room and slammed him into the wall. He didn't fight back, only reached up and pinned her wrists.

"They let me go. I didn't do anything."

507

"Your fucking skid marks cut right in front of him." She struggled to land a punch while he blunted her in a clumsy embrace.

"Do you want me to tell you what happened, or don't you?"

He refused to say anything until she stopped struggling. He sat her on a beanbag chair and tried to give her something to drink. He balanced on a bar stool at a safe distance, brandishing the phone book like a shield.

"We didn't really lie, per se. Technically speaking . . ."

She threatened to kill him, or worse. He started again.

"You were right about the games. We were racing. But it wasn't what you think. We were at the Bullet. Tommy had recently acquired a set of communicators. We went out and started goofing with them. Me and Rupp in Tommy's truck, Mark in his. Just tag. Driving around like we always did, testing the range, chasing each other. You know: hotter, colder, losing the signal, picking it up again. We were a ways away, coming east on North Line, from town. We thought we had him. Mark was giggling into the communicator, something about taking evasive action. Then his signal went dead. Took his finger off the transmit button and never came back. We didn't know what he was up to. Tommy kicked his truck, figuring we had to be close. It was pretty dark out there."

He hooded his eyes with one hand, from the glare of memory.

"Then we saw him. He was upside down in the ditch, right-hand side, just south of the road. Tommy swore and slammed the brakes. We fishtailed and swerved across the center line. That's what you saw: our tracks in his lane. Only, we got there *after* him."

She sat stiff, her spine a spike. "What did you do?"

"What do you mean?"

"He's lying in that ditch. You and your friend are right there."

"Are you kidding? He had three tons of metal on top of him. Every second counted. We did what we had to do. Spun around, ran back to town, and called it in."

"Neither of you has a cell phone? Jacking around with those ridiculous walkie-talkie toys, and no cell phone?"

"We called it in," he said. "Within minutes."

"Anonymously? And you never came forward, after. Never told the story. Changed your tires and pitched the guilty ones in the river."

"Listen to me. You don't know anything." His voice rose. "Those police types bust you first and ask questions later. They go after guys like me and Tommy. We threaten them."

"You, *threaten*? And he went along with it. Your friend Rupp. The Specialist."

"Look. You don't believe me, even now. You think the *police* were going to believe us, the night of the accident?"

"Why didn't they lock you up?"

"They questioned Tommy down at Riley, and he gave exactly the same story. The point is, we got the paramedics there as fast as possible. We didn't have anything to add to the facts. We have no clue what happened to him. It wouldn't have made any difference, our coming forward."

"It might have made a difference to Mark."

He screwed up his face. "It wouldn't have changed anything."

Her need to believe him appalled her. She rose to her feet, rearranging things: the tracks, their order, her memory. Time threaded and rethreaded, slowed, buckled, and slammed into reverse. "The third car," she said.

"I don't know," Cain said. "I've been thinking about it for a year."

"The third car," she repeated. "The one that ran off the road, from behind him." She crossed to him, ready to slam him again. "Were any cars coming toward you as you reached the spot? Any westbound cars, heading back toward town? Answer me!"

"Yeah. We were watching, as we got close. We kept expecting him to blast past us. But then came this white Ford Taurus with out-of-state plates."

"What state?"

"Rupp says Texas. I couldn't tell. We were going a little fast, I told you."

"How fast was this Ford going?"

"Funny you should ask. We both had the impression that it was crawling." The thought sat him up. "Jesus. You're right. This other car . . . this Ford came up just before we did, just after he . . . and they . . . You're saying that they . . . What exactly *are* you saying?"

She didn't know what she was saying. Then or ever. "They didn't stop either."

Cain shut his eyes, clamped his neck in one palm, and threw back his head. "It wouldn't have made any difference."

"It might have," she said. *God led me to you.*

She got home crazy late. Daniel was waiting up for her, beside himself. "I thought something had happened to you. I thought . . . You might have been anywhere. You might have been hurt."

Might have been with the other man. "I'm sorry," she said. "I should have called." To placate him, she told him everything.

He listened, but was no help. "Who called the accident in?

Rupp and Cain? Not the other car? I thought it was this guardian . . . ?"

"Maybe they both called in."

"But I thought the police said . . ."

"I don't know, Daniel."

"But if the other car didn't stop, why the note? Taking credit, for leaving the scene . . . ?"

"I have to sleep," she explained. It was too late to call Mark and Bonnie. She didn't know what she would say, anyway. What her brother could handle.

She woke the next morning to the raging phone. The room was ablaze with light and Daniel had already left for the Refuge. She dragged herself up, out of animal dreams. "I'm coming. Hold on a minute, please. You checking up on me or something?"

But when she lifted the receiver, the voice at the other end was thin and spectral. "Karin? It's Bonnie. He's having some kind of seizure, and I can't get him out."

It had to be the hospital, again. A year's long loop back to where he was, this time last March. Some migrating thing that can't know any better. Mark Schluter back in Good Samaritan, not the same ward, but close enough. Restrained in bed, post-toxic, 450 mg of olanzapine flushed from his body.

A dead man has tried to kill himself: the only way to fit things back together. Dystonic by the time the paramedics reached him. Intubation and gastric lavage, rushed to the hospital for intravenous fluids and cardiovascular monitoring, watched over by a staff who will ensure that he won't try leaving again.

He comes out of his second coma, a mere figment of the first. Conscious again, he refuses all attempts to communicate except to say, "I want to talk to Shrinky. I'll only talk to Shrinky."

Dr. Hayes calls Weber with the news. Weber receives the report like a verdict, the fruit of his long, self-serving ambition. He calls Mark at once, but Mark refuses to talk. "No phones," Mark tells the shift nurse. Every phone line is tapped. Every cable and satellite. "He's got to come here, in person."

Weber makes several more efforts at contact, all without result. Mark is out of danger, at least for now. Weber has already entered into the case beyond the bounds of professional correctness. His last trip almost finished him. Any more involvement, and he'll be done.

But something in the neuroscientist now sees: responsibility has no limits. The case histories you appropriate are yours. If he does nothing, if he refuses the boy's one request, if he abandons now what he has bungled so badly, then he surely is what his darkest voices already declare him. *Tried to kill himself, because of me.* No choice but return. Some long loop, back again. Tour Director makes him.

No way to tell his wife. Tell Sylvie. After what he has already told her, any given reason will seem the worst of self-deceptions. She, who would not stretch out a hand now if Gerald Weber, celebrity author, tainted saint of neural insight, were burnt in effigy for bogus empathy: no possible way to explain to her.

He braces for her response, but nothing prepares him for how badly his announcement shakes the woman. She takes it like some numb Cassandra who already guesses everything he hasn't yet admitted. "What can you do for him? Anything the doctors out there can't?"

She asked him that question, a year ago. He should have listened to her then. He should listen now. He shakes his head, his mouth a mail slot. "Nothing I can think of."

"Haven't you done enough, already?"

"That's the problem. The olanzapine was my idea."

She sits down hard in the breakfast nook. But still she masters herself, horribly true to form. "It wasn't your idea that he take two weeks' dosage at once."

"No. You're right. That one wasn't mine."

"Don't do this to me, Gerald. What are you proving? You're a good man. As good as your words. Why won't you believe that? Why can't you just . . . ?"

She stands and circles. She waits for him to raise the issue. She extends him that grim respect, wholly unearned. She will assume the woman is nothing, irrelevant, until he tells her otherwise. Will believe in him, even without trust. He must say something. But he can't grace the fact, even by dismissing it.

All things come down to belief. Belief in a gossamer too ephemeral to fool anyone. That will be the holy grail of brain studies: to see how tens of billions of chemical logic gates all sparking and damping each other can somehow create faith in their own phantom loops. "He's in agony. He wants to talk to me. He needs something from me."

"And you? What do you need?" Her eyes probe him, bitterly. She looks palsied and pale, suffering from her own overdose.

He answers, almost. "It costs me nothing. Some frequent flyer miles, a couple of days, and a few hundred out of the research account." She shakes her head at him, the closest she can come to derision. "I'm sorry," he says. "I need to do this. I'm not an exploiter. Not an opportunist."

She has stood by, supportive, kept a hard-won poise these last few months, throughout his steady dissolving act. Every drop in his self-confidence has hammered her. "No," she says, fighting

513

for composure. She crosses to him; her hands scrabble at his shirt. "I don't like this, Man. This is wrong. This is messed up."

"Don't worry," he says. As soon as the words leave his mouth, he feels the ridiculousness. *The self is a burning house; get out while you can.* He sees his wife, really sees her, for the first time since he stopped believing in his work. Sees the pea-green amphibian puckers under her eyes, the withering of her upper lip—when did she grow old? He sees in her flinching gaze how he frightens her. She can't make him out. She's lost him. "Don't worry."

She shrinks from his words in disgust. "What the hell do you need? You need Famous Gerald? Famous Gerald can go hang himself. Do you need people to say that you . . . ?" She bites into her lower lip and looks away. When she speaks again, it's like a newscaster. "Will you be doing any sightseeing while you're there?" Her face is bloodless, but her voice is casual. "Any old friends?"

"I don't know. It's a small town." And then—the debt of thirty years—he corrects himself. "I'm not sure. It's likely."

She pushes away and crosses to the refrigerator. Her businesslike movement destroys him. She opens the freezer and removes two pieces of tilapia, to thaw for dinner. She takes the fish to the sink and runs cold water over them. "Gerald?" Idly curious, trying for acceptance, and missing by a cold mile. "Can you just tell me why?"

He deserves her fury, even desires it. But not this calm acceptance. Gerald: just tell me why. *So you will think well of me again.* "I'm not sure," he tells her. Repeating that in his mind, until he makes it true.

Mark left no note before swallowing his antipsychotics. How could he, already dead? But even that lack of message accuses

514

Karin. All this year he has called for her help, and all along she has failed him. Failed him in every way: failed to confirm his past, failed to permit his present, failed to recover his future.

The old Schluter craziness settles on her, the inheritance she's never been able to shed. Her first identity: guilty and deficient, whatever else she manages. She visits Mark in the hospital. She even brings Daniel, Mark's oldest nonimaginary friend. But Mark refuses to talk to either of them. "Can you two just respectfully leave me to rot here in peace?" It's Shrinky or no one.

She surrenders him again to the health professionals, to the chemical correctives now dripping into his limp arms. She slips down her own Glasgow Scale. She can focus on nothing. Her concentration strays for hours at a stretch. At last she sees why her brother stopped recognizing her. Nothing to recognize. She has twisted herself past recognition. One small deceit laid on another, until even she can't say where she stands or who she's working for. Things she's waffled on, denied, and lied about, things she's hidden even from herself. All things to all people. Doing a conservationist and a developer at the same time. Making herself over, personality du jour. Imagination, even memory, all too ready to accommodate her, whoever *her* is. Anything for a scratch behind the ears. Scratch from anyone.

She is nothing. No one. Worse than no one. Blank at the core.

She must change her life. From the mess of her fouled nest, salvage something. Anything. The slightest, drab, creeping thing: it makes no difference, so long as it's uncompromised and wild. She may be too late to get her brother back. But she might still rescue her brother's sister.

She buries herself in legwork for the Refuge, researching

her pamphlets. *Something to wake sleepwalkers and make the world strange again.* The least dose of life science, a few figures in a table, and she begins to see: people, desperate for solidity, must kill anything that exceeds them. Anything bigger or more linked, or, in its bleak enduring, a little more free. No one can bear how large the *outside* is, even as we decimate it. She has only to look, and the facts pour out. She reads, and still can't believe: twelve million or more species, less than a tenth of them counted. And half will snuff out in her lifetime.

Crushed by data, her senses come weirdly alive. The air smells like lavender, and even the drab, late-winter browns feel more vivid than they have since sixteen. She's hungry all the time, and the futility of her work doubles her energy. Her connections race. She's like that case in Dr. Weber's last book, the woman with fronto-temporal dementia who suddenly started producing the most sumptuous paintings. A kind of compensation: when one brain part is overwhelmed, another takes over.

The web she glimpses is so intricate, so wide, that humans should long ago have shriveled up and died of shame. The only thing proper to want is what Mark wanted: to not be, to crawl down the deepest well and fossilize into a rock that only water can dissolve. Only water, as solvent against all toxic run-off, only water to dilute the poison of personality. All she can do is work, try to return the river to those we've stolen it from. Everything human and personal horrifies her now, everything except this doomed pamphleteering.

Water wants something from her. Something only consciousness can deliver. She is nothing, as toxic as anything with an ego. A sham; a pretense. Nothing worth recognizing. But still, this river needs her, its liquid mind, its way of surviving . . .

The world fills with luxuries she can't afford. Sleep is one of them. When she does succumb, she and Daniel still share a bed. But touching has stopped, except by accident. He meditates more now, sometimes an hour at a shot, just to escape all the damage she has done him. She has battered him with betrayals; he absorbs the battering, as he absorbs all the race's insults. He seems to her now a man who might absorb anything, someone who, alone of everyone she knows, has put away vanity and looked past himself. And this is what she has so resented in him. Of all the men she has ever been with, he now seems the only one fluid enough to be a decent father, to teach a child about everything outside us that must be recognized. But he would sooner die than bring another estranged human into this world. Another like her.

He should have thrown her out months ago. No reason why he hasn't. Maybe only residual love for her brother. Or just the care he extends to any creature. She must seem hideous to him, clutching, a brittle little shell of need. He can't want her, and never really did. Yet he remains stubbornly if silently decent to her in all things. Her brother has almost died, and this man alone knows what that means. This man alone might help her cope. She lies in bed, her spine eight inches from his, aching just to reach back with one blind palm and touch the warm of him. Prove that he's still there.

The third day after Mark's attempt, the Development Council indicates its willingness in principle to grant the Central Platte Scenic Natural Outpost the right to purchase water shares. She has dreaded the decision for weeks, but never really believed it would come. The combined Platte preservation groups respond in numb disarray. They've lost their footrace with the developers' consortium, and in a series of hasty meetings, the alliance begins to crumble.

If the decision demoralizes her, it crushes Daniel. He says nothing about the judgment but curt, stoic maxims. He finds the council beneath condemning. Something withers in him, some basic willingness to go on fighting a species that won't be rehabilitated and can't be beaten. He won't talk to her about it, and she has lost her right to press him.

She needs to square things by him. To fix one thing, for one real person, in all the debacle of recent days. Redeem his ill-placed trust and return something to the one man who loves her brother as much as she does.

She has one thing she can give him, one thing only. The thing water wants. She almost talks herself into believing that she has worked toward this, all these months, just to be able to give it to him now. She knows what the gift will cost her; he will learn who she is, and wash his hands of her. The other man, too. She will lose them both, everything that she has perjured herself to get. But she can give Daniel something worth far more than herself.

She spends the day preparing him a vegan feast: broccoli almond seitan, skordalia, and coriander chutney. Even tahini rice pudding, for the man who considers dessert a sin. She flies around the kitchen, mixing and assembling, feeling almost steady. Blessed distraction, and the most effort she has expended on him since moving in. She's done nothing for him, while he has tended to her every crisis. She has let their life be overgrown by the weed of her personality. Is it so impossible to be someone else, to make him a grateful meal for once? Even if it is their last.

Daniel blows in on a cloud of distraction. He struggles to make sense of the feast. "What is all this? Some occasion?"

It stings, but she needs it to. "There's always occasion."

"True. Well." His smile is crucified. He sits and spreads his hands, stunned at all the food. He hasn't even taken off his coat. "My separation party, then."

She stops licking rice pudding off her finger. "What do you mean?"

He's placid, head bowed. "Quit the job."

She holds the counter, her head shaking. She drops onto the stool across from him. "What do you mean? What are you saying?" He can't stop his work. Impossible: like a hummingbird on a hunger strike.

He's expansive, almost amused. "Split with the Refuge. An ideological parting of the ways. They seem to have decided that this whole crane theme park isn't so bad after all. Something they can work with. Compromise is the better part of valor, you know. They're circulating a memo saying that, properly run, the Outpost might even be beneficial for the birds!"

A thing she herself believed in, well past the public hearing. "Oh, Daniel. No. You can't let this happen."

He tilts an eyebrow at her. "Don't worry. I've covered for you. Already talked it out with them. You can go on working there. They won't hold it against you that you're my . . . that you and I . . ."

"*Daniel.*" She can't take him in. They've lost. That's what he's saying. The fight is over. The river will be developed; more staging ground will vanish. He's saying . . . but it's impossible, what he's saying. Quitting the Refuge. Leaping off into nothing. Death by disengagement.

"You can't quit. You can't let them give in to this."

"What I can and can't let happen does not seem to be the issue."

She can make it the issue. Can get him back into the battle. One word from her and the Refuge will rescind whatever deal they have chosen to cut. But that one word kills any love he's ever felt for her. He will see her in full light, at her most hideous. Stay silent, and she might even keep him, broken like this, needing her. He'd have nothing else but her care.

She thinks, for an instant, that she does this for the birds. For the river. Then she tells herself it's to save this upright man. But she will save no one, no living thing. She will barely slow the humans, who can't be stopped. She chooses from pure selfishness, as selfish as every human choice. He will hate her now, forever. But finally, he will know what she can give.

"It's worse than you think," she says. "The Outpost people, they're planning a Phase Two. I know how the consortium will make money on the crane cabins, out of season. It's . . . going to be called the *Living Prairies Museum*."

She describes it to him in all its banality. "A zoo?" he asks. He can't figure it. "They want to build a *zoo*?"

"Indoor-outdoor. And it gets worse. I've found out why they need the extra river allocation shares. There's also a Phase Three. A water park. Slides. Hydraulic fountains and sculptures, all with nature themes. A giant wave pool."

"A water park?" He rubs his scalp, forehead to crown. He tugs at his ear, his mouth twisted. He giggles. "A water park, in the Great American Desert."

"You have to let the Refuge know. They have to stop this."

He doesn't answer, only sits on one heel, the Virasan position, and stares at all the elaborate dishes she's prepared. Now it will come out. Now she will pay, for all this saving. "How do you know about all this?"

"I saw the blueprints."

His chin rises and falls and rises again. A kind of pungent nodding. "And you were going to tell me . . . when?"

"I just told you," she says, palms up, pointing at the food, her proof. She's ready to give him all the brutal details. But he doesn't need them. He sees everything. He knows now what she's been doing, all these weeks, better than she has known. She sits looking on herself, through his eyes. Almost a relief, his fatigue. He must have known for a long time. She braces for his recrimination, disgust—anything to feel clean again. His words blow her bracing away.

"You've been spying on us. You and your friend? Trading secrets. Some kind of double . . ."

"He's not . . . Okay. I'm a whore. Say what you want. You're right about me. A lying, devious bitch. But you have to believe one thing: Robert Karsh isn't what I want in my life, Daniel. Robert Karsh can go . . ."

He looks at her as if she's dropped on all fours and started barking. What she and other men have done is meaningless. Only the river matters. He looks at her, appalled. He can't make out, let alone count, all the ways that she has betrayed the river. "I don't give a fuck about Robert Karsh. You can do whatever you want with him."

She reaches out with her palms, backing him up. "Wait. Who are you talking about?" If not Karsh. "Who did you mean, 'your friend?' "

"You know who I mean." He has lost all patience. "Their private investigator. Their hired researcher. Your friend Barbara."

Her head snaps back. He has some lesion, some sickness worse than Mark's. Cold little hands stroke at her. "Daniel?" She will run from the house and call for help.

"Pumping me at the hearing, to see how much I might have guessed."

"What *investigator*? She's Mark's old aide. She works at the rehab . . ."

"For what? Three dollars an hour? A woman who talks like that? A woman who *acts* like that? You make me sick," he says, human at last.

A fork of panics. What is Barbara to him? She imagines some longstanding, secret explanation, something that locks her out. But the other fear is greater. Her face a snarl, she backs toward the apartment door.

He sees her confusion, and wavers. "Don't tell me you don't know . . . How much do you think you can hide?"

"I'm not hiding . . ."

"She *called* me, Karin. Her voice sounded familiar, the first time we ran into her. I talked to her on the phone, fourteen months ago. She called me, right around the time the developers started planning this thing. She pretended to be working on some news story. She asked me all about the Refuge, the Platte, the restoration work. And like an idiot I told her everything. When people want to talk about those birds, I trust them. More fool, me." He stares past her, stilled, like some small thing dying in a blizzard.

"Wait. Daniel. That's crazy. You're saying she's, what? An industrial spy? That she works at Dedham Glen as some kind of cover?"

"Spy? You would know, wouldn't you? I'm saying I spoke to her. I answered her questions. I remember her voice."

Birding by ear. "Well, you're remembering wrong. Trust me on this one."

"Yes? Trust you? On this one?" His head comes about, luffing. "And what else should I trust you on? You've been ratting me, laughing at me with your old sweet fuck for months . . ."

She swings away from him and presses her ears. His right cheek twitches. He squints and shakes his head.

"You're going to sit there and deny this, after everything? Her name never came up, in all the secret conversations you were having with him? When you were meeting with him, telling them about us? About the Refuge?"

She moans and starts to break. He stands and crosses to the far side of the room, as far from her as possible, holding his elbow and pinching his mouth, waiting for her to be done. She breathes in, mouthful by mouthful, grappling for calm, pretending she is him. "I think I should go."

"You're probably right," he says, and leaves the house.

She wanders about the apartment for a long time. Eventually she drifts to the bedroom and stuffs her clothes into a bag. He will come back and stop her, listen to her explanation. But he is as gone now as her brother. She goes to the kitchen, packs the meal in old bean sprout containers and sticks them in the refrigerator. She sits on the toilet lid in a daze, trying to read one of his meditation books, a crash course in transcendence. She sits at the front door, on the bags she has stuffed with her things. He's outside somewhere, tracking, watching the building, waiting for her to go.

At twenty minutes to midnight she at last calls her brother's friend. "Bonnie? I'm sorry to wake you. Can I crash at your place? Just a night or two. I'm nowhere. Nothing."

Gerald Weber pulls alongside a cash machine in his third Nebraska rental. His hands shake, withdrawing far more money than he intends. From the airport, he heads on instinct back to that hotel where he is now a regular. *Welcome Crane Peepers*. Only now, the lobby is crawling with heavy, aging people in knit clothes carrying field guides and light binoculars. He himself has way overpacked, three times what he would ordinarily bring on a professional trip. He even carries the cell phone and digital recorder, a professional habit that should have died months ago, along with his professional pretenses. In his Dopp kit, alongside the Band-Aids and fold-up sewing sampler, he has packed ten different ingestibles, from ginkgo to DMAE.

Once, he'd studied an otherwise healthy man who thought that stories turned real. People spoke the world into being. Even a single sentence launched events as solid as experience. Journey, complication, crisis, and redemption: just say the words and they took shape.

For decades, that case haunted everything Weber wrote about. That one delusion—*stories came true*—seemed like the germ of healing. We told ourselves backward into diagnosis and forward into treatment. Story was the storm at the cortex's core. And there was no better way to get at that fictional truth than through the haunted neurological parables of Broca or Luria—stories of how even shattered brains might narrate disaster back into livable sense.

Then the story changed. Somewhere, real clinical tools rendered case histories merely colorful. Medicine grew up. Instruments, images, tests, metrics, surgery, pharmaceuticals: no room left for Weber's anecdotes. And all his literary cures turned to circus acts and Gothic freak shows.

Once, he knew a man who thought that telling other people's stories might make them real again. Then others' stories remade him. Illusion, loss, humiliation, disgrace: just say the words and they happened. The man himself had arisen from doctored accounts; Weber had invented him out of whole cloth. The complete history and physical: fabricated. Now the text unravels. Even the case's name—*Gerald W.*—sounds like the feeblest of pseudonyms.

He finds himself standing beside Mark's bed, looking for

redemption. The boy pleads with him. "Doc. What kept you? I thought you were dead. Deader than I was." His speech is slow and fumbling. "You heard what happened?" Weber doesn't answer. "Tried to off myself. And as far as anybody can tell, maybe not for the first time."

The words pull Weber down onto the bedside chair. "How are you feeling now?"

Mark opens his elbows, displaying the IV tube running into his left arm. "Well, I'm going to start feeling better real soon, whether I want to or not. Yep, they're going to bring me back to myself. Mark Three. You know there's talk of electroshock?"

"I . . ." Weber starts. "I think you must have gotten that wrong. Misunderstood."

"Yep, EST. 'Very mild,' they tell me. I'll walk out of this place happy as a clam. Good as new. And I won't remember the first thing of what I know now. What I've figured out." He flails and grabs Weber by the wrist. "Which is why I have to talk to you. Now. While I still can."

Weber takes the heel of Mark's hand in his, and Mark suffers it. The boy is that desperate. When Mark speaks, his voice is pleading.

"You saw me, not long after the accident. You ran tests on me and such. We talked all about your theory, the whole lesion idea, the right posterior thing getting split off from the almond thing. The Miggy?"

Weber sits back, shocked at Mark's recall. He himself had forgotten their conversation. "Amygdala."

"You know?" Mark pulls his hand from Weber's and fakes a feeble grin. "I was sure, back then, when you told me that, that you'd lost your fucking mind." He squeezes his eyes and shakes his head. Time's running out. He's losing his insight to

525

a chemical cocktail seeping into his arms. He can't quite name the thing he needs to say. The struggle runs the length of his body. He wrestles to grasp the thing that stands just three feet out of reach. "My brain, all those split parts, trying to convince each other. Dozens of lost Scouts waving crappy flashlights in the woods at night. Where's *me*?"

Weber could tell stories. The sufferers of automatism, their bodies moving without consciousness. The metamorphopsias, plagued by oranges the size of beach balls and pencils the size of matchsticks. The amnesiacs. The owners of vivid, detailed memories that never happened. *Me* is a rushed draft, pasted up by committee, trying to trick some junior editor into publishing it. "I don't know," Weber says.

"*Now* you tell me . . ." Mark's face crumples again, twisted by thought. No question he might come up with could be worth so much distress. But this is what Weber has flown thirteen hundred miles to hear. Mark's voice drops, concealed. "Do you think it's possible . . . ? Could somebody be completely messed up and not have the slightest notion . . . ? And still feel just like they've always . . . ?"

It isn't possible, Weber wants to say. It's certain. Obligatory. "You'll feel better," he says. "More whole than you do now." Reckless promise. He'd be on the drug himself if that were true.

"I'm not talking about me," Mark hisses. "I'm talking about everybody else. Hundreds of people, maybe thousands: cases where, unlike mine, the operation actually worked. Everybody walking around without the foggiest idea."

Weber's hairs stiffen. Piloerection, old evolutionary holdover—*goose flesh*. "What operation?"

Mark is wild now. "I need you, Shrinky. There's no one else can tell me. All the little brain parts, chattering to each other? Those packs of Cub Scouts?"

Weber nods.

"Can you cut one out? One? Without killing the troop?"

"Yes."

The relief is immediate. Mark slips down on his pillow. "Can you put one in? You know. Kidnap a Scout, stick another in his place? Same basic crappy flashlight, waving around in the dark?"

More goose flesh. "Tell me what you mean."

Mark drapes his palms over his eyes. " 'Tell me what you mean.' The man wants to know what I mean." He twists his head bitterly. The voice drops again. "I mean transplants. Cross-species mix and match."

Xenotransplantation. An article on the subject in *JAMA*, last month. The growing body of experiments—bits of cortex from one animal transplanted into another, taking on the properties of the host area. Mark must have heard about these, in the bastardized, garbled way that science reaches everyone.

"They put ape parts into people, right? Why not birds? Their little almond thing for our little almond thing."

Weber needs only say no, as gently and fully as possible. But something in him wants to say: no need to swap. Already there, inherited. Ancient structures, still in ours.

He owes it to Mark, at least to ask. "Why would they want to do this?"

Mark's all over the question. "It's part of a bigger deal. A whole development thing, on the drawing boards for a long time. Bird City. Capitalize on the animals. The next big business, you see? Figure out how to move bits back and forth. Cranes to humans. Vice versa. Like you say: a Cub Scout more or less and you're still the same troop. Still feel like yourself. It would have worked on me, too, but something went wrong."

Something communicates through Mark. Something primeval that Weber must hear before the dripping chemicals seal this boy-man back up into the human. There's only this minute. Only now. "But . . . what is the operation trying to accomplish?"

"They're trying to save the species."

"Which species?"

The question surprises Mark. "Which species?" Shock gives way to that booming, hollowed-out laugh. "That's a good one. Which species?" He falls silent, deciding.

In Bonnie Travis's turn-of-the-century hip-flask of a bungalow, the two women barely have room to slide past each other. Karin apologizes at every chance, washes dishes that aren't even dirty. Bonnie chides her. "Come on! It's like camping. Our little soddie."

In truth, the girl has been a blessing, mindlessly cheerful and distracting. Bonnie keeps them entertained with reading tarot cards or roasting s'mores over the gas stove. "Comfort food," she calls it. At night, Karin fights the urge to curl up in bed with her.

On the second evening, she comes back inside from smoking half a pack out on Bonnie's deck, to find the girl distraught. She won't say why at first, just keeps repeating, "It's nothing. No problem." But she can't stay on task and ends up carbonizing the potpies. Karin finds the culprit on Bonnie's coffee table: Weber's new book, which the girl has been dutifully plowing through at the rate of half a page a day over the last several months.

"This is what's upset you?" Karin asks. "Something in here?"

One more denying shake of the head, then the girl breaks

down. "There's a *God* part of the brain? Religious visions from some kind of epilepsy storm?"

Karin is all over herself, comforting the girl. And the girl takes some comforting.

"You can turn God on and off with electric . . . ? It's just some built-in structure? Did you already know this? Does everybody? Everybody smart?"

Karin shushes her, strokes her shoulders. "Nobody knows. He doesn't *know.*"

"Of course he knows! He wouldn't put it in a book, if he didn't. He's the smartest man I've ever met. Religion is just a temporal lobe . . . ? He's saying belief is just an evolved chemical thing you could gain or lose . . . ? Like what Mark decided about you. How it's not him anymore, how he can't even see that he . . . Oh shit. Shit. I'm too stupid to get this!"

And Karin, too stupid to help. Some part of her—some temporal storm—wants to say: What we sum to is still real. The phantom wants our shaping. Even a God module would have been selected for its survival value. Water is up to something. She says none of this; she has no words. Bonnie's doubt must have been long in coming, a slow-growing tumor. She's shaken enough to entertain any wider belief system Karin might suggest. For a long time, they look at each other, caught in some shameful secret. Then, on nothing but grim smiles, they make a pact, joined in the trick of belief, novitiates in a new faith, until damage changes them.

Karin hasn't stepped out of the toy house except for one more unsuccessful attempt to talk to her brother in the hospital. She hasn't been to the Refuge since leaving Daniel's. All her life, she has secretly suspected that everything you learn to want, everything you really make your own, gets taken from you. Now she knows why: nothing *is* your own. Last night she dreamt herself aloft, high above the oxbows of the Platte. Crusts of ice studded the flats, and stubble filled the fields. No large life of any sort, anywhere. All large creatures were gone. But life was everywhere—microscopic, vegetative, humming in the hive. Voices without language, voices she recognized, calling on her to see. She woke refreshed and filled with baffling confidence.

Now she preps for a venture outside, borrowing Bonnie's best non-pioneer dress, a sage-green fitted silk that could cause whiplash on Chicago's Gold Coast. She even gets Bonnie to theme her makeup. An older, grimmer Bonnie holds color chips up to Karin's face, studying them through squinted eyes.

Touching the girl's elbow, Karin asks, "You remember painting Mark's toes when he was still in Trauma?"

"Frostbite," Bonnie remembers.

"Frostbite," Karen agrees. "Do me."

They work together, like technicians. Bonnie steps back to admire her handiwork. "Killer," she says, which must be good. "Armed and dangerous. You could eat men like a frog eats flies. He won't know what hit him. Killer, I'm telling you."

Karin sits still and cries. She takes the crestfallen makeup artist and hugs her. Bonnie hugs back, clutching, an accomplice before the fact.

Then Karin is downtown, the same spot where she first flushed out Robert Karsh. Early evening, and his office empties onto the street. He's among the last. When he glides out the door and sees her, he stops in surprise. She turns and closes the distance to him, trying not to think, humming the word *killer* to herself, a protecting spell. He comes up to meet her. His chin is out, and his eyes are everywhere.

"Jesus," he says. "Look at you." He wants her, even now, even after what she's done. Maybe more, because of it. He wants to take her off behind the burning bushes and do it right there, like lower vertebrates. "Well," he says. "Your friend Daniel seems to have gotten the Development Council's attention." He doesn't need to add: *mine, too*. He smiles, his scary, wholesale smile. The smile is so *Karsh* she can't help smiling back. "You gave away the whole show. Spilled pretty much everything I told you in confidence. Okay: maybe not everything. But all the business stuff." He's still smiling, as if at his little Ashley, the girl Karin has never been allowed to meet. "Maybe this was *all* about business, huh? From the beginning?"

"Robert?" Her voice flies a little, until she rides it down. "I wish I could take credit for that. I wish I'd been that smart."

"Well, you've certainly set us back. Complicated the game. Major personal embarrassment, for me. A scramble to keep my ass out of the fire. Hey: keeps things interesting. The price of learning what I mean to you."

She shakes her head. "You always knew that. Better than I did."

"But, hey. If this project doesn't happen right in Farview, we'll do it somewhere downstream. You think you're going to stop us from *building*? You think growth is just going to go away? Who are you? You aren't even . . ."

"I'm not even anyone," she says.

"I didn't say that. I'm just saying that whatever the community needs is going to get built. Eventually. If not next year . . ."

Too self-evident even to counter. Even now, his eyes say, *Let's go somewhere. Get a room. Twenty minutes.* Silk dress, doing its job. And she feels nothing, a nothing that fills and lifts her. She stands dead still, unable to stop shaking her head. "I erased myself for you." Bewildered that she did; bewildered that she still might. She looks at him, scavenging for her past. "You think you knew me. You think you know me!" Years of effort, and she might pass him on the street and not feel a peep. Karsh, too: mimetic Capgras, a smile that fails to acknowledge anything, standing there grinning like he's just bribed the grade school teacher with an infected apple.

And still, they are connected. She turns and slices a straight line back through town, this town she hates and will never be rid of. And all down the block, at her back, she hears him calling, half amused, "Babe? Come on, Rabbit. Hey! Let's talk this out." Easy, understanding, sure she will be back, if not now, then this time next year.

They talk for longer than Weber can say. And with every answer Mark needs, Weber grows less certain. That pack of Scouts, waving faulty flashlights in the woods at night, is scattered. All his life, he has known himself to be just this makeshift troop. Only now, something undams in him, and knowing goes real.

They talk until Mark's theories start to sound plausible, until Mark believes that Weber has grasped the size of the facts. They talk until the chemicals in the IV drip dampen the activity of his synapses, calming him.

But something in him still struggles. One palm on his temples, the other on his nape. "You know, they can do anything that they want to me. Drugs. Electroshock. Even surgery, if that's what it takes. I'll happily let them inside again, if they just get it right this time. I can't live with this halfway bullshit anymore." He closes his eyes and growls like a cornered wolf. "Hate this feeling that I've made everything up. That I'm some totally invented asshole. But there's one thing I *know* I did not invent." He contorts his body, reaches to his bedside drawer, and pulls out the note. It refuses to decay; the lamination has turned it permanent. He throws it down on the sill. "I wish to God I did invent it. I wish there were no guardian. But there it is. And what in God's name are we supposed to do about it?"

Weber does nothing except wait until the chemicals take Mark, and he sleeps. Then Weber totters down the hospital hall. He sits for a moment in a glass terrarium of a waiting room, filled with individuals all promised a high-tech miracle. A girl, twenty at the outside, sits in a cushioned orange chair, reading aloud from an oversized, garish picture book to a four-year-old on her lap. "Did you ever wonder how the miracle of you began?" She reads sweetly, reassuringly. "You didn't come from monkeys. Not from some jellyfish in the sea. No! You began when God decided . . ."

He looks up, and it's as if he has willed her into being, there in front of him. The sister, in green silk. "Did you see him?" he asks. His voice sounds strange to him.

Karin shakes her head. "He's sleeping. Unconscious."

Weber nods. *Un-conscious*. Wrong, that the negation should stand for something so many billions of years older than the negated.

"Will he be all right?"

There's something in the question he can't penetrate. Will anyone? "He's safe. For now." They stand near each other, saying nothing. He sees the hundred small muscles around her eyes reading his, even as his fit to hers. "He's under the impression that he might be part bird."

She smiles in slow pain. "I know the feeling."

"He feels that the emergency room surgeons swapped . . ."

Her brusque nod cuts him off. "Old story," she says. "Not surprising, given the look of them."

She has gone demented—something in the water supply. "The surgeons?"

Her face creases like a child's, a girl who has just discovered the total hoax of words. "No, the birds."

"Ah. I've never seen them."

She looks at him, like he's just said he has never felt pleasure. She checks her watch. "Let's go," she says. "We've just time."

They hide in an abandoned pit blind as dusk comes down. They sit on an old trysting tarp she had in her trunk, she still in Bonnie's green silk dress, he in coat and tie. She's taken him to a roost that only natives know—a private farm, a secret uninhabited trespass. The pit is chilly, the field around them littered with last year's brown corn stalk stubs and waste grain. Just beyond the field, the sandy banks of the river serpentine. A few birds already gather. She folds her hands in front of her face, like a kid learning to pray. He looks at the thicket of birds a hundred yards from them, then back at her. *This is it? The mythic spectacle?*

She grins and shakes her head at his doubt. She brushes his shoulder: wait. Life is long out here. Longer than you think. Longer than you *can* think.

For a moment in the chill dusk, he lifts. The sky slips from peach to garnet to blood. A thread ripples across the light: a kettle of cranes home in from nowhere. They make a sound, prehistoric, too loud and carrying for their body size. A sound he remembers from before he hears it.

He and the woman crouch on the ground. His spine hums with cold. Another thread floats down on the still air. Then another. The fibers of bird catch and join, an unraveled cloth coming back together. Threads appear from all compass points, the sky crimson, shot through with veins of black. The wings bank and yaw, slip or skate up again, before winding back in a slow cyclone. Soon the sky fills with tributaries, a river of birds, a mirror Platte meandering through heaven. And every part of it, calling.

The birds are huge, much bigger than he imagined. Their wings pump slow and full, the long primaries arcing high above the body, then drooping well below, a shawl perpetually resettled over forgetting shoulders. Necks stretch out while legs dangle behind, and in the middle, the slight bulge of body, like a child's toy suspended between strings. A bird lands twenty feet from the blind. It shakes out its wings, a span longer than Weber. Behind this one, hundreds more fall in. And the roosting in this private field is just a sideshow, nothing compared to the climaxes in the larger sanctuaries. The calls collect and echo, a single splintering, tone-deaf chorus stretching miles in every direction, back into the Pleistocene.

He thinks: Sylvie should see this. The most natural thought in the world. Sylvie and Jess. Not Jess, but Jessie, at eight or nine, when a city of birds would have astounded her. Did he ever come close to that child? Did that self-shaping little girl deserve some more feeling father?

In threaded clumps, the birds coast back to earth. They collapse from grace into earthbound stumbling. The diminishment would be comic if it weren't so painful. A thousand floating cranes succumb to gravity. They spot the humans and carry on, deep in the constantly meandering present. For as long as there have been prairies and sandy banks and the idea of safety here, birds have gathered in these braids. This century, they graze on field corn. Next century: whatever scraps this place might still supply.

The icy ground numbs him. He jumps at the sound of her voice, from a distant planet. "Look! That one, there." He lifts his head to see. It's him, in the roadside dance house, alongside

Barbara Gillespie, wrestling his body into joy. The crane dances, weirdly deliberate. It tosses twigs into the air. It cowls its fingers and kinks itself like a rapper. Then the bird and its mate rise to the alert, necks extended, eyes on something invisibly far off, their beaks parallel, signing the air. They alternate, then synchronize, looping their calls into unison.

He locates something in the pirouetting pair. Some clue to his own dissolve. And then, in trivial telepathy, something even science could explain, she reads his thoughts: "Why did you come back? Was it for Mark? Or for her?"

He can't even play dumb.

Her grin twists into a sneer. "Everybody saw. Obvious."

"Saw what?" They can have seen nothing. He's only just seen, himself. But even his slow science converges on the obvious: the *first person* is always the last to know.

She talks to someone out in the field. "Daniel says she called him. A year ago, before Mark's accident. Asking him all sorts of questions about the Refuge. He says she's a spy. A researcher, working for the developers. Does that sound crazy to you? Like one of Mark's theories?"

He would say something if he could. He'd have a thought, and even give it, but he is slipping back down, underneath words.

She examines him, the two of them reversed, she the doctor and he the subject. "Something's happened to you."

"Yes," he says. He sees that something, thousands of it, combing the fields, a whisper away.

She closes her eyes and lies down on the frosty ground. He eases back beside her, on his side, his head in his crooked arm. He looks at her, at the open country of her, as the last amber flecks of light die, searching for the woman of a year ago. Now she looks back. "I don't know what I needed from you. Writing you about Mark. I don't know what I needed from *him*. From anyone." She flicks her palm out at the damning evidence, the bird-crammed field. What is there possibly to *need*?

She looks away, self-conscious. She sits up, points at a nearby pair: two large and agitated birds, walking with their wings out, jabbering. One bugles a melody, four notes of spontaneous surprise. The other picks up the motive and shadows it. The sound stabs him: creation chattering to itself, locking him out. True speech, beyond any but a crane's ability to decode. The speaking pair fall silent, scouring the ground for evidence. They could be detectives, or scientists. Life incommunicable, even to life.

He looks at the woman, her face lined with the same thought, as clearly as if he has put it there: What does it feel like, to be a bird?

"There," she declares, nodding at the walking pair. "That's what Mark's talking about." Her nose flares, red and raw. Her head shakes in disbelief. "They used to just unzip, and be us. Or we'd peel off our skin and go with them. Oldest story in the book." She takes his profile, but when he turns back toward her, she swings away. "The sad thing is, though, they can't love. They mate for life. Follow their partners every year for thousands of miles. Raise their young together. Fake a broken wing to lure a predator away from their chicks. Even sacrifice themselves to save their young. But no. Ask any scientist. Birds can't love. Birds don't even have a self! Nothing like us. No relation."

He can only begin to see all the things she holds against him. He would apologize, if he could speak.

The larger of the walking pair turns and fixes him. Something looks out from the prehistoric bird, a secret about him, but not his. A look of pure wildness, all the hard intelligence of simply *being* that Weber has forgotten.

But the woman is talking. She is saying things, faraway things, with great urgency. She tells him about the water wars. How the preservers have won for a moment. How they will lose, forever afterward. She has seen all the numbers, and no power exists large enough to stop them. Her face sets into an ugly mask. She shakes her arm at the staring bird, who takes fright and skims away. "How can we not want this? Just this, exactly as it is. If people only knew . . ."

But if people knew, this field would be buried in crane peepers.

"How long do you suppose we have?" she asks. "God, what is *wrong* with us? You're the expert. What *is it* in our brains that won't . . . ?"

The sky is dark now, and he can't see what she points at. Each of them sits sealed off in their own private pit blind, looking out on an unthinkably long night.

She speaks out loud, as if already there were only memory. "I remember the first time my father took us out here. We were little. Me, Mark, and my father, sitting in this field. *This* one. Early morning, before the sun was up. You have to see these creatures in the morning. The evening show is pure theater. But the morning is religion. The three of us at dawn, still happy. And my father, still the wisest man alive. I can hear him. He told us how they navigated. He was a small-plane pilot, and he loved how they followed landmarks to find this exact spot, year after year. How they recognized individual fields. 'Damn straight, cranes remember. Hang on to things like a bat hangs to a barn rafter.' And the first time I saw those birds circle up into the air and disappear, I kept looking at the sky, thinking, *Hey, me too. Take me with.* Awful feeling. Empty. Like: *Where'd I go bad?*"

Her fingers brush her eyebrows. He knows her now, the

thing in her that had once so repelled him. Her weakness. Her need to do right by the world.

"Some kind of lesson for us. His idea of fatherhood. Going on and on about blood, family, how even the birds take care of their own. Scared the crap out of both of us. He squeezed us both until it hurt, made us swear. 'If anything ever happens — and it will — you two never, *never* give up on each other.'"

These last words are so swallowed, Weber must supply them. Then she looks away, strong again, more composed than he can even fake, gazing across the wetlands, past the progress that will destroy them.

"He was wild, my father. Totally lost touch with the rest of the race. He always told me I would come to nothing. Pretty much ensured it." She turns and grabs Weber's arm in the dark. She needs him to contradict. Needs him to say it's not too late to change her life. Not too late for real work at last, the only work that matters. "If you had raised me . . . If you had raised Mark and me? Someone who knew what you know?" She might have come to this calling sooner, while there was still time.

Weber stays silent, too scared to confirm or deny. But she's already taken what she needs from him. She shakes her head at him and says, *"Unsponsored, impossible, near-omnipotent, and infinitely fragile . . ."*

He struggles to place the words, written by someone who once was him. Her face, flush with the idea, begs him to remember. If all forged, then all free. Free to play ourselves, free to impersonate, to improvise, free to image anything. Free to weave our minds through what we love. What lots we all might learn about this river. What places water might still get out and see.

He spends the night awake in his rented cubicle, his brain on

539

fire. His cell phone rings twice, but he doesn't take it. He stares at the hell-red LED of the bedside alarm, watching the minutes hang. He will go to Dedham Glen, ask to see her file. No: they would deny him access. He isn't authorized. He could ask her supervisor: When did she come to this facility? What job did she do before this one? But the supervisor would just stonewall him, or worse.

He's out in front of her bungalow at 4:00 a.m. He sits in the rental in total darkness, all the time in the world to decide not to torch his life. But then, it's burned already—Chickadee, Conscience Bay, Sylvie, the lab, his writing, Famous Gerald— all consumed, months ago. He cannot even fake the role now. Not even his wife would believe the act. He wills himself downward, falling. There *is* a need to be no one, one that will forever hide its precise location from neuroscience's probes. He steps from the car and wanders to her stoop, into the chaos he has made.

Barbara comes puffed and bleary to the door, the first hint of awareness on her. She tilts her head and smiles, almost expecting him. And the last, solid part of him dissolves in air. "You okay?" she asks, inviting and uncertain. "I didn't know you were back."

His head rocks, as easy as breathing.

Wordless, she lets him in. Only when she flicks on the dim overhead light in a bare foyer—an abandoned vacation cottage on the shores of a northern lake, circa 1950—does she ask, "Have you seen Mark?"

"Yes. Have you?"

She drops her head. "I've been afraid to."

But that can't be. The boy-man's most devoted caregiver, who has seen him in far worse shape. He catches her eye. Her look is renegade, running out over her left shoulder. She's wearing a green-and-red plaid flannel men's bathrobe out of which her legs and arms protrude like fresh mistakes. She puts a hand to her puffy face. "Am I awful?"

She is beautiful, the beaten kind of beauty that guts him.

She leads him into a tiny cupboard kitchen where, wobbly, she puts a kettle of water on the gas ring. He hovers next to her. "There isn't much time," he says. "I've something to show you. Before the sun rises."

Her hands snake up and push his chest, first gently, then hard. She nods. "I'll just get dressed. Please . . ." Her palms extend, offering the three small rooms to him.

There's nothing to take possession of. The kitchen has service for one, a ragged collection of dented pans and jelly jars. The table and chairs in the front room could only have come from an auction. Oval rag rug and crocheted curtains. A heavy, old oak farmstead hutch and matching writing desk. Above the desk, taped to the wall, is a well-thumbed index card, written in pen: *But I do nothing upon myself, and yet I am mine own Executioner.*

On the desk sits a paperback: Eiseley's *The Immense Journey*. The evening reading of this nurse's aide. The back cover identifies the author as a local boy, born and raised in the bend of the Platte. Scores of adhesive colored arrows stick to the pages. He flips to the last: *The secret, if one may paraphrase a savage vocabulary, lies in the egg of night.*

Next to the book sits a portable disc player and ear buds. Alongside the player, a short stack of discs. He picks up the top one: Monteverdi. She chooses this moment to come too quickly out of the bedroom, rushing to button her cobalt cotton blouse. She sees him fingering the disc. She's caught; her eyebrows pinch, guilty. "The Vespers of 1610. But for you, 1595."

He holds it out to her, accusing. "You misled me."

"No! I bought that . . . since our evening. A keepsake. Believe me, I can't make heads or tales of it."

He places it back on top of the stack without looking. He doesn't want to see the other discs. His belief can't bear more tests.

She crosses the room and circles him. Inside her arms, he comes apart. A fist at the base of his brain stem opens into a palm. He surges on the dopamine, the spikes of endorphins, his chest jerking. The wildest research in the most reckless journal . . . He has wrecked himself, and it's good beyond saying. No writer, no researcher, no lecturer, no husband, no father. *He* has precipitated out. Nothing left but sensation, the warm, light pressure against his ribs.

The room is cold and every inch of her burns. He slips down into limbic back alleys, corners that survived when the massive neocortex came through like a superhighway. He feels his skin against her hands, skin too white and papery, his bare arms a blotchy mess of veins, his flanks rude humps. One heartbeat, and he's strange to his body, all those nested ghosts invisible to this woman who has never seen him any way but this.

Then stranger still: he does not care how she sees him. Does not want her to see him as anything but what he well and truly is: hollow and graceless, stripped of authority. Borderless, same as anyone.

"Wait," he says. "There's something you need to see." Something not his. *The evening show is pure theater. But the morning is religion.*

They drive back out to Karin's field in the first hint of dawn. He finds the way there, lefts and rights stored in his body. The night before has scattered. But the flock is still there, wading. He and this woman take their place in the blind, not ten feet from the nearest clump of birds. They strain for silence, but their movements alert those cranes left on guard. Awareness spreads through the flock. The cranes stir, singly and together, then settle when the danger passes. In the growing light, they begin the ordinary stutters of morning, flaring up here and there in tentative bursts of ballet.

"I told you," she whispers. "Everything dances."

One by one, the birds test the air, first in short hops, like scraps in the breeze. Then thousands of them lift up in flood. The beating surface of the world rises, a spiral calling upward on invisible thermals. Sounds carry them all the way skyward, clacks and wooden rattles, rolling, booming, bugling, clouds of living sound. Slowly, the mass unfurls in ribbons and disperses into thin blue.

What joy there is in this life. Lifting past us always. What pointless joy.

He hears his own voice coming out of him, broken counterpoint to this honking morning chorus. *"Not to be separated, not by the thinnest curtain shut out from the measure of the stars."*

"What is that?" she asks.

He struggles to call it back. *"Innerness—what is it if not amplified sky, shot through with birds and deep with the winds of homecoming?"*

A book of Rilke he bought for Sylvie, lifetimes ago, right out of school, when they still made time for pointless elegies.

"The scientist is a poet," this woman says.

But he is neither. He's no profession he can recognize. Nothing he ever thought he might become. And this woman: What is this nurse's aide? A woman so alone she wants even him.

She puts her hand down inside the collar of his coat. He touches her back. They trace the skin, the trap between them.

543

His hands shake against her breasts, and she would let him, would lead him forward into everything, right here in this bird-filled field. Her rib cage presses against his palm. They blunder into something startling to them both. Their mouths are on each other and thinking goes. Everything goes except this first need.

Something huge and white streaks across the field. He jerks up, and she with him. He spots it first, but she identifies. "My God. A whooper." Ghosts in that flash of light, some private terror. She squeezes his arm, a tourniquet. "We can't be seeing this. One hundred and sixty of them left. Jesus, that's one!"

The ghost glides shining across the fields. Neither can breathe. He grasps at a last hope. "That was it. What was in the road. He said he saw a column of white . . ." He studies her face, science wanting so badly to be confirmed.

She follows the bird, afraid to look at Weber. She has the chance now, to clear everything. Instead, she says, "You think?"

They watch the phantom bird until it vanishes through a line of trees. They crouch and watch, long after the field empties.

Both are frozen and caked in mud. She pulls him back to her, mindless again. They flood each other, waves of oxytocin and a savage bonding. Release—vanishing in mid-prairie, lifted free of everything—hovers just out of his reach.

A broken laugh comes from too nearby, something not belonging to the Platte's dawn chorus. A cricket chirr, months too early. It chirps again, from inside his shed jacket at his feet. He glances at her, bewildered. Her look tells him: your phone. He fumbles to find the pocket that hides the device. He looks at the number on the caller ID, the first time ever. He shuts the ringer off and folds back into her. Everything will be panic, from now on. Strange as birth. He would write it up—first case ever of contagious Capgras—if he could still write. He seems

544

to be nearing, and she is taking him. Thoughts flow through him like a brook over pebbles, none of them his. There comes the emptiness of arrival. Then there is just holding, and bracing for endless vertigo.

Wordless, they head back to her car.

"Which way?" she asks.

No choice, really. "West."

No other compass for the two of them. She drives at random. They cross some dry stream. "Oregon Trail," she says. Scars in the land confirm her, despite the century and a half of erosion.

They drive for miles in silence. He waits for her to say what at any moment he could make her say. But he is perjured now, too, and deserves nothing. When they get light-headed, they stop for something to eat in a town called Broken Bow. "Another ghost town," she says. "Most of the towns out here peaked a hundred years ago. The place is emptying out. Heading back to frontier."

"How do you know these things?" He knows already, how she knows.

She dodges. "Around here? Only the dying stick around."

They buy water and fruit and bread and carry it into the sandhills. They picnic on a dune that drifts downwind even as they sit on it. Some part of them is always touching. The land is abandoned, a worldwide contagion. In the middle distance, the pitch-bending minor chords of an endless freight.

She touches his ear in surprise. "I just remembered last night's dream. How beautiful! I dreamt we were making music. You and me, Mark and Karin, I think. I was playing the cello. I've never touched a cello. But the music coming out . . . unbelievable! How can the brain do that? I mean, pretending to play an instrument: fine. But who was composing that music? In real time? I can't even *read* music. The most gorgeous harmonies I've ever heard. And *I* must have written it."

He has no answer, and he gives her as much. All he can do is touch her ear back. His dream last night was one he hasn't had for months: a man, plunging headlong, frozen in the air in front of a smoking column of white.

They sit in the middle of a drifting nowhere. His phone vibrates in his pocket. If the thing rings here, it could ring in outer space. He knows who it is before he answers. The ID confirms him: Jess. His daughter, who only calls in extremity and on holidays. He has to answer. Before he can even ask what's wrong, Jess howls at him. "I just talked to Mom. What the fuck do you think you're doing?"

He can't attach himself. He feels every mile between here and any coast. He says, "I don't know," perhaps several times. It only makes his daughter crazier. *Grow up*, she screams. Perhaps she is having an insulin attack. The signal starts to die. "Jess? Jess. I can't hear you. Listen to me. I'll call you back. I will call you . . ."

When he hangs up, Barbara is still there. She cradles his cheek, tentatively, and he lets her. The first of his punishments. Her hand says: Whatever you need. Closer or farther. Yours to keep inventing or to send away.

He is a case he has forgotten until this moment: the woman with the shattered insula, lost in asomatognosia. Now and then, for brief periods, all sense of her body disappeared. Skeleton and muscles, limbs and torso would fade to nothing. And still, without a body, she kept to the lie, believing that kapo in the temporo-parieto-occipital junction, that lackey of the system always ready to take charge.

They drive some more, the only thing for it. Another

dozen miles down the road, she says, "There's a place up ahead I've always wanted to see."

"How far?"

Her lips pucker as she calculates. "A hundred miles?"

There's nothing left of him to object. He points through the windshield, some invisible target.

She grows careless behind the wheel, even giddy. They have no future, and even less past. For two hours, they say nothing about themselves. Nor do they talk much about Mark. The closest they come is when she asks him to tell her ten essential things that neuroscience knows for certain. He should be able to list dozens. But something has happened to his list. Those that are essential no longer feel certain. And those that are certain can't possibly be essential.

He sees their destination from a distance, rising up out of a field of winter wheat. Salisbury Plain. Megalithic monument. A wrong turn somewhere, but here they are. She laughs as he makes it out. "This is it. Carhenge."

The huge gray stones turn into automobiles. Three dozen spray-painted junkers stood on end or draped as lintels across one another. A perfect replica. They are out of the car, walking around the standing circle. He manages a pained imitation of mirth. Here it is: the ideal memorial for the blinding skyrocket of humans, natural selection's brief experiment with awareness. And everywhere, thousands of sparrows nest in the rusted axles.

They dine in nearby Alliance, at a place called the Longhorn Smokehouse. A television suspended above their corner booth breaks the news. Operation Iraqi Freedom has begun. War has been so long in coming that Weber feels only mild déjà vu. They watch the cycling, impenetrable footage, the president, looping over and over: *May God bless our country and all who defend her.* He watches her stony face as she watches the screen. She watches as only a reporter can. He has known for some time. Only now he sees her, unmistakable. Her voice catches a little when she talks. "Mark is right, you know. The whole place, a substitute. I mean: Is this country anyplace you recognize?"

They sit too long, watching too many frenzied reports packed to exploding with no content. When they get back into the car, the light is already fading.

"Should we find some place to stay?" She doesn't look at him. She means shelter, but shelter is long gone.

He wants nothing but the blank slate. Erased from what he has done, from what he is doing. Nothing waits for him anywhere. *Find some place to stay*: yes, night by night, foraging, the two of them, even with the worst confirmed, even knowing about her what he now knows. No more reporting from a distance. No more case histories: only make himself as culpable as she. Yet the words out of his mouth kill even this possibility. "We need to go back."

She can't mask the half-second of fear. Her shoulders flinch in the snare. "Oh, Heart!" she says. Whose name is that? Someone else's endearment. Some earlier escape that she mistakes him for. She does not want him; she only wants to avoid detection. She starts to object. "My house is so small . . ."

And the earth so large. "We need to," he repeats. Yes, life is a fiction. But whatever it might mean, the fiction is steerable.

She knows what is happening. Still, she pretends. She starts up the car and points it southeast. After a few miles, her voice pure invitation, she asks, "What are you thinking?"

He shakes his head. He can't do this in words. His silence unnerves her. She grips the wheel, her face braced for the worst.

He grazes her upper arm with his knuckles. "I was thinking, I feel I've known you my whole life."

Her face turns to his and breaks. She doesn't believe him, but she will take it. Some part of her knows, already, where he's bringing them. Some part already suffers the sentence, before he levels it.

He chooses that moment to ask, "What story were you covering? When you first came here."

They ride an awful mile in silence. Something in him hopes she'll say nothing. Something in him doesn't want the facts. He feels what he first knew in her, the dread just beneath her fake composure. Out of the corner of his eye, she is someone else. Like that woman he examined once, call her Hermia, whose only symptom was seeing children in her left visual field, even hearing their laughter, only to see them disappear when she turned to look at them . . .

"What do you mean?" she asks at last. Her voice is bright enamel on ashes.

He has no right to force her. He is not justice; he is duplicity itself. "Who were you working for?" No real need to know. But a proven neurological phenomenon: activity in the verbal center has a suppressing effect on pain.

She grips the wheel and steers the ruler-straight road. "Dedham Glen," she says. "I worked for them every day for a year. I cleared twelve hundred dollars a month."

At last the anomalies on Mark's chart make sense to him. He knows what happened. "Karin's friend," he says. "The conservationist. You interviewed him over the phone, a year ago."

Her eyes are a mess and her red nostrils quiver like a rabbit's. Something still tenacious in her frees that last little part of him that did not yet love her. "Water," she says. Matter of fact. Journalistic. "The story was about water." They roll another quarter mile in the dropping dark. She speaks into a machine. "Most stories will be, soon." She rallies, shakes her hair, turns the full force of her emptiness on him. She shoots for a fashion-magazine insouciance. It would repel him, but for that thing he recognizes in her, and shares. That desperate hope of evading discovery. "I'll tell you everything. How much do you want to know?"

He wants to know nothing. Even now, he would disappear with her, someplace words can't reach.

"A journalist," she tells the windshield. Another three-street town flashes by. "Producer for Cablenation News. You know: find a colorful topic, work it up, conduct the groundwork, screen the interviews, cull the research. I always tried to . . . be as big as the story. I always tried to dig, to immerse in the material. That's what killed me, I think. I'd been an editor for seven years, producer for three and a half. I could have moved up to a major desk, coasted until they turned me out to pasture."

He stares at the age marks in her neck that he has never noticed. The tendons flare under her clenched jaw. Her face will crack open and a grown thing emerge.

"I was in trouble. Flameout, they called it. It should never have started. I was superwoman. I mean, Jesus: I'd been at Waco, with those rows and rows of lawn chairs, all the good American citizens turning out to watch the human barbecue. I produced a series on the crèche babies at Oklahoma City. I did Heaven's Gate—three successive days of collaborative suicide. Nothing bothered me. I could tell it all. Walked around lower Manhattan, sticking a video camera in people's faces after the towers. A week after that, I started to lose it. We're out of control, aren't we? And we're pulling everything down on top of us."

She still needs him to contradict. What she has always needed from him. And even here, he fails her.

"My boss made me see a pill peddler, who put me on the same stuff the rest of the nation is already taking. It smoothed me out a little. But I lost my edge. Got dull and sloppy. I couldn't get the job done anymore. They took me off news and put me on human interest. Harmless pieces. Pathetic. The pauper custodian who dies and leaves a million dollars to the local community college. Twins reunited after forty years, and still behaving identically. That's what the trip to Nebraska was supposed to be. A little rest and recuperation. A can't-miss, please-everyone story, one that even I could handle."

"The cranes," Weber says. The only story out here. Endless return.

On a flat, featureless stretch three miles out of town, she turns to look at him. Her face searches his, bargaining. "They wanted Disney. I tried to make it bigger. So I dug a little. It didn't take much to find the water. I dug a little more. I learned that we were going to waste that river, no matter what I wrote. I could tell a story that broke people down and made them ache to change their lives, and it would make no difference. That water is already gone."

Kearney appears, an orange dome of light on the horizon. He waits for her to finish. Only when she glances over her right shoulder, a wild, fugitive, pleading look, does he realize she's done. "So you quit," he says. "And became a nurse's aide?"

Her shoulders jerk. But recovery comes fast enough. "They took me as a volunteer, at first. I had some experience . . . years ago. In high school. I got the nurse's aide license within three months. It's not . . . you know, brain science."

Even now, she will not tell him. Not by herself. So he tells her. "You knew they would be sending him there?"

Her eyes steel. She grows brutally calm. "Is this some kind of theory? What do you think I am?"

I is just a diversion. His science has known that for some time. He has suspected her, long before Daniel's positive ID. Maybe since the day he saw her. He sensed her deception at once, as she sensed his: the lie that joined them, that drew him to her. But here is the part he still can't understand. "I think I must have seen you once before. Some years ago. When your network interviewed . . ."

"Yes," she says, controlled, making the right onto Highway 10, just outside town. She speaks like a producer again. A journalist who might report any story. "So why did you keep coming back? To test your memory? You thought you'd use me. A little thrill, a little mystery. Public hostility was breaking you down. Take a quick escape trip; rewrite your life. Out-of-body experience. Expose a crime. Entrapment. Then pass judgment on me."

He shakes his head, for both of them. Something bigger than judgment brought him back. The winds of homecoming. Now, worse than ever, even as she turns cold and horrible, he knows her. Her face flares and she slams the wheel with her palms, her eyes everywhere, flushed into the open. With a flick of his head, he will force her to turn, not toward her bungalow, not toward an anonymous motel room. Back to where the story started. When he finally speaks, his voice isn't his. "I don't know what you ever could have felt . . . what I might have been to you. But I know how you feel for that boy."

At the second-to-last traffic light before Good Samaritan, she sees where he is forcing her. She reaches out her right hand and grabs him. One last preemptive seduction: we could still escape, the two of us. Disappear somewhere on that long river.

He thinks of what she has already lost: her career, her community, such friends as she had, a year of her life, and as many more as the boy might want to take. It's not enough. "Tell him," he says. "You know you need to."

552

She turns her head, strewing explanations. "I tried," she claims. "I would have. But he didn't recognize . . ."

"Which time?"

All pretense between them dies. Stripped bare, they know each other. She spits venom. "Why are you doing this? Am I another *case*? What do you want from me? You smug, self-righteous, self-protecting little . . ."

He nods in recognition. But he has grown light, empty, a committee of millions. "You can do this." He looks down into the fact, the one thing left that he knows for certain. "You can do this. I'll go with you."

A cold February night on a dark Nebraska road. She is alone in the car, driving at random. Hours ago, she filmed the evening spectacle. But the cameras failed to capture the full force of the otherwordly gathering. Tonight's birds have shaken her so badly she can't return to her hotel. The crew has long ago disbursed, and she is alone, at loose ends, as brittle and flimsy as she felt in New York last fall. Maybe she has gone off the medication too quickly. Or maybe it's the cranes, those threads floating in, massing and trumpeting, misled by millions of years of memory. The end will be instant. They'll never know what hit them.

She herself would never have known, except in following this story. The silent, invisible new war on wetlands: she has hunted down the details, background for this report. Her species is running amok, and now more than ever, it's every life for itself. Her nerves are jagged, the rental is suffocating, and this straight slash of road unnerves her. She has tried for hours to calm herself, sitting in a restaurant, then a movie theater, walking through the dead downtown, driving these deserted country roads, and still she's in no state to sleep. If she can make it just a few more hours, just until dawn, and the birds again . . .

Even the ancient polyphony coming out of the car speakers shreds her. She shuts it off, her fingers frenzied. But silence on this black and freezing February night is worse. She can take only thirty seconds of it before she flips the radio back on. She trembles up and down the dial, trying to land on something solid. She finds a station and fixes on it, no matter the content. It's talk, and only talk might help her now.

Some woman's satin voice crawls up intimate into her ear. For a moment, it sounds like Christian revival—no believer left behind. But these words are worse than religion. Facts. The woman's voice recites a litany, somewhere between a shopping list and a poem. *It took the human race two and a half million years to reach a billion people. It took 123 years to add a second billion. We hit three billion, thirty-three years later. Then in fourteen years, then thirteen, then twelve . . .*

Shaking, she pulls over onto the shoulder. Alone in this nowhere with these numbers. A storm breaks somewhere in her head. Signals surge, triggering one another. Nothing in evolution prepares her for this. Sheets of electricity cascade through her, fact-induced seizures, and when the headlights appear in her rearview mirror, the most rational thing in the world is to open the door and step out into them.

Now she enters the hospital again. The year before, they stopped her outside the sealed ward. *You're his sister?* One unthinking nod of the head was enough to get her through. This time no one challenges her. Anyone at all is free to go see him. Even the person who first put him there.

He is sitting up in bed, struggling with an old, familiar book. She can tell by his posture that the fog is lifting. His face lights up at the sight of her, that mix of ideal and instinctual gratitude. But it fades as fast, with a look at her face.

What's happened? he asks. Who died?

She stands at the foot of his bed. Her stance alone might trigger his memory. That trace is still in there, in the weights of his synapses. But still, she must tell him. Her tracks were first. The car that was behind him was in front of him. *She* was in the road. He rolled his truck to keep from killing her.

How? he asks. Why? The pieces won't fit together.

She is alive because of him. He is brain-damaged because of her.

You are my guardian? *You* wrote the note?

No, she tells him. Not me.

She stands in front of him again in memory, only hours after the first time, out in the empty road. He is still intact, still responsive. Strung with tubes, but not comatose yet. That will come later, with the excitotoxicity. The shock of this visit will bring it on. Now, as she stands by his bed in the trauma unit, he recognizes. He looks on her, terrified. She has come back, the white pillar he swerved to avoid. She's some supernatural creature, rising up from death. But her face is molten, and choked sounds stream out of her. He recoils before he realizes: she's begging for forgiveness.

He tries to tell her. Nothing comes out his throat but a dry hiss. She leans down to his mouth, and still nothing. His right hand scratches in the air, gesturing for paper and pen. She fishes these out of her purse and hands them to him. Already half-paralyzed by pressure rising in his skull, his bruised lobes swelling against the fixed bone, in a damaged hand that isn't his, he draws the words:

I am No One
but Tonight on North Line Road
GOD led me to you
so You could Live
and bring back someone else.

He fumbles the note into her fingers. As she reads it, a blinding spike hits his right hemisphere. He falls back onto the bed, his cry cut short. Then he is still.

She has destroyed him twice. In reptile panic, she drops the note on the bedside table and vanishes.

His anguish comes on, too stunned to stop itself. Even as she pleads with him, his eyes deny her. In his stare, the saint disintegrates and she turns back into herself.

You let me hunt for a year, and never said shit. How could you? You were my . . . You would have done anything . . .

She stands in front of him, erased. She has lost even the right to defend herself. He tears the note out of his bedside drawer and waves it in the air, slapping the stricken handwriting.

If that's what happened . . . what the fuck am I doing with this? Get it away from me.

He throws the scrap of laminated paper at her. It falls to the floor. She bends down and clutches it to her.

This is yours. Your curse, not mine.

Her mouth works, asking, *How? Who?* But no sound emerges.

His rage bursts. *You're the one who's supposed to go do this. Go bring back someone.*

Someone stands mute in the doorway, brought back by a note that will forever circulate. *So you might live.* And now that curse is his.

PART FIVE

AND BRING BACK SOMEONE ELSE

As for men, those myriad little detached ponds with their own swarming corpuscular life, what were they but a way that water has of going about beyond the reach of rivers?

—Loren Eiseley, *The Immense Journey*, "The Flow of the River"

What does a bird remember? Nothing that anything else might say. Its body is a map of where it has been, in this life and before. Arriving at these shallows once, the crane colt knows how to return. This time next year it will come back through, pairing off for life. The year after next: here again, feeding the map to its own new colt. Then one more bird will recall just what birds remember.

The yearling crane's past flows into the now of all living things. Something in its brain learns this river, a word sixty million years older than speech, older even than this flat water. This word will carry when the river is gone. When the surface of the earth is parched and spoiled, when life is pressed down to near-nothing, this word will start its slow return. Extinction is short; migration is long. Nature and its maps will use the worst that man can throw at it. The outcome of owls will orchestrate the night, millions of years after people work their own end. Nothing will miss us. Hawks' offspring will circle above the overgrown fields. Skimmers and plovers and sandpipers will nest in the thousand girdered islands of Manhattan. Cranes or something like them will trace rivers again. When all else goes, birds will find water.

When Karin Schluter enters her brother's room, the man who has been denying her is gone. In his place, a Mark she has never seen sits in a chair in striped pajamas, reading a paperback with a picture of a prairie on the cover. He looks up as if she's late for a longstanding appointment.

"It's you," he tells her. "You're here." His tongue cups the roof of his mouth, the first half of a K. But a shudder passes through him, and he turns away.

The muscles of her face revolt. A wave breaks over her. He is back again; he all but knows her. The thing she has needed all these months, worse than anything. The reunion she has dreamed about for more than a year. But this is nothing like she has imagined. The return is too seamless, too gradual in coming.

He looks up at her, changed in a way she can't identify. He grimaces. "What took you so long?" She crumples on him, pulls his neck up into her face. Rapids course between them. "Don't wet me," he says. "I've bathed already today." He pulls her head off him and holds it between his hands. "Jesus. Look at you. Some things never change."

She has to stare back for a second before the difference hits her. "God, Mark. You're wearing glasses."

He takes them off to inspect them. "Yeah. They're not mine. Just borrowed them from the guy next door." He replaces them and lays the book down on the windowsill on top of another. *A Sand County Almanac.* "Been boning up."

She knows the copy. It shouldn't be here. "Where did you get that? Who gave that to you?" More bite than she intends. Despite herself: brother and sister again, too soon.

He looks at the book, as if for the first time. "Who do you

think gave it to me? Your boyfriend." He turns to her, expanding. "Complicated guy. But he's got a lot of intriguing theories."

"Theories? About what?"

"He thinks we are all hosed. That we've all gone schiz or something. Kind of out there, wouldn't you say?"

The medication is working, the mild shocks, but so gradually there is almost no threshold. The same spin-doctor subsystem that cut him out without his knowing now blinds him to his own return. She watches him turn back into Mark, old Mark, before her appalled eyes.

"We've screwed up down here, so your man Danny is looking into Alaska."

She sits down in a chair next to him, arms across her chest to still them. "Yes. I've heard."

"Getting himself a new job. Be with the cranes all summer long, on their breeding grounds." He shakes his head at the riddle of everything living. "He's had it with us all, hasn't he?"

She starts to explain, then leaves it at "Yes."

"Doesn't want to be around, when we finally wreck the place."

Her throat closes and her eyes bitter up. She just nods.

He rolls on his side, his fist up to his ear. Afraid to ask. "You going with him?"

She should have long ago habituated to this pain. "No," she tells him. "I don't think so."

"Where you going, then? Home, I suppose?"

Her brain is loose and feral. She can say nothing.

"Sure," he says. "Back to Siouxland. Sioux City Sue. So sue me already."

"I'm staying, Mark. The Refuge says they can still use me. They're a little shorthanded, now." Water is not done with her.

561

He looks off, as if reading his words printed on the sealed window. "Makes sense, I guess. With Danny gone. Hey— somebody has to be him, if he won't."

So this is how it ends. So gradually that neither of them can feel the gears catch. She wants him to shake free all at once, to rise from his fever dream and see where they've been. But he'll crush her again, this time from the other direction. Claim he knew who she was, all along. No firmness floods back into her. If anything, the whole structure seems even flimsier, with no injury to blame.

He stretches out his legs and crosses them, the imitation of repose. "So is Cain going to the slammer, or something? No, I forgot. Totally innocent. Know what they should do with that guy? They should send him to the next Iraq. Use him as a hostage." He looks up, uncomprehending. "It was Barbara. Barbara out there, all along."

He is six again, terrified. And she is everywhere, trying to comfort him. For once, he lets her, so fully broken. He squeezes his forehead, then shakes it. He covers his eyes with his hands.

"You know about all this?" She nods. "You know it was her?" He grasps his skull, the source of all confusion. She nods again. "But you didn't know . . . before?"

She shakes her head hard. "No one knew."

He tries to figure this. "And you were here . . . all along?"

He collapses into himself, not wanting an answer. When he pulls himself together again enough to talk, his words stun her.

"She says she's finished. Says she's nothing, now."

She flares up, insulted that her brother should still care. Disgusted that the woman should give up on them, having come this far. More fraudulence. More wasted godliness.

"Jesus Christ," she spits. "A woman with her skills! Just because she fucked up, does she think the world can't use her? We're down to gallons here. Hours and ounces. And she's going to roll over and die?"

Mark looks at her, bewildered. Some possibility lifts him up. His own loss means nothing. The accident gives him this. "Ask her," he begs. Afraid to suggest even this little.

"Not me. I'll never ask that woman for anything again."

He sits up, clenched in the terror of animals. "You gotta ask her to work for you. I'm not just saying. This is my *life* we're talking about." He slows himself and breathes. He squeezes his eyes again. He points apologetically at the IV drip. "Man! I need to get back in the driver's seat, here. What are they doing to me? Mr. Emotion all of a sudden. With the shit they've got figured out now? They could probably turn anyone into anyone else."

It no longer seems to her like a delusion. Tomorrow will be worse.

He looks at her, forgetting everything but the immediate need. He circles her forearm with his fingers, measuring. "You haven't been eating."

"I have."

"Food?" he asks, skeptically. "*She's* not that thin."

"*Who?*"

"Come on! Don't give me *who*. My sister." And at her flash of panic, he laughs clear and deep. "Would you look at you! Relax. Just busting your chops."

Mark leans back in the chair, stretches out his black cross-trainers, weaves his hands behind his head. It's like he's sixty-five, retired. In three months, her brother will be gone again, or his sister will, someplace the other won't be able to follow. But for a little while, now, they know each other, because of their time away.

"At least somebody else is sticking around. That's what I'm doing. Hang where you know. Where else can you go, with all hell breaking loose?"

Her nostrils quiver and her eyes burn. She tries to say *nowhere*, but she can't.

"I mean, how many homes does one person get?" He waves his hand toward the gray window. "It's not such a bad place to come back to."

"Best place on earth," she says. "Six weeks, every year."

They sit for a while, not exactly talking. She can have him for her own, recuperating, for one minute more. But he grows agitated again. "This is what scares me: if I could go so long, thinking . . . ? Then how can we be sure, even now . . . ?"

He looks up anxiously, to see her crying. Frightened, he draws back. But when she doesn't stop, he reaches over and shakes her arm. He tries to rock it, at a loss for anything that might calm her. He keeps talking, sing-song, meaningless, as to a little girl. "Hey. I know how you're feeling. Rough days, for us two. But look!" He twists her around to the plate-glass window—a flat, overcast, Platte afternoon. "It's not all so bad, huh? Just as good, in fact. In some ways, even better."

She fights to retrieve her voice. "What do you mean, Mark? As good as what?"

"I mean, us. You. Me. Here." He points out the window, approvingly: the Great American Desert. The inch-deep river. Their next of kin, those circling birds. "Whatever you call all this. Just as good as the real thing."

There is an animal perpendicular to all the others. One that flies at right angles to the seasons. He makes the check-in, getting through security on instinct. Navigates on muscle memory. Only the drone of automatic reminders focuses him: *Passengers are required to accompany their baggage at all times. Government regulations prohibit . . .*

The airports are thick with war. In the waiting area in Lincoln, television monitors assault him. The twenty-four-hour news program forever loops its twenty-four seconds of news, and he can't look away. *Day Three*, the deep bass keeps intoning, over synthesized brass, at every segment break. Magic drawing boards, tellustrators, computerized maps with movable battalions, and retired generals doing the play-by-play. Embedded journalists, prevented from reporting facts, pour out meandering speculation. All other world news stops.

In Chicago, more of the same: A taxi drives up to a checkpoint north of a city that may or may not be under occupation control. The driver waves for help. Four soldiers make the mistake of approaching. Even on his sixth time through the story, Weber sits transfixed, for the seventh time might end differently.

Airborne again, dragging back east in the skewed flyway, he grows transparent, thinner than film. A voice says, *Please do not move about the cabin or congregate in the aisles.* He grasps at the words, a life jacket. Something in his species is cut loose. The boy-man was right: Capgras truer than this constant smoothing-out of consciousness. He had a patient once— Warren, in *The Country of Surprise*—a thirty-two-year-old day-trader and weekend rock climber who rolled down the face of a steep ravine and landed on his forehead. Coming from his coma, Warren emerged into a world peopled by monks, soldiers, fashion models, movie villains, and creatures half human and half animal, all of whom spoke to him in the most natural way. Weber would destroy every copy of every word that bears his name for a chance to tell Warren's story again, now that he knows what he's talking about.

He is surrounded. Even the sealed cabin around him has grown septic with life. Everything is animate, green and encroaching. Dozens of millions of species seethe around him, few of them visible, even fewer named, ready to try anything once, every possible cheat and exploitation, just to keep being. He stares at his shaking hands, whole rain forests of bacteria. Insects burrow deep inside this plane's wiring. Seeds abide in the cargo hold. Fungus under the cabin's vinyl lining. Outside his little window flap, frozen in the airless air, archaea, superbugs, and extremophiles live on nothing, in darkness, below zero, simply copying. Every code that has stayed alive until now is more brilliant than his subtlest thought. And when his thoughts die, more brilliant still.

The man in the seat next to him, debating all the way to eastern Ohio, at last summons up the courage to ask, "Don't I recognize you?"

Weber flinches, a lopsided, phantom grin stolen from one of his patients. "I don't think so."

"Sure. The brain guy."

"No," Weber says.

The stranger examines him, suspiciously. "Sure. *The Man Who Mistook His Life for a . . .*"

"Not me," Weber insists. "I'm in reclamation."

Stewardesses skitter up and down the aisle. A passenger across from him scoops mashed animal into her giant mouth. Weber's body crumples inside his stain-wrecked suit. His thoughts skim like water striders. Nothing is left of him except these new eyes.

Inside his own teeming head, the last day's images come home to roost. In his seat behind the wing, Weber plays the last scene repeatedly—reframing, rethreading, returning. Mark in his room at Good Samaritan, watching the same vacant, embedded broadcasts of war as the rest of the clueless world. Watching relentlessly, as if, should he watch these armies long enough, he might recognize an old friend. The cognitive neuroscientist stands at bedside, flinching under the wall-mounted television, forgetting why he's there until the patient reminds him. "Leaving already? What's your hurry? You just got here."

He is spread as thin as life. He holds his hands up to apologize. Light passes clean through them.

Mark gives him a used paperback, *My Antonia*. "For the trip. I read it in a little book club I was in. Kind of a chick-flick thing. Needs a good helicopter chase to become a classic. Naked scuba scene, or something. But real Nebraskaland. I kind of bought into it, finally."

Weber reaches to take the cast-off story. A hand snakes out and grabs his.

"Doc? There's something I can't get. I saved her. I'm . . . that woman's guardian. Can you believe that? *Me*." The words are thick and foreign in his mouth, a curse worse than the misread note. "What am I supposed to do with that?"

Weber stands still, frozen in the glare. His question, too. She will be with him, unshakable, wherever he heads. Accidental turned resident. Nothing anyone can do for anyone, except to recall: We are every second being born.

Mark begs Weber, his eyes flashing with the dread that only consciousness allows. "They need her at the Refuge. Ask my sister. They need a researcher. A journalist. Whatever the hell she is, they need her." His voice would deny all personal involvement. "Man, she can't just walk. It's not like she's some free agent. Some separate . . . She's hip-deep in this place now, like it or not. Do you think I could . . . ? What do you think she'd . . . ?"

Powerless to know what anyone else might do. To know what it feels like to be anybody.

"My sister won't ask her. And I don't dare. The way we left it? After the things I said to her? She'll hate me forever. She'll never want to talk to me again."

"You might try her," Weber says. Pretending again, on no authority. On no evidence but a lifetime of case histories. "I think you might try."

He himself tries only to prolong. If Tour Director even remembers Weber, he is taking no calls. But something else is messaging, too soft to hear. Through the plane's plastic window, the lights of unknown cities blink beneath him, hundreds of millions of glowing cells linked together, swapping signals. Even here, the creature spreads countless species deep. Flying, burrowing, creeping things, every path sculpting all the others. A flashing electrical loom, street-sized synapses forming a brain with miles-wide thoughts too large to read. A web of signals spelling out a theory of living things. Cells by sun and rain and endless selection assembling into a mind the size of continents now, impossibly aware, omnipotent, but fragile as mist, cells with a few more years to discover how they connect and where they might go, before they gutter out and return to water.

He fingers Mark's book throughout the flight, flips through at random as if this buried record might still predict what's coming. The words are more obscure than the most intricate brain research. Whiffs of prairie, a thousand varieties of tallgrass come off the pages. He reads and rereads, retaining nothing. He scans Mark's margin notes, the desperate scribbles next to any passage that might lead forward out of permanent confusion. Toward the end, the swathes of shaky highlighter grow wild and wider:

> This had been the road of Destiny; had taken us to those early accidents of fortune which predetermined for us all that we can ever be. Now I understood that the same road was to bring us together again. Whatever we had missed, we possessed together the precious, the incommunicable past.

He looks up from the page and fractures. No whole left to protect, nothing more solid than braided, sparking cells. What the scans suggest he has seen up close, in the field: older kin still perching on his brain stem, circling back always, down along the bending water. He blunders toward that fact, the only one large enough to bring him home, falling backward toward the incommunicable, the unrecognized, the past he has irreparably damaged, just by being. Destroyed and remade with every thought. A thought he needs to tell someone before it, too, goes.

A voice calls to disembark. In the rising crush, he stands and grapples for his carry-on, shedding himself on everything he touches. He stumbles down the jet bridge into another world, swapped out by impostors at every step. He needs her to be there, on the other side of the baggage claim, though he has lost all right to hope it. There, holding his name on a little card, printed cleanly so he can read it. *Man*, the card must say. No: *Weber*. She will be the one holding it, and that is how he must find her.

www.vintage-books.co.uk